I0675548

PHOTO BOOTH

"Quick," I say, "what should we do?"

A flash of light. Picture one down. Both of our mouths were hanging open, blank stares straight ahead.

We burst into laughter and can't stop. A second flash. Picture number two: both of us laughing.

Our gazes meet and we pull ourselves together, his eyes never veering from mine. He leans toward me, coming halfway before pausing, his eyes seeking permission. I regard him with equal parts terror and anticipation, the intimacy of the situation whispering a thrill. He closes the distance between us and glides his nose through my hair. My heart rattles around as though this is the first boy I've ever been close to.

"Now smile," he whispers into my ear. Even if I should be creeped out, forget it. My cheeks burn despite myself and I feel the corners of my lips tugging upward.

A flash of light signals the third picture and I am totally seduced.

Also by Laura Johnston

Rewind to You

BETWEEN NOW & NEVER

LAURA JOHNSTON

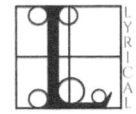

LYRICAL PRESS
Kensington Publishing Corp.
www.kensingtonbooks.com

LYRICAL PRESS BOOKS are published by

Kensington Publishing Corp.
119 West 40th Street
New York, NY 10018

Copyright © 2015 by Laura Johnston

All rights reserved. No part of this book may be reproduced in any form or by any means without the prior written consent of the Publisher, excepting brief quotes used in reviews.

All Kensington titles, imprints, and distributed lines are available at special quantity discounts for bulk purchases for sales promotion, premiums, fund-raising, educational, or institutional use.

Special book excerpts or customized printings can also be created to fit specific needs. For details, write or phone the office of the Kensington Special Sales Manager: Kensington Publishing Corp., 119 West 40th Street, New York, NY 10018. Attn. Special Sales Department. Phone: 1-800-221-2647.

Lyrical and the L logo are trademarks of Kensington Publishing Corp.

First Electronic Edition: March 2015
eISBN-13: 978-1-60183-352-5
eISBN-10: 1-60183-352-0

First Print Edition: March 2015
ISBN-13: 978-1-60183-353-2
ISBN-10: 1-60183-353-9

Printed in the United States of America

For KC

Acknowledgments

This book was an adventure to write, and I have many people to thank.

First, thanks to former Special Agent KC Johnston for help in fine-tuning the plot. Also for answering my basketball-related questions and even coming to some Highland High School games with me (perhaps his favorite type of book research).

Everyone at Kensington Publishing has been nothing but wonderful. Special thanks to Alicia Condon, my editor, for encouraging me to write this novel and for providing valuable feedback. Also to Ellen Chan for all of her help in promoting my work!

A big thank you to Dr. Andrew Evans and Dr. Nicholas Hatch for answering my medical-related questions.

Thanks to Dr. Mike Strayer, professor of Latin American literature, as well as David Quinn Nixon for helping with some of the Spanish segments in this novel.

Sincere appreciation to Yuvonie Johnson for being so willing to provide information about the Miss City of Maricopa pageant.

As always, thanks beyond measure to my critique partners: Kay Lynn Mangum, Britney Gulbrandsen, Kelly Nelson, Jennette Green, Mischa Borgnaes, and Becky Rohner. To my online critique group—thank you. Also, major thanks to everyone in the American Night Writers FBA critique group for listening to, laughing along with, and cheering on this book. I appreciate everyone's feedback and encouragement!

To the bloggers who were so supportive in promoting *Rewind to You*—thank you all!

Last of all, to everyone who has been such a support to me and my writing. I have some amazing family and friends. Thank you.

CHAPTER 1

Cody

Being the son of an FBI agent sucks.

I'll admit there was a time when it used to be cool. All I wanted was to wear the suit. Flash the badge, catch bad guys, throw out words like "informant" and "counterintelligence" and wield a gun. All in a day's work. I used to pin that gold paper badge on with pride, the one Jimmy and I laminated in clear duct tape so it would hold together. Those were the good days.

I walk through the front door behind Vic, my newest friend in this new town. We're moving from Scottsdale to Gilbert next weekend, a difference of about thirty miles.

"Hey, bro," Vic calls out, already at the fridge, framing the open door with his jacked arms. After witnessing the way Vic held a ball in a gladiatorlike death grip during our basketball tournament this week, I quickly assumed he could crush a human skull in his palm.

I started playing club ball back in third grade and I've worked my butt off ever since. Meanwhile, Vic dribbled around city courts. If you know anything about Division 1 high school ball in Arizona, you've heard of Vic Schultz. The guy's a natural.

"Coke? Dew?" he asks.

"Anything cold," I say, wiping perspiration from my forehead and checking for any sign of central cooling in this apartment, town-house, whatever it is. It's June in Gilbert, Arizona, and I swear these people don't have AC on.

My eyes catch a wall of pictures, some framed, a few not, and something catches my attention. I step closer. A younger version of Vic stands surrounded by family: a girl with glasses and some serious hair—his sister, I assume—and a dad with blue eyes who looks nothing like him. Vic takes after his mom, with dark skin, hair, and eyes. His *mom*.

I blink. Do a double take. I swear I've seen her before. Can't place her.

"Catch."

A can of Dew spirals toward me and I turn just in time.

Vic has already polished his off. He crushes the can in that grip of his and adds it to the stack of aluminum and other junk on the kitchen table. Wire, metal, and bottle caps. Heaped up like a pile of trash on the table. But it looks intentional. Arranged, even. Art is one thing I've never understood.

Vic catches my stare.

"That's cool," I lie. I pretend to analyze it, like I'm seeing a deeper meaning in the monument of trash. "It's kinda . . . abstract, you know."

Vic lets out a whoop of laughter. Punches my arm. "You're such a bad liar."

I take this as an insult. I'm no habitual liar, but come on. This is a dis on my skills. I stare at the sculpture of crap again, standing tall and regarding it as though it was my own.

Vic's laughing smile dissolves into an amused smirk. "You're serious."

"Oh, yeah."

Vic cocks an eyebrow up, totally falling for it. Guess I'm not such a bad liar after all. He shakes his head and opens another can. "My dad's a sculptor. Total loony. At least this project comes with perks. An endless supply of soda. So long as I save the can."

"Thanks for this," I say, holding up my Dew.

"Nah, man," Vic says and waggles his eyebrows. "Thank me later tonight when we get a real drink at Connor's. We've got the hard stuff."

Vic is not my typical friend, that much I already knew. I'm the son of two ambitious and highly successful parents, raised to be an over-achiever, if not a law-abiding citizen. My friends up in Scottsdale are the same. It goes without saying that no one wants to move to a new city—*a new high school*—the summer before their senior year, especially when it's their last chance to prove themselves to college scouts.

"Lakers or Heat?" Vic asks, shoving a pile of mail off the couch. He plops down and flips on the TV.

"Neither."

"*Either, or*," he clarifies, as though I'm dumb. *"Comprende esé?"*

I chuckle at his slang term of endearment, *esé*, like I'm his Mexican homeboy. Vic is half Mexican. Green eyes and blondish hair make me about as white as they come. But that's what's so great about Vic. He treats everyone like his equal on and off the basketball court, which is saying something, considering he's number two on the *Tribune*'s Top Boys' Hoops Prospects.

"I'm a Bulls fan," I say, remembering how loyal my little brother Jimmy was to the team of our childhood home. "Suns aren't bad either."

During our tournament in Vegas, a few of the guys on our team started joking about a homeless guy outside the burger spot where we were eating. One comment led to another, and eventually the guy hunched over outside begging for money was proclaimed a mentally retarded fag. "And he's got herpes," Shawn said, which earned a round of laughter from the guys in return.

Not Vic. While the other guys pitched a porn card from the street into the guy's hat, Vic—the big guy, the team's revered power forward—handed the guy an extra burger. I followed up with spare change from my pocket. No one else saw. They were distracted by the bright lights.

"Your dad sculpts," I state and glance around. Piles of junk cover counters, the smell of dirty dishes chokes the air, the guitar in the corner gathers dust, and the inside of the fridge is about empty. Details. Something I was taught to look for. "And your mom?"

I grab the guitar and blow on it, sending dust billowing up before I sit on the other couch. I take a swig of my drink.

"She's dead," Vic says.

I almost choke on the flood of Dew. "Sorry," I cough out.

Vic laughs. "Nah, man, I'm kidding. She's still kicking."

I'm usually good at reading people. Vic is an exception, and I don't like it one bit. I find an uncluttered corner of coffee table and set my drink down. Start strumming a tune.

"She's in prison," Vic offers.

I peel my eyes away from the guitar and focus on Vic. A minor chord teeters in the air as my fingers hover over the strings. I watch him, waiting for a crack in his façade. But Vic merely stares at the TV, avoiding eye contact like people do when masking how hard the truth is to admit.

Vic isn't lying.

The doorbell rings. Vic stands. "Jewel," he calls up the stairs after opening the door, "for you."

I scoot some stuff aside on the side table to reveal another picture of Vic's mom. I study it, searching for that hint of familiarity I saw earlier. At first, I figured she might be some parent I saw in passing at a local basketball tournament. Now I wonder, the idea of even partial recognition driving me crazy.

Someone runs down the stairs. I quickly slide everything back into place.

"Yeah, yeah," a girl says. Vic's sister, I assume. I tilt my head but can't quite glimpse her around the corner. "I'll take good care of Daisy and the puppies while you're gone."

The door closes and she whirls around. She's wearing cutoff shorts and a T-shirt, her hair in one of those buns girls wear. She looks like she's about to weed a garden or clean out a toilet. Still, she sucks my attention her way. There's something about a girl who can wear grunge and strut around with confidence regardless.

I find myself sitting up straighter.

"Victor Jonathan Schultz," she snaps. "Where is it?"

"Where's what?" Vic asks, his eyes settling on the TV with obvious disregard as he sinks back into the couch.

"You know what I'm talking about."

"No, drama queen, I don't."

"How original, Vic. Calling names. What are we, in junior high? Oh, yeah, you *did* fail eighth grade. And I've been stuck with you in my class ever since."

Vic is on his feet now, too. "Shut up, Julianna!"

"No!" she yells, impressively fearless at five foot five, maybe, at the mercy of Vic's six foot three. I've already sunk back into the couch, a bit intimidated myself. Of her, not Vic. "You stole forty-five dollars from my underwear drawer and I want it back. Now."

"I didn't steal your money or your panties, tramp; get your facts straight."

Julianna gasps.

I sit in the middle of all this, wide eyes ping-ponging from Vic to his sister and back. I certainly haven't seen this side of Vic. Didn't imagine this side of his sister when she first walked in either.

I wisely keep my mouth shut as Julianna digs one hand into her hip, her elbow cocked out at a determined angle. "You didn't steal it, huh?"

"No, but now I know where to go looking if I need some."

Julianna shifts her jaw to one side and narrows her eyes. " 'Fess up, Vic; it was you. Who else in our family is a lying thief?"

"Mom," Vic says.

Shock and rage tighten the small features of her face. That's when I notice her eyes—blue. A shocking contrast to her dark hair and golden tan. Something about her eyes reaches through me, puncturing all barriers. "How dare you," she says, her eyes glossing over. "Mom wouldn't even be . . . be . . . where she is if it weren't for you."

"Prison, Julianna. Just say it. Mom. Is. In. *Prison.*"

"Shut up!"

"*You* shut up. You still think Mom's perfect. She stole hundreds of thousands—"

"Because of *you,*" Julianna shouts over him.

Something kicks on inside me; shock for sure, and a gut instinct that launches my brain into action. Vic's mom, a convict. She stole money. Lots of it. And my dad works in white-collar crime. I dig through my mind for tidbits of her story. And that's the worst part. *There's a good chance I might know it.*

I fling a glance toward the door. Even if I could slip out discreetly—which I can't—I'm not sure I want to.

Vic's last name: *Schultz.* Dad always uses the offender's last name to identify his cases once they go public and he can tell us about them. The Miller case, the Baer case, the Howard case. I rake through my memory. The *Schultz* case?

"Well," Julianna says, jerking me out of the chaotic sea of thoughts. She buttons it up, an invisible mask hiding her emotions as she holds her chin high. "Don't forget to water Mom's lantanas. It's your turn. And don't miss any of the bushes."

Vic stands and puts on a mocking grin. "As you wish."

"And next time you come back from a tournament," Julianna calls after him, "don't leave a trail of gym socks all the way up the stairs. This place stank when I got home, *stank!*"

She turns to the mirror on the wall and whips something out of her purse. Standing on her toes, she puts mascara on her eyelashes. Vic mutters something, whispered curses that peter out as he slams the patio door behind him. Julianna finishes both sets of eyelashes before I consciously realize I haven't looked away.

She yanks out whatever is holding her hair up and it all tumbles down her back. I soak in everything about her. Her lips visible in the reflection of the mirror as she puckers to wipe some glossy pink stuff on. Her hair: long, dark, thick. It swooshes around as she straightens up. My eyes follow her hair all the way down her shoulders, down her back, and keep on traveling down toward those cutoff shorts until she spins around.

My eyes snap up.

I put on my best smile and offer a wave, a casual flick of the hand.

She snags her purse without so much as a glance my way and vanishes out the front door.

The water spigot outside lets out a high-pitched hum. I peek through the blinds. Vic sprays water at full blast from the hose onto the plants. Mud splashes up on the window. I seize the moment.

I slip my iPhone out and pull up the *Arizona Republic* news site. Type in *Schultz*.

Injured rock climber chooses to end life support.

Deadly crash in Phoenix, authorities report.

Too vague. I need a first name.

Dad's a bit of a fanatic when it comes to details. Always told us that having an eye for key facts is invaluable. "Open your eyes"—one of his favorite sayings, always delivered with a wink—"See everything."

My eyes settle on a magazine on the coffee table. I pluck it out of the mess and search for the addressee's name. *Jonathan Schultz.* Dang. Then I see it, a corner of leather visible beneath the pile. I shift things aside. Bingo. A wedding album.

I pull it from the pile, praying Vic doesn't pop his head in. Hoping Julianna doesn't dash back for something she forgot. I flip it open.

Jonathan and Sonia

I close the album and slip it back under, my heart hammering a guilty beat. Snooping. I can't believe I'm doing this.

My thumbs fly over my iPhone. *Sonia Schultz.*

This time, my query nails it.

Woman indicted on fraud charges. I scan the blurb. *Sonia Ana Schultz.* The hairs on my arms stand up as I take in the keywords. *Arrested on charges of mortgage fraud. $300,000. FBI.*

Clicking on the article link pulls up one last irrefutable piece of evidence: her picture.

I sit alone in the Schultzs' living room, like prey in a den with lions who haven't yet realized I'm not one of them.

The glass door slides open. I jolt.

"Hey, man," Vic says.

I close the article and sit back. Relax. Fake it.

Vic shuts the door behind him. "You ready to go?"

"Yeah," I say and stand, trying my best to smile. I slide my phone in my pocket, the image of that article seared in my memory, an article I've seen before.

I know Vic's mom all right. My dad put her behind bars.

CHAPTER 2

Julianna

The moment the door closes behind me, I feel it: less space, less sunshine, less air. Well, I'll admit: in Phoenix, Arizona, less sunshine this time of year is a good thing. But I hate this place. Hate it.

"Name?" the officer at the desk asks.

"Julianna Schultz," I say, folding my arms in front of me with every ounce of the Latina attitude I was brought up with. Makes me feel better somehow. I won't let this place give me the creeps. "I'm here to see my mother."

The officer raises a brow, looking past my shoulder. "And you, sir?"

I glance at my dad, his blue eyes, scruffy chin, and bean-pole figure. I almost forgot he was here.

Dad steps forward and mumbles, "Jon Schultz."

Officer Pugmier clucks his tongue as he scans the approved visitor list. Not only do I recognize him from our last visit, I remember his name. I never imagined I'd know the inside details of prison like I do now. Pugmier stands and hoists up the belt at his hips with a grunt. At least we're all uncomfortable to some degree. "Step over here."

We go through what's becoming "the usual." Pugmier checks my driver's license, which sports a dreadful picture of the old me. A lot can happen to a teenage girl in one year, and thank goodness. As I approach the metal detector, my heart races. Officer Pug watches me, stares. He, of course, is clueless about the nickname I've given him. Pug: it fits him, and it makes his stern face not quite so fearsome.

Pug clears his throat and I snap to, focusing on the detector ahead. I walk through without a beep, but Pug asks me step aside for a pat down.

"Don't worry," he says when I give him a pointed look. "It's a random search."

Why does this place make me feel like a criminal? I'm no angel, but I've never stolen, never cheated, nothing. Still, this place has my skin crawling. When my lovely pat down is over and I'm walking down the long hallway with no purse, no car keys, and no cell phone, I understand why. Even for a visitor, entering a prison means giving up a piece of your freedom.

The door opens and Dad hangs back. "I'm gonna grab something at the vending machine."

Good. I told him on the drive up that I wanted a moment alone with Mama. I know what I need to say. Even in prison, my mom is way easier to confide in than my dad. I sit and scoot closer to the table, the chair legs scraping the floor with a screeching echo. And then she walks in.

I pop back up, a myriad of emotions unfurling within me. The first genuine smile I've felt for weeks tugs the corners of my lips upward. Words evade us as she approaches the table. So not normal. My mother is Mexican, and I like to claim the same, even though I'm only half. She's everything to me.

She wraps her arms around me in a crushing embrace.

"Mama," I say, burying my face into her bony shoulder, hugging her back. Taking her in. Her dark hair, light brown eyes, warm smile, and her scent—like a fresh breath of air. Yet something is different. I pull back, then glance around. Excessive displays of affection are prohibited. One hug, one kiss, that's all. It's the craps.

We sit on opposite sides of the table. Normally, we'd kick back side by side on the living room couch for hours, exchanging stories and outbursts of laughter.

That's when I realize what's different: *everything*. I take in my mom's uniform, my gaze drifting down her baggy outfit before snapping back up. Mama notices.

"It's ugly as sin," she admits and then shrugs. "But really, it's not that bad."

I raise one brow, giving her a look that says otherwise. This earns a crack of laughter from her. At least I made her laugh. Mission one accomplished.

She leans forward and clasps my hands from across the table. Her nails have been chewed off. "Oh, *mi joya*, I have missed you."

How I've missed *her*—her voice, her rich accent. *Mi joya* is her own way of calling me her "jewel." Only Mama can call me that.

I bite back the crude words that would accurately describe how much the past three weeks without her have sucked, settling for a grin instead.

"I've missed you, too."

My eyes sweep the cinder-block-walled cafeteria, the fluorescent lighting making my eyes wig out. I blink, then glance down at the ratty edges of her nails again. "How's it going in here?" I ask, diving right into mission number two.

She doesn't budge, just glances away for a nanosecond and flashes a smile. "I can watch TV. Read books. They have a library."

This breaks my heart, Mama looking for the positive. She's too optimistic, too sweet.

"Come on, Mama."

"What?" she says.

"Cut the crap."

"It's not crap." The hitch in her voice betrays her. Mama never was a good liar.

I take in the angular line of her jaw, her hollow cheeks. She's always had a fast metabolism, but this is something else. "How's the food?"

She diverts her gaze with a grimace. I got her. We Mexicans know food. "Bland," she admits. "All right, it's like going to a *really* awful restaurant."

"I knew it."

"But let's not dwell on these things," she says.

"Fine," I say.

"How was your last week of school?" she asks.

"Fine."

"And work?"

"Good."

"Are you sick of chocolate yet?"

I give her an incredulous look.

She throws a glance upward in defeat. "How dare I ask?"

It's a good thing I've got a good metabolism, too, or working at The Chocolate Shoppe would stink.

"I'll bet you're already looking forward to soccer this fall," Mama says, trying to keep the conversation light.

"Yeah," I say, ignoring the stabbing reminder that she won't be around to see any of my games.

Mama pauses, no doubt fishing for another trivial question I'm not about to let her ask.

"How's your roommate?" I ask. "You said you were getting someone new?"

"Good, good," she says twice.

"You sound like you're trying to convince yourself."

Mom feigns innocence. "Really, there's nothing to say."

"Mama," I say with a dramatic folding of my arms to make my point, "this is me you're talking to. There's always something to say. Out with it."

She laughs, a weak chuckle with no life in it. "Okay, okay," she concedes with a roll of her eyes that lets me know something big is coming. Something she'd rather not talk about. "My roommate," she begins and lowers her voice, "was convicted of second-degree murder."

"What?" I shriek.

"I know."

"How? How did she get into a minimum security? And why does she have to be *your* roommate?"

"We all share a dormitory. I have many roommates."

"But this murderer—"

"Shh, keep it down," she snaps in a voice pitched for my ears alone.

"This *chick*," I correct myself, unable to control my volume, "shares a bunk with you?"

Mama nods. "She was in a maximum security for nineteen years but got transferred here because of good conduct. She's got health problems, too. We have better medical facilities."

"I didn't know they could do that," I say, floored. And enraged. The US justice system is so screwy. So much for mission number two. Mama is *not* okay. No wonder she was trying to keep the conversation light. Protect me, even. I have the sudden impulse to drag her out the door and make a run for it.

I try to think of something consoling, something positive, like she would. Something validating like, *Gosh, it sucks that you're bunking with a homicidal maniac.* Or perhaps, *Hey, it could be worse.* Neither seems quite right, so I keep my mouth shut.

Mama shrugs. "Who knows, maybe I can get a few months shaved off my sentence for good conduct as well."

Hope springs up. But hope can be a cruel thing because it often leads to disappointment. I dare to let myself feel it though, grasp it, hold on tight.

"What about the pageant, Julianna?" Her eyes light up with sudden interest. "How is everything coming along for that?"

It's like a splash of cold water in the face, this hairpin turn in the conversation. "The *pageant*?"

"Yes," she urges and leans forward. "It's only a few months away."

"Mama," I say, sounding like a seven-year-old being asked to clean her room. Terrifying images of my Little Miss Arizona days flash before my eyes, frizzy hair and all. Let's get one thing straight: I am not beauty pageant material. If this were anyone besides Mama here, I'd shout *absolutely not.* "I'm . . . well . . . you're in *here.*"

She must be joking. I never wanted to compete in the pageants she put me up to even when she was around to help. I don't want to go near the Miss City of Maricopa Pageant this fall without her. This was perhaps the only bonus about Mama going to prison. Guilt latches on with that thought, but it's true.

Wearing the crown was what teenage Mama lived for, even though her *papi* told her she wasn't good enough to compete. Believe me, I feel her pain. She went ahead and competed behind his back. And lost. Now she wants me to suffer likewise? Yes, she must be joking.

One look at her pleading eyes shatters that hopeful conclusion.

"So?" she says. "You're still going to do it, right?"

I stare at her with dawning horror as I realize how serious she is.

The hope that lit up her eyes shrivels as she watches me. "You're at least considering it, aren't you?"

Getting out of the pageant and letting her down easy is all I've ever considered. The dark circles under her eyes flag my attention. I try to forget the fingernails she's bitten off in the past few weeks behind bars.

"I'll . . . think about it," I lie. Like I said, I'm no angel, but lying to my own mother?

Her posture deflates like a flat tire, the air of excitement seeping out with one prick. It hits me with a pang, the guilt. Oh, the guilt. But how could I set myself up for failure again? I'm a magnet for this type of thing, getting my hopes up and failing miserably. Like my solo piece in *Guys and Dolls* back in junior high. Like running for student council last spring.

Mama's eyes float upward and a signature smile settles on her lips. I glance back and spot Dad holding a box of Junior Mints. Always Junior Mints.

"How is your *papi*?" Mama asks, breaking the painful silence.

I clear my throat and try hard not to pull a face. This conversation keeps going from bad to worse. *Drunk as ever. Losing it without you.* "Fine," I say.

Mama nods. She misses him, too; that much is as plain as day. You see, it's not like we're the falling-apart-at-the seams type of family. Mama shouldn't even be here, if you ask me. This all started because my brother Vic had a drug problem. We thought he was getting better. Then one morning he was gone, along with the Blu-ray player, the flat screen, Dad's laptop, Mama's jewelry, my hard-earned iPhone, and even my piggy bank. My piggy bank! Okay, so maybe we *are* falling apart at the seams.

That's when Mama decided to take matters into her own hands. She's smart, you see. She cooked up a plan at the bank where she worked to bring in some extra cash. It paid for Vic to get proper rehab. Only problem? It was illegal.

Mortgage fraud.

I still remember the jerk FBI agent who put her away. Tall, with a square jaw and the type of blond hair that adult men usually outgrow. He was as cocky as you'd expect any fed to be, too. The type of guy who has no idea what true desperation will do to a person.

Mom waves Dad over. I sit upright, about to protest. Mission number three. I didn't tell her yet. This was the reason I insisted on a moment alone with her in the first place.

Dad sits. They hold hands across the table and start talking.

I think about the money, the forty-five dollars I kept hidden away in my underwear drawer. I can close my eyes now and see them: one five, two tens, and a twenty. They were there. I know it.

And then they were gone. I searched the entire drawer. Double-checked. Triple-checked. Dumped everything out and raked through it all. No money.

Vic. The jerk.

He denied it, but I know better. If Mama only knew what I'm worried he's up to again. She thinks rehab wiped drugs out of Vic's life—our life—for good. Only one thing intimidates me more than this place: Vic on cocaine.

I tune back into my parents' conversation in time to hear Dad telling Mom about his newest sculpture. Heaven help us all, he turns our house into a scrap yard whenever a creative high pulls him into the clouds. Most people get rid of spare junk and try to keep mud outside the house. When your dad is a sculptor those items are easier to come by than a clean fork at lunch.

"This is the one," he says. I almost forgot how contagious his smile can be. "This piece is gonna be big. I've got a good feeling."

"That's wonderful, Jon," Mom says, practically glowing.

I don't buy it for a minute.

Dad has had plenty of "big projects" and "good feelings." He used to work as a design sculptor for General Motors. Good salary. We left the apartment and bought a house of our own, the house we're currently hanging on to by a thread of late-paid bills. Good salary or not, Dad decided he hated his job. Said his creativity couldn't "soar." Whatever.

"Julianna and I were talking about the pageant," Mom says. I snap to. She pats my dad's hand like he's supposed to pipe in and help the cause.

Dad shifts in his chair and avoids eye contact, like we're discussing brands of tampons at a grocery store. "Oh," he mumbles with fake interest.

Mom doesn't notice, just smiles. Everything goes silent.

I start chewing my own nails.

"Was there something else you wanted to tell me, Julianna?"

Both Mama and Dad are looking at me now. My throat dries up like a weed in the Sonoran Desert. I ache to tell them about Vic, that he's about to do something stupid. But Mama's roommate is a second-degree murderer and Dad's creative juices are flowing again. And besides, it's all just suspicion. I don't know for sure that Vic is on drugs.

I look down. "No."

"You sure?" Dad asks.

I look up into his blue eyes. Whole weeks have gone by when he's been too engrossed in sculptor la-la land to notice I exist.

"Yeah, I'm sure."

We exchange hugs as the disturbing scent of questionable cafeteria food drifts our way. Like bad spices and burned meat. Mama's face ages ten years by the time she steps back. Her eyes bleed pain, ooze regret. I've got a feeling things will only get worse for her, too.

She'll spend every holiday for the next two years in prison. She won't see me or Vic graduate. And even when she gets out it will be more of the same. She'll never live a day without scraping by. She won't live her big dreams. She never wore the crown. Stupid prison. Stupid homicidal roommate. Stupid Vic. Stupid, stupid pageant.

"I'll do it."

The words are out before I think better of them.

A little of the old Mama leaps back to life now. "You . . . you'll do it? The pageant?"

Curse this reckless mouth of mine. "Yeah, yeah," I say twice. Now who sounds like she's trying to convince herself?

"That's wonderful!" Mama beams and looks at Dad. "Oh, Jon, you'll have to help her."

Dad throws on a grin that disappears as soon as she looks away.

"I can't wait to hear all about it." Mama runs her hands down my hair, cupping my face.

I take heart despite the knot of dread lodged in my gut, proud that I could give her some source of excitement, unpromising as it is.

"You are beautiful," she says and presses her lips to my forehead, lowering her voice. "Keep on living, *mi joya*. Keep on loving."

It feels like the end of the world when I let go and watch a guard escort her back to her cell. The idea of floating—more like *tripping*—across a stage in heels and an evening gown with a smile plastered on my face like some Barbie doll is enough to end my world.

What have I done . . . ?

Sunshine sears my skin when we step outside. Dirt spotted with cactus as far as the eye can see. Not even weeds stand a fighting chance here. Don't get me wrong, I grew up an Arizona girl through and through. And loved it. But lately I find myself longing to hit the road in search of air I can breathe without cooking my lungs. A place where I can be anyone, become anyone. A weed that stands a chance.

Dad tosses me the keys. I make the catch.

"Figured you could use some practice."

I'm not sure whether he's trying to be nice or slamming my skills.

I unlock the driver's side and slip into Rusty. Vic took our nicer Yaris on a date.

Thick lashes and blue eyes meet my reflection in the rearview mirror. Not quite as blue as Dad's, but blue.

Still, maybe Mama is right. At least I'm easier on the eye than I was a year ago. Glasses have been swapped for contacts. A few miracle products from the hair salon and I was a new woman by Valentine's Day, my poufy mane tamed into shiny black locks. Lucas asked me to my junior prom two months later and we've been together since.

Dad starts tapping his thumbs on his legs, drumming out a tune. Visiting Mama sure cheered him up. Hopefully it lasts.

Maybe Mama *will* get a couple of months shaved off her two-year sentence. I take a deep breath of hot air as I shove the key into the ignition and coax Rusty to life, feeling a liberating sense of freedom seep into me. Mama doesn't have that luxury.

Shifting the car into drive, I exit the parking lot with fresh resolve. A promise is a promise, and I'll sing a song or do a little dance onstage if it means not letting her down.

CHAPTER 3

Cody

Cody's Room: Jimmy's things. I stare at the label on the box, just me and this box in a big empty room. This is all that's left: one box. A time capsule from better times. And I have no idea what's inside.

Mom saved some stuff from Jimmy's closet, said it was for me. Moving here was a new start for Mom. After seven years of Jimmy's side of the room sitting as it always had, she tackled it like she feared her resolve would buckle to grief any second. She ripped the sheets off the bed, wiped dust from the furniture, and boxed up the baseball decorations, art supplies, and LEGO creations that hadn't budged since Jimmy put them together.

When all was said and done, Mom sat on Jimmy's bed, her hair crazy. She looked around at the boxes on the floor, the empty shelves on the wall, the bare mattress, and cried.

I don't blame her. I wasn't ready to say good-bye to any of it either.

I shove the box of Jimmy's things in the corner of my closet and finish bringing in box after box. Dad wasn't about to hire a moving company at the expense of a "good family project," and Mom didn't want to move last weekend, while I was at the tournament. Forty-seven boxes later, Dad waltzes through the garage door wearing his official POLICE T-shirt, the black one with gold letters that he wears to execute search warrants and arrests. "Warrant's over," he announces. He has the nerve to smile. "What can I do to help?"

My cell buzzes in my pocket. New message from Vic Schultz.

Call me a wimp, but telling my parents about Vic and his mom hasn't happened. Maybe it's the thought of Dad going special agent on me with that frown of his or the idea of Mom second-guessing our move here and bursting into tears again.

YO ESÉ, Vic's message reads. CONNOR'S HOUSE TONIGHT. TOURNAMENT FILM IS READY TO WATCH. PARTY ON AT 9. I'LL PICK U UP.

I help Dad move in the furniture, unsure how to walk this dicey line with Vic. Coach was happy to take me on, especially after my luck at the Reebok Classic Run last month. Top performer. Schultz and Rush: It's already created some buzz, which is good for me. I'll take any help I can get attracting scouts this summer, this fall.

Still, I already miss my team at Desert Mountain High. Telling my coach and the guys I was leaving to play for another team sucked. I still wish I could commute up there for my senior year, but Dad wouldn't have it.

"Give me a hand with this mattress," Dad says.

I walk up the ramp behind him, wondering how he'd react if I told him everything. About Vic and his mom. Would that change his mind?

"We'll move this in before I jump in the shower. I feel like I've got meth all over me. Not the most pleasant search warrant."

I cinch up the drawstring on my basketball shorts and grab the mattress. "Drug warehouse?"

"No," he says and shakes his head. "It was a home. They had kids, too. Those are the worst kinds, the warrants and arrests when kids are there to watch it all."

I think of Vic. I think of Julianna and wonder if they were there when it all went down with their mom.

"These drugs," Dad says with a grunt as we lift the king-size mattress, "they mess with the head. You get a guy on drugs with a weapon and you're in a different ballgame."

My sister Rachel is stealing glances at her phone, smacking her bubble gum and bobbing her head to the music plugged into her ears while pretending to wipe down a kitchen cabinet. Eight-year-old Lizzy is flying her flutter fairy, her bright eyes and carefree smile reminding me of what Rachel used to look like. Blond hair free of pink streaks.

Dad and I set the mattress down in the master bedroom. He heaves a deep breath, his blue eyes clouded by the ill effects of knowing too much. Seeing too much.

"Son, stay away from—"

"Drugs," I finish before I have to hear it again. "Got it."

"They're everywhere," Dad says, the inflection in his voice rising like I'm not taking him seriously. I've only heard this speech a million times.

I take my hat off, scratch my head. "Got it."

"You're starting up at a new school, Cody, and although it's a good school, you can find trouble anywhere."

My point exactly. "Then why don't you let me finish my senior year at Desert Mountain?" I protest.

"That's out of the question."

"Why?"

"I won't have you driving up there every day; it's dangerous," Dad says, as protective and stubborn as ever.

"You drive all over the valley every day."

"Because I have to," he says.

"Do you realize how many people I've upset, moving from one Division 1 school to another?"

Dad's stern brow line is unrelenting. "Basketball. Isn't. Life. I put my hopes on pro baseball, son, and it didn't pan out."

I get it. He's trying to protect me from the same disappointment he faced. Dad was a short stop for the Arizona State Sun Devils. He doesn't need to say it; I know he always wished I had stuck with baseball. But that was Jimmy's sport.

"Look," he says, "you can do whatever you put your mind to. But you're a genius, Cody. You speak three languages, you have great people skills, and you're manipulative when you want to be."

"Is that a compliment?"

Dad's voice lowers, becomes almost a growl. "Not to mention you have a smart mouth. And you're stubborn."

"That makes two of us."

The vein in Dad's forehead bulges. "You've held a 4.0 GPA. . . ."

So what is he worried about?

"What about the FBI?" he asks.

"Dad—"

"I thought you had your heart set on it," he says. "You *and* Jimmy."

"Jimmy's *dead*."

His gaze wavers, drops to the ground. I look down, too, wishing I could take some things back. I wonder when this started—me and him arguing. It didn't used to be like this.

"Just choose your friends wisely," Dad wraps up the conversation before hitting the shower.

"Sounds good," I say, thinking better of my earlier impulse to tell him about Vic's mom. My phone buzzes again, reminding me of the text I never responded to.

Yo man you got my message?

Connor's house, nine o'clock. Specks of dust float around me, catching the light from the setting sun streaming in through the window.

Sounds good, I text to Vic. I'll meet you there, though.

I'll pick u up, Vic replies.

I can drive.

On my way to get u bro, Vic sends. See you in a few.

I check the clock, confused. It's not even eight o'clock. I text Vic the five-digit gate code, jump in the shower, and fly down the stairs before Dad gets done with his. I'm still pulling my shirt over my head as Vic's clunker rolls up.

Mom is already at the front window, peeking out.

"I'm heading out," I say.

"Oh, good," she says, eager for me and my sisters to make friends here. Settle in to her hometown of Gilbert, Arizona. "With who?"

"Vic." I leave it at that.

"Oh, from your team! Well, I'd love to meet —"

"No!" I push the door closed, eyeing the master bedroom door at the top of the stairs.

Her eyebrows pull together.

"We're in a hurry," I lie. More like we have an hour to kill.

"Oh," Mom says, checking her watch. She tugs my shirt down into place. "All right then, next time."

"Yeah, maybe so."

"Have fun," she calls as I scoot out, "and be safe."

"I will."

I jump in.

"Sweet house," Vic says.

I glance back at the huge house, situated in the corner of Chadwick Estates, where Grandpa and Grandma Chadwick's farm used to be. Dad steps outside.

"Let's go."

Vic pulls away. I watch Dad from the side mirror. He gives a little wave, and nerves twist in my gut.

Vic and I sit in silence for a while, both lost in our thoughts.

"Why are we so early?" I ask.

Vic switches lanes. Grips the wheel.

"Vic?"

"Huh?"

"You texted: nine o'clock."

"Oh, uh, yeah. Well, we're meeting at Connor's at nine."

"Yeah, and it's eight fifteen."

"Yeah."

I give him a questioning look, but he doesn't look my way.

I wait a good minute for him to reply before deciding he didn't hear me right. Or didn't understand. Or plain isn't listening.

"Look, man," Vic says, "you got my back, don't you?"

I stare at him. "Your back?"

"Yeah," Vic says with a forced smile.

"What do you mean?"

He mops up the sweat from his forehead with the back of his hand. It's hotter than sin outside, that's for sure, but I get a feeling he's sweating over something else.

"Vic, what's the deal?" I ask. "You're dripping sweat."

Vic checks his rearview mirror for the fifth time in a row.

"Aw, nothing, man. I just need you to hang around for a bit. Watch my back."

Whoa now. "Watch your back?" I repeat, not liking the sound of this.

My eyes sweep the interior of the car. Doors unlocked—check. Empty chip bags, some tinfoil, BIC pens with no ink barrel or tip, and a car jack that could be used as a weapon in a bind.

We turn down Power Road heading north. Away from Connor's.

The car accelerates and so does my pulse. Vic darts a glance at the setting sun, his fists clenching and unclenching on the wheel.

I piece together the two odd items: tinfoil and pen barrels—a *straw.*

Ah. "What kind of *stuff* are you doing, Vic?" I ask. "Weed? Meth? Coke?"

A bit of the apprehension dissolves from Vic's expression and his gaze meets mine with eager curiosity. "You got a preference *esé*, because I can hook us up."

It hits me hard: Vic's raw talent, his height and strong build. A rare combination of size and offensive skill. He's a good jumper, too. Huge, and yet he has a soft touch. Everything a ball player should be. And all for *this*?

"No, Vic. Just . . . no. You're shooting up?"

"Hey, I'm no needle junkie."

I glance at the foil and straws. "Smoking."

"Yeah, man. You in?"

I close my eyes. Let out a deep breath.

"Some foil and a straw, and *bam,*" Vic says, "we're set. You got a lighter?"

"No."

"We'll snag one at the store on our way back."

"Our way back from *where*?" I ask. "Where are we going?"

Vic pulls behind a store not far from the Superstition Springs Center. Kills the engine.

I grab the door handle in case.

Bushes and a low brick wall line the alley. A streetlamp puts off a weird glow. No other cars in sight. No eyes. Only me and Vic and whoever else is on their way here. I swallow hard. Ready to split.

"You seriously never been smacked, have you?" Vic asks.

Smacked? I almost laugh. "No desire whatsoever."

"That's what they all say. Just wait *esé*. These dudes got the good stuff."

I think about Vic and the list of basketball scholarships he's already been offered, offers I'd kill for: Arizona, Arizona State, Cal, Oregon, Texas A&M, Utah, Virginia. I look Vic square in the eye. "I'm gonna walk home if you don't start the car back up."

Vic jabs at my arm like I'm teasing. "Come on, man."

"Get out of here, Vic," I say, one last attempt to talk some sense into him. "You don't want this."

Vic shakes his head, one elbow on the door, his thumb brushing his chin, his other hand still holding the wheel. "Nah, nah, man. I got no choice. I gotta get the money to them, bro. They'll come for me."

"Wait, *what?*"

"The *money*. This was my first time selling and I didn't get enough dough."

I didn't think this could get any worse. "You're using *and* selling?"

"Yeah," Vic says, sounding like I shouldn't act so surprised.

I pull out my wallet. "How much do you need?" I pull out one twenty. Two. Three. "I got sixty bucks."

"Try a grand."

I stuff the cash back in. "A grand."

Vic lowers his forehead into his hands and stretches the skin above his brows with his palms. Like he can make it all go away if he pushes hard enough. "Yeah, a grand. I got about three thou. I owe them four."

I massage my own forehead. "Vic, come on. Let's get out of here. Talk to the police—"

"Psh," Vic mumbles a sound. "Cops? You serious? And get myself into more trouble than I'm already in?"

"Why did you need the money so bad in the first place?"

Vic regards me with disbelief. "You ain't holding nothing back, are you, rich boy?"

I glance around at the narrow back alley, noting a jumble of grocery carts near a Dumpster. "Well, since you dragged me out here and I assume there's a drug deal going down any minute, I figure I might have the right to ask."

"Fair," Vic says, "and if you know some guys who need a fix, we can split it fifty—"

"*Why,* Vic?" I ask, yanking him back on track.

"Because I stole from my family," Vic blurts out. He brushes his thumb along his chin again, a nervous habit, I figure. Julianna's outburst about stolen money the other day slides into place. Maybe she wasn't making it up.

"That was during a low point, a'ight? So don't freaking lecture me. I know where to draw the line now. How to use, when to stop. My mom freaked, though, and signed me up for rehab—expensive rehab. And she got herself in prison trying to fund it. Feds took it all when they took her down."

I let out a deep breath. Heat mounts, silence stretches on. A cross hanging from the rearview mirror sways back and forth like it, too, is being pulled in opposite ways under the tension. Some moments feel surreal. You ask *why* and get nothing. Your question hangs in the air.

When I was a kid everything seemed black and white. Now I wonder if sometimes the bad guys aren't always what they seem.

I open the door, my gut twisting as an underlying principle wars against that thought. I am who I am—a straitlaced FBI agent's son. The agent who put Vic's mom away. And I have no interest in drugs. I step out of the car.

"Where are you going?" Vic asks, popping open his door and jumping out.

I slam mine shut. "Home."

"Just like that, you're out?" Vic huffs. "Some friend, Cody. Some friend you are."

I turn. "Some friend *I* am? You dupe me into a back-alley drug deal and then dis on me as a friend?"

"Yeah."

"You don't make sense, Vic. None of this does."

"You're right, Cody. None of this makes sense to *you*. Rich boy. Got everything you ever want. You don't understand a thing."

"Yeah, okay, let me tell you what I understand," I say. "Your mom's in prison. She got herself there trying to get you off drugs. And you do what? You sell *drugs* to pay back for your mistake?"

"Shut it!" Vic yells. "Just shut your pretty-boy mouth and run on home."

Headlights flash around the corner of the building, signaling an approaching car. We both jerk back. I freeze.

Shadows outline Vic's eye sockets, making them look dark and hollow. "Get back in."

Fear rides on his voice, setting my nerves on edge. Vic has no idea what he's doing. He's terrified. Where does that leave me?

I scoot up against the brick wall and give Vic a pointed look, adrenaline pulsing through my veins. "Trust me, Vic, I'm the last guy you want to be a part of this."

One call. That's all it will take.

"Get outta here," Vic says.

The rumble of the car amplifies as it makes the turn and starts toward us. If I bolt now, they'll see me. At the last moment I slip around the corner of the building. I duck behind a jumble of grocery carts near the Dumpster and duck down. The car pulls up alongside Vic and stops. Red. A Porsche. Tinted windows. I can't quite make out the plates.

Trapped. I've pinned myself into a corner. I can't make a run for it now.

Dad is going to *kill* me.

I second-guess my impulse to hide here. I second-guess everything.

The passenger door opens and a man steps out. Black tank and jeans, flat-billed hat, a tattoo sleeve covering his entire arm. Caucasian. Strong. He actually doesn't look much older than us. A second, shorter guy steps out from the driver's side. Pale skin. A head of thick hair—a mullet. A cloud of smoke seeps from his mouth after he takes a long drag on a joint. "Vicky boy."

I whip out my iPhone. My thumb hovers over it, hesitating. My dad, police, my dad, police: the options ricochet in my mind before I go for something else entirely, the choice my brother Jimmy would have rooted for.

I press record.

My phone makes a bleep right as the driver slams his door shut, masking the sound. Quietly, I let out a long-held breath, fully aware that I'm doing what an eight-year-old Jimmy would have done in this situation: record the drug deal like a special agent wannabe—the last thing I want to be. *Smart, Cody. Real smart.*

My finger slides over to stop the recording, but I think better of it at the last moment. I flip the switch to silent first. Still, even if I call the police, the dealers will hear my voice.

I focus on the conversation late, knowing I should have tuned in long ago.

The dude in black says something I can't quite make out.

"So when do I meet Ian?" Vic asks.

"You don't," the guy in black says.

Ian, Ian, Ian . . . I convert the name to memory.

"You deal through us," the mullet guy says, flipping through a stack of cash Vic handed him. I keep my breathing in check. Silent. Vic doesn't have enough. My mind reels at the harsh reality. And this *is* real.

Mullet reaches the end of the cash pile and pauses, his chest deflating with obvious disappointment. He pulls the joint from between his lips and flicks it, sending it straight at me. "Where's the rest of the money, Vic?"

The joint tumbles to the asphalt and rolls under the grocery carts, losing momentum when it touches my foot. Silently I pick it up, the distinct smell reaching my nose. Weed for sure.

"We're cool, man, we're cool," Vic says. "I'll get you the money."

The dealer in black, intimidating in build, shifts his weight from one foot to the other, his silence telling me all I need to know. I drop the joint.

"The money, Vic," dude in black growls, holding his hand open. The streetlight casts enough of a glow on his features for me to get a quick shot of his face on camera.

Vic mumbles something I can't make out, a confession. This whole thing went from bad to worse fast, as I expected. I feel it in the air. I can't see very well behind these carts, so I lift one foot and touch it down. Toe, heel, toe, heel, dodging pebbles and rocks scattered over the pavement. I stay hunched down step-by-step until I can look around the shopping carts. I refocus on the scene as Mullet pulls something out. I peer around the cart for a better look as the slide of a gun snaps into place, releasing an echo that shoves my nerves into overdrive.

Freak.

I panic, all concentration lost. Dad had me training with firearms by the time I was seven. Still, nothing can prepare anyone for this.

Think.

A bullet is in the chamber now. Means there wasn't one there before. This guy is trying to intimidate Vic and it's working. It's working on me, too. At best, these guys want to scare Vic, get what they want from him. But these dudes could very well be high on drugs, screwed up in the head, like Dad said.

The meaty guy in black seizes a fistful of Vic's shirt. He's a good three inches shorter than Vic, yet he still manages to spin him around and shove him up against his car.

"Get the money, Vic," he says, his lips curving into a twisted grin. "That sister of yours, the one with the tight little body? I wouldn't mind getting my hands on that."

Julianna. Something lurches inside me as his words ring loud and clear. Vic shoves against him in a flash of rage. Clearly pissed, the dude in black smashes Vic's face, knuckles thudding into flesh with a nauseating thump.

He sinks punches into Vic's ribs and stomach. The sight guts me out, leaving me immobile. Useless. Staring.

My hand wraps around one of the rocks at my feet before I think about what I'm doing. I'm officially crazy. Desperate. No time to back down now.

Vic isn't putting up a fight and he's smart. He's outgunned.

One, I count and swallow hard. *Two.* No way is this going to end well, but I wind up anyway, committed to instinct against what is probably my better judgment. *Three.* I pitch the rock over the carts, sending it flying in a high arc toward the other end of the empty alley. It crashes into the rocky landscaping at the edge of the asphalt.

Both dealers reel around toward the sound, facing away now. Vic turns and looks straight at me.

I shake my head slowly. Twice.

"We got company, Vic?"

"No." Vic shakes his head. "Not that I know of."

Mullet walks to the edge of the alley, his grip tight on his gun as he investigates. Dude in black has both hands knotted into fists. Vic looks like he's holding his breath. I realize I've stopped breathing altogether. I take a shallow breath in, a quiet, controlled process that makes my lungs burn. In . . . out. In . . . out.

"It's nothing." Mullet returns, giving Vic a death look. "I want the rest of the money in hand by next Friday."

"You got it," Vic says, wiping at the blood on his lip.

The dude in black pulls out what looks like a sucker and hands it to Vic. "To tide you over." He laughs, his open hand smacking Vic's cheek twice.

Mullet flicks his wrist. "Get outta here."

Vic doesn't waste time. He's in his car the next second, his clunker roaring to life. Then there's a pause, like Vic's second-guessing, holding back. For me.

Don't, Vic. Get out of here. Get out.

At last he takes off, and the dealers move toward their car.

I grip my phone, ready to catch their license plate. Call the police.

My phone makes a deafening beep, a discordant echo that shakes every cell in my body and puts my pulse on hold. I muffle the sound too late. I glance down.

EMERGENCY ALERT: Dᴜsᴛ Sᴛᴏʀᴍ Wᴀʀɴɪɴɢ ɪɴ ᴛʜɪs ᴀʀᴇᴀ ᴛɪʟʟ
11:00 ᴘ.ᴍ. . . .

The realization of how loud it was hits me in slow motion. I look back up, veins surging, my senses heightened as I find both dealers' full attention drawn my way.

Buh boom, buh boom. My heart thrusts against my rib cage. Emergency alert—stupid message intended to save lives is about to end mine.

Both guys hunch down, their guarded expressions curious, agitated . . . hungry.

Buh boom, buh boom. It beats in my ears now, rushing blood. Raw fear. Every nerve ending charged with pent-up adrenaline.

Run. *Run.*

Their eyes strain for a nanosecond before zeroing in on me. It's time.

My feet hit the pavement, rocks kicking up as I push off into a full sprint.

I jump the half brick wall, glancing over my shoulder to find the dude in black in hot pursuit behind me.

I pick it up like I never have before and dart into the road, headlights blinding me as an SUV screeches to a halt. My arm flies out, muscles clenching with fear. The hood meets my hand, sending a shot of pain through my wrist and knocking my iPhone from my grasp. My phone crashes to the pavement, flips up, and collides into the ground again. I scoop it up. The SUV driver lets his horn wail, long and loud.

Can't let it shake me up. No time. I sprint through the parking lot, arms pumping, legs flying. This is no video game.

I imagine a bullet whizzing past my head. I imagine worse.

This is not happening.

Any sane person wouldn't shoot, right? Not out in the open like this. But sanity could be long gone for these guys, like Dad said.

Dad

911

I bring my phone up to eye level as I dash around a row of cars. A crack slices through the screen and tiny fissures radiate out from it. I curse.

I dare a glance behind me as I approach the mall entrance, relieved. I've lost my tail. I hope. He's nowhere in sight. For now.

I whack my phone against my other hand. Nothing. I curb my speed at the last second and swing the door open, sliding in. A lady jumps aside and gasps. I pant, my throat burning, a sensation of hot liquid trickling down.

"Sorry," I breathe out and tear down the empty hallway. I scan for security and push the power button on my phone to no avail. Shattered. Useless. Dead.

I slow my pace and look back. I imagine guns in a mall. *A shooting.* Because of me. No.

They can't find me.

A memory springs up, a story my dad told me about a fugitive he and two other agents stumbled upon. It turned into a chase. Through a mall. The fugitive was smart. Bought a new outfit, slipped out through a utility door, and got away.

I slide into Buckle and grab the first hat I walk past. Snag a shirt. I'm at the register four seconds later with my wallet in hand.

The employee smacks her gum, looks me over like we have all the sweet time in the world. I realize I'm panting, sweating, and starving from moving forty-nine boxes and escaping a gun-wielding drug dealer.

"You know," she says, "there's still twelve minutes before the mall closes if there's another store you're trying to get to."

"No, I'm just . . . sort of in a hurry."

She scans the hat as I glance behind my shoulder. Still no one. I wonder if I could be this lucky.

"This is snaz."

I whirl back around. "Huh?"

She holds up the hat, alternating glances between it and me. She smiles. Giggles even.

Oh, jeez.

"I love fedoras," she says and winks.

"Fedo-what?"

"Fe-dor-a," she breaks it down like I'm dumb and holds up the plaid hat. "This is a fedora hat. The green and blue will go good with your eyes."

I slap my debit card down on the counter and she gets the hint, picks up the pace. "Thank you," I say, trying my best not to be rude. An idea springs up. "Hey, can I use your phone?"

"You don't have a cell?"

I hold up my shattered iPhone. She makes a sad face at it. "That sucks. Here," she says, and holds out the store phone. "What number do you want me to call?"

I pause. Saying *911* might not go over so well. I check the entrance behind me again, wondering if 911 is even necessary. Or I could call the nonemergency police number, a number I don't have. I could ask this girl to look it up for me, but she'd think I was a nutcase after I dashed in here like I did.

Or I could tell her everything. Maybe she'd think it was cool, like she's part of something big. People love this stuff. Usually.

I think about the dealers, what their next move might be.

Would they care if I got away? Would they give up? Hopefully they think I'm no real threat. But I am. I have their voices—their faces—recorded.

The recording.

I take my phone in hand and locate the SIM tray.

"Do you have a paperclip?" I ask, knowing I'll need something small to pop it open.

Her eyebrows scrunch together.

"Actually . . ." I say, snagging a pair of earrings from a stand. I poke the end of an earring in the hole of the SIM tray to pop it open. The tiny card falls into my palm. I shove the useless phone back in my pocket.

The employee snaps her gum again, pulling me back. Both of her eyebrows are winged upward now. "What number?"

"Huh?"

She holds up her phone again. "You still wanna make a call?"

I could call Dad. I curse the fact that he had every right to lecture me on drugs and friends. That and Mom's farewell warning to be safe makes me realize how messed up this is. They'd kill me.

"You know what?" I say. "Never mind. Thanks anyway."

I grab the neck of my T-shirt behind my head and whip it off with one pull. I grab the shirt and hat from the girl staring at me with wide eyes. "Thanks."

I walk out, pulling the new shirt on and situating the hat. I toss my old shirt and shattered phone into a nearby can. Walking to the nearest retail kiosk, I hide behind it and peer down the emptying hallway, SIM card in hand. Still no drug dealers. I glance down the hallway behind me, pretending to be immersed in shopping. I reach for the first thing at hand, touching something fluffy. That's when I turn and realize I'm at a stand of stuffed animals.

"Which one you want?" the employee at the kiosk asks, a Vietnamese lady who has to crane her neck to look up at me.

"Uh," I stammer, throwing a look around. If I'm lucky, the dealers didn't see me recording them. But what if they did? I don't want this SIM card anywhere near if they find me. My eyes settle on a row of potted plants. Do I hide it? Not here. But where?

"I say, which one you want?"

I snap to, redirecting my attention to the lady smiling up at me.

"I'm just looking," I say, scanning the stand for a polar bear, Lizzy's favorite. No polar bears. I snag a white dog instead—close enough—and glance behind me again. I give the dog a quick once-over, my eyes settling on a small opening in the seam where part of the stuffing inside can be seen—and I get an idea.

"Actually, do you deliver?"

She looks at me like I'm stupid. After everything I've gotten myself into tonight, I'd have to agree.

"What?" she asks.

I hold up the dog. "Do you deliver? You know, like a flower delivery only with a stuffed dog instead?"

She shakes her head.

I pull out a twenty. "You know what, I'll buy it anyway. Keep the change."

I start down the hall, tugging the seam in the stuffed animal to make it wide enough. I search right, left. I begin to think I might have lost them for good.

I shove the tiny SIM card inside the dog, wedging it deep into the stuffing. I walk alongside what few shoppers remain in the mall. Blending in. Hiding. I pull the brim of my hat down, glancing from side to side. They're gone. Gone.

That's when it all crashes in: the nerves, the adrenaline, the gun, the sprint away from my closest brush with real danger. I grip the dog between my palms and my hands begin to shake.

And here I thought moving to Gilbert would be boring. Ha. Senior year has already thrown out more action than I bargained for and it hasn't even started. I stretch the muscles in my neck, heading for the nearest exit. And then I see her.

Her smile lassos my attention, dissolving everything else around me. Long dark hair. She blows a strand away from her eyes as she works. She hands something to a customer, her eyes flashing a stunning blue under the bright lights of the mall.

Staying out—and I mean way out—of her life is for the best. Distancing myself from Vic, preventing the inevitable clash. My dad, the FBI agent. Their mom, the convict. But then I remember Vic's drug dealers, the way they threatened her, and something kicks in, an inborn drive to step in and protect. I curse Vic's name, sizing him up in my head and wondering how a throw down between the two of us would end.

I almost walk away, but I hesitate. At the very least, I should make sure she gets to her car safely after work. I almost take the first step toward her, but something holds me back. Gut instinct? Or maybe fear that I'll cause more harm than good. I dither back and forth, unable to make up my mind. Unable to take my eyes off Julianna.

CHAPTER 4

Julianna

I hand the lady her chocolates: last customer of the day, thank heavens. "Have a better day."

She looks up, offers a weak smile. "Thanks."

Her nose is red, her eyelids a bit puffy. I see this from time to time at The Chocolate Shoppe. Her smile spreads into something more genuine and she shakes her head, like she's brushing off the last of her tears. "I will."

This is what I love about working at The Chocolate Shoppe: everyone leaves happier than when they arrived. At least that's my goal. People don't walk into a store full of chocolate to check a chore off their to-do list. Emotions drive them in. Excitement on a special occasion, satisfaction after an accomplishment, love at the best of times, cravings at the worst of times, and depression during those worst of the worst of times (ahem).

I heave a deep breath when she leaves, gearing up to close down for the night.

Suz, my boss, steps in from the back. "Here you go," she says and plops down a few rags and cleaning supplies. "You tidy up the front and then I'll take care of the rest, okay? You don't want to miss your bus."

"Thanks," I say as she disappears again, and I recall our earlier conversation. Her daughter Ginger and her niece Lily will both be old enough to work here once school starts. What does that mean for me? Fewer hours this year. I slide a jar of sprinkles and a bottle of caramel aside and start wiping down the ice cream showcase, ready to go home. I can't afford fewer hours, not with Mom in prison and Dad dragging his feet on his projects. Not with Vic stealing money again.

I grit my teeth and reach out for an extra rag, bumping the bottle of caramel in the process. I gasp, my lungs placing all demands for air on hold as I watch the bottle teeter. I lunge for it, but it dives off the other end of the counter before I can reach it, rousing visions of myself on hands and knees wiping caramel from the checkered tile. Missing my bus. Walking home.

"No!" I choke out.

A hand flies in, catching it like it was nothing. I breathe out, amused at the terror spiraling to a halt within me. I grip the counter, catching my breath and feeling like an idiot. But oh, so grateful that I won't be on my hands and knees tonight.

I look up to find two very green eyes staring into mine. I blink twice. *Green.* Such an unusual, captivating color. Maybe because, in desert Arizona, we don't see it much.

He smiles, a flash of white perfection that's enchanting enough to disarm anyone.

"Got it," he says, one side of his smile lifting into a crooked grin with killer dimples. Dimples are dangerous.

"Thanks," I say. "I owe you."

"Rough day?"

I should be offended. *I look like crap, huh? Do I, buddy?* But for some reason, his deep, concerned voice takes the edge off. My brother Vic could be on drugs again, my hours at work are being cut down by half, my mom is in prison, and my dad is being his normal self (enough said). Oh, and in a little over four months I'll be competing in a—drumroll: look at me now in my chocolate-splattered apron and picture this—*beauty pageant.*

I blow my side bangs away from my eyes and almost laugh. "You have no idea." I check the clock. Three minutes until closing. "What can I get for you?"

His eyes lock on mine and he keeps smiling that curious grin of his, like he sees something amusing. He gives me a look, a slight arc of the brow like he's waiting for me to say something. Almost like he's waiting for me to remember him.

"Have you been in here before?"

His smile broadens, his eyes flashing with anticipation. "No, why? Do I look familiar?"

Something's definitely funny to him and I'm not catching on. Is he toying with me? He's supercute with that fedora hat and all, but he's not my type. At all. Way too clean-cut. Probably shaves first thing every morning and shines his shoes, a bag of potato chips and an ESPN game constituting his highest form of adventure. A jock. Perhaps even a player, one of those dudes who hunts for chicks at the mall. A mixture of irritation and embarrassment rushes in at that thought, making my cheeks burn.

"No," I say, getting my spunk back on.

My cell phone vibrates in my pocket. I ignore it. It's probably Trish or Mindy or even Lucas, calling to see if I can hang later. It buzzes again and again.

"Go ahead," he says.

"No, it's fine," I say as it stops. "I should have turned it off anyway. Sorry."

As if on cue, it starts buzzing again.

He shifts over to the displays of chocolate and puts on a mischievous grin. "No, really, go ahead. I need a minute to decide."

I peel my eyes away from his dimples and sneak a look at who's calling. *Vic.* What the weird? Vic never calls. If I hadn't already ignored four text messages from him within the past twenty minutes, I wouldn't even consider this. *What if it's about Mom?*

I step back and answer, keeping my voice light, "Vic, what's up?"

"Jewel, where are you?"

"Work."

"At the mall?"

Duh, where else? "Uh-huh," I say instead. "Everything okay?"

"Uh . . . I . . . yeah," Vic says, like he's out of breath, agitated. "Everything's cool."

Please tell me he's not on crack. "Is Mom okay?"

"What—yeah," Vic says.

"Look, Vic, I gotta go."

"I'll come pick you up."

"What? Why? I'm fine taking the bus," I say, confused at the undercurrent of concern in his voice. So not like Vic. Maybe he's worried about the whole dust storm warning that came out. "I'll see you at home."

"Be carefu—"

I hang up and turn my phone off, embarrassed. "Sorry, that was my brother."

"Vic?" he asks.

Good ears. I laugh it off. "Um, yeah. You know, the whole *rough day* thing? That would be Vic."

"You guys don't get along?"

I scramble for a light way to sum it up, a bit surprised at how attentive—how bold—this guy is. "Vic's just . . . trouble. And his friends?"—I let out a little laugh and roll my eyes—"Don't get me started. *Total* losers."

His Adam's apple slides up and down. Usually I'm the one who lets the customers do the talking and vent their frustrations, not the other way around.

"So what do you want?" I ask him. "Are you buying for yourself or someone else?"

"Someone else."

"Someone special?"

"Mm-hm."

I pull on a new pair of plastic gloves and ask, "Girlfriend?"

Suddenly I know he has one. He's gorgeous in a preppy yet rugged sort of way, if that's possible, and holy Jamaica, he's ripped. I tear my eyes away from the swell of muscles beneath the tight fit of his shirt.

He hesitates, darting a quick look behind his shoulder. "Ah, this is for a girl, yes."

I can't help but note his evasiveness. "Not your girlfriend."

His lips twist up into a cute expression of thought. Man, his eyes are beautiful. "Mm, that's to be determined."

"Ah," I say and throw him a wink for good measure. "Well, chocolates will sway her verdict in your favor."

"Yeah?" he asks and smiles like I just delivered a hard fact. Man, I'm good at selling chocolate. I sure hope I'm not giving him false hope. But come on, this guy is gorgeous, in a suffocatingly neat-and-put-together sort of way. I picture his girlfriend-to-be, some J. Crew model with perfect hair, coordinated accessories, and a pricey bag dangling from her arm. Yep, she'll fall. Hard.

"Well, chocolates would certainly sway me."

"Sweet," he says and resituates something under his arm. A stuffed animal?

"So what's her dessert of choice?"

His eyes scan the array of chocolates behind the glass. "Ah ... shoot, I wish I knew."

Guys these days. "She likes chocolate, though, right?"

"I sure hope so," he says, his expressive eyes flashing an incredulous look. "Who in their right mind wouldn't?"

I like this guy already.

"I sort of just met her," he offers, all dimples.

"Okay, well, tell me a bit about her. What you know, at least. Maybe I can point you in the right direction."

He exhales, an almost dreamy look flickering over his face. He's toast. This chick has him wrapped around her finger.

"Well," he says, "she's beautiful for starters. Full of life."

"All right," I say.

He gets this faraway look, like a kid staring up at a cookie jar he's nowhere close to reaching. "She's got these big blue eyes that are, well, *incredible*. She's assertive. Tons of spunk." His gaze meets mine now, the intensity in his eyes reaching right through me. "Yet she's vulnerable and doesn't know it, and I think she needs someone to look after her."

My insides turn to the consistency of melted butter and I realize my mouth is hanging open. I snap it shut. "You should tell her that sometime."

A dimple accents his cheek before he even smiles. "Maybe I will."

I clear my throat, channeling my inner creative flair. "Well, you said she's spunky, so I can almost picture her with a butterscotch lollipop or maybe a mocha truffle. Some maple cashew brittle could be nice, too, something with a little snap. Assertive makes me think she's used to getting her way and is maybe even borderline bossy, in which case I'd suggest anything *Rocky Road*." I pause, hoping that wasn't offensive, relieved when he starts to chuckle. I start laughing, too. "But if you ask me, what any girl needs every once in a while is some good old-fashioned milk buttercream."

"Perfect," he says. "I'll get some of those."

He checks over his shoulder again, like this girl is going to show up any moment. Is that sweat on his brow?

I bag three of our milk buttercream chocolates. "Does she work here?"

Again he laughs. "Yeah, she does."

I think through the other girls I've seen working down the hall, wondering if I know her. Not that I care. "Anything else?" I ask. "Cupcakes? Truffles? Ice Cream? We do sell our ice cream in tubs."

He takes off his hat and scratches the back of his head like it will help him think, his biceps bulging in the process. I focus on his face instead, his even five o'clock shadow, thick eyelashes, and the manly jawline that saves him from looking too pretty.

"I don't know," he says with a cute twitch of his lips, "I thought I was good at reading people, but you're giving me a run for my money. I never knew there was so much behind chocolate."

I smile, a little laugh escaping my lips, aware of the effect that he's having on me. "I've got a suggestion."

His eyes slide back up to meet mine.

"Ask her what she likes next time you see her. She'll appreciate it."

His crooked smile returns, a trace of humor twinkling in his eyes again. "All right, I will," he says. "What do *you* like best?"

I get this a lot, and I tell every customer the same thing. "Our white chocolate Bordeaux can't be beat. I also love our milk chocolate chew and, above all—I should be ashamed to admit this—the Rocky Road truffle."

This receives a weakly restrained burst of laughter from him.

I laugh, too, humbly aware of my rocky road, feisty personality. "Oh, and if that's not enough, I must say that I do appreciate these German chocolate cupcakes because I spent a good hour frosting them."

"You *made* those?" he asks, visibly impressed.

I nod. I can't lie; his reaction means a lot. Baking is an art, one that is consumed all too quickly.

"Well then, I'll take it all."

"Come again?"

"Everything you listed," he says. "I'll buy it all."

I get to work boxing up all of my favorites, eyeing the clock. Five past nine. I steal glances at him every now and again, absentmindedly noting little details and making inferences. Brand-name shirt. *He's rich.* The dignified set of his jaw and his sturdy bearing. *He's confident.* The stuffed dog under his arm. *He's sentimental, or maybe plain weird.* The subtle shine of perspiration on his forehead. *He's worried.*

About what?

That's when I notice a tag still hanging from the back of his hat. Did he steal it?

I ring his purchases up at the register, keeping one protective hand on the over-thirty-dollars of chocolate until he whips out the correct dollar amount in cash and pays. I relax, telling myself off for being so guarded.

I hand him his bag and smile. "Have a good night."

I force myself not to watch him leave. We girls fall hard, and I hate it. Cute, charming guy comes along, makes us laugh, and we're still thinking about it hours later. I grab my rag and start cleaning, completing five circular motions before noticing he hasn't budged. I look up.

"Ah," he stammers, looking around the store before throwing his killer smile back on full display. "Do you want some help?"

"Huh?"

He laughs, his timid chuckle petering out as he gestures to the store in general. "I was just wondering if you could, you know, use some help cleaning."

I stare at this guy, at his bag of chocolates and stuffed dog, trying to figure out if he's for real. And why he's still here. Whatever his reason, I have less than twenty-five minutes to finish up and catch my bus.

"Sure," I say, highly amused as I retrieve the broom.

He gets to work. Suz walks up, her eyebrows pulling together as she spots the random hot guy sweeping our floors. She throws me a curious look. I shrug and so does she. Everything is tidied up a few minutes later. I bid Suz good-bye and walk out behind the guy.

"Thanks for the help."

"No, thank *you*," he says, earning a curious glance from me in return. He holds up the bag of chocolates. "For your help, I mean. This will be perfect."

I pull my purse strap on my shoulder and smile. "I'm sure she'll love them."

Suddenly it's that awkward moment when you both realize you're heading in the same direction. I give a courtesy laugh and he echoes my sentiment. We make it a few steps before his feet come to an abrupt stop. I glimpse a flash of apprehension on his face before he grabs my arm and pulls me into a photo booth.

"What the—"

"Shh," he says, dead serious, his arm taking a protective grip around my shoulders. Panic bubbles up. He smells like manly after-shave and expensive laundry detergent, like cologne mixed with sweat. He smells like danger.

He peeks out the opposite curtain before spinning back toward me. We're face-to-face on this booth bench—totally enclosed—side by side. Inhaling the same air. His lips a breath away from mine. A host of emotions spiral through me. I'm not sure whether to be creeped out or seduced. As it stands, I think I'm a little of both.

"I'm sorry," he says, pulling his arm away in a gesture of inno-cence. Somehow I'm holding his stuffed dog now. "I've always wanted to try one of these, you know?" he says with a nervous laugh and pulls out his wallet. "Have you ever taken pictures in a booth?"

"Uh . . . yeah," I say, wondering just how nutso he is and deciding to tread carefully. You never know these days. I peel back the curtain on my side. "I really need to go, though."

"No!" he says, and I jump. Then it all clicks into place.

"Is this about your girlfriend? Your to-be-determined special someone?"

He hangs his head and shakes it, his shoulders deflating. "No, I promise, it's not."

For some reason I find myself believing him.

His green eyes plead with mine, one brow arching up as his dim-ples sneak out to convince me. I repeat: Dimples are dangerous.

"All right," I concede. "One quick round of pictures." He did, after all, sweep my floors.

"Sweet," he says and inserts his card.

We listen to the monotone voice reel off instructions. Four pic-tures. A light will flash before each picture is taken. Etcetera. How I ended up in this position I'm not sure. We both sit, staring at our re-flections on the dark plastic and, no doubt, both stuck on the same thought that crosses everyone's mind when they're on this seat.

"Quick," I say, "what should we do?"

A flash of light. Picture one down. Both of our mouths were hang-ing open, blank stares straight ahead.

We burst into laughter and can't stop. A second flash. Picture number two: both of us laughing.

Our gazes meet and we pull ourselves together, his eyes never veering from mine. He leans toward me, coming halfway before pausing, his eyes seeking permission. I regard him with equal parts terror and anticipation, the intimacy of the situation whispering a thrill. He closes the distance between us and glides his nose through my hair. My heart rattles around as though this is the first boy I've ever been close to.

"Now smile," he whispers into my ear. Even if I should be creeped out, forget it. My cheeks burn despite myself and I feel the corners of my lips tugging upward.

A flash of light signals the third picture and I am totally seduced.

He turns to the screen and puts on that smile of his, patiently waiting for the next picture as if whatever just happened between us didn't happen at all. Or at least didn't faze him.

The fourth flash snaps me out of it and I return to reality. I think of his J. Crew model and how she would feel about this.

He peers outside the curtain again, inching out before pulling it open for me to exit. I'm anxious to scram, but he stays by my side, giving me the extra copy of all four pictures as we walk out. I hold his chocolates and stuffed dog as he opens the mall door and we step out into the hot night.

I spot the bus, still shaken up from that third picture.

"Is that your bus?" he asks.

"Uh, yeah," I say. A prideful instinct nudges in, making me want to spout off something snippy to assert the fact that this night meant nothing to me. My life, my happiness, don't depend on guys. This was my mom's fatal mistake, one I won't repeat.

He starts to back away; toward his car, I guess. He pinches the brim of his hat and tugs it down old-fashioned style. "It was a pleasure."

Who says that? It's rare, I guess. Classy, even. One wink from him as he backs away convinces me I loved it all: his engaging smiles, our playful banter, the photo booth. Even if it didn't mean a thing to him. They come through all the time, cute guys stopping in for something at the mall, never to return. Somehow this one felt different, and despite myself, I'm sad to see him go.

What's his name? Did I even ask?

"Hey," I call after him, surprised at how far away he is now. He turns, still walking away as I hold up his chocolates and stuffed dog. "You almost forgot."

He shakes his head, walking backward with a wide smile. "They're for you," he calls out, as though I should have known this.

I look at the bag of chocolates in my hand—all of *my* favorite chocolates—and the dog, stunned. Confused. Still processing the fact that he gave them to me instead of the girl he likes. What on earth? I wonder why he changed his mind, and when. And then I realize. *Rocky Road, spunky, full of life, a girl he just met . . .*

I open my mouth to call out to him, to say something—anything. Get his name perhaps. But his figure disappears around the corner. Gone.

After a prick of disappointment, something warm stirs inside, sending little sparks up and down my skin. I steal a glance at my bus, which is about to leave, and then back to the corner he disappeared around, my gaze toggling back and forth. Reluctantly, I turn, staring down at the gifts in my hands as I make my way to the bus. I smile, still shocked, wishing I knew his name, his number, *something*. These chocolates, this dog . . .

They were for me all along.

CHAPTER 5

Cody

Vic has everything: a magic touch with the ball, scholarships to boot, and a mom who loves him so much she went to prison trying to get him off drugs. And then he put Julianna in danger.

I should have turned him in.

I second-guess my last-minute decision to give Julianna the dog. Vic's got to be pissed, too, after getting beaten up by that dealer, ready to turn them in. He'd better be. Maybe I'll tell him where to find the video so he can come clean and put this all behind him.

I look over my shoulder to see Julianna's bus lurching to a start. Safely on its way.

I was almost sure I'd lost that drug dealer. Then I caught a glimpse of someone down the hallway, all in black. I pulled Julianna into that photo booth before whoever it was could spot us. Who knows if it was even him? I was probably just jumpy. Still am. I haven't seen the dude since, but I needed to get Julianna out. I went in there to make sure she got to her car—bus—safely, and she did. Still, what if I was drawing added danger her way?

That whole thing with Julianna was too perfect to resist, though. And she fell for it, thought I was talking about some other girl the whole time. I smile, remembering the way her full lips pulled to one side as she tried to figure out the best chocolates for my special someone.

But she has the dog.

This might not be good. I'll have to call Vic and tell him where the recording is. Let him fix this whole mess he dragged me into. And then I'll keep my distance. For real this time. The Reebok Classic Breakout camp in July will be a good excuse. I can feel that scholarship on the horizon. I put my all into the Classic Open Run last month and got a coveted invitation to the breakout camp in Philadelphia, one of the best places for upcoming seniors to score a scholarship.

Walking is about the last thing I feel like doing after the sprint of my life, but what was I going to do? Take Julianna's bus? Whoa now. That has stalker written all over it. She'll flip enough when she finds out I'm one of Vic's "loser friends."

I cross Power Road, eyeing the fast-food restaurants where I could use a phone. Call my parents. But what am I going to say? *I recorded a drug deal, ran away from some guy with a gun, hid the evidence in a stuffed dog I don't have anymore, and now I need a lift.* That would be rich.

My stomach growls, making a convincing case for stopping anyway. I hesitate before turning and heading south, deciding to stop at a restaurant on the other side of the freeway. I could use the extra minute to think, to make sense of everything that happened tonight and figure out what I'm going to tell my parents.

A block or two into my walk, I notice it. Again. An image my subconscious picked up moments ago in the parking lot. Not just any car. Dad's Vette is nice, but this is something else. The car purrs a rich hum as it glides slowly across the road in my peripheral vision. Under speed. I keep my eyes on the ground, stealing a glance or two.

First look: black, Jaguar. My mind picks up the details. Logs them away.

Second: tinted windows, shiny hubs, six spokes. Supernice. This ride could go from zero to sixty in six seconds. Maybe five.

Third glance: F-Type, two doors. This guy is loaded.

The deep hum of the sports car fades as it drives ahead, its rear lights blending into a dozen others at a traffic light.

I tell myself off for being paranoid. Nonetheless, I let my gaze follow the car's progress as I cross the bridge over the freeway, unable to ignore my gut. Something twists inside, knotting up. A hunch.

Something about that car is all wrong. And the night is calm, too calm—eerie.

An SUV pulls off to the side of the road, hazards blinking. Then a truck. More hazard lights. Superstrange. I struggle to keep my eyes on the Jaguar as it shifts lanes a couple hundred yards ahead. It makes a turn and disappears, cutting my focus and redirecting my gaze to the dark sky ahead. I should have been watching this all along.

I freeze, my heart lurching at the sight.

I recall the weather alert on my phone that almost got me caught. Dust storm.

They weren't kidding.

It stretches from the horizon up into the sky, a thick brown wall of dust illuminated by city lights. I've lived in Arizona for twelve years and seen plenty of dust storms, but this is unreal. One, two miles high? From northeast to south as far as I can see.

The hairs on my skin prickle one by one. This thing is incredible—huge. Like something from a different country, another time. Like I should seek refuge behind my camel and use my turban as a mask.

It billows inch by inch. Swallowing the city whole.

Something flicks up and hits my leg, a cricket that scurries away. I stand, my eyes glued. In awe. Then fear slithers in and clasps on, imbedding a respect for Mother Nature, which man is powerless against. Vulnerable.

And here I am.

I reach for my phone before remembering it's gone. I want to get this on camera. Put it on YouTube. I feel it coming. Trees rustle in the distance. I watch the domino effect. Tree by tree, until the hot breeze whips past me. I hesitate. Glance back. I have time, but not much.

I turn around and start back over the bridge, kicking myself for not appeasing my growling stomach sooner. I could be biting into a cheeseburger instead of swallowing dust. Another gust of air hits me sideways, plucking the pricey fedo-whatever hat from my head and sending it flying across three empty lanes of road.

I look over my shoulder. The horizon shrinks before my eyes, drawing closer. Dust covers car after car on the freeway below. It's coming quick.

I increase my pace, but the wind picks up faster. One car pulls to the side of the road ahead while others proceed slowly. At any rate, the road clears around me. Here I am, the only idiot pedestrian who's stupid enough to screw the weather alert and start home on foot. Straight into what has to be the dust storm of the decade.

Wind whips around me, picking up debris. A plastic bag, a Styrofoam cup, and, of course, *dust*. More and more of it. A strange feeling settles over me and I brace myself. What I wouldn't give for my camera.

It's here.

I punch the crosswalk button as it encompasses me, a thick haze that blurs the sky, the mall, the road ahead. Everything within thirty, maybe forty feet. The signal switches from red hand to white stick figure. Not that I needed to wait for any cars. Looks like everyone besides me is playing it safe, pulling off the road or hunkering down at home.

A coughing fit erupts before I feel it coming. I pull the neck of my shirt over my nose and jog down the sidewalk, keeping my eyes peeled for the nearest building.

Trees twenty feet ahead blur into an orange haze. There and gone. Darkness closes in, so dense it's almost palpable. Particles of dust cling to my skin, creeping through my shirt and up my nose. I cough. Throw a wild glance around, recognizing this for what it is: zero visibility.

Apprehension claws its way in and I stop running. Can't see where I'm going. I shield my eyes but too late. Bits of dust lodge under my eyelids, jabbing my eyes. Stinging.

My shirt thrashes around, my shorts flapping against my legs as the wind threatens my foothold. I widen my stance and wait it out, my heart making its presence known as I stare at the inside of my shirt. Hammering. Pounding. A rush of blood through my ears harmonizes with a deep rumble approaching from behind. A familiar sound. A rich, chilling purr.

The Jaguar.

I whirl around, barely see it coming.

Tires squeal. My heart hurdles into my throat. I leap into action, bolt to get out of the way, but too late. My gut sinks as part of my brain comprehends/accepts what's happening. The drug deal. The recording. It has to be.

I hadn't lost them.

Headlights blind me in the instant before the bumper rams into me—my leg.

Muscles, a bone.

A shattering pain.

A bottled-up scream.

I hit the hood, my shoulder ramming the windshield before the car brakes and sends me flying in the other direction. Thrown several feet ahead until I slam into the ground, the asphalt scraping off the side of my face before my skull meets something hard and unforgiving.

And everything goes black.

Buh boom, buh boom.

A splitting pain, a longing to slip back under. Let everything go dark again. Push it all away.

Buh boom, buh boom.

My heart thrusts with a force that takes me by surprise. Telling me something I don't understand. It beats on, won't let me embrace the darkness, a deep-rooted fear trapping me between layers of consciousness. Dirt digs into my flesh.

Dirt?

Pain stabs me from all angles. Sounds drift in. Wind. Lots of it. I'm outside. A car door pops open and slams shut. Two car doors. A hand grips my shoulder and I know this is it, that something I need to remember.

A deep rumble echoes, shaking the ground. Shaking me. Adrenaline flares. Thunder? Dirt, darkness, thunder, and pain unlike I've ever had before; if I'm dead, surely this is hell.

"Is he dead?" a bottomless voice asks.

The hand turns me over, sending shoots of pain radiating outward. A sound shakes my core; a groan. Me?

I pry my eyelids open briefly, glimpsing a silhouette through my lashes: a man. Come to help?

"That's him all right," the same voice says. Distant. He's farther away.

The guy at my side says nothing. Two hands rove over my chest, pat down my sides. It hurts. A lot.

My leg, my leg, I want to yell. He must see it. My shin—it burns. Can't think of much else.

What happened to me?

Dread weaves in as I realize what this guy is doing. Searching under my arms where I have no injuries. Searching my pockets. Going for my wallet? No, he skips right over my wallet. He pulls something else from my pocket, pausing.

"He must have taken these at the mall," one of them says. "With her."

I force my eyes open, anger simmering. Dark hair, square jaw, and those eyes. So light, so piercing, they're not even blue.

His fist crashes into the bones around my eye.

My head whirls in confusion. My heart responds to panic, slamming against my rib cage.

What's going on?

Why?

Some composed part of my mind realizes he didn't want me to see him. A foot wedges under my shoulder and kicks me back over, rocks digging into open flesh as I hit the ground. Warm liquid oozes from my face. Instinct kicks in and I pry my eyelids open. I tuck my chin down, dirt lodging in my scraped flesh as I look for the car, the license plate.

Hot air blows against my ear. "Where is it?"

A voice so warm yet so chilling. I doubt I'll ever shake the memory of this.

"Your phone," the other guy says, his tone urgent, angry. "Did you take pictures back there? Were you recording us?"

Nothing they say makes sense. Pictures? Recording?

I blow out an excruciating breath of air, lungs aching. Feeling like I'm about to retch, I try to focus on the car. I search for the license plate, but it's too blurry.

"Who did you send it to?" the chilling voice at my side asks. "Did you take a picture?"

His tone is so unnervingly persuasive, I want to give him an answer. But I have none. What picture? What recording? I weave through the pain, reaching for something, anything. Some kind of recollection.

I hear a voice saying the same thing over and over.

"I d'n know. I don't know."

Me—I'm the one speaking. My voice is hoarse, barely there.

"Yo, Ian, maybe he really doesn't remember," the other guy whispers, a hopeful lilt to his deep voice. "He's been knocked retarded."

Ian. The dark hair, the piercing eyes.

"What's your phone number?" Ian asks, his cool voice devoid of emotion. A challenge.

I part my lips, but nothing comes. No numbers. Not that I would tell him, but I can't remember a single digit, which isn't like me. If there's one thing I'm good at, it's numbers.

I twist my head at great cost, cement scraping what remains of the skin on my cheek as I spot the license.

Arizona plate. SNT . . .

"I don't know," I keep saying, a pathetic confession. It's the truth.

SNT1039

I will it into memory. The numbers are easy; it's the letters I'll forget. A drop of moisture hits my cheek.

SNT for scent or spent or . . . *saint.*

Irony of the century. I remember my initial thought about these freaks, how I took them for good guys stopping to help.

I glimpse the frame around the license plate, black with white letters in caps. ACKLEN MOTOR GROUP.

Rain sprinkles down, hitting the back of my neck.

"Yo, Damian, should we finish him off?" the other guy asks.

In that instant everything stops. My thoughts, my heartbeat—even the pain.

Damian, the guy at my side—*Ian* for short?—stands up. "And have homicide charges following us? Nah; the kid doesn't remember a thing."

I try to recall the letters and numbers of the plate, but they're already gone.

"His lucky day," one of them says.

Then something smashes into my head—a shoe—and I embrace the darkness at last.

I'm swimming. No, I'm walking. Through rain. Or perhaps I'm running; I can't tell. It's a dream, that much I'm aware of, but I'm too tired to pull myself out of it. And this feels so real, like it really happened before. And then I realize it did.

It was raining outside—pouring—one of the few days each year when storm clouds actually gather above Scottsdale, AZ, and let loose. A monsoon. Rain came down in buckets, angry pellets of water hitting the dry ground like bullets. I ran up the stairs—seventeen of them, taken two at a time—with the excitement of a reckless seven-year-old high on sugar and focused on a mission. No time to waste.

"Jimmy," *I panted after barging through his door.*

Jimmy whirled around, a scrawny six-year-old with curly hair and more energy than a live wire.

Jimmy.

Paper, glue, scissors, and gold glitter covered the floor at the base of his bed. His hands were flying in a frenzy of creative invention. Even then, at only six years old, Jimmy was the artist in the family.

"One minute," *he shouted, scrambling to scrape up what glitter he could from the carpet and apply it to his project.*

"Jimmy, now!" *I grabbed him by the arm.* "The rain will be gone soon. It's our only chance to get the bad guys."

Jimmy resisted my pull as he pressed the last bit of glitter onto his paper cutouts. "Done! Here, put this on."

He held up two glittery gold badges. FBI. US Department of Justice. *Jimmy had outdone himself this time. They looked like Dad's badge. Plus glitter.*

"Come on, Jimmy. Glitter?"

"It's all Mom had!"

"Oh, well," *I said, ripping off a strip of clear duct tape and strapping the badge to my belt loop. This was why I kept Jimmy around. He made me look official, and besides, a good special agent never leaves his right-hand man behind.* "Let's go."

We scrambled down the stairs with Nerf guns and dashed out the front door, flying past the crickets and lizards scurrying toward the porch for refuge.

"Fan out," *Jimmy called above the pelting rain.* "Trust your instincts."

One of Dad's lines and one of Jimmy's favorites—trust your instincts. Bad guys were always easier to catch during a storm. I don't know why. Our instincts told us so, I guess. At least it was more exciting that way. And anytime a monsoon or other storm hit, Special Agents Cody and Jimmy Rush would rise to the call of duty, strap on our badges and guns with pride, and run out into the rain to answer the demands of justice.

A dream—*that's all this is. Yet I feel as though I could open my eyes and Jimmy would be there, sitting on his bedroom floor as though he'd never left.*

CHAPTER 6

Cody

The fissure of light between my eyelids is too bright. My head throbs. Sounds flutter in: some beeping, distant voices, a cupboard closing. Shoes squeak on tile. I let each noise drift around and settle in, a small corner of my mind trying to catch up.

Where's Jimmy?

Gone.

The force of it nails me down, not that I was going anywhere fast. But it hurts. Kills all over again. My brain wants to stop, to block out the light and dive under, back to that darkness where there is no pain.

So much pain.

He's gone.

Nothing new. Jimmy's been gone for a long time. But I feel it all in full again.

Muscles ache, my arms reduced to dead weights at my sides. A burning sensation runs from my shoulder down into my elbow. Skin on fire. I try to swallow but can't. My tongue sticks to the roof of my mouth. Every nerve along the side of my face throbs. Pulses. *And my leg.*

"He's waking up again!"

I recognize the voice: my mom.

I start to say her name, but my lips are pasty, stuck together.

"He's trying to say something," Mom says.

"Probably the same three questions again. Round five," another voice says: Rachel.

My lips part. "Wh-wh—"

"What happened?" Rachel fills in, exactly what I was about to ask.

Mom shushes her. "Rachel, be nice."

"Let him talk," a deep voice resonates. *Dad.*

I try to see him, want to tell him something. Blinding shafts of light flood in as I open my eyelids, and something scrapes my eyes. Almost like I have sand wedged in there.

"Dad," I say. He leans over and offers a reassuring smile. I take in his blond hair and blue eyes and my own smile spreads. Safe. The feeling surrounds me and I hold on to it. Shaken up. Scared even.

"I—" The rest of whatever I was about to say flies away. Here and then gone. Or did I even know what I wanted to tell him in the first place?

Lizzy's face pops up, inches away. "Hey, Cody!"

I wince, my head aching with every sound.

I'm in a hospital; that much I can tell. I scour my memory, starting at the present and scaling back. Lizzy's face, Dad, Rachel's and Mom's voices, the splitting pain, the bright light, running in the rain with Jimmy—a dream—and then . . . nothing.

My head throbs as I throw a glance around the room. "What happened?"

Rachel's eyes roll upward and then settle on my mom.

Mom pats my hand. "Oh, here we go again. Honey, you were hit by a car."

"What?" I say, blown away. "In the Vette?"

"The Corvette is fine," Dad says and heaves a deep breath. "You were walking when the car hit you. In a dust storm."

I take it they've explained this to me before. But this is news to me. "A *dust storm*?"

"Mm-hm."

"When?"

"Last night," Dad says.

I take a deep breath myself and let it out, my shoulder pinching with pain, my head aching anew, my leg hurting the worst of all. I take in the sight: the splint around my shin. My swollen leg.

"Ah, shiz."

"Cody!" Mom exclaims, never one for foul language.

"He said *shiz,* Mom." Rachel comes to my defense.

My heart rate flips into high gear as all I can think of is *basketball.*

"When will it be better, Dad—my leg?"

I reach for my face to assess the damage but think better of it. Feels like I got the tar beat out of me in a fistfight. For now, it's the least of my worries. *My leg.*

Dad still hasn't replied, which can't be a good thing.

It all crashes in, pushes me back down. My leg. Basketball. The team I left at Desert Mountain. Everything I've worked for. How did this happen?

"He needs more pain meds," Mom says on her way out the door. "I'll get the nurse."

I'm all light and dizzy, like I've been pumped full with meds already. For all I care, they can medicate me into oblivion. Knock me out so I won't have to face reality.

A doctor arrives, a guy in scrubs with a stethoscope around his neck. Doc has a warm smile and a wrinkly forehead, like he's analyzed one too many charts in his day. He looks smart, and that's good, I guess. Still, I wish I wasn't here.

He asks how I am. I understate by saying I've been better.

I try to pull pieces of my memory back into place. Senior year. New school. New team. *The Reebok Classic Breakout camp.* "How's my leg?" I ask.

Doc sits down. "We ran a number of X-rays and found a small fracture in your left fibula. You were lucky; an isolated fibula fracture in a pedestrian versus car accident is rare. Typically, both the tibia and fibula are broken and require surgery. In your case, we're dealing with a nondisplaced fracture, so you won't need surgery."

"Good," I say. "When can I walk on it?"

"You'll need a cast for up to six weeks."

My heart plummets.

Doc seems to sense this. "But you're young. There's a chance you'll recover quicker. I've seen casts for these types of fractures come off as soon as four weeks."

I think about the breakout camp in July, my best shot at getting a scholarship.

"But you'll be in a boot for a while after that," he says. "The boot will be removable and will enable you to start strength and flexibility exercises with a physical therapist to reduce muscle atrophy."

A boot. Physical therapist. Muscle atrophy.

My head spins and I think I'm going to be sick.

Doc talks with my parents. I run through the basics; what I can remember at least. Our move from Scottsdale to Gilbert, Mom's hometown. Grandpa Chadwick passed away two years after Grandma, leaving Chadwick Manor in my mom's care. Mom loves the place, loves the land she grew up on, so we moved to be closer. I left my team at Desert Mountain High to go to Highland High. My mom, the floral designer. My dad, an FBI agent. *FBI* . . .

"What is it, son?" Dad asks.

My brows are pulled together, creating tension that makes my headache worse. "Feels like there's something I was about to tell you, but I can't remember."

Dad offers an all-knowing smile.

"I've said that before?" I ask.

He nods. "It'll come. It'll come."

"Why was I walking?"

"That's what we're hoping you can tell us."

Out late at night walking alone through a dust storm? Doesn't make sense. "A *dust storm*?"

"Yeah," Dad says. "Biggest one in years. Delayed flights at the airport. Power outages. Trees uprooted."

"Wow," I say, shocked that I can't remember it. I dig for memories, but my head hurts. It must be there somewhere, buried. I would have caught a dust storm like that on camera.

"I take it I didn't call you guys?"

Dad's lips press into a stiff line. "You didn't even have your phone on you."

Now this really doesn't make sense. "I always have my phone on me."

"Yeah, well, it was nowhere to be found. We searched the scene of the accident."

"Where was it—the accident?"

"On Power Road by the mall."

"But why? Why was I even there?"

Dad throws me a sharp sideways glance, about to pop with irritation. Patience isn't his best virtue.

Mom walks in and apparently senses the tension. "Let me do the talking, Ryan."

I must have been driving them crazy, question after question, over and over. I got a concussion once in the fourth grade, playing soccer. All I kept asking was whether we won or not. I look at my family and note the signs of sleeplessness: rumpled clothes, bags under their eyes, crazy hair. Lizzy even has her pillow, a few ponies, and those polar bear slippers of hers.

I picture myself wandering around the streets last night like some mental patient, confused. No. Definitely not. There had to be a reason.

"I'm sorry," I say to all of them.

"Oh, don't be, sweetie," Mom says. Dad shifts a restless gaze to the floor like he doesn't share her sentiment. Rachel too. Lizzy is wrapping a latex glove around one of her ponies like a saddle blanket.

"Cody," Dad says, "you left the house yesterday with your friend from the basketball team."

"Vic," Mom chimes in.

I remember now: Vic. At least I remember our basketball tournament in Vegas. I recall seeing the picture of his mom in his kitchen and figuring it out. My dad put her behind bars. I recall Vic's living room. Playing the guitar. And Julianna.

She didn't even glance my way.

The memories end there, my train of thought fizzling out into a big, wide-open nothing.

"I was with Vic last night?" I ask. Mom nods.

I thought I had decided to keep my distance. For his sake, for mine, for everyone's. He's bound to figure out who my dad is at some point.

Dread gives me a hard jab as I wonder if he already knows. Did I give it away? Could Vic have gotten mad last night, really mad? I think of his jacked arms and wonder if he threw a punch. Knocked me senseless? Vic's sure to have a vicious swing. But no, it was a car.

"Wait a minute. Who hit me?"

Dad is all eyes on me now, his gaze calculating. He's no longer just Dad; he's the special agent. I've seen that look, the look he gets when something doesn't add up and he's determined to figure out why.

"We don't know," Mom answers. "They must have driven off."

"A lady drove by as the dust passed and saw you lying on the sidewalk. She called 911," Dad explains. "She said she didn't see any other cars near you when she pulled up."

"No one saw the car," Rachel says. "I'm surprised she even saw *you*, the dust was so thick."

"Detective Ferguson seems to think the lady found you pretty soon after you were hit," Dad says.

Rachel stands. This is the first time in forever that I've seen her without her eyes rimmed in black. "Here, look at this," she says and pulls something up on her phone.

She shoves her iPhone in front of my face as a YouTube clip starts. It's a video taken at night, the lights of Phoenix dotting the screen. A huge cloud piles up along the horizon, dust that grows higher and higher and then sweeps over the entire valley.

"Holy—" I stop there, speechless.

"Yeah," Rachel says and takes her seat on a chair, curling her legs under her. "You were in that. Dust all over you."

"Your lungs took in quite a bit," Mom says, her face drawing into a frown.

"I called Vic," Dad butts in.

My ears perk up. "You did?"

"Mm-hm. Called your coach and got his number. I spoke to him on the phone about an hour ago."

"What did he say?"

"I told him about the accident and your concussion, how you spent most of the night repeating the same questions."

"And?"

Dad watches me, reading my every expression. I force myself to relax.

"To his credit," Dad says, "he sounded genuinely concerned."

"Of course he did," Mom says and throws my dad a sharp glance.

A light knock pulls our attention to the open doorway, where a police officer stands.

He extends an encouraging grin in my direction. "Detective Ferguson."

Dad shakes his hand. Detective Ferguson requests a moment to ask me a few questions. I assure him I'm with it now. I hope I'm right.

His balding head reflects the bright lights of the hospital room. He asks questions, most of which I can't answer. Still, he manages to jot plenty down on his report.

"His friend, Vic, will be here any moment," Dad says.

"He's the one you were with last night?" Detective Ferguson asks me. I shrug. "I guess so."

Vic arrives as promised, his hands jammed in his pockets. He wears a careful smile and a small cut lines his bottom lip, spiking my curiosity. Seeing him is a relief for some reason, a sort of reassurance that the pieces of the puzzle will come together in time.

Vic shakes Mom's hand and offers a wave to Rachel and Lizzy.

When Vic extends his hand to my dad, I watch for any crack in his friendly front, a clue that he might know who my dad is. I see nothing.

Vic smiles and introduces himself to my dad. "Thanks for calling me," he says before turning to me. "Hey, Cody. You—ah—you've looked better."

I laugh, and it hurts everywhere. "It's weird, man, I can't remember a thing about last night."

"Yeah?" he asks.

"I need to ask you a few questions," Detective Ferguson intervenes, pulling Vic aside. They stand outside the doorway, out of earshot. Almost. I listen in as Vic relays the story of how we stopped for something to eat on our way to Connor's house.

"We both wanted different fast food," Vic says.

Dad stands at the door, listening in as well. He nods once, like he's heard this all before. Vic must have told him over the phone.

Vic tells the detective how I wanted Wendy's but he wanted El Pollo Loco. Sounds like Vic, I guess. Vic tells the detective he dropped me off at Wendy's and when he came back for me, I was nowhere in sight.

None of this sounds familiar, but then again, nothing from last night does.

"And that cut there on your lip," Detective Ferguson says. "How did you get that?"

Rachel snaps her gum and Dad shushes her.

"Got an elbow playing basketball," Vic replies.

Detective Ferguson jots it all down. "Who elbowed you?"

Vic rubs his chin. "It was pickup ball. At the park. Don't know his name."

Fergusson nods. Finishes up.

"Hey, Vic," I ask when the detective is gone, "do you remember if I had my cell phone on me last night?"

"Nah, man. I called—you know, after we got split up—but you never answered."

Vic tells me he would have called my parents but didn't know their number. Couldn't remember where my house was either. Said he'd deleted the text with my address. He figured my phone had run out of battery and I'd found another way home.

I nod, letting it all process and hoping it sticks.

"We were headed to Connor's house, remember?" Vic waits too long for me to answer. "Sorry. 'Course you don't. Anyway, you were hungry after moving in, so we stopped for food."

"Do you remember moving everything into the house yesterday?" Mom asks, hopeful.

A vague memory of it floats around. In reality, though, I could be trying so hard to remember my mind is making it up. "Kind of."

"Anyway," Vic continues as he rubs the scruff on his jaw, his thumb a little shaky, "I'm sorry, man. About your head and all."

I nod. "No worries. It's not your fault."

More chin rubbing. A scratch on the back of his head.

We exchange small talk and then Vic leaves. It makes sense. Sort of. Dust storm came through and a car veered. Happens all the time in storms like that. Whoever hit me must have been spooked and driven off. Or maybe they were drunk on top of everything. Had a little too much at happy hour. It was Friday night.

Lizzy hands me a drawing she made. A stick figure of me in a cast is dunking a basketball in a hoop. I try to smile. "Thanks, Lizzy."

She and Rachel leave with Mom.

I sleep the rest of the afternoon and dream about basketball. The stadium is alive, the crowd wild, and my heart pumping as I jump to make the winning slam dunk. Something heavy locks around my leg at the last second, anchoring me to the court. A cast. Frustration latches on and I start coughing, dust choking me.

And then Vic is there. Vic in his house, Vic in his car and on the court. Nothing in particular, just Vic wearing that careful smile, his thumb stroking his chin. I've seen that before, that motion. His thumb gliding along his jaw down to his chin and then back. Can't remember when or where. Or why it's even important.

When I wake up my dad is there. He sits on a chair, his elbows on his knees and his fingers interlaced. His gaze is pinned on me like he's been watching me for some time.

"He seemed nervous," Dad says.

Vic. His thumb rubbing his chin: a nervous habit. His tell. I can't remember when I recognized this as his physical tell, but that's exactly what it is. Vic was worried.

"Do you trust Vic?" Dad asks.

I look at the window. Light breaks through the edges of the shade. "I don't know," I admit.

"Do you believe his story?"

Again, I pause. "Yeah?" It comes as a question, like I'm trying to convince myself. "Dad, there's something I have to tell you."

Dad raises a brow, clearly unconvinced.

The skin on my face burns as a reflex smile stretches my lips. "I promise, this time I remember what I want to say."

"Okay, shoot."

"The other day—well, I don't know how many days ago—but I was at Vic's house and I saw a picture."

Dad's brow remains arched.

"It was Vic's mom," I say. "She looked familiar, and then Vic said his mom was in prison. I looked up her name while Vic wasn't watching and there it was: her picture and her story. Mortgage fraud. The FBI put her away."

The muscles in his face unwind, his lips parting into a thoughtful *o*. Or is he shocked?

"What's her name?" he asks.

"Schultz." I scrape around for her first name. "That's it, *Sonia* Schultz."

Dad blinks, a long and deliberate drop of the eyelids before they flash back open. "Humph."

"You know her, right?"

"Yeah." Dad's tone drops. "Probably know more about her than Vic does. That was my case. I indicted her."

"Yeah, that's what I thought."

"Does Vic know this?" Dad asks.

I shrug before remembering how much it will cost me. Pain tears through my shoulder. "I can't remember anything from last night. Nothing."

Dad nods, his eyes piercing through me. "I want you to stay away from him, okay? The defense attorney in that case mentioned Vic had a drug problem."

Drug problem? Vic? Arizona's Division 1 basketball star?

I nod. Dad's gaze roves over my face, studying, contemplating.

I dart a nervous glance side to side before looking at him again. "What?"

"Cement and asphalt are unforgiving," he says. "They tear the flesh."

Kind of random and pretty obvious. "Yeah, I figured that out last night."

"But the bruise over your left eye looks like nothing more than that, a bruise."

I consider what he's saying. "Like a shiner?"

Dad shrugs.

"You think Vic hit me?"

"Do *you*?"

I pause for a moment too long. "No." Regardless, it's the truth. I realize that now. "No, I don't think Vic hit me."

Dad nods. Just once. "Yeah, your head probably hit the hood of the car."

"Yeah," I say. "Could be that."

"All right." He stands, stretching out his arm and scratching his head. "We'll talk more about this later. I'm going to get something to eat. You want anything?"

"No, thanks."

He starts for the door but stops halfway. "Oh, yeah," he says, reaching into his pocket and pulling something out. "This was in your pocket."

He tosses a card—no, a photo—on my lap.

"Who is she?" Dad asks.

I pull the picture up, finding four images. It's one of those photo-booth type cards in full color. And *I'm* in the pictures. Me and . . . I blink once, twice.

Julianna.

It's her; there's no denying it. In the first picture we look like we've seen a ghost, but in the second we're laughing like two best friends.

My mind reels, my head buzzing with questions. How can this be? The third picture stirs up even more questions. I'm leaning into her ear, whispering something that has her smiling. That or I'm kissing her neck. She's hot, that's for sure, and I'd gladly kiss her neck or whisper something that would make her smile again. But that's all I know about her—she's beautiful and she's Vic's sister. At least that's all I can remember.

I glance at my dad, almost forgetting he's here.

One side of his lips twists into a grin and he gives me a look, the man-to-man kind. "You can tell me later."

He walks out, leaving me in the dark hospital room with this strange puzzle piece. I look at the fourth and final picture of me and Julianna sitting side-by-side in the photo booth. I'm smiling at the camera in this picture, not a scratch on my face. Julianna's head is turned, however, her blue eyes fixed on me. She looked at me. Last night? But where?

The mall. I was there with her?

I shake my head, nothing adding up besides the unrelenting throbbing against my skull. Julianna actually looked my way—something I can't imagine forgetting. Yet I don't remember a thing.

CHAPTER 7

Julianna

Two Months Later

I walk into the main office on the second week of school and find a zoo instead.

"Patsy," Carol from records calls to the secretary, "can I borrow your TA this morning?"

That would be me.

Patsy yanks a crinkled paper from the copy machine. "I'll send Julianna back as soon as things settle down," she says. "Julianna, can you work on this copier? Mr. Gerrard needs to sign off on these papers."

She grabs a clipboard of documents for the principal as the phone rings. I set my bag down and get to work on the copier.

"Ah, *sí, sí*. Hold on," Patsy says and then waves the phone at me. "Julianna, they only speak Spanish."

"I got it," I say, abandoning the copier to take the phone.

"Real quick," Patsy says. "A parent is dropping by any minute to collect some missed assignments for his kid from the first week."

Patsy hands me a stack of worksheets, disclosure documents, and a textbook.

I nod and Patsy takes off. *"Aló, esta es Julianna,"* I say into the phone. *"¿Cómo puedo ayudarle?"*

Some guy in a suit walks into the main office as I talk to the lady on the other end about her daughter's lost library book. *"Un momento,"* I tell the lady, about to transfer her over to the librarian, who luckily speaks Spanish.

Visible in my peripheral view, the man's black suit and imposing stance suck my full attention his way. Recognition slices through, slowing the pulse of blood in my veins.

I drop the phone.

"Ryan Rush," the middle-aged man introduces himself and flashes a smile. Blue eyes, blondish hair, and those cocky dimples. Subtle wrinkles line his forehead, though, shaping his features into a permanent stern expression. Like he could uncover all your secrets with one interrogating glance. "I'm here to pick up some homework for my son?"

If it weren't for that smile of his, I'd either burst into tears or throw the paperweight at his face. My throat is so dry it gets a tickle and I cough, realizing my mouth is hanging open.

"Are you okay?" he asks.

Another call comes in, a flashing light on the phone. I'm too shocked to answer him or the phone. I can't pull my eyes away from him. Can't move.

He's the one who arrested my mom.

I grab the stack of assignments and the textbook Patsy left before memories of that day can assault me.

For Cody Rush is scribbled on a Post-it in Patsy's handwriting.

OMG, *his son goes to my school.*

My heart sputters, shaking me from the inside out.

"Thanks," he says. "And thank—oh, what's her name—Patty, that's it."

I'm too speechless to correct him.

"Thank Patty for me. It's sure nice of the teachers and staff to help us out."

He slings the textbook under his arm, inadvertently pulling the opening of his jacket back enough for me to glimpse his gun and badge. My pulse stops altogether. He slips on a pair of shades as he opens the door, exiting the building in full federal agent glory. I sink into the chair, forcing some fresh air into my lungs. I didn't even say one word. Couldn't.

A second ring from the phone signals another call as I try to convince myself this isn't real.

Patsy rushes back in and surveys the scene with wide eyes.

I scramble to pick up the phone and discover it's been off the hook this whole time.

"¿Aló? ¿¡Aló!?" the lady on the other end hollers in my ear.

"Oh ¡perdón!" I apologize again and again. I had dropped the phone and left her hanging. *"Un momento."*

I transfer her to the library for real this time.

The rest of first hour passes by in a daze punctuated with the rude reminder of one name: *Cody Rush. Cody Rush, Cody Rush, Cody Rush.* As soon as the bell rings, I grab my bag and proceed down the hall with caution before reminding myself that this Cody guy is obviously not here today. Like he'd even know who I am. I breathe with a bit of relief, determined to stay as far away from him as possible. Maybe he's a freshman. A scrawny freshman with glasses. And pimples. I feel better already.

The next few days go much the same. I walk, I scan, I jump every time someone calls out my name, as though my subconscious is determined one of these times it will be him. *Cody Rush.*

"Julianna."

I jump. Again.

Lucas slides through the crowd to my locker and slips his arm around my waist. I'm so relieved, I throw my arms around him, a public display of affection he wasn't expecting. His posture loosens after a beat and he puts his arms around me, too, obviously liking my gesture of affection out in the open like this, something I'm not good at.

For Lucas's sake, I glance around to make sure Vic isn't near. I pull away from him. Vic's locker is right next to mine: Schultz and Schultz. Another lovely bonus of having your brother flunk eighth grade and bump down to your class. His locker is now forever right next to mine. Just wonderful.

At first it was pranks. Vaseline on the locker combination, embarrassing pictures of me taped to the front, a condom sticking out between the cracks. Now he's taken it upon himself to "protect" me. Basically, I think he's looking for any excuse to pound on another guy.

A thought slides in: an image of Vic pushing a puny Cody Rush up against a wall of lockers. I hold on to that image. Agent Rush and his punk freshman kid don't stand a chance of ruffling my feathers.

"I'll see you at lunch," Lucas tells me with a kiss on my cheek, his hand sliding dangerously low on my back before I whack him. He walks off, throwing a smile over his shoulder.

I grab my calculus textbook; stupid calculus. I drag my feet. I spot Holly Rusell several lockers down from me. *Rusell—R.*

"Hey, Holly."

Her head of bouncy blond curls turns my way. "Oh, hey, Julianna."

I point to the locker next to hers. "Whose locker is this?"

"Oh, that's Nathan Rury's."

I point to the one on the other side of Holly's now. "And this?"

Holly's lips twist to one side. "Huh; I don't know. But the next one is Samantha's."

"Samantha Rusnak's?" I ask, and she nods.

I stare at the locker between Holly's and Samantha's and fill in the formidable last name via alphabetical order. Between *Rusell* and *Rusnak.*

"Have you seen anyone at this locker?"

Holly shakes her head. "Nope. I'd better go before I'm late."

The one-minute warning bell rings. Crap. Calculus. I start speed walking down Hawk Hall, not about to breach the unspoken cardinal rule of coolness: one should never run in the halls, not for something as nerdy as attendance.

Screw that. I sprint up the stairs to Mr. Mortimer's classroom, rounding the corner and spotting his door as the tardy bell rings.

I slip in and sink into my chair as inconspicuously as possible.

"Settle down, everyone," Mortimer says from his desk. I let myself breathe when it's obvious he didn't notice me. "Pop quiz, people. Get out a piece of paper and a pencil. Oh, and Juliane?"

I look up, veins surging from exertion. And fear. "It's Julianna."

Mortimer tips his nose down to look at me over the rim of his glasses. "You must complete the quiz, but it will count as a zero on your grade thanks to your tardiness. That's warning number . . ."

He holds up two fingers and whispers, "two," as though it will save me from the added humiliation of my peers overhearing him. In reality, it only drew attention to the fact that I'm on my second warning. A couple of people snicker. Candace and her entourage. The beautiful, over-tanned trio of cheerleaders in the back of the room. Candace and I have a history and it isn't good. Seventh grade. Drama class. I've lived the past five years trying to forget it.

"Don't make me go over the disclosure again, people. Three warnings will earn you an afternoon in detention."

Now I'm on fire, burning with embarrassment. Mortimer writes the quiz questions on the whiteboard and a hush falls over the room. I swear Chinese would be easier to understand. I haven't the slightest clue how to begin any of the problems. Mom is the one who got me through every level of math up to this point. One problem now: *she's not here.*

That's how I got warning number one. I failed three of the first five homework assignments. *Failed.* I am so dead.

Mortimer assigns us the even problems—again. Jerk. Answers to only the odd problems are in the back of the book, so I can't check any of my work. Like I'm going to cheat. Have a little faith! Blasted AP Calculus can't end soon enough, and when the bell finally rings I shove my beastly textbook in my backpack and hoist it up.

The sound of splitting fabric doesn't go unnoticed. My mouth drops as I take in the sight of my backpack strap hanging on by a few threads.

I hug my backpack—the one Mom bought for me freshman year—and make my way out. I check the locker between Holly's and Samantha's every time I pass until I drive myself crazy.

"Hey, Julianna," Patsy says as I approach the reception desk for first hour TA the next day. Thursday, thank heavens. One day closer to the weekend.

"Hey," I say as I sit down and unwind. School in Arizona starts at the beginning of August, which means that flip flops and light-weight clothes are the only way to survive. Our AC unit has been working with a mind of its own lately in record-breaking heat, so I relish the slight chill in the main office.

"Ms. Quinn wanted to talk to you," Patsy says. "She said she has a new—"

The door opens and in walks Ms. Quinn.

"There you are," Patsy welcomes her.

Ms. Quinn balances a stack of clipboards, all smiles. I sit up, a mixture of dread and anticipation converging in my gut.

Ms. Quinn reigns over the student council. Awesome lady. My best friend Trish and I ran for student government at the end of last year. Unlike me, Trish made it. Ms. Quinn has been more than nice to me, though. She helped me put out an ad soliciting my services as a tutor. The pageant claws its way to the forefront of my mind and I cringe.

Every pageant contestant needs to have a "platform"—basically, a cause—and a number of service hours. My quick Google search on pageant platforms yielded a carnation-pink Web site bedazzled with glittering jewels titled *Pageantry—Where True Beauty Shines.* Save me now. My heart started tapping out the Morse Code distress call right then.

The Web site listed a number of typical platform topics: all the usual, including literacy, breast cancer awareness, and so on. So, pretty much, I don't have a cause. Not a one of them jumped out at me.

It was Dad's idea, the tutoring. "Just get the service hours in and BS the rest."

Dad was perhaps cooler in that instant than ever. It was a great idea. I printed off a few flyers and spoke to Ms. Quinn the next day. She agreed to forward any prospective students who need help in school—in any subject *but* math—along to me.

Ms. Quinn sets her clipboards down and tucks her short blond hair behind her ear. "I have a new student for you to tutor."

The last student Ms. Quinn passed along didn't speak a lick of English—or at least pretended not to—and while I tutored him in English he spent his time peering down my shirt. Perv.

"What subject?" I ask.

"He needs help with his art class," Ms. Quinn says.

"*Art?*"

"Yeah," Ms. Quinn replies and leans against the counter, "and he might need some help getting from class to class."

"What do you mean?"

"He's in a wheelchair."

Ah, special needs. I picture a clubbed foot, a sweet smile. I was a peer tutor in junior high and loved it.

"Great; how do I get in touch with him?"

"He's planning to meet you in my room at the end of class."

"*This* class?"

"Yep, my room is open," Ms. Quinn offers. "This is my prep hour."

Patsy flicks her hand before turning to the ringing phone. "Go ahead and leave early if you need to. Hello?" she says into the receiver.

Ms. Quinn's room is down the same hall as my locker. Perfect. I can grab a few things after meeting this kid and still make it to math. *On time.*

"Awesome. Thanks, Ms. Quinn."

I tidy up the front desk before grabbing my fraying-before-my-eyes backpack and heading outside toward Ms. Quinn's room, which is in another building.

The lantana bushes spotting the rocky landscape along the sidewalk catch my eye: my mom's favorite flowering bush. Each blossom has several tiny yellow flowers clustered together, like a minibouquet for Barbies. I used to pick them for Mom. She'd put them between paper towels and slide them into the pages of her Bible to make pressed flowers.

I bend down and pick a few to send to her in my next letter. That's what all of this is for: encouraging Dad to finish his project, keeping Vic out of trouble, getting straight As—here's to hoping—and the pageant . . . the *pageant*—ugh. Yes, this is definitely all for Mom.

I hear Ms. Quinn's laugh clear down the hallway. The light in her room is on. Sounds like my special-needs pal has a sense of humor. *Special needs*—that's it! Why didn't I think of it before? That's a great platform. Maybe it's not too late to rearrange my class schedule. I'd love to be a peer tutor again. I pick up my pace, feeling everything fall together.

Ms. Quinn walks out of her room with a lingering smile and heads down the hall. Her eyes light up when she spots me. "Julianna, there you are," she says as she passes me. "Cody's waiting for you."

"Great," I say and smile, taking three more steps before a mental red flag brings me to a halt. I spin around. "Wait, what's his name?"

"Cody," she says and turns, her forehead creasing. "Cody . . . something with an *R*."

My nerves spring into a frenzy. *Cody Rush.*

"I gotta get to the counseling office and back before second hour," she calls out in a hurry. "Let me know how it goes."

I stare at the open door, panic billowing. My lungs take in shallow breath after shallow breath while my mind fights reality.

No way.

I don't care if he *is* special needs. I don't care if he's flunking art. *No way.*

I'm about to turn and bolt when a throat-clearing sound resonates from the room, making me jump. It was too deep, too rich, and . . . masculine. I step forward, refusing to panic but failing miserably. I take two steps back, a tumult of indecision whirling within. One step forward. Another step back. Irrational curiosity wins out and I brave the remaining distance to the door.

I pause. Can't breathe. Standing tall, I suck in a deep breath. I grasp the lantana stems in my hand, my palms a sweaty mess. I gather gumption. I've got this.

I cross the threshold with no idea what I'm going to say. Holding my head high anyway, I stride in. I turn and spot the figure in the wheelchair, my hold on the lantanas deteriorating. Yellow flowers flutter to the floor and my jaw slides down, my mouth gaping open as my eyes play tricks on me.

Yes, no, yes . . .

It's *him.*

Only broken. A scar running down the side of his face.

It's *him.*

Questions race. A cluster of heated words trip inside my mouth, leaving me at a complete loss for anything to say at all.

"*You?*" I say at last, my heart dropping, anchoring me to the spot.

His green eyes flicker to the door and back, his intense gaze nearly undoing me. Anger flares.

I point a finger at him, my throat swelling. The mall, the chocolates, the photo booth . . . the *photo booth*! He nearly kissed me. *Cody Rush* nearly kissed me. And I let him, the son of the FBI agent who put my mom in jail. She should be the one cheering my dad on, keeping Vic out of trouble, helping me with math, welcoming me home. When I get home from school now there's no one.

"*You're* Cody Rush?"

He hesitates. Clearly, I've made him nervous. Good.

"Yes": his voice waivers with a tinge of uncertainty. Or is it regret?

Fighting off a strike of anxiety, I take him in with new eyes and see the differences between now and our last meeting, weeks ago at the beginning of summer. His sandy-colored hair is longer, wavy. A thick layer of scruff covers the chiseled features of his strong face. Fatigue and something else weigh his eyelids down—pain?—giving him a tired, albeit manly look. A smolder, even. Actually, it's quite seductive.

I blush, scolding my imagination as it goes wild picturing him rolling out of bed like this. No shirt. *Julianna!* I shove my thoughts back on track. He looks awful—*awful*. Those dimples of his can't even be seen under all that scruff. He's worn out, beaten up . . . almost like he needs help.

Sympathy twists my heart.

The wheelchair. The scar on his face. The boot on his leg.

What happened?

The hot sting of tears burns my eyes. Not for him, though. That guy at the mall who made me feel like a million dollars is Cody Rush. And to think I watched for him at work this summer, wondering if he'd ever show up again. Only to be let down.

Stupid, stupid Julianna.

"What was that, huh?"—it all comes out in a rush, unplanned and uncensored—"Weeks ago at the mall? The chocolates, the photo booth . . . what, were you toying with me?"—my voice rises as my heart pounds out each fuming syllable—"Did you know who I was? And your *dad*? He put my mom in jail! Was it a bet? Your buddies put you up to that stunt at the mall? *Jerk*. I'll bet you all had a royal laugh at my expense afterward."

His jaw drops. He has the gall to shake his head, like he's in some state of shock. He almost has me convinced, but it's nothing more than a charade. Oh, he's good. Preppy, beautiful boy woos me into thinking I'm something special. How typical. I should have seen this coming, should have known it was all a joke.

No more.

I cross my arms, the quiver of my chin settling as self-control wins over. "Well, you know what? The joke is *over*, Cody. Stay *away* from me." I turn and start out the door, resisting the urge to flip him off.

I crush the lantana flowers under my foot on the way out and start down the hallway as the bell rings. People flood the halls. I push past them, my veins pulsing, my heart pounding. My mind reels. I try to grasp what just happened, what I did—*what I said*.

There's a chance Cody didn't know who I was that night at the mall weeks ago. But what are the chances of his walking into The

Chocolate Shoppe, transferring to my school, and then requesting me as his tutor? No, he bought those chocolates *for me.* What kind of sick joke is this?

I think about Mama. I think about Dad and Vic, the endless laundry, the stench of vomit in the bathroom after one of Dad's rough days, and my mom's six o'clock dinner tradition I'm trying to keep up. I think about calculus and school and the pageant, all of the things I'm supposed to keep on track, hold together. And I accept the fact that perhaps I, like Cody, am putting on nothing more than a charade.

I can't even hold myself together.

CHAPTER 8

Cody

I squeeze through the open doorway, crushing my knuckles between the wheelchair and the door frame on the way. Freaking wheelchair.

Shaking off the pain, I continue wheeling myself down the crowded hallway. Stuck.

"Excuse me," I say, shifting to peer through the chaos of bodies and backpacks. So far, my first day at school has sucked even more than I thought possible.

That isn't how I envisioned my conversation with Julianna going. At all. She knows about my dad. Obviously. I just need her to answer questions about this photo booth picture, about the night I can't for the life of me remember.

I glimpse her through a narrow opening in the crowd and call out, "Julianna."

She hears me; she has to.

"Julianna," I call again.

She flinches, just a quick pause.

Some guy big enough to be a football lineman notices me. "Hey, watch out," his voice booms, "wheelchair coming through."

People see me now, slide out of the way. Two girls smile. Julianna's about to pass my locker.

"Thanks, man," I say and take off through the opening. "Julianna, wait."

I've almost caught up to her now. I'm getting good at this wheelchair thing.

Her posture goes stiff and she dares a quick glance back. Forces her gaze forward again. Picks up her pace.

Oh, come on. She's gotta have a heart in there somewhere.

I stop wheeling myself forward and rest my arms. "I'll make it worth your time," I say over the hallway commotion as she ignores me. "You name the price, babe, I'll double it."

She jerks to a stop, her spine zipping up with tension.

She whirls around, red with embarrassment. People stare. Some snicker. One guy woops out a supporting holler and whistles, offering some man-to-man props. A couple of girls give Julianna the once-over with a look of disgust and I almost feel guilty.

She slinks back to my wheelchair, the color draining from her face as she darts an anxious look around at our audience. Or maybe she's searching for the nearest open locker to disappear into.

She stops in front of me, her full lips drawing into a tempting little furrow as she regards me through narrowed eyes. I see why I couldn't help but notice her the first time I saw her. Her arms cross one over the other, her hip jutting out at an indignant angle. "Do you realize what everyone thought you were implying?"

I hear the daggers behind her words. I shift back in my seat despite myself. She strikes terror into my soul and drives me crazy all at the same time. I can't decide if it's the good kind of crazy or the annoying kind.

I slide a deliberate glance from her lips back to her blue eyes and raise a half smile. "I don't mind one bit."

Her eyelids fly wide open. "Ugh." She utters a disgusted sound and makes as if to storm off again. "Just-just leave me alone."

She's a piece of work, that's for sure, with more attitude than a bull in an arena. And I'm obviously the red cape.

I recall the scar down the side of my face and this stupid wheelchair, realizing that sweet-talking probably isn't my best-played move. I don't look like the guy in the photo booth pictures: the guy she laughed with, smiled at. I don't feel like the same person either.

To say that I slept most of the summer away wouldn't be an exaggeration. Don't get me wrong, I'm not proud of it. My accident made the local newspaper. Sports section. On one hand, I was glad to be viewed as a key player, enough for people to take note. On the other, it was depressing to realize that would be the last sports article I'd be in.

The week I was scheduled to be in Philly for the Reebok Classic Breakout was the worst. Didn't want to look at the cast on my leg. Didn't want to do anything. Slept through the first few days of school, too.

"I was referring to the tutoring," I lie before I lose her. "I *will* pay you."

Not that I was even planning on her tutoring me at all; it was just the quickest way of getting to her. I'm seriously starting to wonder what I could possibly have seen in her at the mall. She's a fireball. Nothing but trouble. In fact, once she answers my questions, I don't care if I ever see her again.

She pauses, her irritated façade wavering. Could she be considering it?

"Why do you want me to be your tutor anyway?" she asks.

Maybe I should have gone about this differently, shouldn't have played the tutor angle. But Mom was right: walking through the front doors this morning felt like a fresh start. Okay, so I was wheeling myself in and I had to use the automatic handicap door, but the fresh-start effect was still there.

I saw Julianna's ad on the bulletin board and couldn't resist. I was more than ready for answers. Like what's up with Vic? He didn't call or text all summer. Julianna and the photo-booth pictures seemed like the best place to start.

"I need answers," I say.

"Answers?"

"*Help.* I meant help."

She tucks her lower lip between her teeth, looking anywhere but at me.

"Listen," I say, genuine concern kicking in now, my voice dipping lower as I remember her mom, "I'm sorry. For everything."

Her gaze meets mine with the first hint of something besides distaste, a shadow of the look in her eyes I see in that picture. I wait for more. She turns to the locker beside her with a huff instead and starts spinning the combo.

She's like Mentos in an overshaken liter of Coke: the last girl I want to get anywhere near, but I have no choice. She has the answers

I want and I plan on getting them. Since I'm stuck with her, I figure I might as well enjoy the view unnoticed while she's opening her locker: her proud posture, nice curves, and the strand of hair teasing her jawline.

I look from her locker to mine and smile, amused.

I wheel myself around and use the combination they gave me this morning: 36, 15, 04. Right, left, right. Open. The textbooks I placed there this morning rest where I left them.

I turn to Julianna and find her eyes on me, her fingers hovering over her combination in midspin. Her dropped jaw snaps shut and she rolls her eyes. "Of course," she mumbles.

She pulls a few things from her locker and shoves them into her joke of a backpack. The thing looks like it survived a war. She slams her locker shut. Pauses.

"Why didn't you tell me your name that night?" she asks.

I hesitate. No idea what to say. I never told her my name? If only she'd hear me out, listen to my fragmented side of the story, and tell me more.

"It's . . . complicated," I say.

Someone reaches for the locker beside mine and I shift out of her way. "Hi," the girl says, her blond hair whipping around as she does a double take. No doubt a little freaked out by the scar. "Hi," she repeats and smiles. Friendly enough. "So this is *your* locker." She glances up at Julianna. "We were wondering whose it was, huh, Julianna?"

Julianna yanks her gaze away like she's been caught.

"Cody," I say to the girl with a nod in greeting.

She smiles. "I'm Holly."

Julianna heaves her backpack over her shoulder as the one-minute warning bell rings. I wheel over to her before she can get away.

"Julianna," I say, my lungs deflated. "You gotta help me."

She starts walking away.

"Just give me a chance," I call out. "Let me show you I'm not the jerk you think I am."

She pauses. Turns. Her lips remain pinched, but I see the smile in her eyes. She tears her gaze away from me, her indignation slowly giving way. "You really need a tutor?"

"I'm way behind," I say, the only truth I can give her. "Missed the first week."

She presses a finger to her eyebrow and massages outward. "With *art*?"

"Big time," I say; nothing but truth in that. The reason I've held a 4.0 GPA throughout high school is because I've put off this art requirement until the last minute.

"Can't help you there," she says.

I flick a glance to her backpack, which is covered top to bottom with colorful doodling. Flowers all over. Looks like I'm not the only one who isn't being totally truthful.

She shifts it behind her back. "Fine, I'll help you this once. Just today and then we're done."

"Sweet," I say. I'll take what I can get. The fact that she's not yelling at me anymore is a step in the right direction. I smile as her eyes linger a moment too long, bugged that I can't remember what our first real conversation was like.

"Uh," she says, jerking her gaze away, "I gotta go."

The hall is clearing out fast, the bell about to ring. She takes off down the hallway in a full out I-don't-care-if-I-look-like-an-idiot-running-to-class sprint. Makes me smile.

"Meet me outside the lounge," she calls out over her shoulder. "Right after school."

I smile, ready for the challenge. Game on.

CHAPTER 9

Julianna

I sprint into Mortimer's classroom as the bell rings.

"Late, Julianna," his monotonous voice announces.

"No!" I declare, breathless. "I made it in, I swear."

"Students must be in their assigned seat when the bell rings," Mortimer says, his beady eyes finding me over the rim of his glasses. "You signed the disclosure document like everyone else. That's warning number three, and don't make me give you another warning for attitude. Warning number four would put you one third of the way to detention number two."

"Please, Mr. Mortimer—"

"Sit," he says.

I obey like a good dog.

"As it stands," he continues, walking over to my table and slapping down a blue detention slip with my name already on it, like he was waiting for this, "you will meet me in my room directly after school."

I pull out my textbook and keep my eyes down, embarrassment, frustration, and a host of other emotions rushing up to burn my cheeks. "Yes, sir."

It's too quiet for too long. I look up and find Mr. Mortimer's bushy brows raised. "Is that more attitude, Miss Schultz?"

"No, Mr. Mortimer," I say, secretly satisfied that he took my "yes, sir" for attitude even though I didn't mean it as such.

He returns to the whiteboard and finishes scribbling the pop quiz questions—which I won't get any credit for. Curse that Cody Rush. I should have slapped him in the face while I had the chance. He deserves it. But slapping the new, wheelchair-bound kid would have earned me a fast-track ticket to the hallway gossip column. If I'm not there already after that whole debacle.

Thank heavens Lucas didn't stop by my locker to see that. On second thought, perhaps witnessing Cody's persistence would have given Lucas a reason to start treating me like more than a convenient girlfriend.

Shock deals me a hard slap. Am I devising scenarios to make my boyfriend jealous of the new kid in the wheelchair? I'm losing it.

Despite this, Cody Rush has the kind of good looks and unnerving cocky tilt to his chin that would suggest he's gotten his way far too many times in his life. A wheelchair doesn't hold that type of guy back. Lucas definitely would have been jealous.

Something in my peripheral vision catches my attention, catches everyone's attention. I turn in time to see a wheelchair sliding through the open doorway. I bury my face in my palms, knowing this day couldn't suck any worse.

"Mortimer?" Cody asks. "AP Calculus?"

AP Calculus—what was I even thinking, registering for this? That was back when Mom was still around to help me.

"Ah, you must be Cody Rush?" Mortimer says. "Right over here."

I glance up to see the table along the side of the room Mortimer is gesturing to, a wheelchair-accessible one unlike the individual chair desks we all sit in.

"It's great to put a face to the name that's been on my roll," Mortimer says. That's it. No warning for tardiness, no stern glance. I guess the guy *is* in a wheelchair.

Cody rolls in with a smug smile, like he hasn't a care in the world. His eyes find me and he pauses. I fold my arms on my desk and let my forehead flop down.

"I'm sorry to hear about your accident," Mortimer says, kindling my curiosity. I lift my head enough to steal a glance. Cody wheels himself into position at the table. "I hope you fully recover in time for the basketball season. Coach Layton told me what a valuable player you are."

Cody nods. "Thanks."

Basketball player. That's all I need to know. No one makes it onto the team without his parents being rich enough to pay for him to play club sports his entire life. Vic is a rare exception, not that Vic is a shining example of high character either.

I peel my eyes away from Cody. I've seen enough. Stuck up. Full of himself. And I took his bait, fell for him weeks ago when he showed up at The Chocolate Shoppe. Most likely he's never been told no in his life. I cringe, irritated that I gave him the satisfaction of yet another yes in his favor today when I agreed to tutor him.

Mortimer turns to the class. "Would anyone like to volunteer to be Cody's helper until he's up to speed?"

A hand in the back shoots up. "I will," Candace's voice rings out.

Of course.

Wheelchair or no wheelchair, Cody Rush exudes hotness. And apparently, he's quite the athlete, which is totally Candace's thing.

Candace pops up, her hair bouncing as she makes her way to Cody's table. She slides into the chair beside him, reminding me of a cat ready to pounce. She lifts a flirtatious shoulder to her chin. "I'm Candace."

I can practically see her fake eyelashes fluttering from here. I should have seen how fake she was back in seventh grade, should never have trusted her. To think that at one point I wanted to be her friend.

I prop an elbow on my table and rest my cheek in my palm so I'm facing away from them, trying to ignore Cody's voice and the way Candace laughs at everything he says—with no warnings or detentions served. Evidently, everyone thinks he's quite funny. Candace is no doubt scoping out the fresh meat that will be on the team she cheerleads for. *Go ahead and have him.*

When the bell rings I snag my things and jet. I lose myself in music during chamber choir, nearly forgetting what a crappy day it is until Mrs. Hughes pulls me aside and mentions the possibility of a solo part in our next concert, as though I'd be interested in trying out.

"Uh," I mutter and swallow hard, memories of my last solo performance back in junior high flitting back to mind with haunting clarity. I force those memories away, remembering how I vowed never to take a solo part onstage again. "I'll think about it."

A lie.

"I hope you'll do more than just think about it," Mrs. Hughes says, not letting me off. "Your voice is so full and warm—just what we need."

The minute bell rings.

"Thanks," I mumble.

"Class," Mrs. Hughes says as I head back to grab my backpack, "one last thing."

If it weren't for the sad undercurrent in her tone, I'm sure everyone would keep talking. As it is, a hush falls over the choir.

"If any of you have ever considered taking AP Music Theory, this year is your last chance. The district is making some major cuts in the visual and performing arts classes offered."

A rumble of low voices spreads over the choir.

"How come?" an alto asks.

"Budget cuts, of course," Mrs. Hughes says, "and added requirements in core subjects that leave less time for extracurricular courses."

The bell rings and some of the less enthusiastic choir members file out.

"We'll discuss it more tomorrow," Mrs. Hughes says.

"That's awful," Stacy, the soprano beside me, blurts out.

"Will other classes be cut?" Riley pipes up.

I don't have an answer. No one does. Stacy is beside herself, lost in the thought of cuts in the arts along with the rest of the choir members, hanging back, dragging their feet. I realize I'm one of them.

I scoop up my things and barely make it to AP English in one piece. Collapsing into my chair next to Trish and Mindy, I try to push choir, math, Candace and, most of all, Cody Rush, from my mind.

"Did you walk through a mosh pit on your way here?" Trish asks.

"Pretty much. Honestly, how do you stand Candace?"

Trish's eyebrows draw together before understanding erases the question on her face. "Oh, no; what did she do this time?"

Trish is a cheerleader, too. She and Mindy have lived next door to each other since they were four. From personality to style they're about as different as could be, but they've been lifelong friends nonetheless. Both have been my best friends since junior high, and we've all known Candace for about as long.

I shake it off. "Oh, nothing."

"Uh-uh. You're not getting off that easy," Trish says.

"Yeah, tell us," Mindy whispers with a glance toward the clock as the minute bell rings.

I take a deep breath. "You know the FBI agent who put my mom in jail?"

"No," Trish says.

Mindy rushes in with, "I think she meant that as a hypothetical statement."

I turn to Mindy. "You mean a preface."

"Preface?" Trish grunts. "Stop using words that shouldn't exist. Just tell me the story."

Mr. Davis walks by. "Extra credit, Julianna, for expanding your vocabulary."

At least one teacher likes me. Davis turns to the class as the tardy bell rings. "Everyone, take out your homework assignments on figurative speech."

Class gets underway. I give Trish and Mindy an I'll-tell-you-later look and pull my homework out.

Davis keeps us busy, never letting up. A text to Trish and Mindy won't do my story justice, so I wait.

When two thirty finally rolls around and the last bell rings, I dart over to Mortimer's class for detention, not about to piss him off any further.

Mortimer raises his head and lifts a smile. "Ah, Juliane."

This is the first time he's ever smiled in my direction, almost like this detention is dessert and he's been waiting all day for it. Jerk.

I sit, trying hard not to let any hint of disrespect escape my stoic façade.

He delivers a paper and pencil to my desk. I don't meet his eye.

"Write an essay, front and back, neat handwriting, on what you did to deserve the warnings leading to this detention and why you won't repeat the same mistakes."

I almost smile.

"Is something funny?"

"No," I reply, knowing Mortimer has no idea that to me an essay is a piece of cake; I love them. Dessert for me, too.

"Good," he says. "You have thirty minutes."

A text buzzes my phone as he walks back to his desk. I sneak a peek. Lucas. He's waiting to give me a ride home.

GOTTA STAY AFTER, I text back. **WILL FIND OTHER WAY HOME.**

The screech of Mortimer's chair legs against the unforgiving tile jolts me. "Texting—and phones, for that matter—are not allowed during detention, Miss Schultz."

"Sorry," I say, praying against warning number four. A warning *during* detention? Now that would stink.

I stare at the blank sheet of paper, thinking about my three warnings. The first was for failing my first homework assignments, which wouldn't have happened if Mama were around. My second warning was for being tardy when I got distracted trying to figure out whose locker was between Holly and Samantha's. I'd had a hunch it was Cody's and I was right. The third warning was for being tardy as well. Today. Thanks to Cody. All of this, to some degree, was thanks to the boy who is quickly becoming the bane of my existence.

Cody Rush.

A flash of remembrance makes me sit upright. I told Cody I'd meet him outside the lounge. I dare a glance from Mortimer to the open door and the quieting hallway beyond. Guilt tightens my nerves until I remind myself: I wouldn't even be in detention if it weren't for Cody.

My grip on the pencil solidifies and I attack the essay, filling the paper front and back in no time. When I check for spelling and grammar I find several lines that make me pause, wondering if I should edit them out. Tame it down.

"Time," Mortimer says.

Wow, the time flew.

I gather my things and hand him the paper before making a quick exit, peeking into the lounge on my way. No Cody. After walking home in the forecasted 112 degrees that feels like 115, my front door has never looked so wonderful: blue, like water. I step from the oven outside into an equally hot oven inside and slam the door. I push the button on the air-conditioning dial. Nothing. I punch it with more force but still nothing.

I take a calming breath, regrettably inhaling the musty stench of dirty dishes, grimy floors, and couch cushions in dire need of Febreze. A new pile has turned up on the kitchen counter. Unopened mail, empty chip bags, a half-eaten box of Junior Mints, and a carving chisel. For every pile I clear away two more show up. I don't know how Mama did this.

Throwing my last shred of patience behind, I run upstairs. I snag Cody's stuffed dog from my bed, disgusted with my romantic self for sleeping with it, and hurl it inside my closet. I grab my thick hair and flap it behind me on my way to the bathroom, cooling off my neck as I kick piles of Vic's laundry aside to clear a path. I pull out my phone and dial.

"Hello?"

"Hey, Dad," I say. "Where are you? Our house is so hot. AC is acting up again."

"Oh, yeah," he says. "About that . . . it broke."

Dread cements my feet in their tracks. "Broke?" My voice hitches.

"Mm," Dad mumbles. Sounds like he's driving somewhere.

I throw a prayerful glance heavenward before kicking one last pair of Vic's boxers, my little toe smashing into the door frame in the process.

I double over as pain pulses. "Where are you?"

"Something came up," Dad says, vague as always. "Got a possible project for the Children's Museum."

I perk up. "The Children's Museum?" It's too good to be true—a new project. Money. Probably not much, but still. "Dad, that's great!"

"Eh, we'll see. I won't be back in time for dinner, so you'll have to cook something without me." Said as though he actually helps sometimes.

I wish him luck and hang up, favoring my toe as I limp into the bathroom. A dusting of Vic's hair clutters the sink, his electric razor perched on the edge of the counter. The sharp smell of urine attacks my nose.

I twist my hair into a high bun and attack the bathroom. Washing. Scrubbing. Singing is what gets me through the daily cleaning grind. I hum away as I throw the rug in the washing machine and snag the mop, wiping away who knows what.

A text from Mindy pops up on my cell, inviting me to get smoothies with her and Trish. Sounds so much more appealing than cleaning Vic's mess and doing homework. I almost abandon the mop and run for the nearest exit.

Lamentably, I reply, SORRY CAN'T. WAY TOO MUCH TO DO. NEXT TIME!

Just about the hardest thing I've had to do all day.

My hands clench the mop and I have the sudden impulse to swing it at the wall, the demands of keeping this place up drawing out a violent side of me I was unaware of until now.

I stow the all-purpose cleaner under the sink when everything is done, the cupboard door maintaining a desperate hold by one hinge. Dad said he'd take a look at this cupboard like *three months ago*.

The dead AC unit slithers back into my thoughts with a slam of fear for the hot hours—perhaps days—ahead.

Mama would have fixed both in no time.

I lean against the edge of the clean counter as Cody Rush comes to mind with a drag of frustration. I remember the silly pageant Mama is excited about, and the service hours I have to complete. And Cody actually offered to *pay* me.

I rest my eyelids and mentally scroll back to our conversation, assuring myself that I heard him right. But having Cody pay me to tutor him would negate the whole point of service hours, wouldn't it? Still, I wonder how much he had in mind.

Shame spurs my eyelids open. Was I actually considering his offer?

No, absolutely not.

Accepting his money would be nothing more than a mockery of everything I believe in. Stupid special agent. Stupid government. I smile to myself as I picture Cody Rush alone in the lounge after school today, looking around hopelessly, waiting for me.

And I ignore a sharp prick of guilt.

CHAPTER 10

Cody

She *is* heartless. Set me up and ditched out. And Vic isn't in a single one of my classes.

I set the green liquid down on the desk in my room and lower myself into the chair, positioning the boot that almost feels like a part of me now. It's like a sports cup: super annoying and a pain, but it serves a purpose and you get used to it. Can't say I'm fond of the boot, but we've called a truce.

I sip the foul green liquid. Tastes like pepper and cardboard, but Mom swears it will help the bone heal, so I drink it. The new electric razor is situated on my desk, box and all. Same one I saw in the bathroom this morning. Mom must have moved it in here hoping I simply overlooked it. I slide it aside and set my textbooks down, scratching the scruff on my chin.

Calculus, English, chemistry, history . . . I look through the assignments. It's impossible to start, impossible to care. I don't even crack the thin textbook for my drawing and painting class. I can't avoid this art requirement any longer, though.

Math, science, even English—I've got those down. Working with numbers has always come easy. Even history is a breeze. Dates, timelines, basic facts. Memorizing things in terms of numbers is the key to getting As, the key for me to remember anything. In fact, random numbers have been bugging me lately, jumping into mind like they should mean something.

I grab my notebook and find the page. Numbers are scribbled across it, and they don't make any sense: 621039. The same numbers are rearranged in different orders, but none feels right. Only 621039 looks right for some reason. Looking at this page and listening to my own thought process, I wonder if my brain didn't get knocked loose in that accident.

I slam the notebook shut and crack open the art textbook, only to slam it shut too. If only I had inherited the creative gene from my mom like Jimmy did.

My head turns, my gaze shifting to the box wedged in the corner of my closet, now covered with a duffel and sweatpants. A few ball caps are stacked on top. Being a mess like this isn't me, but then again, growing out a beard and wearing the same T-shirt three days in a row isn't either. Guess that accident changed me in more ways than one.

Cody's Room: Jimmy's things

I've seen the label on the box several times since the hospital. Mom says I moved every last box in here on my own, so I must have seen it before the accident. Still can't remember anything about that night, though. Did I open it? I tap my pencil against my head as though it will help me remember.

Ignoring it all, I crack open the art textbook again. Color, layering, blending, blind contour: words spring out, silent predators I didn't see coming that take me back to when the artist in our family was still here.

Brushes, erasers, a new sketchbook, and pastels were scattered on the kitchen table, presents from Jimmy's eighth birthday. He sat hunched over his sketchbook, a pastel between his fingers.

I grabbed a fork and dug out a leftover chunk of Jimmy's baseball jersey cake, cutting into the black and gold D-backs letters.

"What're you drawing?" I asked, my mouth full. As usual, Jimmy didn't answer. Probably didn't even hear, he was so focused. He'd been at this for almost an hour and I was ready to drag him out to shoot some hoops. Baseball was Jimmy's sport; basketball was mine.

I walked over, took one look at his drawing, and fumbled my fork.

"Holy cow!"

We'd just returned from a spring training game with Dad, and ap-

parently it had inspired Jimmy. I stared at his drawing, an almost perfect replication of the field and the players from our point of view in the bleachers. SCOTTSDALE STADIUM *was penned in caps over the dugouts. Full color.*

No wonder this had taken him so long.

I forked another bite of cake and pointed out the obvious, "Why didn't you just take a picture?"

He picked up a new pastel—blue—and started on the sky. "Didn't need to."

No kidding. *My gaze roved over Jimmy's work, noting the detail he put into everything: the tense stance of each player as the pitcher wound up, the bits of personality evident in each spectator, the tiny wisps of cloud overhead. I swear the guy in front of us had a hat on just like the one in Jimmy's drawing.*

"How'd you do that?" I asked, shifting a new stack of old-fashioned baseball cards aside to set my paper plate down. "How'd you remember everything like this?"

For perhaps the first time since Jimmy had started his sketch, his fingers paused. One corner of his lips tilted up into an impish grin and his eyes met mine. "Just open your eyes," he said, mimicking one of Dad's lines we often repeated, chuckled at, took to heart, "See everything."

That was Jimmy's eighth birthday. It was also his last.

I snap the textbook shut and push myself up before I can think twice about it. I hobble over to the box in the closet. Won't let myself stop. The junk is thrown aside in no time, the box in my hands. Mom told me that she'd found some of Jimmy's things, stuff she thought I'd like to keep. I'm not sure why I didn't open this before, but it's time to get it over with.

Then why am I still staring at it?

My hands slide along the cardboard, my thumb brushing over the words.

Cody's Room: Jimmy's things

Our names, together. Like they used to be. Cody and Jimmy's toys, Cody and Jimmy's skateboards, Cody and Jimmy's friends, Cody and Jimmy's room. We used to share a lot of things. Now there's only one thing left.

I push the box back into the corner, my heart gaining speed. Climbing into my throat.

I throw the duffel on top and pile on the baseball caps. The door is closed and I'm back at my desk a second later, shoving the art text-book off and kicking it under the bed with my good foot. I pull the news article from my desk: sports section.

> *Top Arizona high school basketball prospect sustains*
> *serious injuries in hit-and-run crash during dust storm.*

I will my memory to recall details of the accident that took the Reebok Classic Breakout camp from me.

Jimmy's words echo back to mock me. Were my eyes open that night? Did I see everything?

Trying to remember only leads to frustration. I pull a picture from my wallet, the edges worn from holding it so many times.

I stare at the photo-booth pictures, my eyes initially drawn to Julianna. But something new jumps out at me, something I hadn't noticed before.

The hat I'm wearing.

I sift through my closet, finally finding the hat. Mom bought it for me a while ago, but I've hardly worn it. I compare this hat to the one in the picture, noticing the plaid is different. I look at the T-shirt in the picture, the one I was taken to the hospital in and later threw out because it was so ripped up. I assumed Mom had bought it.

I grab my crutches and start down the stairs, which isn't a fast process. I've lain off my leg long enough. Even took Mom's advice and stuck to the wheelchair as long as possible between physical therapy appointments.

Mom is in the kitchen fixing dinner. I hold the picture up. "Mom, did you buy this hat?"

She takes a glance, her eyebrows arching up. "She's *cute*."

Lizzy skips over. "I wanna see! Rachel, come look. Cody has a girlfriend."

Rachel walks through the kitchen, a shadow of black clothing, iPod buds plugging her ears. She heads up to her room without a glance our way.

I don't miss the look of worry on Mom's face. She shakes her head and shifts the picture for Lizzy to see.

"Was I wearing this hat when they brought me to the hospital?"

Mom narrows one eye like she always does when she's thinking. "Mm, I don't think so."

"The shirt I was wearing when I got to the hospital," I say, "do you remember it?"

"What was left of it . . ."

"Did you buy it for me?"

Mom shrugs. "I assumed you'd bought it, but I'm not sure. It didn't look familiar."

Shopping isn't my favorite pastime. Nothing about that night makes sense. Sometimes I wonder if I wasn't right in the head. Despite this, I look sane in the picture, with it enough to make a move on Julianna. Too bad she obviously wishes I don't exist.

I pull out my iPhone, the newest model—one good thing about losing your phone and your mind in a pedestrian accident. I wonder why I didn't think to do this before. I wasn't with it after the accident, though. Denial. Depression even. I'm pathetic.

I pull up my debit card transactions and scan back to the first week in June.

June 5 – Debit – BUCKLE 6555 E SouthernMesa – $61.95

There it is: proof. I was in the mall. I bought the T-shirt and probably the hat as well, although I have no idea what would possess me to buy another one. Did I run into Julianna at the mall or was it planned? Obviously she didn't know about my dad then or she wouldn't have been sitting next to me in these pictures.

June 5 – Debit – SuperstitPhotobooth 6555 E SouthernMesa – $5.00

The photo booth.

"Cody." Lizzy grabs at my shirt. "You wanna play hair salon?"

I look down at her. This is what my life has come to. Actually, if there's an upside to having this broken leg, it's been getting to know Lizzy better, even if it meant letting her take plastic Barbie salon tools to my head of overgrown hair.

At school Friday morning I wait in anticipation. Search the halls. Watch Julianna's locker. I don't see her, so I have no other choice but to wait until calculus third hour.

The guys from the team give me high fives and fist bumps in the hallway. No Vic, though. I have yet to see him. Connor, Sam, and

Pablo tell me I'll be back on the court in no time. Shawn doesn't seem to share their sentiment, which is no surprise. He's a small forward, too, and only one player per position can start on the team this fall. It should be obvious that he has no need to worry.

Regardless, it feels good to be on at least one foot again. I'm on crutches today and that's a good thing. Coach Layton meets my eyes across the hallway and flags me down.

He gives my shoulder a hard pat and smiles. "How's the leg?"

I stand tall with my best smile and BS it. "Great."

He slaps my shoulder again, satisfied. "Keep it up."

And then he's gone. My posture deflates. After spending an entire summer on my backside, it's hard to imagine myself out on the court again, playing a game that relies so much on momentum.

I sit in AP Calculus, watching the door, trying not to think about the senior year I could have had at Desert Mountain.

People file in, including Candace and her crew, a duo of Candace look-alikes. Aubrey and Laurel, I think. Candace reminds me of my ex from Scottsdale, Erica. I can't decide if that's a good or a bad thing.

"Oh. My. Gosh," Candace says as she takes her seat next to me, coming to a full halt after each word. "Cody, you're like totally coming to the football game tonight, right? I am so excited."

The one-minute bell rings.

"I don't know. Hadn't thought about it."

Julianna still hasn't showed. I alternate glances between the door and the clock.

"Well, I'm cheerleading, so be sure to stop by the fence and say hi if you do."

Julianna dashes in and slips down the aisle, sitting as the bell rings. She sinks back into her chair, her posture collapsing in relief. I wonder if she'll turn my way and mouth a silent *sorry* about yesterday.

"So . . ." Candace continues; I've forgotten what she just said. "Have you asked someone to homecoming yet?"

"Uh, no," I say and turn a smile Candace's way, trying not to be rude. I've probably come off as a jerk to everyone at this school, but I can't help it. Ever since the accident, smiling is about the last thing I feel like doing. All I care about is piecing together the miserable night when this all happened.

One second later I'm watching Julianna again. She hasn't even glanced my way.

"Your hair is so thick," Candace says, reaching up to drag her fingers through my hair. Her eyes follow the motion before looking straight into mine. She grins. Oh, she's good. Definitely had practice. "Who does your hair?"

"An eight-year-old named Lizzy."

She bursts into laughter.

I chuckle, too. It feels good to laugh again. I tell Candace about my summer appointments with Lizzy and her plastic Barbie clippers.

"Oh my gosh," Candace says, her hand on my arm now. "My sister totally has the Barbie hair salon kit, too!"

Glancing over, I catch Julianna's gaze on me and almost don't believe my eyes. I grin, satisfied that I caught her stare. I raise a suggestive brow, the devil inside me wanting to get a rise out of her because that seems to be the only thing I can get from her. She quickly diverts her gaze, suddenly studious.

She's a flake. Worse: a cruel girl who enjoys leaving wheelchair-bound people hanging around after school.

Julianna is hot and cold, a fireball one moment and an ice princess the next. She hates my guts and I want to hate hers. I note the arc of her spine, the way her eyelids fight to stay open. She rakes her fingers through her thick hair. Blinks several times like it will help her concentrate. Tired. Run-down. I know that look. I saw it in the mirror every day this summer.

It isn't easy to follow someone unnoticed when you're on crutches. Nonetheless, I've had enough of Julianna avoiding me. Since my last hour is weight lifting and I can't do much there anyway, Mr. Talbot lets me leave early. I time it perfectly. I watch her walk out to the parking lot and start after her. It's official now: I'm a certified stalker. I have so little pride left anyway; there's not much to lose.

Her feet drag, no life in her step. I'm easily catching up. She approaches a group of skateboarders and slows her pace. One of them slings his arm around her, and I stop.

He leans in and kisses her full on the lips, the plastic spacer in his ear catching the sun. I watch his lips all over hers, my thoughts careening out of control as the image of our photo-booth picture flashes back to mind. Something bitter deals me a hard shove and I start forward again. I chalk it up as protectiveness, although I know I have no right to feel like this.

As I hobble over, I contemplate wedging my crutch between their bodies. Before I know it, that's exactly what I've done.

Their kiss jerks to a stop, their gazes dropping first to the crutch tapping them apart and then up to me.

I raise a grin that I hope doesn't look as fake as it feels.

Horror washes the color from Julianna's face.

"Excuse me," I say, relishing the kind of victory that should only make me feel like a loser. As it is, I'm feeling pretty good about myself. "Julianna?"

"Who is this?" the dude asks, a Spanish lilt flavoring his voice. He throws me a suspicious glance. He's only a couple of inches taller than Julianna. I could rest my chin on his head.

"Es un don nadie," Julianna mutters, her voice loaded with spite. Her cheeks flare that dark red color I like so much. *"Un tipo nuevo en la escuela. Un fracasado."*

A stream of insults. Couldn't have planned this better myself.

"¡Qué pedo! Buey," I say and extend a hand to Julianna's boyfriend. *"Me llamo* Cody Rush, the new guy who's a loser and a nobody."

Julianna has mortification written all over her face, her cheeks on fire, her jaw inching downward.

"Lucas." Her boyfriend introduces himself with a chuckle and shakes my hand, obviously amused by the fact that I one-upped his girlfriend. I may be a gringo, but I'm no idiot, and luckily, I know Spanish.

"You're sick on that board, man. I saw you the other day," I lie. I know his type, though. Probably on that board every day.

His brows furrow at first, like he's not sure what to make of me. When his eyes drop to his board and Julianna looks away in boredom—or annoyance—I seize my opportunity. My hand darts out unnoticed. I drop the piece of paper into Julianna's backpack. Easy when the zipper is hanging down. Probably won't zip all the way, it's so beat up.

Lucas looks back, alternating glances between me and Julianna. "Thanks, yo."

"Yep, see ya."

I step off the curb and start toward the automatic, feeling their stares on me as I limp away. I sense their surprise at my abrupt departure. I accomplished what I needed to, though; no need to hang around. Julianna's boyfriend wasn't a part of the original plan. Good thing I had a backup.

"What was that all about?" I hear Lucas say.

Grateful for my uncanny hearing now more than ever, I block out the sound of people pouring through the gates and into the parking lot. I focus, waiting for Julianna's reply, ready to detect a trace of anger, dismissal, or—worse—annoyance.

"I have no idea," she replies, her voice hinting at nothing but surprise. And maybe, if I'm lucky, a bit of curiosity.

I'd say that's one point in my favor.

CHAPTER 11

Julianna

I'm five minutes late and way underdressed. I stand inside the entrance of the community center, overwhelmed by the scent of too much perfume. Pageant orientation is in full swing. At least there aren't very many contestants. Five, maybe. *With their parents.*

I take a seat alone on the end of the semicircle of chairs and put on a smile.

"Hi," a lady wearing a burgundy dress says with a pleasant smile, offering me a delicate handshake. "I'm Barbara. I'm one of the pageant assistants."

"I'm Julianna."

She's nice to me, even though I'm wearing the type of cutoff jeans and casual T-shirt that might suggest I'd been on my hands and knees cleaning all afternoon, which I was. I look around at the five other girls, at their either flat-ironed or perfectly curled hair, and regret twisting mine into a messy bun.

"Welcome, ladies and gentlemen." The girl up front lobbies for everyone's attention. She doesn't have to try hard. As if the tiara on her head of wavy blond hair isn't enough to suck our attention, her emerald eyes glimmer under the bright lights, her beauty eliciting a revered hush. Or perhaps it's something more. The way she stands, her petite shoulders squared. Her posture emits confidence, as though addressing people in heels and a strappy gown is nothing.

"Welcome to the Miss City of Maricopa Pageant orientation," she says with a permasmile. "I'm Miss City of Maricopa." She lowers her voice to a mock whisper. "But my friends know me as Lacy Baldwin."

This draws out a low chuckle from the meager crowd. I glance around. Moms and daughters smile. Three girls pull out pads of paper to take notes, highly committed and hopeful that the crown will be theirs. Don't get me wrong: it's hard to look at the sparkling tiara on Lacy's head and not want to get a closer look, feel it, try it on.

A phone buzzes, and the typical awkward moment ensues, the one in which everyone casts glances around the room, wondering who was stupid enough to leave their cell on. When I realize it's mine I'm hot with embarrassment. I reach into my bag to silence it. *Mindy.* Probably calling to see if I'm going to the football game. Friday night and I'm at a pageant orientation of all things, not that I'm about to tell Trish or Mindy about the pageant yet. I'll have to call back later.

Lacy continues talking about the competition, making this all sound disturbingly official. The pageant is underway. She's prepared. Everyone else here is, too.

"One year ago," Lacy says, "I sat where you're sitting now."

With her mom, a checkbook, and a stocked wardrobe, no doubt. Still, her words paint an image I can't ignore. A slightly younger Lacy Baldwin sitting here, perhaps in this same seat.

The pageant director is next, an attractive lady with short-cropped hair. She refers us to a pageant calendar, like we're supposed to know what she's talking about. One glance around the room confirms that everyone else does. Matching folders open. Parents help their daughters shift through papers.

Thankfully, Barbara leans over and hands me an extra folder.

Donna, the pageant director, explains each of the workshops, one per week from now until the pageant in October. Interview, photo shoot, choreography, hair and makeup, post, and presentation. She stresses the importance of our platforms and encourages us to get a minimum of five service hours if we haven't already. Parents nod. Girls glance side to side as though assessing the competition. They have service hours already, I know it. As if Donna's reminder wasn't unpleasant enough.

Checkbooks are drawn out. Money must be raised for the Children's Miracle Network. Additionally, each contestant needs to acquire two hundred dollars in sponsorship money from a local business. Oh, and a fifty-dollar entry fee. I think I might keel over with stress. As Donna wraps up her presentation with a pep talk, I realize I shouldn't be here. I don't belong.

I scram as soon as it's over, skipping refreshments. The image of Lacy flashes back. It's hard not to want what she has, and I don't mean the sparkling tiara. Yet as I drive home I acknowledge something I've known all along: I'm the last girl who deserves a crown.

Our home is dark—and hot—when I arrive. I flip on a few lights, ignoring my juvenile fear of being home alone. Opening the freezer door, I stick my head inside to cool off and numb away any lingering pageant-orientation stress.

The sound of the front door swinging open and crashing into the adjacent wall makes me jump. I whirl around to find Dad in the doorway. He grips the door frame as though propping himself up, his head bent, his eyes squinting.

"Turn th' lights off," he says and staggers forward. "I got a headache."

Friday night, happy hour. My stomach drops.

"I thought you had to stay home to start that Children's Museum project."

That was his excuse for not coming to the orientation. Dad sways as he walks in, leaving the door open. I march over and close it, not about to let any more hot air in.

"More th'n five hundred color pencils they want," he slurs, not making sense. His top lip curls up dismissively. "Stupid coral reef: tha's what my career's come to."

His eyelids spring open and he dashes into the bathroom, banging into the sink on his way. The sound of him hurling is the last thing I want to hear. Stress mounts, the kind that no amount of freezer mind-numbing can reduce. One glance in the bathroom and I can see he didn't make it to the toilet in time.

And I thought our house couldn't smell any worse.

I sift through stacks of stuff near the kitchen sink—rubber bands, sheet music, URE-BOND adhesive, a can opener, even a shampoo bottle—finding everything under the moon besides the roll of paper towels I know is here somewhere. My hands stop when I find Dad's sketch of what must be his project for the Children's Museum. Sharpened colored pencils fan out in little clusters to make coral reefs, arranged by color. I see the vision, instantly liking it.

Finally locating a squished roll of paper towels, I throw it into the bathroom. It rolls into the wall, leaving a trail of connected paper towels for him to work with.

"Did you take a look at the AC unit?" I ask.

He casts a dark look my way.

"Forget it. I'm going to bed," I choke out despite the stench, my eyes stinging from exhaustion. I recall the pageant orientation: the smiles, the glittery jewelry, and the intricate refreshments I didn't try. What a different world, a fairy tale so far from reality. "Don't forget, we're going to see Mama tomorrow, one o'clock."

His head hangs in his hands. "I can't . . ."

I ignore him, knowing perfectly well why he gets drunk but not wanting to think about it.

The next day I give Dad a bunch of quarters at the prison with a list of things I want from the vending machine, claiming I'm starving. Vic has to use the restroom, so I have some time alone with Mama to tell her. I sit, waiting for a guard to bring her in. My eyelids feel thick, my eyes dry and irritated from lack of sleep.

The house is in shambles, who knows when Vic came home last night, and Dad's creativity, let alone his sanity, is lost without her. And she wants me to plaster on a smile and compete in a pageant?

The door opens and she appears. I'll tell her first thing, spill it all out. Our life is no fairy tale; it's time we all accept that. I'm not doing this pageant.

As Mama draws near, I sense something is off. Exhaustion weighs down her eyelids, too. Her hair hangs in clumpy strands like it hasn't seen shampoo or water in a while. When I wrap her in a hug, my hands feel too much bone and not enough muscle.

"Mama, you okay?"

"Eh," she mutters as we sit, her dried lips pinching together like she has a bad taste in her mouth. "I'm not sure whether it's the flu or food poisoning, but a lot of us have been sick."

"Oh, Mama," I say and clasp her hand from across the table.

She slips her hand out. "You probably shouldn't get too close."

Forget germs. She's had no one to comfort her.

"I don't care," I say and grab her hand across the table, prepared to spout off the truth about our home life nonetheless. I can't keep it in anymore.

The corners of her lips lift upward to form a wry smile. "If you think throwing up in your own toilet is bad enough, try throwing up in prison."

I hate Vic more than ever. Anger simmers, not just toward Vic but toward Mama for getting herself here. I tell myself off for feeling this, wishing I could stroke her head while she sleeps, like she always did for me when I was sick.

I keep thoughts of Cody Rush at bay, how the son of the FBI agent who put Mama here popped into my life. It's like he's everywhere I turn. Can't get rid of him. That photo-booth picture is still in my dresser drawer. No matter how much I want to throw it out, it remains. My life used to be simple.

"I'm so sorry," I say.

I debate telling her how tired I am as well so we can commiserate together, but that could have the opposite effect. My bed has an errant coil that digs into my back, our AC is blown during record-breaking heat, and our house smells like men who, upon finding the word *sanitary* in the dictionary, would shrug their shoulders and chalk it up as a misprint. But I'm free.

Dad shows up with my heated burrito and his usual box of Junior Mints, putting on an impressive act. Even I have a hard time believing he was hunched over a toilet last night as well. Vic exits the restroom with a casual grin, and Mama wraps him in a hug.

"Oh, my boy," she says on tippy toes, her arms scarcely encircling his muscular torso. Vic definitely got his height from Dad, but where he got all of those muscles is beyond me. Dad's shoulders are about as broad as his skinny hips.

"Aren't you going to eat your burrito?" Mom asks. I realize I haven't touched anything.

"I'm not hungry."

This earns a frustrated glance from Dad.

In the end, I don't mention the pageant. Or Cody or Vic or the fact that Dad has been drinking too much and our house is falling apart. I don't have the heart to tell Mama the truth about how it's going at home, don't have the heart to break hers.

* * *

Only Dad and Mama know about the pageant and I'd like to keep it that way. Not even Mindy or Trish. And Lucas? Definitely not. Lucas once told me he's sick of drama queens. His ex-girlfriend had something to do with this, and I vowed never to be like that. I imagine he figures pageants are prime drama-queen breeding grounds. I can't believe I'm doing this.

"How was your weekend?"

Ms. Quinn's voice catches me by surprise. I sit upright as she approaches the reception desk first hour and try to force some artificial life into my smile.

"Ah, good," I say, my mouth full as I tuck the rest of my Pop-Tart between the folds of a napkin. I remember Mom's buttermilk pancakes, eggs over easy, and banana bread with a pang.

"And Cody Rush?"

I nearly choke on what's left of the Pop-Tart in my mouth. Warring emotions clash within. "Oh, it's not going to work out."

She offers a regretful grin. "Well, I'll keep my eyes open for any other tutoring opportunities."

She's sick of me. I've flaked out too many times. Picky. As soon as Ms. Quinn is gone and Patsy steps out on some errands, I let my head fall to the desk.

"Excuse me?"

I jerk back upright and look at the girl with a long braid and glasses who showed up out of nowhere. "Can I help you?"

She holds up a wallet. "I found this outside. Can you put it in the lost and found?"

"Sure," I say as a call comes in. "Set it there."

When I hang up the phone, I finish my Pop-Tart, reminding myself to search for spare change in the kitchen drawers if I ever want breakfast from the vending machine again. As I finish my last bite, my gaze crosses the wallet. A corner of worn green paper peeks out. It's probably a one. Or a five. But maybe it's a twenty. I intend to look away, but I don't.

The AC unit, my tattered backpack, the broken cupboard, and every other stroke of bad luck rushes back to mind, striking a bitter chord. So unfair. And all of that money needed for the pageant that I have to somehow come up with. The prospect of things turning around in my favor seems dismal. Not going to happen.

Before I know it, my fingers are pinching the corner of green paper and pulling it out far enough to reveal a fifty-dollar bill.

Fifty.

My heart pounds a new rhythm. Heady and terrifying. My mind reels in confusion. My fingers get all tingly, and I wonder what on earth I'm doing.

I give the wallet a hard shove seconds before Patsy walks back in.

The beating of my heart continues its shamed pulse.

"Mrs. Hale from the counseling office wants to see you, Julianna."

Is that disappointment I detect in her voice? I spin around, looking at the counseling office door not far behind me and wondering if Ms. Hale was watching.

"I told her I'd send you over for the rest of first hour," Patsy says.

My eyes refuse to meet Patsy's as I hand her the wallet and tell her it belongs in lost and found. Every step toward the counseling office serves as a heavy reminder of what I was about to do. Not that I would have taken it, right? My mind fights the memory of a situation years ago when I experienced this same feeling of guilt.

It was seventh grade, back when I had frizzy hair and pimples and glasses and no friends. Candace, Aubrey, and Laurel were the opposite. Always have been. They were in my drama class and I idolized them.

Pamela Redman was another popular girl like them. But different. They didn't like each other, Pamela and Candace. I suppose girls always compete. It's in our nature. Only it wasn't in mine. I didn't care to be on top, I just wanted to be liked.

Candace convinced me that Pamela had stolen her sweater and lip gloss, the kind that could only be bought from stores I never dreamed of setting foot inside. She said no one would believe her besides Aubrey and Laurel. Candace showed me a picture of herself wearing that sweater. The three of them were actually talking to me. I felt privileged and I wasn't thinking clearly. Candace was confiding in me. Maybe I was cooler than I thought, worthy of the friendship of popular girls like Candace.

During a hectic day in drama class, when Pamela turned her back on the sweater and her purse was sitting out in the open, lip gloss and all, Candace dared me to steal them back for her. Begged me. My desk was next to Pamela's, so it would be easiest for me to do it. They needed me. They said they'd take me shopping after school if I did it.

This was my chance. I had crooked teeth, insubordinate hair, and clothes bought from my parents' favorite thrift store. I needed help—a mentor. Like Candace. Someone who could help me navigate my way through high school.

It was only right, too. Pamela had taken from Candace. I convinced myself I was doing the right thing.

I enter the counseling office, my stomach churning at the memory. I got caught, of course, and I've never lived it down. To everyone in that class, I was a thief. Whether Pamela really stole that sweater and lip gloss from Candace or not I'll never know. Recalling the little smirk on Candace's face when our teacher caught me, however, I have a good guess.

I sit in Mrs. Hale's private office, looking at the middle-aged counselor with dark hair. Almost the same shade as Mama's. I think about Vic and the money he stole from my drawer. I think about Mama, about what she did, and the possibility that I might be no better.

After that incident in seventh grade, I knew I had been a fool. Hot with shame, I had promised myself I would be different. Now I fear nothing has changed.

The full weight of guilt hits me as I sit here in the counselor's office—a troubled student—and, like Mama and Dad hunched over the toilet, I think I might be sick.

CHAPTER 12

Cody

She's deep in thought. Exhausted yet jumpy. Nervous yet relieved. She's hard to read. I sit at the side table in calculus while Mortimer drones on, leaning over enough to see Julianna.

I feel a tap on my leg. Candace gestures to her notebook. A stick-figure version of Mortimer stands at the whiteboard, his back to the class of stick-figure students with their heads on their desks. Little zs float up from each sleeping student.

I chuckle. Candace bursts into laughter. Everyone looks our way, including Mortimer.

"Settle down, Candace," he says and turns back to the board.

Julianna's piercing blue eyes rest on me.

I straighten up. She never looks at me in class. It's like I don't exist.

Julianna shifts her gaze away, not in an uncomfortable, edgy sort of way. More like she's bored. Almost annoyed.

Frustration settles in as I lean back, propping my textbook open. I look down at the boot, frustrated that I can't remember anything about the night this happened. I hate this school, too; the daily grind and the fact that I'm dumb enough to hope tomorrow will be better than today. And obviously I've let yet another person down.

Something was there between us at the mall that night. I see it in the pictures. How did we come to this? Did I see the Julianna then that I see now? Tired, stretched to her limit. *Maybe even in trouble.*

That was a weird thought. Random.

But true?

A feeling creeps in. The shadow of a memory on the horizon. A memory blocked. Trapped. I get all tense. It begins to fade and I clench my fist, realizing how much I want to recall that night. I grasp for something I can't remember yet feels so close.

Adrenaline courses through my veins. My heart thrusts against my rib cage. Buh boom, buh boom.

Danger.

My eyes zero in on Julianna as recollection of that feeling rushes in. It's strong. Suffocating. Linked to Julianna? This is messed up. I feel a sudden urge to protect, an impulse I've only felt so strongly one other time.

Jimmy.

And now Julianna. Something must be up with the school's AC because it's suddenly way too hot. I close my eyes, the unrelenting beat of my heart hammering a strange feeling through me: *fear*. I've felt this before.

A shiny floor, bright lights, potted plants, a trash bin—the mall.

I walk alongside what few shoppers remain in the mall. Blending in. Hiding. I pull the brim of my hat down, glancing side to side. Searching for something, someone. *Scared.*

And then I see her. Long dark hair. And those eyes.

I almost take the first step toward her . . . to make sure she's okay. She *is in danger.*

621039

Those numbers again.

The hazy awareness of something slipping off my lap and tumbling to the floor yanks me out of it. My textbook lies face down on the floor, pages crinkled against tile. Every eye is on me. I realize I'm sweating.

I push myself up and grab my crutches. "Hall pass?" I ask on my way out, not that I'm really asking.

"Go ahead," Mortimer says, looking a bit taken aback. And no wonder.

I head to the bathroom, not sure where else to go, and run straight into Vic.

"Whoa," he says, kind of jittery. "Hey, man."

He sniffs and wipes his nose, a trace of something red smearing the back of his hand. Blood. This is the first time I've seen Vic at school in the past week and I clam up. He's blinking a lot, like the lights are too bright for him. And he smells, or is it the bathroom?

"Hey, Vic."

"Been a while, man," Vic says. "What you been up to? I see you're back on your feet." He moves to the door, giving me little chance to reply. He's not himself, but then again, would I know? We hardly know each other. This thought reinforces the impulse to guard my trust.

"Hey, I can't remember—which restaurant did you say you drop-ped me off at that one night?" I ask anyway.

Vic rubs his chin. "McDonald's. Something like that. I can't re-member," he says and swings open the door. "I gotta get back yo."

I lean on my crutch. "Maybe we can catch up sometime."

So many questions I should have asked him about that night.

"Yeah, sure, man," Vic says. "Whatever. See ya."

I stand in the bathroom entrance after he's gone. *Wendy's*. At the hospital Vic told me he'd dropped me off at Wendy's, not McDonald's. He very well could have forgotten. And it's obvious Vic doesn't have the answers I need. He dropped me off and left, leaving only one per-son I know of who can tell me what I was doing that night.

Julianna.

Her family is nothing but trouble. Vic is messed up. I remember what Dad told me in the hospital, about how Vic had a drug problem. Is he still using? No. He's Arizona's Division 1 basketball star. Ranked second in the state. There's no way he'd jeopardize those scholarships.

Obviously he wants nothing to do with me anymore, and neither does Julianna. Not that I want much to do with them. But the irrita-tion of not being able to remember something that feels so important is turning me into a nut job. I went out for fast food with Vic, ended up in a photo booth with Julianna instead, and then got hit by a car?

621039

The recollection of those numbers tied to that random flashback in math is proof: they do mean something.

I'm hobbling along toward my locker between classes when I see her. She stands on tiptoe, searching her locker. Her shirt hugs her slender waist and every other curve. She's Mentos in Coke for sure—an explosion of spunk and nerve waiting to happen—but she sure is beautiful. And yet she hides in the shadows. I've watched her long enough to know that.

She hasn't noticed me yet, so I quickly form a plan and move forward before I think better of it. I'm leaning against the locker two down from hers when she sees me and jolts back.

The smallest hint of humor in her eyes disappears as fast as it appeared. Like she was about to smile but composed herself at the last second. Ice princess again.

"I think we got off on the wrong foot," I say, underscoring the words with a smile. My crutch supports me as I offer my hand.

Her gaze drops and she regards my hand like something that could bite if she gets too close. This is not going well.

"Hi," I say, pressing on anyway. "I'm Cody Rush."

She hugs a textbook close to her chest, her lips parted in a speechless albeit enticing little *o* that leaves me wondering what on earth she's thinking. Her jaw snaps shut and she looks around, as if she suddenly realizes there are people walking past. Onlookers.

Her eyes rest on my hand again. The corners of her lips twitch, almost a smile. Fleeting but there nonetheless.

Her hand slides into mine, and it feels good.

"Julianna Schultz."

Our gazes collide as we shake on it. It's not much, nothing more than one step in the right direction after taking so many steps in the wrong one. I smile, heeding the impulse to leave before I do anything that might retract that step. Our hands drop, and for the first time in more than two months I hardly notice my crutches as I make my way down the hall.

"Lace up, Lizzy," I call out. "Ice cream for two. It's on me."

"Yay!" Lizzy jumps up from her pile of homework in the living room. "With sprinkles?"

"Yep, tons."

"Wait a minute," Mom mumbles with a ribbon between her teeth. She's making flower arrangements for a wedding. Vases line the counter. "You have homework, Lizzy."

"I'll help her when we get back," I offer, perfectly fine with the fact that I'm fighting for an eight-year-old's company. Lizzy's the only one for the job, though.

Since I've safely driven the automatic to school and back a couple of times, Mom doesn't argue further.

"I want to push the button," Lizzy protests twenty minutes later at the mall. She reaches for the handicap button for the automatic door as I reach for the handle.

The slick metal glides along my palm and I wait for a flash of remembrance.

"I didn't use the button that night," I say to myself, knowing I wasn't on crutches then.

"What?" Lizzy asks.

"Nothing," I say and stand aside while she pushes the button.

An air-conditioned breeze hits us when we step in. I try to imagine what this place would look like at night. That night.

Lizzy tugs at my arm. "C'mon, Cody. Ice cream!"

"You're on."

An escalator takes us up to the food court. I get Lizzy a huge ice cream with tons of sprinkles and we find a table in the hallway. Only four bites of double fudge ice cream make it down before I'm too preoccupied to care. Definitely not like me. The chair, the table, the lit-up display windows: I take in everything, but nothing comes. No flashback like before.

Giving up, I look down at my ice cream. Light reflects off the tile below.

A shiny floor—tile.

I focus, thinking back on the little pieces I remembered in math that morning. I was definitely here and I was nervous. *Admit it; I was scared.* The feeling rushes back even now. Or do I simply fear what I can't remember? Am I making this up?

To say that some wires got crossed when I hit my head that night is no exaggeration.

Lizzy's lips are covered in pink ice cream when I look back up. "Can I do the carousel after this?"

"Sure," I say. "And then you and I are going to do a photo booth."

"Ooo." Her eyes go wide and she takes another bite of ice cream.

Lizzy rides the carousel three times in a row, switching from a pink horse to a giraffe and finishing off on a zebra before I can convince her it's photo-booth time.

I stare at the photo booth downstairs, the black curtain and ads of people making cheesy faces at the camera, waiting for it to jar a memory. Again, nothing. Julianna and I were here? I glance around, noting a toy store, a women's clothing store, and a hat store. *The hat.*

Buckle.

The sight of the big Buckle sign sets something off inside me. I still don't remember being here, but the debit-card statement is proof that I was. I stare at the sign down the hallway. I study the red logo. *621039*—what do those numbers mean? Sixty-two, ten, thirty-nine? I pair off numbers, trying to make sense of them.

Lizzy lets out a tired breath of air. "Can we take the picture now?"

"Oh, yeah," I say and turn.

Dark hair and blue eyes catch my attention. I do a double take. The same shirt hugs her form.

I almost slip off my crutch.

The chocolates.

Now I remember, not from the night of the accident but from my first day at school, when Julianna walked into Ms. Quinn's room and yelled at me. She mentioned *the chocolates.* It made no sense then. Staring at the store sign now, I understand.

"Aw, look at those stuffed animals," Lizzy exclaims and rushes off.

Julianna works in the mall? I try to imagine her reaction if she sees me standing here, staring at her. I get the feeling I don't want to hang around to find out. Warning: *abort.*

"I wonder if they have a polar bear," Lizzy says, standing at a re-tail kiosk full of stuffed animals. "Can I have an animal *and* photo-booth pictures?"

"Lizzy," I whisper, "we gotta go."

"What about the photo booth?"

"Later, I promise."

"But you said this photo booth is extra cool."

"It is," I say, knowing that Julianna and I sat side by side in there, my lips above her ear, my nose testing out the scent of her shampoo. Suddenly I admit it: perhaps I do want something to do with Julianna. And I'm talking more than just answers. "We gotta go, though."

"Can I at least have an animal?" Lizzy asks, still peering around for a polar bear.

"How about this," I offer as I scoot around the stand of animals, keeping my eye on Julianna from a safe distance. "I'll buy you a polar bear on Amazon. Or another pair of those polar bear slippers; yours are falling apart."

Lizzy's eyes narrow to form her game face. "*And* a bathrobe to go with my slippers," she says. Definitely the youngest child.

"Deal."

We make a clean exit, unnoticed.

"You look angry," Lizzy says as we cross the street.

"I can't remember anything about the night when I got hit by that car," I admit. "I know I went into the mall, but I don't even remember walking in there."

"Well, maybe you were *skipping* in," she says.

I chuckle. "Yeah, maybe."

"*Running?*" she suggests.

I pause, glance back.

"Come on," I say, pushing the unlock button on the car key. "Let's get home."

So many questions, so many things I'm still unsure about. But one thing I'm sure of now more than ever: If I'm going to get close to the buried details of that night, I'll need to get close to Julianna first. And that might not be such a bad thing after all.

CHAPTER 13

Julianna

I organize the bills in the cash register at The Chocolate Shoppe, regretfully reminded of the wallet that tempted me in the school office. There's no light way to put it: I definitely considered it.

I head out after my shift, keeping my eyes averted from the photo booth in the hallway. Being called into the counseling office had nothing to do with the wallet. Mortimer had turned my detention essay in; whether for the pure delight of proving I am mischief or because he's genuinely concerned, I'm not sure. I regret dashing off those truths about my life, writing all about my mom's imprisonment and stress at home, how I can't sleep, can't focus on homework. I even spouted off about how unfair our government is.

Idiot. What did I expect? Regardless of how hard I tried to convince Mrs. Hale I'm fine, she wants to talk again. This only made me feel worse, like a teen in need of intervention.

Then Cody showed up, standing next to my locker like he'd been watching me for some time. The special agent's son, sniffing out trouble. But he smiled that smile of his and even reintroduced himself with charm, offering his hand like he wasn't ashamed of being associated with a nobody like me. Whether I like to admit it or not, that meant something.

But am I kidding myself? Cody doesn't know about the wallet, doesn't know I considered taking someone else's money.

When I get home I find my dad at the darkened living room window, his tools spread out amid piles of laundry and a pizza box. A rusty piece of junk is wedged in the window—the old swamp cooler. Dad had kept it in our garage all these years.

"What's this?" I ask, tapping my foot against a second hunk-of-metal swamp cooler that's even uglier than the first, if that's possible.

"Oh, that," Dad says. "It's a portable swamp cooler. I found it for next to nothing at Goodwill."

"I figured." It was either that or he traveled back in time to get it. *Two* swamp coolers, though. This should help.

Seeing as how Dad went out to buy an extra swamp cooler and even grabbed pizza for dinner, I start to hope our financial situation isn't so bad after all. So I decide now is as good a time as any to bring it up.

"Hey, Dad?"

"Yeah?" he says, using his ratty T-shirt to mop up the sweat on his forehead. The veins on his arms bulge, his muscles reduced to nothing. His hair has flecks of gray where there used to be none and dark circles shadow his eyes.

Stress has done this to him, stress and working hard in the only way he knows how to earn a living for our family. Looking at him now, I almost chicken out and say nothing.

"I need money," I blurt out, instantly aware that I should have crafted my request better. "I mean, it's for the pageant. There's a fifty-dollar entry fee, and we're supposed to donate money for the Children's Miracle Network on top of that. Then there's the two hundred dollars in sponsorship money; I'll need to find a local business willing to sponsor me."

I stop there, leaving out money needed for dresses, makeup, and hair. I'll have to borrow.

If it's possible, Dad looks even older now than he did a second ago. "Do you even *want* to be in a pageant?"

"This isn't about me, Dad."

He heaves in a deep sigh. "For Mom."

"Yes. She wants this. It's the least I can do."

Dad's head drops. "You'll have to come up with the money on

your own. Work a few extra hours at The Chocolate Shoppe or some-thing."

Fears confirmed. I'm on my own. I only have two shifts at The Chocolate Shoppe now, Tuesday and Thursday nights. I could quit and find a new job, but I'm going to be hard pressed to find another boss like Suz, who will work around my busy school and soccer schedule once the season starts.

I haven't bought clothes or jewelry in months. No music down-loads from iTunes. I've even avoided extra school activities that cost. Still, I struggle to afford my Reduced Fare ID card for the Valley Metro and my monthly cell phone payment. Basically, since the breadwinner in our family went to prison, I've had to put a portion of my paycheck toward groceries and other necessities. Shampoo, de-odorant, floss . . . if I don't buy them, they simply don't get bought.

"Fine. I'll figure it out," I say, frustration and hunger compound-ing to give me a headache. "I'm gonna eat and go to bed."

I bend down and open the pizza box, finding crumbs and a dry piece of pepperoni inside.

"Oh, sorry." Dad turns back to the swamp cooler. "Vic and Heidi finished it off before they went out for the night."

I drop the lid, cursing Vic and his girlfriend. I open the freezer and pull out a bag of tamales Mama and I made two weeks before she was arrested. As I take my first bite of reheated tamale, I close my eyes and envision Mama sitting here eating beside me.

The next morning I watch a rugged and annoyingly handsome Cody Rush smile at something Candace says in math. He seems more chipper today. Maybe because Candace is practically throwing herself at him.

A hot flash of jealousy sets my temper on fire, surprising me. I shouldn't care. Why on earth do I? He's not the boy I met at The Chocolate Shoppe. Candace is his type, and I'm fine with that.

Cody says something back in a hushed tone that earns a fit of gig-gles from Candace. When Mortimer slides a glance their way and pretends he didn't notice, anger boils. No detention slips for seem-ingly perfect students like Candace or Cody.

I try to pretend they don't exist, but my insubordinate eyes trail back to Cody. Perhaps his mock "introduction" in the hallway yester-day was a joke. Cody flirts with girls for sport no doubt, reeling in as many as possible. And I'm one of the many fish stupid enough to take his bait.

Candace scoots closer to Cody, shifting in her seat to give him an eye load of her cleavage. I watch Cody studying his textbook, daring him to look at her impressive display. I'm still waiting three minutes later when he glances up at me instead, catching my stare.

I look away. I promised myself I'd be civil today, that I'd at least smile if our gazes met. Now I realize I'd be making a fool of myself. He'd figure me for some hopeless girl crushing on him from a distance.

Despite this, my eyes gravitate back to Cody. And he's still looking at me. One side of his lips quirks up into a grin and he nods, lending my heart a set of wings it shouldn't have.

I stare at my book the rest of the class period.

Trish and Mindy are up to something when I walk into English. Lots of giggling and even a high-pitched squeal from Trish. With two minutes left until the bell rings, I slip into my chair and get straight to the point. "Who's the guy?"

Trish beams. Mindy pretends she's clueless, but her blush deepens.

"Oh my gosh, oh my gosh," Trish says, pounding her desk for emphasis. "He's so freaking hot."

"Who? Trent?"

"No, Trent was so yesterday," Trish says, as though we're discussing boom boxes versus iPods here.

"Then who?"

Giddy is my least favorite word, right up there with *lovesick* and, worst of all, *desperate*—basically not a word I would choose to describe a good friend. Looking at Mindy now, however, it's all that comes to mind.

"The new guy!" Mindy bursts out in the loudest possible whisper, as though admitting her interest cost her a kidney.

Nerves converge in my chest, quickening my pulse. I don't need clarification.

"Who?" it rolls off my tongue anyway, confirming how badly I want to be proven wrong. Anxious, hopeful—*desperate.*

Trish mistakes my desperation for interest, leaning forward and making a low groan in her throat like she just took a bite of chocolate cheesecake. "Mm, Cody Rush."

This is when I realize I never told them about Cody, about the mall or how I figured out who he really is. Maybe it was denial, a subconscious need to pretend he doesn't exist. Here Trish and Mindy are, as good as lovesick, and they didn't even see the tall, confident, unscarred Cody Rush I met months ago. Not even Candace knows that Cody. The girls at Highland High are going to have a heyday with him.

What would Trish and Mindy think if I told them about Cody's offer to pay me to tutor him?

"He is, like, the cutest thing *ever*," Trish gushes as the tardy bell rings.

Mr. Davis makes his way to the front of the room, leaving me no chance to say a word about Cody. I'm not sure I want to. I get a feeling the topic of Cody Rush is going to be one of those things that's never-ending. Like laundry.

I find a quiet hall during lunch and call an AC repair service. When Dad set up the swamp coolers, I let my hopes soar. Last night was a cruel reminder of how much swamp coolers suck. Not one wisp of cool air made it up to my room. We're going on *seven nights* with no AC.

A maintenance check will be forty-five dollars, the guy tells me.

"And what if there's a problem?" I ask. "How much will repairs cost?"

"Mm, hard to say. Could be anywhere from one hundred to several hundred dollars."

My gut sinks. "And what if the whole thing needs to be replaced?"

He tells me a new unit plus installation will run about five thousand dollars and I end the conversation.

I'm in the bathroom a moment later, leaning against the sink. *How are we going to pay for this?* We've been late on utility payments before; I've sorted through the stacks of mail often enough to figure that out.

An idea shifts into place. What if Dad doesn't want to fix the AC? What if we simply can't afford AC anymore? Breathing suddenly feels like a hard thing to do. An idea springs up and I snag my phone again. I dial and luckily, Ms. Taylor answers.

"Hi, Ms. Taylor, this is Julianna."

Ms. Taylor lives down the street. Once she offered to pay me if I was ever interested in washing her windows. I thought I was too busy then, already working enough.

"Do you still need someone to wash your windows?"

"Sorry, Julianna," she says. "I just had them washed."

"Okay, no worries," I rush in. "Let me know if you ever have any cleaning or anything else you're looking to have done."

This is what my life has come to: pleading to clean other people's houses in addition to our own.

Ms. Taylor tells me she'll keep me in mind if something comes up. I thank her and hang up. Right now I'm wishing I had a rich grandparent, a rich aunt or uncle—*someone*. Dad's an only child and his parents aren't well off; my grandpa's failing health and high medical bills are draining what little money they have.

Mama's mother passed away years ago, and her dad is the old-fashioned, work-for-hire type. Besides, he lives in Southern California.

I dab on some makeup, pulling my thoughts away, but my face still looks washed out, tired, hopeless. I shade my face from the bright lighting to see if it makes a difference. When I accept the fact that the bathroom lighting has nothing to do with it, I shove the makeup in my backpack, noticing a lone piece of crinkled paper at the bottom. I snag the paper and head to the trash, my feet cemented to the floor as I find someone else's handwriting there.

In case you change your mind.
Cody (480) 291-0632

The door to the bathroom bangs open and I flinch. A group of girls shuffles in, chatting. I reread the note, terrified at the idea of Cody Rush putting this here without me noticing. When? How? Perhaps my pride isn't all lost, because right now it's putting up an admirable fight, one last-ditch attempt to save my dignity. Mindy and Trish would flip if Cody left a note like this in their backpacks, but I'm not so easily persuaded.

His dad put my mom in prison. Agent Rush started this all—the fear, the financial stress, the shift in roles at home . . . the heartbreak. No, Vic and his drug addiction started this. Then Mama took the underdog's side yet again and went to illegal lengths to help him. Loyalty to family kicks in regardless, urging me to hold firm. But Dad, Mom, and Vic leave me no choice.

With one last bleak assessment of my lack of options, I decide there's only one thing I can do.

CHAPTER 14

Cody

I lift weights in sets of sixty-two, ten, and thirty-nine. Sixty-two crunches, ten shoulder presses, thirty-nine pushups. *621039.*

Dr. Huntington, my physical therapist, is impressed with the progress my leg is making. My leg is one ugly beast, that's for sure. White skin, stiff joints, soft muscles. But the bone is recovering at a remarkable rate. That's all that matters.

It's been almost eleven weeks since the accident, so I'd say it's about time. Six weeks in the cast and now I'm going on six weeks in the boot. It feels good to be building up strength after laying off for so long. Still, it feels like a mean joke, having my leg broken during my best shot at a scholarship. I missed the Reebok Classic Breakout camp.

A bell rings. School's almost out. Everyone is wiping down equipment, talking, laughing. Someone turns off a radio I hadn't noticed was on. *621039.* Those numbers are driving me insane.

I take my time in the shower. Usually I wait to shower at home, but honestly, I have no idea what I'm supposed to be doing these days. My life feels pointless, and as I wrap a towel around my waist, I wonder how I got here. How did everything get screwed up so fast?

Three months ago I was finishing up my junior year at Desert

Mountain. At the top of my game. No injury. So many possibilities lay on the horizon at that point. If only I'd known. If only I hadn't hung out with Vic that night.

Vic. Something doesn't sit right with me about him. Nothing about that night does. And these stupid numbers aren't getting me anywhere. 621039. They probably mean nothing.

I throw on some fresh clothes and head out, shielding my eyes from the blinding sun. Spotting Julianna in the courtyard is about the last thing I expected.

She looks away as soon as my eyes make contact with hers. Obviously she was waiting for me. I feel the corners of my lips twitching upward.

She holds up a little piece of paper, the one I wrote my number on.

I smile. "You found it."

It was meant as a light way to break the ice, but I can tell it was the wrong thing to say.

She puts one hand on her hip and darts an irritated glance sideways, like simply being in my presence is killing her. "Yes, I found it."

I brush the hair off my forehead, still wet from the shower, and flash a smile that feels rusty. Three months. It's been almost three months since I've been out with a girl or even cared to flirt with one.

I take one more step toward her and stand tall, wishing I didn't still have this crutch. "You could have called, you know," I say, extending the invitation again. Judging by the way she's acting, you'd think she's scared of me.

"I don't need your number," she huffs and takes a step back, the color in her cheeks betraying the impassive front she's putting on. She's nervous. "I know where to find you."

I raise a suggestive brow, which makes her blush deepen.

"Don't flatter yourself," she says. "I didn't mean it like that."

"Then why are you here?"

"You, a—" She looks around, like the words she's searching for are hiding under a rock somewhere. "I just . . . wanted to make sure you found a tutor."

Amused, I smile. "You worried about me?"

"No," she says. "I mean, yes. You sounded pretty desperate."

"I am." No lie there. I'm desperate all right. For answers.

"You *are*?"

"Mm-hm."

"So you haven't found a tutor?"

Is she really reconsidering my offer?

"Just answer *yes* or *no*," she demands, her patience breaking.

Equal parts surprise and guilt hit me. I didn't mean to leave her hanging in suspense. She really is on edge, and I wonder why. Photo booth aside, which I don't remember anyway, she's been nothing but rude to me.

"I'm sorry. This isn't how this was supposed to go. *At all.* It's just—" She lets out a little laugh, shaking her head, but it's pretty obvious she doesn't find anything funny. "Actually, *I'm* desperate."

Her voice is a whisper, and I wonder if I heard her right.

She looks up, her candid expression making me think she's finally leveling with me. "What I meant to say in the first place is: if you still want a tutor, I'd love to help."

She starts walking away.

"Whoa, hold up." I slip my hand around her wrist, spinning her back around. "You didn't even give me a chance to say *yes.*"

Her eyes travel up the length of my arm and then search my face, their blue depths hopeful. "Yes?"

She *is* desperate. Why?

"Yes, absolutely."

This was supposed to be about *her* helping *me*. Getting *her* to tell *me* about that night and figuring out what really happened. Besides the service hours that her tutoring ad mentioned she's working for, which I'm still curious about, the only reason I see for her needing me is money. Me paying her was nothing more than a joke initially, a spur-of-the-moment offer in the hallway that first day to get under her skin. I note a rim of redness around her eyes and wonder if she's been crying.

"What are you good with?" I ask. "Ten, fifteen dollars?"

Her jaw inches down. "An *hour*?"

"Twenty dollars then?" I hedge, not meaning to undervalue her help.

"Oh my gosh, no. I mean, I was thinking seven or eight, maybe."

"Fine, fifteen it is," I say. "You won't stand me up again?"

It sounds harsh, but it's a fair question.

Her bottom lip pulls down, forming a sorry little look. "I'm sorry about that."

I nod. "We're on then."

"Okay," she says, a smile outlining her lips, perhaps the first genuine smile I've seen on her face. And it looks good. Her eyes get kind of wet, like something is irritating them. Oh, man, I think she's about to cry. "Sounds good. Let me know when you need help."

"Tomorrow."

"Tomorrow," she repeats. "Sure."

"My house."

The relief that loosened her up a second ago disappears, her posture stiffening. "I prefer the library."

"I prefer my house," I say.

I can see her swallow. "Fine."

"Do you want a ride?"

"*What*?" she asks, like I just offered her my bed to sleep in. This is too much fun.

I laugh. "A ride. To my house. After school?"

She starts to back away. "Ah, no, no, I'll be fine."

"Give me your number then."

"My number—*why*?"

"Don't you need my address?"

"Oh." She laughs. "Yeah, of course."

"I'll text it to you."

She recites her number and I punch it in. I send her a quick text with my address and the gate code. A buzz from her backpack lets me know she got it.

"Great," she says, taking another step toward the front of the school like she can't break away fast enough.

I start toward the parking lot with a smile. "See you tomorrow after school then."

She nods and continues walking away, her steps shaky like she just signed up for her first skydive. She really is scared of me.

I'm on the lookout for Julianna as I drive past the front of the school, wondering if she got a ride from someone. Must have. I don't see her anywhere.

I smile to myself as I drive down Guadalupe Road, thinking maybe the answers will come after all. The memories are there somewhere, buried deep.

A sound nips the edge of my consciousness, the deep purr of a car pulling up as I stop at a red. A silver sports car stops next to me. Driving an automatic is great, I'm not complaining, but I miss the feel of that stick shift in my palm. Dad won't let me drive the Vette yet.

I take another glance and see it's a Jaguar. This car is cherry: mint condition. The driver's hair is just as silver as his car. I take it he's not the type to push his car and I'm right.

The light switches from red to green and he creeps cautiously into the intersection. What a shame. That ride could definitely get up to sixty miles per hour within six seconds.

He picks up speed alongside me, the deep hum of his car echoing in my ears. The sound sets off something inside me, something strange I can't put my finger on. A feeling I can't shake. The Jaguar gains speed, leaving me behind. But the sound resonates in my ears, the rumble underscoring the erratic beating of my heart.

Hammering.

Pounding.

A rush of blood through my ears. A deep rumble approaching from behind. A familiar sound. A rich, chilling purr.

The Jaguar.

A horn wails and I snap to. The car behind me swerves and speeds ahead. I'm going twenty miles per hour in a forty-five-miles-per-hour zone. And my hands are shaky. The memories are close; I want to keep them coming. Picking up speed, I turn down Power Road, knowing where I need to go.

I'm not sure how I feel about this section of Power Road by the mall, but one thing is for sure. For the first time since it happened, the accident feels real. I was *here*. I'm remembering bits and pieces.

I pass the spot on the road where my dad said they found me, but it isn't enough. Hanging a right onto Hampton Avenue, I pass the Wendy's Vic must have dropped me off at. I pull in, park my car near the road, and slip out. I keep my eyes open, trying to see everything.

Cars pass by, birds fly overhead, a dude on a skateboard rolls past, but no memories come. I turn south, facing the freeway and the overpass that leads to El Pollo Loco. Both the mall and Wendy's are behind me now, which means I must have been walking south. Was I trying to meet back up with Vic at the restaurant he wanted to eat at?

That's when two realizations hit me. First, I'm not a picky eater. I doubt I would've insisted on eating at Wendy's. Second, if I was walking south toward El Pollo Loco to find Vic or even toward home, wouldn't the car have hit my right leg?

I look down at the boot on my left leg. I turn around, facing north. Did I get turned around in the dust storm? Or maybe I was looking for cover. And where did my phone go?

I get back in my car, all hope of a colossal breakthrough gone. I swing around the mall before heading home, wondering if I should contact Detective Ferguson and tell him I think it was a Jaguar that hit me. The idea of telling Ferguson makes me second-guess my memory, though. My brain isn't reliable these days, and I'm desperate for memories, desperate enough to be making them up.

I let out a frustrated breath of air, wondering if that's exactly what I'm doing.

Buick GMC, Honda, Toyota: I pass a bunch of dealerships along the Auto Park Drive lined with palms, but no Land Rover Jaguar.

I've turned onto the main boulevard and started for home when a sign catches my eye, a black sign with white letters in all caps: ACKLEN MOTOR GROUP.

Black with white letters in all caps. ACKLEN MOTOR GROUP.

I've seen it before and I can hardly peel my eyes from it now. I focus back on the road in time to see red taillights, the car in front of me at a standstill. I slam on my brakes, stopping inches behind the bumper. Adrenaline tears down my limbs, screeching to a halt along with my car.

Idiot. Not him; me. The line of backed-up cars starts moving, but I pull off the road anyway, right into Acklen Motor Group.

I spot a BMW, a Ferrari, a Lamborghini, and a Maserati. This is no typical used-car lot. I park and get out, leaving my crutch behind as I search for a Jaguar. Can this be coincidence? Each car has a promotional frame around the plate, a black frame with white letters that reads ACKLEN MOTOR GROUP. My gaze is cemented to one of the frames as my heart makes its presence known.

Hammering. Pounding.

Tires squeal. My heart hurtles into my throat. I leap into action, bolt to get out of the way, but too late.

"Can I help you?"

I jolt, the voice breaking me from the memory. I curse.

"Is something wrong?"

"No," I lie to the salesman, some skinny dude in a buttoned-up shirt.

"Can I get you a drink? We have complimentary water bottles in the fridge."

"No, thanks," I say as a bead of sweat gathers on my forehead.

"Are you looking for something in particular?" he asks.

His sleeves are rolled up, but he still looks like he could keel over from heat exhaustion in this 112-degree flat heat. Suit pants and a tie. I'm in way over my head here. This is a luxury used-car lot and I'm seventeen, showing up here in shorts and a T-shirt.

"Do you have any Jaguars?"

Sure enough, his gaze drops down the length of my pathetic outfit all the way to my feet, his brows climbing a notch as he takes in the blue Nike flip-flop on one foot and the boot on the other. "Right this way. I'm Ron, by the way."

I follow him, shaking the hand he offers in greeting.

"We have an XK-Series convertible, and I think we have an older S-Type. Of course there's a newer F-Type coupe in the showroom."

Ron shows me a couple of cars, pouring on his salesman charm despite my apparent lack of age and funds. Listening to Ron pitch away on these cars is a waste of both of our time.

"Do you keep a record of the cars you sell and who owns them?"

The question slipped out without thought, and Ron obviously doesn't know what to make of it. "Uh, yeah, we do. For tax purposes and stuff."

It's suddenly awkward, and no wonder.

"Thanks for your help, Ron," I say, ready to split. "I might be back, you know, with my dad. I've always wanted one of these."

Why am I lying? I shouldn't even be here.

Ron offers his business card and steps back inside. I start toward my car, taking one last look at the license plate frames. ACKLEN MOTOR GROUP. Even if it was a Jaguar that hit me, it could have been purchased anywhere. Maybe Vic and I drove around this side of the mall that night. This sign could look familiar for any number of reasons. The best I can do is tell Detective Ferguson I think the car was a Jaguar, even though it's not much.

The door behind me swings open again and Ron makes his way out. Another customer has arrived: a lady in heels and the type of pricey sunglasses that suggest she'll have no trouble buying a car here. Ron's lucky day.

"I hear you're in the market for a Jag."

I spin around at the voice, my gaze coming level with a set of blue eyes. Lightest blue I've ever seen. This salesman is a lot taller than Ron, almost as tall as me. And built. He wears no tie, though, and the top two buttons of his shirt are undone, the sleeves rolled up.

"Uh, yeah," I stammer.

"You ever been in one?"

I hesitate because the answer is *no*, and the real reason I'm interested in Jaguars isn't something I'll divulge. Luckily, he extends a hand and pretends he didn't ask.

"I own the place," he says with a firm handshake. *Owns* the place. Great, now I'm really going to get a sales pitch. "Ron told me you're looking at Jaguars. Thought I'd come out and introduce myself."

"Thanks," I say, wishing I had hightailed it out of here as soon as Ron gave me his card.

"And your name is?" he asks.

"Cody."

"Cody," he says expectantly, like he's waiting for a last name.

Why do I not want to tell him?

"Rush," I finally add, telling myself off for being mistrustful. That's what you get when your dad is a fed and you hear too many stories.

"Welcome, Cody Rush," he says with a smile I can't decipher. "Have we met before?"

His question catches me off guard. "Uh, no. I don't think so."

He nods, the corners of his lips retaining a grin, his eyes studious. How would I know if we've met before? Maybe Vic and I did come here. "Are you sure? You look familiar."

"Nope," I say with a fake confidence that seems to satisfy him at last.

He waves it off. "My mistake. I must be thinking of someone else. We get a lot of guys like you here."

"Like me?"

"Yeah," he says with an appraising nod. "Good-looking guys like you. Ladies at your heels. World at your fingertips. How about we get you a nice set of wheels under your fingertips as well?"

"I was just stopping by," I cut in and shift toward my car. "I'd have to bring my dad back if I even dreamed of owning one."

"Yeah, I know how it goes," he says. "Once you have Jags on your mind, they're hard to forget."

My head snaps up, my full attention drawn to his blue eyes as his words ring too true for comfort.

"Thanks," I say with finality and a parting handshake, realizing he never introduced himself. "What was your name?"

One corner of his lips turns up into a crooked grin, and I realize how intense this guy is, his eyes never straying from mine. Just as I finish that thought, his icy blue gaze trails down to the boot on my leg and his lips spread into a full grin. "Damian."

I push the unlock button, breaking away at last. "Thanks, Damian."

CHAPTER 15

Julianna

Getting to Cody's house on foot in 116 degrees is not ideal, but I have little choice. Vic disappeared in Rusty after school, even after I told him I needed the car, and I wasn't about to ask Dad for a ride. I don't need him getting suspicious about who I'm tutoring.

Luckily, the Valley Metro took me halfway. Now I approach what I think must be his neighborhood. Hopefully, his AC works a lot better than ours. I hum a song from choir as I reread the address, realizing there's more to Cody's text than I initially saw. He left a gate code—a *gate code*?

I look up, doing a double take when I spot it, the mother of all community gates, intricate wrought iron between stone fences and a sign that reads CHADWICK ESTATES.

I double-check—triple-check—Cody's text, hoping I got turned around somehow. I figured he was rich, but *this* is a whole different level of richness. I wait for cars to clear out before dashing across the street.

My fingers hesitate over the keypad before punching in the five-digit code. I jerk back when the gate responds. It glides open, revealing a fancy road made of brick pavers—not your typical asphalt—and it leads the eye straight to a roundabout complete with water fountain, palms, and planted flowers.

My feet start down the road. I take everything in with a sort of reverent awe. Any neighborhood in Arizona that can keep this much grass alive and so green deserves respect. Trees shade my walk down the path, offering a blessed relief from the beating sun. Flowers in vibrant shades of yellow, red, and purple line either side of the road. A car passes by, a shiny SUV with an engine so quiet I didn't hear it coming.

Weaving through the streets, I navigate my way until I reach the house that matches the address on Cody's text, a two-story brick house—no, a *mansion*—with a fountain and a circular drive that put the community entrance to shame.

It hits me, like it took me clear up until this moment to fully grasp where I am: Agent Rush's house. Cody is intimidating enough, his cocky smile reminding me too much of his dad. He's rich, popular, and almost too pretty, and he won't leave me alone. I hate to admit it, but something about him gets to me every time he's near, and if I were smart, I would be nowhere near his house now.

Cody had to go and be all nice to me yesterday, though, agreeing to have me tutor him after I'd been so rude. I start up the sidewalk, trying to calm my breathing. I knock on the door and then freak out, wondering if I should bolt back the way I came or hide in the bushes. *I can't believe I'm doing this.*

I spin around and dash down three of the stairs before the door swings open. I jolt, whirling back around. My face flushes with a different kind of heat when I see Cody standing there, a funny little smirk on his lips.

His grin breaks into a dimpled smile. "Leaving already?"

Dimples are definitely dangerous.

"Yes," I say, "I mean *no*."

He laughs. "I was starting to think you'd ditched out again."

He had to bring that up. "Sorry I'm late." I point back in the direction I came. "If this isn't a good time, I can leave."

"No, come on in," he says and stands aside, gesturing me inside.

"Okay," I say, hesitating before braving the remaining distance. I slip in past him and scoot off to the side, casting a quick look around. His entryway is ten times the size of my bedroom. And ten times cooler. "Should I take my shoes off?"

"Whatever's most comfortable," he says and shuts the door. "Up to you."

I doubt anything will make me comfortable here. I keep my ears alert for any other male voices, praying that Cody's dad is still at work. I slip my flip-flops off and follow Cody. When my feet hit the carpet—the superplush kind you can sink your toes into—I think maybe I was wrong. I could get used to this.

"You want something to drink?"

I want to say no, but my throat is so dry. I'm not sure which is better: making eye contact to assert my confidence or avoiding it altogether. Looking into his eyes has proven deadly in the past, especially that night at the mall, so I settle for glancing around impassively. "Water's great. Thanks."

He heads to the kitchen. This place is huge, with classy lighting fixtures and crown moldings to boot. All of the furniture looks heavy, made of solid wood. Fans spin overhead without a sound. Not a single pile can be found anywhere on the counter. It feels clean and, yes, even comfortable. It feels like someone cares.

Cody returns with two water bottles and grabs his backpack from a recliner. "Have a seat."

I freeze when I realize this is where we're studying—the living room. Cody pops a squat on the floor at the end of a coffee table that's probably more expensive than our car. This all looks too cozy, like friends kicking back to do more hanging out than studying.

Better get this over with. I sit. "Okay, what do you need help with?"

I look at Cody from across the long coffee table, finding that funny smirk on his face again. He shifts around the table, coming closer, and rests his back against the sofa, his left leg extended to keep his booted foot straight. "It's a lot more comfortable if you lean up against the couch," he says with a suggestive glance at the spot of carpet beside him, like I'm going to heed his beckoning and happily scoot closer.

He's got something else coming at him. "Oh, no, I'm just fine right here. What do you need help with?" I repeat with a quick glance over my shoulder toward the garage door, praying his dad won't walk in any second.

"Art," Cody says.

"*Art?*" I repeat. He mentioned needing help with art before, but I thought he was joking.

"Yeah," he replies and pulls a piece of paper from his backpack.

Who needs help with *art*? And for fifteen bucks an hour?

His head shakes as he scans the paper. "It's our first project. Some 'One-point Perspective Collage.'" He reads off the instructions. "'Create a one-point drawing on cardboard using geometric shapes, checking for a balanced composition. Then pick a color scheme and create an aesthetically pleasing, three-dimensional—'" He tosses the paper on the coffee table without finishing. "Sounds like Chinese."

A chuckle escapes my lips before I can stop it. "That's what I say about math."

"*Math*?" he asks. "That I can understand, but *this*? Sure, I can be dense, but this doesn't make a lick of sense. About the only word in there I understand is *geometric*."

I laugh, although I'm not sure why. Maybe it's his self-deprecating way of blaming himself for not understanding instead of calling the assignment stupid. "Pick a shape," I say and sip from my water bottle.

He thinks for a second. "Square."

I pull out my notebook and find a blank page, sliding marginally closer for him to see. I draw a horizontal line to represent the viewer's eye level and explain the basics of drawing a three-dimensional object. He nods as I explain, taking the liberty of scooting closer as he does. I shift back an inch in response and finish a sketch of a room drawn in one-point perspective.

"Wow," he says, eyes on my drawing. "You *drew* that."

I glance at my rough sketch—and I mean *rough*—and can't help smiling. Everyone in my family is artistic, even Vic. Even Lucas doodles little anime characters from time to time. No one has ever stared at something I've made quite like Cody is now, and it reminds me of how impressed he was of the cupcakes I frosted at The Chocolate Shoppe.

"That's crazy," he says, rubbing the thick stubble along his chin. "Like you're looking right into a room."

"And here I just thought you had a thing for cupcakes," I say.

His brows pull together as he looks at me. "Cupcakes?"

"Yeah. I thought you were just trying to schmooze a free one off of me at The Chocolate Shoppe."

Recognition still hasn't crossed his face, and I realize with a stab of humiliation that he doesn't remember. Duh, Julianna. Obviously that night meant more to me than it did to him.

"Oh, right," he says and smiles, but I know better.

I sit upright and scoot back to my spot at the end of the coffee table.

Cody props himself up on one hand as he leans closer to me than we've been since that night in the photo booth. A clean, strong scent tempts my senses, like aftershave and manly soap. Even as I dare a glance at him, I know it's a bad idea.

His sandy-colored hair is a little crazy, like he just rolled out of bed, and a healthy layer of scruff covers his sharp jawline. He's so different from the clean-shaven guy I met at the mall. Still, Cody is agonizingly handsome whether he's trying or not. And there's something else. He seemed so carefree at the mall. Yet there's something in his green eyes now, laden with doubt and perhaps a few secrets of his own, that makes him all that much harder to disregard. Like a guy who hasn't always had the easy way in life after all.

Which almost makes me want to ask him what happened to his leg.

A playful grin curves Cody's lips as he looks into my eyes. "About that night—"

"Listen"—I cut him off before his flirtatious ways turn me into a puddle of mush at his feet—"for the record, that whole photo booth ... incident ... didn't mean anything, okay?"

He sits up, leaning forward to pull a wallet from his back pocket. He fishes something out and slaps it down on the coffee table.

"Oh, yeah?" he challenges. "What about that?"

I glance down at the pictures—the photo-booth pictures. His index finger taps the third picture, the one of him practically kissing my neck. The nerve! I feel a wave of heat rising up my neck and into my cheeks. Wait, *he keeps this in his wallet*?

"Pulling out that dimple-loaded smile of yours and doing ..." I fish for a term to describe what he's doing in that picture. Smelling my hair? Kissing my ear? It's too intimate, too personal to articulate. "... doing ... *that* ... might win over every other girl who comes your way, but it doesn't work for me."

"Oh, yeah?" he asks again and leans in dangerously close, his tone doubtful. His gaze drops from my eyes to my lips. "What *does* do it for you, Julianna?"

The sound of my name on his lips sinks right to my core, rich and tempting. Like chocolate. He is *such* a player. I wonder if slapping him would make me feel any better. Isn't the admiration of three fourths of the Highland High School female student body enough for him? Why is he toying with *me*?

"You would like to know, wouldn't you?" I ask, loading as much spite into that challenge as possible.

One side of his lips kicks up, like he's thoroughly enjoying this. "Lucas?"

"Yes," I assert, pulling the conversation back into my ballpark. "Lucas is my type."

"So all I need is an ear spacer then?" Cody teases.

"Ew."

"*Ew?*"

Oops. It slipped out. Simply imagining Cody with a spacer makes me cringe. It's all types of wrong. An uppity-uppity like him with brand-name clothes and the kind of cocky smile that's only acquired from years of being too popular for your own good . . . all that and a *spacer*?

"Yes, *ew*."

"Right here," he says and pinches one of his earlobes with a smug smile, his face a breath away from mine. "What do you think, Jules?"

"*Julianna*," I correct him, not about to let him make up his own nickname for me. Who does he think he is?

His smile looks more mocking now than anything. "Fine. What do you think, Julianna?"

"You couldn't pull off a spacer," I assert.

"Oh, yeah, I could."

His arrogance is driving me crazy. "*No*, you couldn't."

"Why not?"

"Because you're a pretty boy!"

The words ring out, filling the short space between us with awkwardness. And remorse. *I can't believe I said that.*

The sound of my lungs moving oxygen in and out is suddenly very loud, the only sound I hear as I wait for him to tell me to *shut up* or *get out and never come back*, either of which I would happily comply with.

He leans back against the sofa, no doubt bruised from my cutting remark.

I am such a brat.

I bite on my lower lip, something I do when I'm nervous. His eyes are locked on mine, his intense eyes dragging me in and swallowing me whole as he gives a fluid wink of his eye.

What the—

"I'm going to remember that," he says and settles back into a comfortable recline with a smile, like he just scored first base with a girl. "You think I'm pretty."

CHAPTER 16

Cody

Dr. Huntington was all praise over my leg this evening during physical therapy. Major progress. It's getting better. Between that and Julianna actually showing up, I'd say it was a good day.

She's hot and cold, though. One minute she was laughing at stuff I said, and I wasn't even trying to be funny. Then she mentioned cupcakes like it was supposed to mean something, and by the time I figured out she was referring to the night of my accident, it was too late. She'd shut down, all irritated and jumpy again, glancing over at the garage door like my dad would walk in any second.

It's got to be weird for her. I imagine what it would be like to have feds barge into our house and arrest one of my parents. Then going through a trial. I'll bet true friends are harder to come by after that. Neighbors give you odd stares, keeping their distance. And here she sat in my living room, knowing the man who brought her mom down could walk through the door.

I whip off my shirt, ready for bed. Maybe I should feel bad for making her come here. After the way she shut me down, though, not giving me a chance to explain what happened that night, I don't care. She thinks I'm conceited, that much is apparent now, and she's been nothing but an ice princess, like she takes it as her mission to keep me in my place.

When I open the bathroom door, I find everything the way I left it. I open the cabinet over the sink. The bristles of my toothbrush stick out at odd angles. A new brush rests on the shelf below mine, unwrapped and unused. I snag both and toss them in the trash, then fish under the sink for two replacements.

I unwrap two brushes, scrub my teeth with one and put both in their place, one toothbrush on the bottom shelf, the other on the shelf above. As soon as my head hits the pillow, I feel myself drifting to sleep. I hope for a restful night with no dreams. Once again I'm not so lucky.

Coach Layton won't look me in the eye when I pass him in the halls. Somehow I'm aware this is only a dream, but it gets to me anyway. He's disappointed in me, and this annoying boot is the reason why.

Then I'm a kid again and I fall out of the big tree on Grandpa's property. This dream feels more real, the details distinct. Both legs are broken after my fall, and Dad tells me I need to have them amputated.

And then Jimmy is there in the next dream, running through the alfalfa fields behind Grandpa Chadwick's ranch here in Gilbert. Like it used to be. The sun is bright, the tip of each strand of grass crisp like I'm seeing everything in real life. Like I'm really here in Grandpa's fields. Or at least I was.

Jimmy ran through the field, dodging rectangular mounds of baled hay. I realize with a start, even as I sleep, that I *was* here. This is no dream. Something between shame and dread settles in as I remember this particular day. It happened years ago and I don't care to relive it. I'm too old to have nightmares.

"You can't catch me!" Jimmy called out over his shoulder, the type of challenge every kid is bound to make at some point. It was a stupid taunt, though, the kind Jimmy should have known better than to dish out. Something wasn't right. Suspicion stirred, I wondered if Jimmy was up to something—a prank of some sort—but there was no time to hesitate.

The race was on.

I sprinted after him, already gaining speed. Jimmy was always the runt in the family. Only a year and a half younger than me. Still, I towered over him. What Jimmy lacked in strength, however, he made up for in smarts and guts. Jimmy had the heart of a lion and the determination of a fish swimming upstream.

"First one to the canal is the winner," Jimmy shouted between pants.

I passed him easily and skidded to a stop at the canal, winging back around with a victory smile. Before I could make a full turn, two hands shoved me good and hard, and I flew into the canal of lukewarm water. I surfaced to the sound of Jimmy laughing as I spewed water.

"Tell me you saw that coming," he spat between chuckles.

"I totally did," I lied.

"Then next time trust your instincts, idiot, and you won't end up with a cow pie in your hair."

I reached up and, sure enough, felt a clump of poo that must have floated down the canal.

Trust your instincts. *Another one of Dad's favorite lines when telling special-agent stories to us at bedtime. Well, there was only one instinct I was feeling at that moment: retribution. I slipped off my shorts and tossed them onto the bank at his feet, one challenge leading to another.*

"I dare you."

"To skinny-dip?" Jimmy exclaimed. He didn't think about it long. Stripped down and jumped right in. Some challenge that was.

The water was borderline warm with a few other questionable brown clumps floating down, but we didn't care. This was why we loved Grandpa's home. The tall trees, alfalfa fields, row after row of cornstalks, and the cow pastures. The Chadwick ranch was acres of carefree living and wide-open possibilities.

Jimmy climbed out, his attention drawn to something on the side of the canal.

I clenched my hand, sending a spout of water soaring into the side of his head. Jimmy didn't flinch.

"Whatcha looking at?"

"Shh." He kept staring. "It's a praying mantis."

Jimmy was like that, naturally curious. Science and math came easily to both of us. One difference: Jimmy actually used it.

"C'mon, let's go back," I said and pulled myself out. "Grandma's making ice cream sandwiches."

That's when I heard it, the cry for help mixed with laughter. I saw Jimmy slipping, his hands reaching for something to steady himself as his feet flew out from under him. His hand grasped a fence wire as his foot hit the water.

And then Jimmy was shaking. Convulsing. His whole body jerking violently. It was a live wire, the ancient kind Grandpa used to keep the cows in. He hadn't updated his fencing with the safer electric-pulse wires.

Every nerve ending in my body jolted at the sight, as if I, too, was being electrocuted. I bolted into action, sprinting toward the house for help. Then I skidded to a stop. Help would arrive too late, I realized. Jimmy would be dead. It was up to me.

Trust your instincts.

I spun around and raced back to Jimmy with no clue what I was going to do. All I knew was that I had to get to him. As I neared his shaking body, I skidded on whatever Jimmy had slipped on and crashed into him, the force of my body breaking the deadly connection.

Both of us tumbled to the ground, rolling through a mixture of weeds and dirt. I climbed onto my hands and knees and scrambled over to Jimmy. He lay with his eyes closed, his head hanging over the edge of the canal, his blond curls dipping into the water. His wet body, like mine, was blanketed in dirt. And he was breathing.

After that I looked after Jimmy a lot more carefully. The canal debacle had shaken me up. I realized not only how fragile life was but how fragile Jimmy was. Both of us went to the same school, sat on the same bus. Jimmy would come down with a cough. I wouldn't.

The incident at the canal had been a close call. After all, it was sheer luck I was able to save him. Jimmy's slip on the wet weeds almost killed him. My slip saved his life.

The whole thing had been my fault in the first place, though. If it weren't for me daring Jimmy to skinny-dip, he never would have slipped and grabbed that wire. I had been the cause of my best friend almost dying, but at least I'd been able to save him. The second time around I wouldn't be so lucky.

Jimmy died eighteen months later.

I awake with a start, short of breath. And sweating. I look down, almost expecting to be covered in canal water and dirt. The dream felt so real, a nightmare relived play-by-play.

I bolt out of bed and pump the AC up in the hallway. My boot is off. My bare foot against the carpet feels weird. The house is dark, everyone fast asleep. I stand in the cool hallway, part of me wanting to jump back into that dream, grab hold of Jimmy, and never let go. The other part of me doesn't want to go back to bed, doesn't want to go anywhere near those dreams of Jimmy.

They're happening all the time now, dreams while I'm asleep and flashbacks while I'm awake. And they all started eleven weeks ago, when I got hit by that car, like that bonk to the head jarred all of these memories to the surface.

Tiredness wins the battle, however, and I crash into bed, falling asleep. I awake to sunlight streaming in through the window.

"Why is it so *cold*?" Rachel's voice sounds from the hallway, her voice grumpy, something that's becoming the norm. It's 6:30 a.m. and probably sixty degrees inside, though, so I don't blame her. "Who turned the AC up so high?"

I pull the covers over my head before the accident and these dreams can bombard me again. Now that I think about it, I realize the harder I try to remember details about the accident, the more I re- member vivid details of Jimmy's short life, which doesn't make sense. There's no connection.

I can think of one convincing reason why I'm having these dreams about Jimmy and it's sitting in my closet.

When I can't stand it any longer, I climb out of bed and head for the box wedged in my closet. *Cody's Room: Jimmy's things.* What- ever is in this box, Mom saved it for me, not Jimmy. He had no time to designate personal items to family members. He hardly had time to say good-bye.

I slide the lid off the box, deciding suspense might do funny things to the brain. Perhaps this will end the dreams. A deck of base- ball cards is the first thing I see, and I'm tempted to stop there. I haven't seen these in years, since Jimmy's last birthday eight years ago, in fact, and they're hard to look at.

Jimmy loved baseball. Would he still be playing baseball if he were alive today? If so, I would have stuck with the sport, too. Dad would have loved that, both of his sons playing the game he played in college. Jimmy was the only kid I knew who still collected baseball cards. He loved old things. Vintage. He was an odd goose, but the kid had class.

A set of Ninja Turtles action figures rests beneath the baseball cards, followed by a LEGO creation we called the time machine. It was only a mock-up, of course, a smaller model of the real deal Jimmy planned to build one day.

A throbbing sensation rises in my chest. Spreads into my throat. The sight of Jimmy's sketchbook beneath the time machine undoes my resolve to look through the box and I slam the lid back on.

I close the closet door and head for the shower.

Mom meant well, but if you ask me, she shouldn't have saved any of Jimmy's stuff.

Some things are best left behind.

CHAPTER 17

Julianna

To say that our first tutoring session didn't go very well would be a megaunderstatement. And the worst didn't even happen; Cody's dad didn't show up. Still, we spent the entire hour driving each other crazy. I should be relieved that Cody took my insult about him being a pretty boy as some twisted compliment, but it confirms what an arrogant piece of work he is.

Regardless, I feel awful. It's like I can't do anything right these days. My life is bound by threads I can't hold together.

I slip into the community center five minutes early and I even had time to fix my hair tonight. It's amazing what you can get done when you ignore the dirty dishes and stacks of laundry. I'm feeling ready for the pageant workshop this time, prepared. A few girls trickle in, each one assessing this new social situation. I imagine my own carefully measured expression mirrors their own.

We all smile and introduce ourselves as we find seats. Rebecca is tall and thin, with auburn hair and a kind smile. Sophie is blond and short: shorter than me, which comes as a relief. Fashion is her obvious strength, her outfit flawlessly coordinated. Denica is a repeat contestant; she won second attendant in the Miss City of Maricopa pageant last year. Then there's Jenny. Five of us in all. Anyone can join the pageant up until a week before the competition. For now I'm relieved there aren't more.

The pageant director and a few other ladies are setting up, chatting. All in all I'm feeling pretty good until Denica brings up the talent portion of the pageant and everyone chimes in eagerly about their respective talents.

"Irish dancing," Rebecca says.

"Oh, *Irish* dancing," Denica says. "I do ballet."

"What about you, Jenny?" Sophie asks. "What's your talent?"

Jenny smiles. "Ventriloquism."

We all stare at her blankly, some in surprise and some perhaps totally clueless, until Jenny holds up her hand like a puppet. A voice comes from somewhere in her throat while her lips remain motionless, her fingers and thumb moving as if her hand is the one talking.

A couple of us laugh. Sophie exclaims, "That's awesome. My talent isn't *nearly* as original."

"What's your talent?" Denica asks.

"The piano," Sophie says. "I'm performing Rachmaninoff's Concerto Number 2."

I'm officially sick to my stomach even before they turn to me.

"What about you, Julianna?" Sophie asks.

These girls are talented and confident and prepared, none of which I'm feeling at the moment. And here I thought I *was* prepared for this workshop.

"Uh," I mumble and start chewing on my lower lip. "I'm going to sing."

The words coming from my mouth surprise even me. Memories of my disastrous solo in junior high flash back. Singing is the only performance skill I have, though.

"Oh," Denica pipes in. "What song?"

"No idea."

Jenny gets all jittery. "I'm, like, *so* nervous for swimsuit, you guys. What about you?"

"Oh my gosh," Rebecca says. "Don't remind me."

"Wait, *what?*" I cut in. All eyes shift to me.

"Swimsuit," Denica says. "Actually, I'm excited. The swimsuit portion was, like, one of my favorite parts last year."

"They actually *do* that?" I ask. "*We* have to do that? In a local pageant like this?"

Rebecca and Sophie offer gentle smiles of consolation.

I start chewing on my lip again.

"Uh-huh," Denica says. "Onstage. Trust me, the worst part isn't the swimsuit. The worst part is having creepos follow you around at all the parades and local events once you win."

"Ew," Jenny says.

Denica confirms any doubts with a solid nod. "It's true. Creeps are an inevitable consequence of winning."

This pageant is sounding better by the minute.

Donna, the pageant director, approaches, and we all look at her. "Welcome, ladies. It's so good to see you again. Let's get our first workshop underway. We'll start out with choreography for our open-ing number."

I go through the motions, pasting on a smile at all the right mo-ments. Mom can't possibly be set on me competing this way. Wearing a swimsuit *onstage*? Even as I go through the motions, I know I won't do it. I can't. This will be my last Friday-night pageant workshop.

I hold my breath the next day, Saturday, as we make our weekly visit to Mama.

"Where's Vic?" she asks right off.

"He said he's got basketball practice," Dad explains, which, come to think of it, doesn't make sense.

"The season hasn't even started yet," I say.

Dad shrugs. He seems to be distracted today, even more lost in his own thoughts than usual. Both Mama and I catch the beginnings of a smile on his face, the kind of smile I've seen on him too many times before. That smile is hiding something.

"I've got good news," he says.

"What is it?" Mama asks, a smile spreading across her face as well.

I glance at the cinder-block walls, the nasty floors, and the other families visiting inmates at neighboring tables, knowing smiles are hard to come by in this place. I can't blame Mama. Still, she's so eas-ily excited when Dad announces good news, as if she hasn't learned anything from past experience.

He takes a deep breath, like he can't contain his excitement. "My presentation proposal was accepted by the SWAEA."

"What?" Mom shrieks.

Dad smiles. "Yeah!"

I'm not following along. "Wait, what's SW . . ."

"The Southwestern Artist Education Association," Mama says.

The name sounds familiar, something I've heard my dad talk about before.

"Finally, Jon!" she says. "After all these years of submitting. Congratulations."

"Thanks," Dad says. "It will be a busy weekend next week."

"It's *next week*?" Mama gasps, earning an even bigger smile from Dad. Now I realize this was his plan all along. Dad likes holding out until the last minute to draw a bigger response from people, and Mama is a sucker for surprises. She loves that about him. Me, not so much.

"Wait, you're leaving next weekend?" I ask.

"Yep," Dad replies. "It's a two-day convention. Friday and Saturday."

"Where?"

Dad's smile spreads as he shifts his gaze to Mama. "The San Diego Convention Center."

Mama muffles another squeal of excitement and then blabbers on about how wonderful it is that people are beginning to recognize his true talent as an artist.

"That means you'll miss out on visiting Mama next week," I remind him.

They're silent for a beat, followed by, "Oh, it's okay, *mi joya*. Dad's been waiting for this for years." Mama's attention returns to Dad before she continues. "I'll be even more excited to see you the following week. You'll have to tell me all about—"

"How long have you known about this?" I ask, cutting Mama off. Really, I'm not getting the excitement here. Dad is leaving us in a falling-apart house so he can spend money traveling to a convention that may or may not translate into future work opportunities.

"They got back to me about two months ago," Dad says, "but I wanted to wait for the right moment to share the good news."

And the right moment would be five days before the convention? Makes perfect sense.

"Oh, this is so wonderful," Mama says and turns to me. "And the pageant is coming up, too."

"I'm not doing it."

Her smile is gone faster than mascara runs on a rainy day. "What?"

"High heels, evening gowns, *swimsuits*, and a crown?" I say. "That was your dream, Mama, not mine."

Mama's shock is unmistakable.

"Julianna . . ." Dad says, a diplomatic voice amid the tension.

I hate to ruin the moment, but it is what it is. At least one of us isn't stuck on high hopes and pointless dreams. I have school and work, not to mention my last soccer season this fall. Add college applications on top of that. My dream of being able to afford college is futile enough.

Mama doesn't say more about the pageant, just bottles up her feelings and turns to Dad. This does nothing to ease my guilt, but I don't let myself think about it.

Dad leaving next weekend isn't such a bad thing, I decide. Vic is eighteen. I'm seventeen. We're old enough to take care of ourselves.

Sunday is miserably hot and I'm left with nothing to do after High Mass but sit and stew about the past forty-eight hours, everything from my less than wonderful tutoring session with Cody to the awkward pageant workshop to Dad's big news about the convention.

Vic is off with Heidi. I think. Dad is fast asleep on the couch beneath the swamp cooler, an empty bag of potato chips wedged between his body and the cushions. Everyone seems to be going along fine with our life the way it is; everyone but me.

Observing this makes me wonder: Is it *me*? Am I the one who needs to change? Everyone bugs me right now. *Everyone.* Especially Vic and Dad. And then there's Lucas, who I usually see at Mass. His family was there, but not him. I wanted to talk. Lucas didn't respond to my questioning text for a good two hours, though, and when he did, he made it brief.

SLEPT IN. UP TOO LATE BOARDING.

Which didn't help my nerves because I was at the skate park with him to the bitter end last night, filming his every jump like any good girlfriend would. Even Mama was beginning to irritate me yesterday. She didn't even ask if Vic and I would be all right while Dad is gone.

Maybe it's due to the fact that I just got back from Mass, but all my thoughts are sounding selfish. I'm starting to see things in a different light, like there's no one to blame but myself.

I brush some crumbs from a barstool and sit, letting my eyes sweep the disastrous house I'm not about to clean. Cody's house flits back to mind—the plush carpet, clean counters, and polished floors—and I hate to admit I wish I was there.

Remembering how I treated him on Friday only makes me feel worse, and I suddenly can't stand myself. Somehow, over the last few months since Mama was imprisoned, I've lost sight of who I am. Heaven knows I was born with the spunk gene, but the way I treated Cody is something else entirely.

Acting civil around the boy whose dad put Mama in prison feels like all kinds of wrong. At least it used to. That's what I hate about getting to know people like Cody Rush. Even knowing what little I do about him makes hating him hard. The boot on his foot and his overall disheveled demeanor claim my sympathies, too.

I push back the barstool and stand, not about to let myself back out now. In so many ways, Cody is different from the boy I met in The Chocolate Shoppe at the beginning of the summer, and I want to know why. I walk to the cabinet, singing a hymn that's been stuck in my head ever since Mass. Dad sleeps like a log regardless. I open the cupboard, feeling good about this decision as I pull out all of the ingredients I need to mix up what I make best.

CHAPTER 18

Cody

The doorbell rings and I smile. Julianna stands on the front porch holding a brown paper bag. Remembering our last tutoring session, I remind myself to be on good behavior. I welcome her in like a gentleman. Mom would be proud, even more so if I'd shaved.

I run my hand through my hair. Mom's right; there's way too much of it. "Go to the mall and get a cut," she suggested Saturday morning, giving me the kind of frightened look she gives Rachel, as if she fears I, too, will get a lip piercing and start wearing goth or emo clothes.

Going near the mall again is a no. After that dream about Jimmy almost dying at the canal, I didn't care to stir up memories of the past, recent or distant. For my messed-up brain these days, they're all the same, and remembering anything only leads to frustration.

Not that I blame Mom. Where I normally would have stayed out with friends on a Saturday night, I hit the sack around nine o'clock. Slept in late, too. I spent the entire weekend with the kind of headache you get from sleeping too much. A bad mood settled in to stay. It was easier to spend my time wishing the accident hadn't happened. Then I could have gone to Philadelphia for the Reebok Classic Breakout. Who knows, I might have been offered a scholarship. If not, I would have been in shape to earn one this winter season.

When I don't see a car parked outside, I wonder how Julianna got here. She scoots inside with a nervous glance over her shoulder, and I realize what's going on. She doesn't want to be seen here. With me.

I should be offended, but I find it amusing. I have to force people—*pay* them even—to visit me these days. What a loser. Which reminds me that I don't need Julianna anymore, not now that I don't want to remember the accident. I should make her day and let her go home.

Julianna is wearing a smile, though, that and the kind of outfit that reminds me how good-looking she is. Jean shorts and a fitted T-shirt. Okay, so maybe it's not the outfit, it's just her. Lucas is a lucky man.

"This is for you," she says and thrusts the brown paper bag toward me. She's grinning from ear to ear and her chest is rising and falling quickly, like this is a brave gesture I'd better accept before she regrets it.

"Thanks," I say and take the bag, curious. I open it and pull out the type of cupcake that probably costs more than a dozen doughnuts.

She points to the cupcake. "I figured after all those chocolates you bought for me, I owed you something."

I gather we're talking about the night of the accident again, The Chocolate Shoppe and the photo booth. I bought chocolates for her?

"So," Julianna continues hesitantly, "I made that for you."

"You *made* this?"

Her blue eyes study me with an odd look before I remember her mention of cupcakes last Friday. She said I'd been impressed with her cupcakes, the ones I must have seen her make at The Chocolate Shoppe.

Right now she must think I'm a mental case. Ever since the accident, I sort of am.

"I'm . . . really impressed," I say, looking at the swooshy frosting and specks of stuff I'm not sure what to call. Looks like a cupcake I'd see at one of the million-dollar weddings Mom decorates for. "You know I'm not going to let you live this down," I say, earning a questioning look from her. "You brought me a treat *and* you think I'm pretty."

She smiles. "Don't let it go to your head."

"I've got a feeling you'll see to it that I don't."

"And anyway," she rushes in to assure me, "you're *not* pretty."

I raise a questioning brow, trying to look hurt.

She keeps tripping over her words. "I mean, you *are*, but . . . you're not, like, *pretty*, you're, you know, just really good-looking."

Her cheeks turn red and I decide to save her. "Thanks for the cupcake." I take a bite, the rich flavor covering my tongue. "It tastes even better than it looks, which is saying something."

She lets out a little laugh.

"Thank you for coming over," I say, "but I actually don't need help today. I'll pay you and everything, but I'm good for now."

"Oh," she mutters, her hands pulling together all fidgety as she glances back at the front door. If I didn't know better, I'd think she actually wants to stay. "So, you finished your one-point perspective project?"

She had to remind me. I spent a good hour on Saturday trying to draw three-dimensional squares and ended up with something that looked more like a defunct robot. I balled up the paper and started again, all the while thinking about Jimmy's sketchbook in my closet and wishing it wasn't there.

Julianna and I sit by the coffee table again and I finish her cupcake. Is this her actually being nice to me?

She keeps a safe distance like before, but she seems more relaxed. She guides me through the steps, but I'm slow, each line taking forever.

I keep at it, suggesting to Julianna that she do her own homework while I trudge along. I picture her spouting off something snappy and looking at the clock like she can't wait to leave. Instead, she looks relieved as she pulls out our math textbook. Meanwhile, the eraser and I are best friends.

I sense Julianna looking at me a couple of times as we work. Each time I look up and catch her stare, she shifts her gaze back to her homework.

"Do you mind if I ask you something?" she asks.

I look up.

"What happened to your leg?"

I glance at it. Dr. Huntington says by next week I should be able to walk on it without the boot.

"I can't remember," I admit.

She offers a courtesy laugh and then waits, like she's expecting the truth now.

"Why do you need service hours anyway?" I ask instead.

Her eyes widen like I'm prodding into a secret. "S-service hours?"

"Yeah," I say. "That's what your ad on the bulletin board said. In the school hall. Said you were looking to tutor someone for service hours."

"It's nothing. I actually don't need them anymore."

So this really *is* about money.

"So, is that your brother?" she asks, continuing what has turned into a game of switching from one unpleasant topic to the next.

"What?"

"Your brother?" she repeats, confirming that I wasn't hearing things. When I fail to respond, she points to the leather photo album on the coffee table. A picture of a younger me and Jimmy occupies the center frame.

"Is that you?" she asks.

"Yeah."

"I figured the other kid was your brother."

"He is. *Was.* Jimmy died seven years ago. Almost eight years now."

Really, I didn't need to explain any of that.

Silence, followed by a soft, "I'm sorry."

I look up, finding her eyes pinned on me with nothing but open sympathy in their blue depths. A lot of people shy away from this stuff. Typically, they trip over an apologetic word or two and then look at anything but you. Not even I know how to handle it, and I've lost someone close to me.

Usually I clam up as well and crack a joke to lighten things up, but nothing comes to mind now. I drag a grin onto my face and look at the picture.

Jimmy and I stand with our arms crossed, striking tough-guy poses with our hips jutted out to show off the real FBI badges attached to our belt loops. One belonged to Dad, the other to his buddy Carl from the bureau.

"I had just turned ten. Jimmy had turned eight that spring. We were close," I say as memories rush in. Sometimes those last days with Jimmy don't feel real, while at other times they seem annoyingly tangible. Lately, it's been the latter. All thanks to that accident. I look at my leg. "The truth is, I really don't remember what happened to my leg, Julianna."

I pull the photo-booth picture from my wallet and slide it toward her. "That picture, that whole night; I don't remember any of it. I was hit by a car afterward during the dust storm. It was a hit-and-run."

Her eyes and mouth have shaped themselves into three unmoving *o*s, her shock unmistakable.

"I got a concussion and a broken leg."

"Oh my gosh," she says. "Cody—"

Several drawn-out seconds pass with nothing but the ticking of too many clocks on the wall. Mom loves clocks.

Getting hit by cars. Breaking bones. Concussions. And here I wasn't going to mention any of it.

The garage door opens and Julianna jumps, literally rising off the floor a few inches. Her eyes fill with terror and she whirls around toward the sound. Mom walks in carrying an empty vase. Lizzy follows, skipping through the kitchen.

"Hey, Mom. Need help?" I ask.

"No, thanks. I just have this one vase I'm trying out for the Montgomery wedding next—" She breaks her sentence off when she sees Julianna. "Oh, hi!"

Her things are discarded on the kitchen counter in a flash and she heads into the living room. Mom's excitement to see that I actually have company is sadly comical. Lizzy jumps onto the love seat, beaming at Julianna like we have a celebrity in the room.

Julianna looks a little shell shocked at the addition of my mom and sister in the house.

Mom waves. "I'm Janice, Cody's mom."

Julianna returns a hesitant wave. "I'm Julianna."

"It's so good to meet you," Mom says with an overdone smile and takes Julianna's hand in a firm handshake.

"Are you Cody's *girlfriend*?" Lizzy asks, drawing out the last word with an impish grin.

"Julianna is helping me with art."

"Oh, good," Mom chimes in, looking at Julianna. "He can use all the help he can get."

Luckily, Mom shoos Lizzy up to her room a minute later and pretends to be occupied in the office.

"Your mom's nice," Julianna says. She looks anywhere but at me, her eyebrows drawing into a slash of confusion, like she's standing at a fork in the road and doesn't know which way to go.

I ball up my piece-of-crap drawing and start with a fresh sheet of paper. Again.

"No, don't do that," Julianna says and lunges for the balled-up paper, a motion that cuts the space between us. I'm not about to complain. I catch a scent of something coconut, her shampoo maybe. She opens the paper, smoothing it out against the coffee table, and accidentally brushes her elbow against my arm in the process.

Her gaze drops to my arm and then jumps up to meet my eyes. "Save it so you can see your improvement."

The distant sound of the garage door opening and Dad's car pulling in fights for my attention, but I'm not about to break eye contact. Julianna's wide blue eyes framed by dark lashes pull me in.

"Dad's home!" Lizzy shouts as her feet drum a rhythm down the stairs.

Julianna jerks away. Panic erases the color from her face. Her things are shoved into her bag a second later and she springs to her feet. "I gotta go."

She slips on her flip-flops and flies out the front door before I can catch her. Stunned by her fast exit, I look out the front window, catching a glimpse of long dark hair as she hurries down the street before a row of bushes blocks her from view.

She didn't drive and no one gave her a ride here. She *walked*.

The jingle of car keys behind me catches my attention and I turn, finding Dad in the living room peering down at my crumpled drawing.

"Nice robot," he says with a thumbs-up before heading to his office.

In all things artistic, I definitely take after him.

CHAPTER 19

Julianna

I'm not sure which was worse, our first tutoring session or our second. Cody opened up about his little brother, sharing snippets of sorrow that wove around my heart. Then his dad came home and I about peed my pants. I ran out of the house like a total idiot.

I look at the photo-booth pictures Tuesday morning before school. I take in Cody's scar-free face and carefree smile, the mystery dancing in his green eyes. Some things make more sense now, everything from the moment he said good-bye in the mall parking lot until now.

He showed up for school that first day with no recollection of me other than a picture in his wallet. How did he even know my name then? How did he put two and two together when he saw my tutoring ad? Questions fizzle out as I recall the way I reacted when I saw Cody in Ms. Quinn's room.

There I stood, accusing him of buying those chocolates for me as some kind of bet. If I remember right, I was *yelling* at him. He was the victim of a hit-and-run and I didn't give him a chance to get in one word. No wonder he looked shocked. Did I actually call him a jerk?

Now that I think it through, I'm amazed he still talks to me.

I sit in Mr. Mortimer's room third hour, nervous prickles coursing up and down my restless legs as I glance at the clock. I avoid looking at the door Cody will walk through any minute, pretending instead to be immersed in a riveting chapter of AP Calculus.

"Any chance of scoring another one of those cupcakes?" His deep voice sends a warm quiver up my spine, drawing my gaze to meet his eyes. His thumbs are tucked under the straps of his backpack, the full bend of his elbows accenting the muscles stretching his short sleeves.

One eyelid drops in a fluid wink as he walks past my desk. His subtle grin is framed by deep dimples. Chick magnets, that's what those dimples are. Lethal.

By the time I realize I haven't responded, he's already at his table.

"Uh," I mutter too late, fully stripped of all rational thinking as my ridiculous grin refuses to surrender. I didn't even give him an answer. Not that he expected one. Did he?

I finally pull myself together before Candace walks in and takes her seat by Cody, firing up a conversation as though they hang out every day at lunch. For all I know they do, and it wouldn't surprise me. She's definitely his caliber, his type.

I'm Cody's tutor.

I keep my eyes safely averted from his table as Candace's muffled laughs carry through the entire class period.

I still haven't said a word about any of this to Trish or Mindy, and that's probably best. At this point Mindy would give me the silent treatment for not telling her sooner, while Trish wouldn't stop talking about it.

I'm spinning the combo on my locker before lunch when two hands touch my upper waist, making me jump and whirl around.

"Lucas," I breathe out in a rush as he slides his arms around me and clasps his hands at the small of my back.

"Were you expecting someone else?"

Truth is I wasn't, but Lucas's mention of a someone else brings one other boy to mind. I instantly force my thoughts back in line.

"No."

"You wanna come to the skate park after school?" His gaze roves around my face and pauses on my lips. "We need you to refilm a few stunts. Josh wants to splice the film tomorrow. With music and everything."

"*Re*film?" I say. "You've got to be kidding. I filmed like forty-five minutes last Saturday. How much footage do you need?"

"I'll get you a burger," Lucas adds as incentive. "And fries."

"Actually, Lucas, I'm busy," I say, the excuse sounding lame. But it's true. My teachers laid it on thick today. "I have twice as many math problems tonight, a report for history I haven't even started, and Mr. Davis assigned us two reports. Due tomorrow."

Lucas's hands glide lower, almost on my butt now. "So what?"

"So what?"

"Yeah, why are you so worried about school?"

"Some people want good grades, Lucas."

He inches back. I hate PDA, but I tolerate it because that's what couples do, right? Really, I would have no idea. Lucas is my first boyfriend, my first kiss besides Isaac Bogert back in the first grade, during a game of kissing tag at recess.

Lucas's fingers touch my cheek and glide up and down. It's a weak spot of mine. He should have started there instead of my butt because right now my annoyance over his flippant attitude is fading. And fast.

The homecoming dance has been the gossip today ever since student council made a big deal of it during announcements. It's three and a half weeks away. Still, I wonder when Lucas will get around to asking me. And *how.*

I imagine him texting me two days before the dance—so Lucas.

A few girls have already been asked, or so I hear; girls like Jentrie Burk and Michelle Walker, who are homecoming queen material.

"How about we go on a real date this weekend?" I say, putting my arms around Lucas this time.

"A date?"

"Yeah," I say, thinking how nice it would be. "You know, like get something to eat or see a show."

I picture Lucas and me at the theater, laughing together and having a great time. A date is just what I need, a brief escape from everything.

Lucas laughs, a breathy snicker that cuts my idyllic visions short. "Girls," he says with a roll of his eyes, pushing away from my locker and leading me along by the hand. "Too busy to hang out, but never too busy for a fancy date."

I raise a grin. Perhaps I should laugh along, but I don't feel like it.

"Come on," Lucas says. "Let's get lunch."

I glance back to make sure my locker is shut, my eyes instantly drawn to a tall figure walking away from the locker a few down from mine. Despite the boot on his leg, he walks steady, his head of sandy blond hair held high. I shouldn't care, but I do. Lucas and me back there, his hands all over my backside in a blatant display of affection; Cody saw it all.

Once again I have no car after school to get myself to Cody's. Dad is running errands in the Yaris, Vic hasn't answered his phone, and I don't see Rusty anywhere in the parking lot. Driving old Rusty into Cody's gated community isn't exactly appealing, but it would sure beat walking.

As I start out on foot, a bush of lantana flowers near the front of the school catches my eye, reminding me that I never sent the ones I picked for Mama. That was the first day I saw Cody at school. I dropped them, shocked, and stepped on them. Guilt hits me as I realize how long it's been since I sent a letter. I bend down to pick a few.

A chorus of giggles behind me draws my attention. I turn to see Candace, Aubrey, and Laurel in full black and teal cheerleader costume. They exchange devious glances as they walk past. I almost wonder if they don't see me crouched down here.

Candace practically snorts as they walk through the school gate, their backs to me now, like she couldn't hold a laugh in any longer. "There's one I haven't used before"—her mocking voice rings out—"hashtag: loser picking flowers."

I feel myself sinking into the cement as Aubrey and Laurel cackle away. To make matters worse, a shiny sports car pulls up along the curb beside me. Probably one of Candace's friends stopping by to join in on the laugh.

"Hey," the liquid voice snaps my attention toward the car.

Cody sits behind the wheel of a sporty convertible. From the bold orange paint to the shiny black wheels and leather interior, everything about this car is striking.

The expensive-looking sunglasses he wears are so dark I can't tell if he sees me here, squatting down by the bushes. I glance over at Candace and her friends, wondering if he's trying to get their attention. One look at their short skirts and I decide it's more than likely.

Candace spins around, flashing a million-kilowatt smile of bleached teeth, and I suddenly wish these bushes were big enough to disappear behind. He's going to flirt with her.

"I'm not about to let you walk again," Cody says.

I look over in time to catch a smile spreading over his lips.

"Hop in, Jules."

There's that nickname again, the one he used at our first tutoring session, that I couldn't stand. Clutching the lantana flowers, I walk to the passenger door and slip into the cool leather seat. Cody revs the engine and we pull away, leaving a very shocked Candace in the dust.

"Thanks," I say. He has no idea what he did for my self-esteem back there.

"No problem," he says, shifting the car into third gear as we gain speed, his arm close.

I'm pressing myself up against the passenger door and yet this snug car refuses to allow a safe buffer of space between us. Being this close to someone who, for so many reasons, should be nothing more than an enemy is anything but comforting.

"Is this *your* car?"

"Nah," he replies, his wavy blondish hair blowing in the wind. "It's my dad's."

Makes me feel so much better.

"I think it was a midlife-crisis kind of purchase because he hardly drives it."

"He hardly drives it?" I exclaim.

"He takes the government car to work," Cody explains, venturing too close to the topic of his dad's line of work for comfort. A dimple outlines his knee-weakening smile as he glances my way. "Not that I'm complaining."

For the next two days Cody gives me a ride to and from tutoring. I dash inside my house each time, hoping Cody drives away before anyone sees his ridiculous convertible in a neighborhood like ours. It's a nice-enough neighborhood, but it's no Chadwick Estates.

On Thursday we pull into my neighborhood to find a police car parked outside my house. My gut sinks, my suspicions thrown into hyperdrive. Cody doesn't say anything, but I sense his curiosity nonetheless. And then I notice the tow truck.

"You going to be okay?" Cody asks.

"Yeah," I say, keeping my voice light as I step out. I've kept things distant and professional the past few days, as they should be. Nonetheless, here he is glimpsing the ugliness of our personal life.

This can't be good.

I dash up the sidewalk, willing Cody to take off fast, but I'm not so lucky.

"Who was that?" Dad asks as he opens the screen door, his forehead pinched up in curious concern as he watches Cody's convertible drive off.

"Just a friend," I say and deflect the attention. "What's going on?"

Dad runs a hand over his head. His thinning hair stands out on end like he's done this nervous motion a hundred times in the past hour. A police officer stands at the curb. Another guy, wearing a grease-stained T-shirt and work gloves, is pulling equipment from the tow truck.

"Dad," I say again, my heart skidding around. I glance at our blue Yaris parked on the curb. "What are they doing?"

Dad heads back toward the house. "They're taking the car."

"*What*? Why? The Yaris?"

"Yes, the Yaris."

I follow Dad inside. "It wasn't parked illegally, was it? That curb isn't painted red."

Dad heads to the kitchen table, where the early stages of a new creation rests next to his hunk-of-scrap-metal sculpture. Red-colored pencils stick out from a central point, creating half of a coral reef.

"No, it wasn't parked illegally," Dad says, his voice rising in volume like it does when he gets mad. Which is rare. "We've been late on our car payments."

"So, what now?" I say as the reality of what's happening sinks in. "They can't take that car. We're barely getting by with two cars and you were supposed to go to that convention this weekend."

I look at the clock before remembering the battery needs replacing. Dad planned to leave this evening for San Diego. Perhaps now he'll realize what a mess we're in and skip the convention. I've always hated the idea of wake-up calls, the disasters that make people redirect their lives for the better. Now, however, I'm hoping this will startle Dad out of his complacency.

"I'll have to take Rusty," Dad says.

Our house is suddenly quiet, not a sound besides the rickety fan overhead and the chirp of a cricket stuck in the AC vent. Dad turns and starts for the stairs.

I take in a measured breath, a last-ditch attempt to remain calm. "You're still going?"

"Of course I'm going," Dad snaps over his shoulder, his typically mild tone coming out so sharp it feels like a slap in the face. Which only flips up the heat beneath my pot of boiling rage.

"Dad—"

"I've got to pack." He cuts me off.

"But Vic and I won't have a car."

Dad trudges up the stairs. "Find a ride. Take the bus. It'll be good for you two to stay home on Saturday anyway. You need to clean up around here and actually get some work done."

I halt on the third stair, anger soaring to an all-time high. Remembering my resolve on Sunday to change perspective, I bottle it in and spin around. I fling open the sliding glass door and step out into our little side yard, reminded of Cody's plush carpet and silent overhead fan.

His dad took everything from us and they have everything. Mama had a good job, a regular salary that kept us afloat. Really, it's all Vic's fault.

Everyone regards Mama as a criminal, and technically it's true. She committed a crime. But they didn't see the hurt look in her eyes every time Vic crashed through the door high on drugs. They didn't see the medical bills after Vic got those stomach ulcers, or the stack of late notices on utility bills. They didn't wake up one morning to find their house robbed, only to discover the thief was a member of their own family. They don't know what it feels like to live in fear like this, to have no one to help you get out of this tight spot besides yourself.

I flip on the hose to water Mama's lantanas and turn to find three sickly-looking bushes instead, their vibrant leaves shriveled. How long has it been since I've watered them? I can't seem to keep track of anything lately. I douse the bushes, stepping closer before something on the dirt near my toe catches my eye.

A scorpion.

An ugly-sounding yelp bursts from my lungs as I leap into the air. My feet rise only to touch down again, my flip-flops providing little protection from a possible sting.

I flip off the water, dash back inside, and slam the door.

Dad stands near the front door with an old suitcase. He's silent, standing there looking at me like he expects something. A good-bye, perhaps? A hug and well wishes on his way?

I'm speechless, and in the end he simply turns and walks out without a word, Rusty's deafening engine signaling that he's gone.

With the kind of stress coursing through me that only God or food can help, I turn toward the fridge, starved. Lunch was hours ago.

Our car is gone.

The only thing I could scrounge up for breakfast was a piece of stale bread.

We have a scorpion problem.

I recall what everyone says, how scorpions come in packs.

Forcing these thoughts away, I open the fridge, hoping Dad grabbed my favorite yogurt at the store this afternoon. Empty food-stained shelves greet me, mocking my hunger. Ketchup and mustard and a container of expired leftover food constitute my only options. And I don't have a car to go get groceries.

I move to the freezer, grateful more than ever for the tamales Mama and I made last April. Half a bag of hash browns, three freezer-burned hamburger buns, a can of orange juice concentrate: I sift through everything, panic taking over the longer I search.

Slamming the freezer door, I accept the truth: the tamales are gone. Vic or Dad must have finished them. I spin around and lean up against the fridge. My stomach growls and my eyes well up with hot tears.

It's only a bag of tamales, but right now it feels like losing Mama all over again.

CHAPTER 20

Cody

The same foggy, I-don't-care-about-anything feeling won't let up. Some would call this mild depression. I call it life. Sure, I put on a smile during school and at the kitchen table, but I can't shake it. For the few short moments Julianna is here helping me with that dang art project, I almost let myself forget.

She needs help; that's about as obvious as the fact that I need help with art. I see the strain, the fatigue in her eyes. She's been distant lately, keeping to her usual end of the coffee table. It makes me miss her laugh, her spunk.

Every once in a while she'll lean up on the coffee table and look at the picture of me and Jimmy, like she's waiting for me to tell her more. Telling her about Jimmy *and* the accident on Monday didn't help, though; it's about all I can think of now.

It's hard not to replay every detail of the past events that marked me. Like Jimmy's death. When I was younger, I used to think through what happened. Over and over. Every night. Just me, alone, in an empty bedroom that used to be occupied by two. It was easier that way, easier than putting words to the story and giving it a voice.

As I lie in bed now, I feel myself slipping back into my old ways. It's too hard to try to stop. I drift off to sleep, feeling the memories of those last days with Jimmy slithering toward some deep corner of my brain where dreams are made.

It happened only a year and a half after we skinny-dipped in the canal. I had just turned ten, Jimmy was eight, Rachel was six, and Lizzy—the surprise child—was one. Dad had bought me my first airsoft gun for target practice. It was a super low-velocity gun, safe for beginners. I was thrilled, Jimmy even more so. Mom wasn't quite so sure. Once the airsoft gun proved useful in pest control, however, she changed her mind.

Mom hated lizards. They came from the open fields beyond our backyard in Scottsdale, thriving on water from the drip hose beneath our bushes. So long as Jimmy and I wore long sleeves, gloves, and goggles and vowed to shoot lizards, we could use the airsoft gun all we wanted.

It was an unseasonably cold day for the beginning of November, and Jimmy had already been coughing.

He should go inside; *I remember thinking that. Jimmy was always coming down with something, though, and we were having too much fun.*

We pelted lizards left and right, Jimmy shouting his usual orders to fan out *and* trust your instincts. *Neither of us was about to stop, even when thick clouds overhead opened up and rain began to fall.*

Nothing beats an Arizona rainstorm. We were loving it. After all, bad guys were always easier to catch during a storm. Even though we were getting a little old for that kind of play, some lingering nostalgia linked to shooting imaginary bad guys as kids kicked in and we were Special Agents Rush and Rush again.

One last time.

Our goggles fogged up before long, covered in so much water we couldn't see a thing. Jimmy shot at a rock he thought was a lizard. We both started laughing. Jimmy's laughing turned into a coughing fit. Mom called us in, upset. She'd thought we'd come in long before.

Jimmy spent the next hour on the couch in front of the TV and then the next twenty-four hours in bed. He'd spiked a high fever. Couldn't stop shaking. Then the headaches started. And nausea. He said he was stiff all over. His neck hurt.

A doctor's appointment turned into a hospital visit. It all happened so fast.

Meningococcal meningitis: an infection had taken over, causing swelling in his brain and around his spinal cord. Somehow Jimmy had been exposed to the meningococcus bacteria. The doctor told us Jimmy had to have been infected through direct contact with a carrier of the bacteria. Everyone in the family was tested. Only one of us tested positive as a carrier: me.

Turns out, some people can carry the bacteria and never get sick. They can pass it on to others without even knowing.

We all received the antibiotic and we did everything we could for Jimmy. Doctors did everything they could. Jimmy was always the runt. Jimmy was already sick, his immune system weak. Within seventy-two hours after our airsoft adventure in the backyard, Jimmy passed away.

He should go inside. *That instinct haunted me for days, weeks, months. Years. The little brother I'd vowed to watch over after that close call at the canal was gone.*

Jimmy and I shared everything. Same bedroom, same toys, same bathtub, same tube of toothpaste. Jimmy even had a bad habit of using my toothbrush every once in a while. "So what?" he'd say to my protests. "You afraid of a little spit?"

It was Jimmy who should have been afraid of a little spit. My *spit. Just like that day at the canal, I was the one who put my best friend's life in danger. This time I couldn't save him.*

I throw the covers off. Hot. Sweating. Again.

A foul taste coats my mouth, the kind you get when you forget to brush before falling asleep. The air-conditioning vents cool me down on my way to the bathroom, but my mind is still on fire with memories and the knowledge of one very hard truth I learned to accept years ago, back when hopeful thoughts of heaven and a life after death were put to rest where they belong: Jimmy is gone.

I floss and brush, placing my toothbrush on the second shelf from the bottom, just above the toothbrush that lies unwrapped yet unused. Untouched.

Some habits are hard to break.

After all, Jimmy isn't here anymore. He isn't here and he isn't there. He's nowhere.

CHAPTER 21

Julianna

I wake up to a hot, clammy feeling enveloping my body. Sunlight barges through the broken slats of the blinds over my window, making me squint. A dull headache swells, and I'm tempted to roll back over and sleep through school.

Vic came in late last night, and it wasn't Heidi or one of his usual friends who dropped him off. At least it wasn't a car I recognized. He shoved open the door, letting it bang against the opposite wall and asked why Rusty wasn't parked out front. I told him why, still upset about our no-car situation myself, in addition to our new scorpion problem and our very empty fridge. That's when the yelling started.

He left no foul word unsaid, and when he rammed his fist through the drywall in the living room, I ran up the stairs and locked myself in my bedroom. I'd seen enough. Vic had been agitated the moment he walked through the door, his eyelids twitching like the lights were bugging him. Was he on drugs? Please, no.

Some people assume I like confrontation. In reality, my spunk is something learned rather than inherited. Acting strong is what I've had to do to survive.

The portable swamp cooler I'd wheeled in earlier kept me company as I worked on homework until midnight. By the time I finished my back ached from hunching over and my throat was dry. Imagining the possibility of a scorpion lying in wait along my path to the kitchen, I decided sleeping thirsty wasn't such a bad thing.

Then the electricity went out during the night. I know because I woke up in a hot sweat, my sheet tangled around me. The clock wasn't working and neither was the swamp cooler. My room had to be ninety degrees. I flipped the light switches on and off to no avail. The only good news to be had during a power outage at 2:00 a.m. came in the form of a text message from Dad letting me know he'd made it safely. Exhaustion won despite everything and I passed out on my bed.

Blinding overhead lights tore me from sleep sometime later. The clock was blinking 12:00 a.m. and my lights were on. The swamp cooler was out of water, but the idea of getting up to refill it made my mounting headache worse. I checked the time on my phone—3:14 a.m.—and reset my clock. Peeling back my sheet, I inspected my bed for any scorpions, remembering a story Trish had told me about one stinging her butt in the night.

I flipped off the lights and somehow fell asleep again despite the heat. And morning came too soon.

Mindy's horn honks as I'm finishing my hair. I check Vic's room on my way out. His bed is empty, the house silent. I jog downstairs, relieved to find Vic on the couch, sprawled out beneath the window swamp cooler. Beads of sweat glisten on his brow and he's out cold. I almost feel bad for him before I see the hole in the wall and remember the foul names he called me. Still, I refuse to believe he's on drugs again.

I leave without breakfast—let alone dinner the previous night—but I'm not even hungry anymore. I debate calling Dad and ratting Vic out, but calling Dad on the morning of his big presentation to tell him about the hole in our wall doesn't sound appealing. I call anyway, only to get his voice mail.

My stomach feels weird all morning and the school day passes in a haze. Seeing Lucas with Tina East in the hallway after first hour doesn't sit right either. It's just the two of them in a corner, and he's standing close. Leaning. Close enough to look down her shirt. And she's laughing. I figured Tina was with Josh, Lucas's friend. I shake it off, telling myself it's nothing, and head to class. None of the chairs are comfortable enough for my back, and all I want to do is lie down on my desk and sleep.

Lucas slides his hands around my waist while I'm at my locker.

"I hear your dad's out of town tonight," he whispers in my ear, the feel of his hot breath against my already hot neck making me flinch away.

"Who told you?"

"Mindy," he replies.

I nod.

"Why didn't you tell me?" he asks as I turn around into his loose embrace. His lips spread into a grin. "So, the master bedroom is open?"

I shove him away. "Don't be sick."

He's joking, like guys do. At least I think so.

We've never been past second base. Or first base; I'm not sure. Who even knows which base is which? I sure don't. I'm new to this whole relationship thing.

"I'm so, *so* tired, Lucas, and I have a headache," I say and wiggle away, still unnerved at his suggestion, even if it was a joke. "I'm going straight to bed as soon as I get the chance."

Lucas doesn't look put out, which reassures me it was a joke. Still, it has me thinking about our relationship, about where it's going. Right now I need a friend. Someone who will listen.

The first time my aching back feels any kind of relief is when I sink into the black leather seat of Cody's convertible.

"You okay?" he asks as he works the clutch. His boot rests on the tiny backseat. If I had a car like this, I'd take a boot on and off to drive it too.

"Yeah, I'm fine," I say, resisting the urge to ask more about his leg. Somehow, over the past four days, the two of us have settled into something of a routine. Cody drives; I flip through songs on the radio.

A song I've heard a couple of times catches my attention. I lean back and close my eyes, letting the cool air and melodic tune suck away the tension. "I like this guy's voice."

"Tyler Ward," Cody says. I open my eyes enough to see him looking my way. He turns the volume up.

The song is tender, the kind that reaches inside and pulls everything to the surface. Not the type I'd choose to listen to with the son of Special Agent Rush. The melody is rich and moving though, each chord of the piano lifting my cares higher until they are almost out of reach. Almost.

A tear slips from my eye and streams down my cheek. Surprised and more than embarrassed, I mop it up. Actually, why should I be surprised? It all crashes back now: the tiredness, the stress, the car, Vic possibly messing with drugs again, the late bills, and Mama in prison.

I catch Cody's stare again, humiliated at the idea of him catching me crying.

"Can I borrow these?" I ask and reach for an extra pair of sunglasses resting on the skinny console between us.

"You bet."

I snatch them up and put them on, keeping my head turned away.

The song slows to an end—thankfully. Music always does this to me. It cuts through my defenses, leaving me weak. The car turns off the main road, and I flip my attention back to Cody.

We pull into an empty lot near a gas station where a little stand with a sign that reads SUNGLASSES $10 is set up.

He puts the car in park next to the stand. "Pick any one you want."

He must be joking. One look into his eyes, however, and I know he's serious.

"I don't need any."

"Do you even have a pair?" he asks.

The way he phrased it, like he highly doubts I have my own pair, grates on my nerves. The frustrating truth is, I don't. Another tear pushes its way to the edge. I look away. What's my deal?

This unrelenting headache reminds me of how crappy I've felt today. I want to go home. With nothing but another hot and restless night ahead, I remember how much I need this job as Cody's tutor. I need the money.

I look over at the stand of sunglasses, surprising even myself when I say, "Fine."

"Yeah?" Cody says, looking genuinely excited that I'd let him buy me a pair.

A smile works its way onto my lips.

Cody opens a small drawer in the console, revealing a collection of money that puts a whole new definition on the term *spare change*. Coins clink as he sifts through the mass, pulling out dollar bills and change by the handfuls. "I've been trying to get rid of some of this anyway."

He proves how much he wants to get rid of it when he starts tossing pennies out the window. I catch a glint of silver flying out his window and sit upright. He's throwing *nickels*, too? When a quarter soon follows, my hand dashes out instinctively. "No!" I say, shock swinging my voice into a high pitch of desperation. "Not *quarters*."

He turns to me, and I realize how close we are. Our faces are a breath away as I hold his wrist firm, saving the next quarter from the pavement. His eyes burrow into mine, the intensity of his gaze crumbling any last defense the song failed to break through.

A moment of irrational curiosity elapses as each of my senses takes him in at once: the thick stubble along the sharp contours of his jaw, his shower-fresh scent, the warmth of his skin on my palm, and even the subtle sound of air passing through the lungs of this very alive and masculine form beside me. His gaze slides down to my lips, and in this insane second of weakness, I'm tempted to lean forward and give that last sense of mine a taste of Cody Rush.

I jerk away, returning to the scant buffer of space my seat offers. "The vending machine, the food—everything at the prison during visitor hours," I say, the words stumbling from my lips uncensored as I try to catch my breath. "Quarters only."

I wait for him to make a verbal jab, to laugh off my desperation so I can push him away and hate him forever.

Instead, he nods, a solemn bob of his head before he begins picking quarters from the jumble of coins. He takes my backpack from the backseat, opens the front zipper, and dumps a boatload of quarters in.

I sit in my usual spot of plush carpet in Cody's house thirty minutes later, my new pair of sunglasses resting on the coffee table beside an impressive spread of colored pencils. Cody is almost finished with his one-point perspective project. Finally. Watching this boy with a ruler and a pencil is painful.

He's come a long way, though, and it fills me with satisfaction I wasn't expecting. Mrs. Hughes's announcement about upcoming cuts to visual and performing arts classes drifts back to mind. What a shame.

I shiver, wondering if it's always this cold in Cody's house.

I gesture to a fuzzy blanket stowed beneath a side table. "Can I use this?"

"Sure."

The point of a green colored pencil in Cody's hand snaps off. He lets out a grunt of frustration and flings it aside, adding it to the collection of broken colored pencils dotting the carpet.

My eyes shift to the pile of broken pencils at his side. "You know, there *is* such a thing as a pencil sharpener."

He shrugs, all of his concentration zeroed in on the new colored pencil between his fingers like he's willing those impressive muscles of his to take it easy on this one. "Nah. I'll just get a new box."

"A new box?" I repeat, wrapping the blanket around my legs. "Of pencils?"

"Yep."

"What, and throw those away?"

He glances up, his inquisitive stare revealing that he caught the undeniable hint of interest in my voice. "Do they take colored pencils at the prison, too?"

For some reason this makes me burst into laughter. I'm so tired, though, I don't even try to hold it back. My unrelenting headache throbs worse the harder I laugh, so I rein it in. The leather couch draws my attention its way. The cushy form is too inviting to resist. I scoot between the coffee table and the couch, closer to Cody, and rest my head back.

"No," I answer him as my eyelids surrender to fatigue. I'm not sure if it was the song or the tears or the fact that I already mentioned something as personal as Mama in prison, but I open up and tell Cody why.

"My dad took our only car to San Diego this weekend for an art convention. When what he probably should be doing is working on this new sculpture he's been hired to make for the art room of the Children's Museum. It's a coral reef made of colored pencils." I let out a laugh. "Thing is"—and here it is, nothing more than a few subtle words packed with the truth of our pathetic financial situation—"we don't have any colored pencils."

A beat of silence, followed by, "Do you want some water?"

I nod, and he stands.

My raw throat aches at his offer, and it suddenly dawns on me that

I'm coming down with something. I should have put this together hours ago. My achy back, headache, sore throat, and tiredness. I should have gone straight home after school.

My head droops to the side and jolts upright, my reflexes working to keep me awake. I try to open my eyes but can't. I feel so relaxed on this spread of clean, plush carpet where I don't have to worry about a scorpion stinging my butt. That errant coil in my bed isn't digging into my back and Vic won't barge through the door any second with a hot temper.

The song Cody and I heard in the car drifts through my drowsy mind, the rich voice and gentle stroke of piano keys lulling every worry into oblivion. And I give up. Here I rest in the home of the man who played such a big part in turning my life upside down; a home that, ironically enough, feels like a safe haven.

CHAPTER 22

Cody

I return to the living room to find Julianna's eyes still closed, her head resting back against the couch. I hold out the water bottle and sit. "Here's your water."

No response. I grab a coaster and set the perspiring bottle down, my eyes glued to Julianna. Still nothing.

"Jules?" I ask.

Her lips part, her jaw inching down. She's totally asleep.

I smile.

I start coloring again, glancing up every few minutes to check on her. Her head has tilted to the side, like at any moment it's going to fall the rest of the way and jar her awake.

I scoot closer. "Jules?" I whisper. Nothing. "Julianna?" I ask.

If she wakes up now and finds me this close, she'll freak. Still, she looked exhausted today. I guess there's no need for her to wake up yet. If only I could slip a pillow between her head and her shoulder. Or better yet . . .

I close the distance between us, leaning up against the couch. I'm almost finished with my project when her head slides the last few inches and rests against my arm.

Her head is on fire.

I toss my project onto the coffee table and look down at her head of dark hair resting on me. Slowly, I inch my cheek down to touch her forehead like my mom always does when I'm sick. Yep, she's definitely got a fever.

Just like Jimmy.

I don't let myself think about that.

We sit like this for a while, long enough for me to think back on the tears in Julianna's eyes on our drive over. She can pretend to be strong all she wants; I know better. She needs someone. Help. *Protection.*

Her smile lassos my attention, dissolving everything else around me. Long dark hair. She blows a strand away from her eyes as she works.

The mall. I'm in my living room next to Julianna now and yet I can picture her across from me in that chocolate store, the lock around my memory breaking loose.

She hands something to a customer, her eyes flashing a stunning blue under the bright lights of the mall.

Staying out of her life is for the best. My dad, the FBI agent. Their mom, the convict. Yet something kicks in, an inborn drive to step in and protect.

Music blares, cutting the stream of memories short. Rachel. Her room is overhead. I glance down at Julianna to find her in the same position, her chest rising and falling slowly. If that music doesn't wake her up, nothing will.

Mom hurries into the kitchen and I hear the jingle of car keys. "Hey, Cody, I've got to hurry and pick up Lizzy from her dance class."

The love seat is blocking me and Julianna from her view, so I guess she doesn't see the cozy position we're in.

"Don't forget," she says on her way out, "I'm hosting book club tonight at seven."

Which means Dad and the rest of us need to clear out. And this living room needs to be spotless. I look at the stack of colored pencils on the floor.

The garage door slams and I freeze, sliding a glance down to Julianna. She slept through all of it. How long has she been asleep? Ten, fifteen minutes?

Dad will be home soon. Imagine how much Julianna will freak

then. Would he recognize her? Probably not. I can understand why Julianna would never forget him, but my dad arrests people all the time.

I slide my arm between the couch and Julianna's back before I think twice about it. If this wakes her up, I'll drive her home. If not . . . well, she might as well sleep comfortably. I get my feet under me and lift her into my arms. Man, she sleeps deep. I'm about to set her on the couch, but then I look at the clock and realize it's almost dinner time. And then book club.

I look down at Julianna's sleeping form, curled up in my arms, and I start for the stairs instead. I navigate the staircase despite the boot, keeping her as still in my arms as possible.

My room is the farthest from Rachel's loud music. I nudge the door open. Carrying a girl into my bedroom and laying her down on my bed isn't something I foresaw happening today. Especially a girl like Julianna, who hates me. At least she used to hate me.

As I lay her down and look at her sleeping form, I think back. She seems less jumpy now. In fact, sometimes she looks happy to be here. Relieved. She's not all hard as nails like she acts either. She mentioned her mom today, something I imagine was hard. Even her blushing smile when I bought her those sunglasses is evidence. She doesn't hate me, not anymore.

Man, I want to kiss her.

Not like this, though. Asleep. Sick. Of course not.

Still, I'm tempted to gather her up in my arms again. Run my hands through her hair. Down the side of her waist.

I back up before my imagination gets away from me.

"So, Julianna . . ." I say at the dinner table forty-five minutes later, "the girl who tutors me—"

"She's purty," Lizzy says with a mouth full of mashed potatoes. "Can I have some chocolate milk, Mom?"

"You've got a tutor?" Dad asks, his forehead gathering up over a confused stare. "Since when do you need a tutor?"

"He needs help in art, honey," Mom cuts in with a light whack on his arm. "There's no shame in that. Rachel, take out your earbuds."

Rachel doesn't hear. It's almost six o'clock and Julianna still hasn't woken up. She's been asleep for over an hour and a half. I've checked on her several times, wondering if I should wake her. Each time I chicken out.

"Ryan, say something," Mom whispers, her eyes shifting between Dad and Rachel.

"Rachel. Earbuds. *Out*," Dad orders.

Rachel's eyes snap up to meet his gaze and she yanks the earbuds out.

"Anyway," I say, "she's sleeping in my bed."

Now all eyes are on me.

There's a real possibility Julianna might walk down any minute, so I figured it was best to get this out in the open. It was either this or wake her up and sneak her out. Now, with everyone staring at me and Lizzy's mashed-potato-covered mouth hanging open, I wonder if that wasn't the better option.

Dad drops his silverware and directs a firm hand toward me to emphasize whatever point he's about to make. "Son, I know we've discussed the importance of using protection, but I figured it went without saying that bringing a girl into our home—into your bedroom!—is out of the question."

"Ryan!" Mom snaps. "Lizzy, cover your ears. Cody, save it for marriage."

This is the first dinner conversation Rachel has been interested in for months. She snorts back a laugh.

"It's not like that," I say, hardly able to hold back a laugh myself as I realize I should have phrased this better.

Dad's lips form a stern line. "This is not a laughing matter, Cody."

"She fell asleep, okay? While I was working on my art project."

"Your art put someone to sleep?" Rachel says. "What a surprise."

"Rachel, cut it out," Dad barks.

Mom simply looks grateful to have Rachel participating at the dinner table.

"How did she end up in your bed?" Mom asks.

Lizzy's wide eyes ping-pong from Mom to me.

"I carried her."

"And she didn't wake up?" Rachel asks.

"She was pretty out of it," I say. "I think she isn't feeling good."

Mom looks at the clock. "Won't her parents be worried?"

"They—" I say and pause. "Aren't home."

A muscle in Dad's jaw flinches. He picks up his fork and knife and starts cutting into his meat again. An awkward silence with no end in sight falls over the table.

"Can I have my chocolate milk now?" Lizzy asks.

I'm not sure how I figured this conversation would go, but this certainly wasn't it.

CHAPTER 23

Julianna

I'm lying on a fluffy cloud, a cool breeze sweeping over me—must be a dream. A soft dream I don't care to awaken from. My eyes open and adjust to the darkness. A sliver of light from the door behind me lights a portion of the wall I'm staring at. I wonder if Dad is up late working on projects. But wait, he's gone. Vic, then? Actually, where am I?

The bed beneath me suddenly feels too soft. No errant coil digging into my back. And the silky smooth sheets have a thread count way above what I can afford.

I bolt upright, nerves stacking up as I realize I'm not home.

A clock near the bed says 9:10 p.m. I scramble toward the lamp beside it, fumbling to turn the little knob before I have a heart attack. *Where am I?*

Light illuminates the room and I squint before my eyes rest on a framed picture on the wall. A bare-chested Cody Rush stares back at me with nothing but shorts, a backpack, and a pair of hiking shoes covering his chiseled body as he poses on beautiful Camelback Mountain.

I fly out of the bed, bottling up a scream.

Cody's bed. Cody's *sheets*. Oh my gosh!

It flits back to memory now: the car ride to Cody's, the sunglasses, the broken colored pencils on the floor. And then what? *I ended up in his bed?*

I remember leaning up against the couch. I was exhausted and sick. Yes, I fell asleep. But that was at, like, four fifteen in the afternoon. Now it's nine o'clock at night?

My head feels so much better. Still, I can't believe I did this. And where's Cody? Thank goodness not in here.

I find a mirror on the wall, cringing at my ratty hair and smeared makeup. Escape plans quickly form in my mind. I picture myself darting down the hallway and through the front door hoping no one notices. Plan B involves me crawling out Cody's window and running like mad. Neither option looks promising. I bite my lower lip, unable to make up my mind.

A blue comforter covers Cody's queen-size bed, matching the oversized beanbag in the corner as well as the drapes. This room is immaculate, so different from Vic's. A desk is situated nearby, a key chain collection decorating the wall above it, along with a poster of a pro basketball player. When I realize someone is standing in the far corner, staring at me, I let out a muffled scream for real this time and jump.

He wears a cowboy hat and boots, the whole getup. It's only a stand-up. Of John Wayne. Guys' rooms are so weird.

The collection of pictures on the wall snags my attention again, first the one of Cody's impressive bare chest and then the others. One picture of a little boy holding a bat over his shoulder tugs at my heart. Jimmy.

He draws me in, won't let me go. He was a photogenic kid, his eyes containing that clear quality that Cody's have. They look alike but different, Jimmy's hair curlier and blonder than Cody's, his frame skinnier. In several of the pictures, both boys are wearing overalls and they're standing in fields of corn or on top of bales of hay like they used to own land.

A soft rap at the door sends me running for the window.

"Hey," his voice greets me.

I whirl around, feigning composure. Cody leans up against the door frame and casually slings his hands in the pockets of his basketball shorts, like finding me in his bedroom is completely normal.

He *carried* me in here. He had to have.

"Sleep well?" he asks.

"It's, like,"—I gesture to the clock—"nine o'clock. And I'm in your *bedroom*."

"Yeah, you looked pretty tired. And your head was on fire. I put some medicine on the nightstand. Here—"

He crosses the room to the nightstand, his shadow against the far wall stretching as he draws closer. Now I notice the glass of water and little bottles of medicine clustered around it.

"Headache reliever and fever reducer," he reads from the first bottle and then picks up another. "I wasn't sure which one you'd want, if any."

I watch him fish through the medicine that he set out for me while I was sleeping. This is so unlike Vic or Dad, so unlike Lucas or any other guy I've met, and I suddenly have a very hard time swallowing.

He reaches up toward my face, his intent gaze nearly undoing me. My heart flings a stream of flutters against my rib cage and I hold my breath. His thumb brushes my cheek, that weak spot of mine that turns me to mush. And this is *Cody Rush*.

"Here," he says, his eyes shifting to follow the motion of his thumb. "You have something under your eye."

Mascara. Makeup everywhere. Ratty hair. "I've got to get home."

He takes a step back. "I'll take you. Let me change my shirt real quick. I made Lizzy laugh when her mouth was full of chocolate milk and I learned my lesson."

I glimpse the specks of brown covering his shirt before he whips it off in one swift motion right in front of me.

I spin away, looking anywhere else. "Ah . . ."—I motion toward the door—"I'll just, you know—"

"Come again?" he says, pretending not to hear me. I'm well acquainted with that playful tone in his voice by now and I turn to meet his eye, instantly knowing it was a mistake. The dim lighting of the lamp casts shadows in all the right places along his defined chest and abs. His mischievous smile sneaks out to tease me right before he pulls on a new shirt.

"Come on," he says with a wink as he heads to the hallway. "Let's go."

"Your parents," I venture as I follow Cody down the stairs. "Will they be upset?"

"Nah, they're cool with it."

"Really?"

"Oh, yeah."

At which point I run into Special Agent Rush himself.

I gasp and step back, nearly tripping over the bottom stair I just stepped off.

"Hey, Dad," Cody says.

Agent Rush slides a pair of glasses down the rim of his nose. His lips are unmoving, his blue eyes sliding between Cody and me as he shifts a stack of papers from one hand to the other. It's weird to see him here like this all dressed down, puttering around his home office.

"Are you feeling any better?" Cody's mom asks, and I turn, realizing she has company. Two other ladies stand in the living room with her, and one is Candace's mom.

"Yes, thank you," I say.

"There's some leftover meat and potatoes in the fridge," Cody's mom tells me. "You're probably starved. Cody, make sure she gets some."

Candace's mom is one of those involved moms, so I've seen her a lot in the past six years. She looks at me curiously, like she recognizes me as well.

When I glance back to find the same quizzical stare on Agent Rush, crippling fear threatens my already shaky knees. *He recognizes me.*

"That's right," he declares as his face lights up with recognition. I nearly keel over. "You're a TA in the front office, right?"

Relief washes over me, too good to be true. "Right."

"I'll be back," Cody says and snags a set of keys.

My heart hasn't slowed its frantic pace five minutes later as we drive to my house under a starlit sky in Cody's convertible.

"Can I ask you a question?" Cody says. "About that night at the mall?"

I take a deep breath and resituate the container of meat and potatoes on my lap, finally relaxing. He shifts the gear and we pick up speed, his knuckles only inches from my knee. I picture those hands sliding under my legs and around my back, lifting me up and carrying me upstairs. To *his bedroom.*

"Jules?"

"Hm?" I reply. There's that nickname again, like he and I—the convict's daughter and the FBI agent's son—are actually friends. Should I be okay with this? I slept in his bed, for heaven's sake.

"That night," Cody repeats as we near my neighborhood, "at the mall."

"Oh, yeah, sure. What is it?"

"Was Vic there, too?"

"Vic?" I ask, caught off guard.

"Yeah, or did I mention him?"

"Wait, my *brother* Vic?"

Cody hesitates. "Yes."

"How do you know Vic?" Seriously, now that I think about it, I've hardly mentioned Vic.

Cody pins a questioning stare on me before focusing on the road again. He pulls into my neighborhood. "Ah, we met at a basketball tournament at the beginning of the summer."

This piece of news is a total shock. "Like, *before* you and I met in the mall that night?"

"Yeesss," Cody says, his brow lifting curiously. "I didn't mention any of this to you at the mall?"

"No."

The rich rumble of Cody's car dies down as he pulls up beside my house and parks. He studies the dashboard. "How long were we together at the mall?"

"Well, you showed up at The Chocolate Shoppe—"

"I remember that," he says.

"You do? I thought you said you didn't remember anything."

"Bits and pieces are coming back."

"I don't know, Cody; you just sort of showed up out of nowhere a few minutes before closing. We talked for a while and then you bought some chocolates."

"And I didn't tell you my name?" he asks.

"No."

He shifts his probing gaze to me. "And you didn't ask?"

I drop my chin and give *the look*. "Does *every* girl have to ask for your name and number?"

"But somehow we ended up in a photo booth together," he counters. "How did *that* happen?"

"You pulled me in there."

"Really?"

"Yeah. Like, total creepo-dragging-me-in type thing."

He leans toward me, resting his elbow on the narrow console between us. "But you didn't protest, did you?"

There's that naughty grin of his again, the devil inside of him sneaking out to drag the confession from me.

"No," I admit reluctantly.

"How come?"

He is so full of himself. He knows very well why. "Because, Cody, I think I could already tell . . ."

It hurts my pride to give in like this.

"You could already tell what?" he asks when I fail to finish.

He's gorgeous, that's why. But it was more than that, and I realize this now. "I could already tell you're a good guy."

There it is, the truth stripped down and in the open. This is the part of Cody that keeps my curiosity hooked, the part that makes him hard to ignore. He's not only a handsome face and an athletic body. It would be so much easier to hate him if that was all he was. The past several weeks have shown me how very real he is, a person with pain and weaknesses and mysteries not even he knows about.

"Thanks," he says with a genuine grin and leans back in his seat. "Vic and I were on our way to a post-tournament party that night. All I know between that and waking up in the hospital is that somehow I ended up in the mall photo booth with you."

I'm not sure what to make of any of this, it's so bizarre. "*You* and Vic," I say. *"Friends?"*

"Is that so hard to believe?"

"Kinda," I say. Okay, big-time. I picture the rich, tidy, straight-arrow Cody Rush hanging with Vic, my pothead brother who can sink ball after ball into a hoop but can't seem to get a single gym sock in the laundry hamper.

"Here, I'll get this," Cody says and reaches for my backpack in the backseat.

"I can get it."

"No, I got it," he says, beating me to it.

I look at my house, the faded stucco and darkened windows, and admit that it was nice for once to be the one being cared for today instead of the other way around.

"Thanks," I say and get out.

When we reach my door, Cody looks up at my darkened house. "You going to be okay?"

"Yeah."

Darkness masks his face from view. A beat of silence passes, during which time my eyes adjust enough to glimpse a grin on his face, his eyes focused on me.

This is the first time someone besides Lucas has dropped me off on my porch like this.

Cody's gaze travels over my face, and when his eyes pause on my lips, I hold in a breath, split between want and trepidation.

"Take care, Jules," he says, and then he's gone.

I watch him walk back to his car. I'll never admit it, but the nickname is growing on me.

"Jewel!" Vic's voice roars downstairs.

I set the novel down on the edge of the bathtub and sit up, bubbles covering me from the neck down. It's nearly midnight. After enjoying the meat and potatoes Cody's mom sent home with me, I cleaned the bathroom, wired after all that sleep I got at Cody's. Not even Vic's filth could spoil my good mood, and when I found the long-forgotten bottle of bath bubbles in the cabinet, I decided a cool bubble bath in a clean tub with a good book was long overdue.

The front door slams, shaking the whole house, and I stand.

I wrap a towel around me, knowing that edge in Vic's voice all too well. I recall his bloodshot eyes last night, the hole he punched in the wall. Is he high? No. *No.* He can't be. I wish Dad had answered my call earlier today, wish I had called him again. I grip the door handle and swallow hard, fear making my heart flicker out of rhythm.

I open the door and start down the darkened hallway toward my room, peeking into Vic's room on my way and looking back up to find the shadow of his intimidating form right in front of me.

A scream escapes me as I jump back. My shaking hand flies to the light switch on the wall. A flash of light followed by a loud pop and a return to total darkness makes me scream and flinch again. I grab the towel around me before I lose it. Great, now the lightbulb is out and we probably don't have a replacement.

"Vic," I say, the quiver in my voice giving my apprehension away, "what's wrong? Where have you been?"

"Where have *you* been?" he shoots back.

I'm at a complete loss, wondering what he's getting at. When has he ever cared about where I go? He has no right to treat me like this.

"Since when is it your business?" I ask, my big mouth getting away from me. Bring it on.

He pulls something from his pocket and holds it up. The shiny paper in his hand catches a trace of light from the bathroom behind me, and I recognize it at once.

The photo-booth pictures.

"You *thief.*"

One hand flies out on instinct—my other still clutching my towel in place—and shoves him hard in the chest. He barely budges.

"You stole that money months ago and now you went back for more."

"No," he says. "You told me where to go looking for money months ago when you *accused me* of stealing from you."

"Liar!" I shout and shove him again. "You're nothing but lies, Vic. And *your* lies put Mama in *prison!*"

His hand captures my wrist before I can push him again. "Shut up!" he roars, the force of his voice driving me back. He pins me against the wall and thrusts the picture in my face again. "When did you take these pictures? How do you know him?"

"Cody?"

"Yes, Cody."

"He goes to our school, Vic. And he told me you guys are *friends.*"

"Not anymore," Vic says, the faint bathroom light highlighting the stern set of his jaw. "Stay away from him, Jewel."

I snag the picture from him with my free hand. "Why?"

"His dad," Vic starts, "is the FBI agent who put Mom behind bars. I met him."

I say nothing. When Vic's eyebrows drop down to accent the rage in his eyes, I realize he was expecting a bigger reaction from me. "You *knew?*" he roars.

"Not at first."

"Jewel," he yells, "his dad put our mom in prison."

"No, Vic, *you* did that, and everything has been falling apart since."

"And I'm trying to fix it!"

"What?" I shriek. Confused. Doubtful.

"What's going on between you and Cody?"

"Nothing," I say, knowing it's a lie. I slept in his bed and I spent the past half hour reading a romance novel in the bathtub replaying every detail of the evening, from his thumb brushing my cheek to him taking off his shirt.

"Good," Vic says and backs off at last. "Keep it that way."

"Just because his dad is an FBI agent—"

"Stay away from him!" Vic lashes back. "I have a plan, Jewel. I can fix this. I can get us money, but you have to stay away from Cody Rush."

This above all strikes fear into me. "What are you talking about, Vic? What are you up to?"

He brushes me off, like he's already said too much. "Just go to bed."

He slams his bedroom door. I dash to my room and do the same. I throw on pajamas and climb into bed. I check my phone and find four new text messages.

MISSED YOUR CALL, Dad wrote at 4:45. WILL HAVE TO TALK LATER.

And then three messages from Lucas, the first one received at 6:23 p.m.

WHERE ARE YOU? I'M ON YOUR DOORSTEP. ASLEEP ALREADY?

Eight minutes later: CALLED VIC. SAID HE JUST LEFT THE HOUSE AND DIDN'T SEE YOU COME HOME AFTER SCHOOL.

Forty minutes later: CALL ME.

I toss my phone aside and force myself to sleep, trying to ignore my heart and its tangled mess of emotions.

CHAPTER 24

Julianna

I hide in my room most of the day Saturday. Like, *all day* with my nose in the book I started last night, one of Mama's romances I thought I'd never read. Vic comes and goes without a word, thankfully. I reply to Lucas's texts, telling him I'm still under the weather.

When I can tell Vic is gone for the evening, I sneak downstairs to raid the pantry. I find some crackers wedged behind a stack of board games and head back upstairs to finish my book. I can't lie; my little escape from reality yesterday with Cody was refreshing and I don't want it to end.

As the sun goes down, I check my phone yet again, denying my disappointment when I find no new texts. Not like Cody would have any reason to text. I'm hooked on the romance until the last page, finishing the final line before a soft tap on my door drags me back to the present.

I sit up. It's eleven o'clock. "Yeah?"

The door opens and Dad's head of graying hair peeks in.

"Dad," I say, relieved to see him home.

"Ready for bed already?" he asks and steps in.

I look down at my pajamas, the same ones I put on last night and haven't changed out of. "Yep. You made it home fast."

"I left as soon as I could," he says. "I've got good news."

"What?" I say, doubtful.

"Some repair guys are coming Monday morning to fix the AC."

I'm speechless. Actual good news was the last thing I expected. "How?"

"I made some calls to clients who still owe me. It was a really productive weekend."

Dad seems different today.

"That's awesome, Dad. I tried to call you yesterday. It's about Vic. He punched a hole in the wall."

"I saw it," he says. Not quite the reaction I was expecting.

"And?"

"Vic apologized. I can understand. I was upset about the Yaris being taken, too."

"But Dad, it's not just that . . ." I pause, not ready to admit the possibility of Vic being involved with drugs again.

"Right now," Dad says before I can finish, "I'm concerned about you."

To say that I'm confused doesn't begin to describe this moment.

"*Me?* Why?"

"Is it true?" he asks. "What Vic tells me—is it true?"

I fail to temper the sudden jumpy rhythm of my heart. *Vic*, that tattletale. It's like they're all ganging up on me. Now I realize, however, this was inevitable. How did I ever think tutoring Cody was going to work? This is Mama we're talking about, the person whose absence has left a huge void in our home. We all miss her, Dad perhaps the most.

"That was him, wasn't it?" he asks. "The other day in that sports car."

I close my eyes and nod. "Dad, we hardly know each other. He just needed my help with art and we barely started—"

"Good," he cuts me off with a commanding finality in his tone I've never heard from him before. "Then make sure it ends now."

I head toward math Monday morning, remembering well the warnings Vic and Dad issued. Cody didn't call or text. Checking my phone every half hour did nothing to lessen the letdown. I couldn't help it. Spending so much time with him, listening to him talk about Jimmy and the accident, waking up on his soft bed with medicine neatly laid out and feeling his thumb gently brush my cheek—no wonder I was confused about what was going on.

Now I know. Nothing is going on. It's for the best. Cody is just a good guy, and I happened to be the recipient of his kindness.

Only a few people are sitting in Mortimer's room when I arrive. I start toward my seat, my gaze instantly drawn to the huge pile of school supplies on my desk. I count the desks, making sure I'm at the right one before poking through the mysterious heap.

Colored pencils, colored pencils, colored pencils. Box after box of brand-new colored pencils. And five rolls of quarters.

"Good morning."

I whirl around toward the voice, a smile breaking loose when I find Cody standing over my shoulder. He smiles, the thick stubble covering his face unable to hide his deep dimple.

"Feeling better?"

"Yes," I say. "Tons."

He starts toward his desk with a smile, walking backward with his thumbs tucked under the straps of his backpack. "Didn't happen to have anything to do with the sleeping arrangements, did it?"

I laugh. "It might have."

With less than two minutes until class starts, people start flooding in.

"Hey, Cody," I say, "thank you."

He nods with a grin before Candace strolls in and takes up her usual spot beside him. I shove box after box of colored pencils in my backpack as class starts, remorse yanking me back to reality as I realize this makes what I'm about to do all that much harder. Why does he have to be so nice?

The jangle of colored pencils in my backpack on my way to my locker after math takes me back to my elementary school days. I wait by my open locker, split between hoping Cody shows and dreading what I'll have to say when he does.

He rounds the corner for better or worse, and I remind myself that none of this was supposed to happen: me and him, friends. I never should have agreed to tutor him.

"Hey," he says as he draws near.

"Hey," I reply and take a deep breath to gather courage as I extend the stack of colored pencils to him. "And the quarters. I can't accept them."

His lifts his arm to the wall of lockers and leans against them. "And I won't take them back."

"Listen," I say, short of breath as nerves stack up around my lungs, "I have a ton of my own homework to do today so I won't be able to tutor you."

"Math?" he cuts in.

"Yes, math."

"I'll help you."

Cody is the perfect solution to my failing math grade. He aces every pop quiz and Mortimer loves him.

"Thanks, but I can't. Besides, you don't need my help. You're not that bad at art."

He drops his chin, giving me an incredulous look. "Uh-huh, right. Out with it, Jules. What's going on?"

I bite my lip, hating the way this will sound. "I can't tutor you anymore."

He pushes away from the lockers, standing tall. "How come?"

"Well, my mom, you know—"

"I know, Jules."

"And you act like it doesn't matter."

"I wish it didn't," he replies.

"Vic found out, Cody."

"Found out about what?"

"The photo-booth picture," I say.

"And?"

"He wasn't happy," I say, receiving a puzzled look from Cody in return. "He sure acted like you guys aren't friends. Not anymore, at least."

Cody looks more than confused.

I see it now, subtle similarities between Cody and Vic that could serve as common ground for friendship: athleticism, a love for basketball, and a good heart at the core of both of them.

"I'll talk to him," Cody says.

"No."

"Come on, Jules. You can't let Vic make your decisions for you."

"I'm not," I snap. Is he accusing me of being weak? I'm doing the hard thing here—the right thing. Family first. Doesn't he see this?

Cody tucks his thumbs under his backpack straps. "I thought you needed the money."

"I shouldn't have agreed to tutor you in the first place. It was a mistake and I'm done." I close my locker and turn to leave.

"I'll up it from fifteen an hour to twenty," he says.

"Yeah, and how exactly are you going to pay me? With your *dad's* money?"

"No, my own."

"Your own?" I repeat, highly doubtful. "You don't have a job."

"No," he agrees.

"Then it's not your money."

"You're right, it's not. It's Jimmy's."

"Jimmy's?"

"It's ours, I guess. Definitely more his than mine, though."

The one-minute bell rings and I curse it, wanting to hear more.

Frustration shapes the features of his face, drawing emphasis to the faint scar that runs from his eyebrow down into his cheek. "If you don't believe me, look his name up on YouTube."

Cody starts down the hall, the boot slowing him down on his way to the class he's already late for. He gave me a lot of reasons to reconsider, which can only mean one thing: For some reason, Cody Rush wants me around.

Nothing stands a chance of getting Cody off my mind until cool air sweeps over my skin when I step inside our house after school.

"Dad?"

"Yeah?" he grumbles from the kitchen.

"The AC is fixed."

"Yep."

"That's wonderful," I say.

When I find him at the kitchen table working on the coral reef, I unzip my backpack and unload the boxes of colored pencils in front of him. By the third box Dad's attention is effectively pulled from his work. His lips part when I finish, and I see the obvious question in his stare.

"Don't ask," I say and start for the stairs.

"Jewel," he calls out, and I turn. His gaze sweeps over his project. "Would you . . . well, do you think you could help?"

"Help?"

"Yeah, with this coral reef."

Dad's never asked me to help. When I was a kid pestering him to let me help with his projects, it was just that—pestering. He'd shoo me off. My loyalty to my family runs strong, a force like gravity that keeps my feet planted here, and yet I hardly spend time with them.

"Sure," I say and take the seat beside him. Neither of us says a word. Dad doesn't even give me instruction, but he doesn't need to. Creative instinct takes over as I scan the two clusters Dad has already finished and open a box of pencils.

I'm in the computer lab during English three days later, finishing a report. Mindy and Trish are at the printer, waiting with a few others for their papers to print. When I send mine to print as well, I wait for a feeling of satisfaction. I'm caught up on my assignments. No homework today. This should at least make me feel relieved, but my mind is preoccupied.

Cody and I haven't talked since I told him I couldn't tutor him anymore. I've busied myself with work and school and even the coral reef project with Dad.

I even went to the skate park with Lucas and his friends last night, filming the last of their stunts for the clip Josh is putting on YouTube.

Which reminds me . . .

My eyes sweep the row of computers I'm sitting at—the back row. Only Dan and I are still here. With four minutes left of class, he's typing frantically, immersed. Everyone is either finishing up, waiting by the printer, or at the door, talking loud enough to cover any sound.

Before I think better of it, I pull up YouTube and type in *Jimmy Rush*. I glance up as the page loads, unable to ignore the jumpy beat of my heart as I make sure no one is watching. Visiting any Internet page not related to a school assignment is against policy.

A list of videos pops up. The first one looks like an ad for yogurt. Then I see him, the scrawny boy with curly blond locks I recognize from the pictures at Cody's house. And there are several of him.

I click on one titled *Six-year-old Baseball Prodigy*, making sure the volume is low. Cody appears on the video first, and I feel the familiar flicker in my heart that his smile always elicits. He's young, maybe seven or eight, yet I see the Cody Rush I know in the boy before me.

"All right," I hear their mom's voice call out. She's filming. "Let's see it, Jimmy!"

Cody stands on a makeshift pitcher's mound in the middle of a field. Jimmy stands a ways off, perched with a bat over his shoulder. Cody winds up and sends a baseball soaring toward Jimmy, an impressive throw for a kid his age. When Jimmy's bat strikes the ball, however, I see who the real star of the show is.

As the camera follows the high arc of the ball as it rockets into the pasture of cows behind Cody, I realize he had some mad skills.

Over and over, Jimmy bats what could be a home run, the film spliced to show each swing in rapid succession. Cody flings his ball cap into the sky, both boys laughing and celebrating as they clash into a side hug.

And then Jimmy is on a real home base with Cody on a real pitcher's mound on a baseball field. Jimmy hits home run after home run, a small crowd on the bleachers cheering louder with each successive ball Jimmy hits over the outfield fence, their disbelief understandable. Only a few balls skid to the ground in the outfield. The kid was amazing.

The video ends, and I notice for the first time how many views the clip had: over *twenty-five million*. The next clip is of little Jimmy in a huge stadium, the stands filled with cheering spectators. It's a pro ball game, part of a pregame show perhaps. The clip is titled *Jimmy Meets His Favorite Baseball Player, Chipper Jones*. Jimmy hits a ball into the outfield, the crowd cheers, and, as the title suggests, he meets Chipper Jones.

I spot a video with an even higher number of views than the first. *Mentos in Coke: A Slam-Dunk Experiment*. It has over two hundred thousand likes.

I click play with one minute left of class. The filming is a little shaky, and I quickly realize Cody is the one behind the camera. Jimmy shows the camera how to fix a row of Mentos on a piece of string. He drops it into a liter of Coke, screws on the cap, and shakes it.

"Cody, Cody, take it," he shouts, his panic evident as he grabs the camera from Cody and switches off. "Go, go, go!"

Now the camera is on Cody. He runs up to a basketball hoop, the overshaken Coke held in one hand as he jumps up and makes a slam dunk. The rim is on the lowest setting, but Cody can't be older than eight, and he slams the Coke through the hoop with authority.

The Coke bottle hits the cement and a spray of dark liquid splatters the screen as it rockets into the air. Cody loses his footing and crashes to the ground as Coke showers him.

"Cody!" his mom shrieks, the screen door of the house behind them swinging open to reveal an enraged Janice Rush. Jimmy is laughing.

Obviously, Janice decided to post Cody and Jimmy's video anyway because here it is, and the boys already had enough of a following to make some decent money off their little experiment. Lucas has told me all about how people can make money from getting a high number of views on their YouTube videos. He and his buddies keep hoping one of their skateboard videos will take off.

"Hey, Julianna," Trish calls out. "You ready?"

"Yeah," I say and close YouTube, grabbing my document before heading out.

A hand covers my eyes in the hallway after school, blocking from sight my open locker before me. Lucas, of course, or so I think until my nose picks up the scent of expensive cologne, a smell that throws me back into the living room with Cody.

I whirl around, finding Cody standing over me, his hand resting on the locker above my head like a guy who's about to lean in and kiss his girlfriend.

"It sucks doing homework alone," he says with a suggestive grin.

I swallow hard, the sight of his incredible eyes and perfectly sculpted lips in such close proximity threatening my resolve. I see the little boy in him, the carefree eight-year-old Cody Rush I saw in those videos who made up half of the menacing duo that was he and Jimmy. And yet he's so different now, the green of his eyes containing new depths, the scar along his brow a clue to the pain he's been through.

I slam my locker, giving in to the swell of emotions within. "Come on," I say and grab his hand. "I've missed that car of yours."

CHAPTER 25

Cody

"I want to show you something," I say as I open the garage door for Julianna and walk in behind her. When I place my hand over her eyes again, she naturally tenses. I lean toward her ear, happily eliminating any buffer of space between us. Her shoulder meets my chest, and I whisper, "May I?"

She nods, a silent smile shaping her lips.

I guide her to the back door and into the backyard, helping her navigate the steps down the back porch.

"You know I only have a half hour tops to help you with art," she says before losing her footing on the last stair.

I catch her and she laughs.

"It's worth it," I say. For me, at least. Forget homework. "Ready?"

I've built this up far more than I should have for such a lame surprise. Really, I just wanted an excuse to get close to her and see how she'd react.

She relaxes into me, her back molding into my chest as she nods.

I lift my hand, certain that this is the most anticlimactic surprise ever.

She gasps anyway. "No way! This is your backyard?"

I look around at the huge lawn surrounded by flowers and bushes, with what remains of Grandpa Chadwick's fields beyond. This is where he and Grandma used to live. This is where Jimmy and I spent lazy afternoons together, getting into trouble, with Rachel in tow half the time. The canal Jimmy was nearly electrocuted in has long since been covered, but we still irrigate with it and the water is on now, dousing the plants that have seen far too much sun.

Looking at this now, I see why Mom wanted to come back. Leaving Desert Mountain High and breaking my leg in that accident—not much good has come from moving to Gilbert. However, with the recent surfacing of memories of Jimmy and all the good times we had here, I see this place with new eyes.

"I know you like those yellow flowers," I say, trying to explain my lame surprise.

She nods, her eyes jumping from bush to bush of those yellow flowers she dries between the pages of her math textbook. "Lantanas," she says. "They're my mom's favorite."

"Well, if you ever want to pick more, you're welcome to these."

She smiles up at me. "Thanks, Cody."

We walk through the bushes, treading the stone pathway carefully so we don't get our shoes—and my boot—wet.

"Jimmy and I used to splash around in this stuff all the time. Boat races. Mud fights. All of it."

Julianna turns around to face me with a playful smile. She dips the toe of her flip-flop into the water and flicks it up at me.

I flinch back, looking down at the splatter of mud on my legs, boot, and shorts.

She lets out a laugh, switching her expression to a mock frown when I look up.

"Aw," she says with a fake pout. "Too much of a pretty boy now for a little mud?"

Game on. "Pretty boy, my eye," I say and wrap my arm around her.

She lets out a squeal as I pick her up and march into the muddy water, sufficiently getting my payback. More mud covers her legs and knees the more she kicks and screams. She reaches down and splashes mud up into my face, laughing. Within seconds it's a full-out mud war—twisting, pushing, splashing.

We run into the open lawn after we're covered, laughing. It's hard to tell who won. We're both wet from head to toe, mud caking our skin and clothes.

"Come here," I say as I grab the hose and flip on the water.

She backs away with her hands out defensively, still laughing. "No you don't."

I grab her wrist and pull her in. "Relax," I say, my voice lowering as she draws near.

Her laughing dies down as she steps closer, her eyes glued to mine. I wash her arm first, my fingers working the mud from her skin. Then I start on her hair.

"Will your mom be upset?" she asks, her chest still rising and falling quickly as she catches her breath from our mud fight.

"No," I say, my eyes tracing the line of her jaw to her lips, then down to the wet shirt that hugs her figure in all the right places. "She's pretty chill."

"She wasn't happy about the Mentos and Coke, though," Julianna says. "I saw it," she continues when I look up. "I saw all the videos. Jimmy was a really good baseball player and you dunked that Coke with authority."

I smile, the memories of our excitement over our YouTube success crashing back. The best of times, the worst of times; Dickens nailed the entire human experience with those words. Jimmy never got to enjoy the profits from those clips.

Slowly, I brush at a streak of mud on Julianna's cheek and lift the hose.

"Close your eyes," I tell her. She does, her lips parting slightly before water glides down the contours of her face. The onslaught of memories has torn me open inside, leaving me weak.

Julianna does this to me somehow. When I'm with her, I feel like there's a chance of things falling back into place somehow. It all links back to her, to that moment in the mall I can't recall in full, and I can't help but want to wrap my arms around her and lose myself in those lips.

My fingers find hers, pulling her hand up to eye level where our fingers interlock. She opens her eyes. Drops of water wet her thick lashes. I look at our hands, liking the feel of her fingers between mine. She grips my hand like she doesn't want to let go either.

I drop the hose and brush a strand of wet hair from her face, ready to answer the plea in her eyes that tells me she wants this, too.

"Cody?" my mom calls out from the back door.

Julianna draws back, her hand pulling away from mine. "I'd better go," she says, her words yanking my head back to a rational plane. I'm covered in mud, I haven't shaved in the last two days, and I was one move away from kissing Julianna. And she has a boyfriend.

"Yeah?" I call back. Mom can't see us from there, and that's good. Julianna is already blushing deep, her feet shifting farther and farther from mine.

"Candace stopped by, but I couldn't find you," Mom says. "I told her I'd let you know."

Julianna takes a noticeable step back. Timing couldn't be worse.

Candace lives down the street and our moms are in the same book club. Sometimes she stops by, but that's it.

The drive home is awkward. I handed Julianna the money as she got into my car, a stack of twenties to pay her for tutoring. She said thanks, avoiding eye contact. Despite what I'd hoped, paying her as I promised only seemed to make things worse.

I try to think of what to say as I drive, how I can explain. As I run through the options, none sound right. Julianna says nothing.

"You can drop me off here," she says as soon as I pull into her neighborhood. "Stop. Stop!"

I slam on the brakes, confused.

She pops open her door and raises a smile. "I'm sorry about your seat."

It's wet, but I don't care. I'm about to blurt out what I want to say before she can get away, but I'm too late. She sprints off down the road with her backpack, her clothes, and her hair still damp from the hose. Then she disappears around the corner, leaving the honest feelings I was about to confess jammed up inside.

CHAPTER 26

Julianna

Cody Rush almost kissed me—*almost kissed me*—and I almost let him. There's no denying how heated that moment in his backyard was, the short distance between us charged with an inescapable force drawing us together.

Unfortunately, someone else was knocking at his door, ready to fill in for whatever I wasn't willing to offer. Candace. I knew something was up between them. Apparently, I'm not the only girl Cody has over and I shouldn't be surprised.

Then he paid me, and don't get me wrong, I'm grateful for the money, but it served as a reminder of what I am to Cody. I'm his tutor who happens to be around a lot. Proximity does stuff to two people. We're like magnets that shouldn't have been placed within close range.

The following evening I pull on my favorite lacy top, shorts, and strappy sandals, then tie my hair up with the teal and black ribbons Trish insisted Mindy and I wear. Tonight is the second Highland Hawks football game of the season.

The bleachers are packed, the student section alive with noise. Girls sport short shorts with green and white handprints painted on their legs. The guys are less decked out in general, other than the dude covered in white paint.

"Julianna," Trish calls out, snagging my attention, "Mindy."

Mindy and I head over to the gate as Trish bounces over to meet us.

"Looking hot, girl," I tell her as she pulls us both into a tight squeeze over the chain-link fence.

"You too," she gushes, her eyes raking up and down in approval.

"I know," Mindy chimes in with a sideways glance toward me. "First time I've seen you in anything but sneakers or flip-flops in weeks."

"Is Lucas coming?" Trish asks and nudges me with her elbow.

"Uh, no," I say.

I spot Aubrey, Laurel, and, of course, Candace, all decked out in cheerleader form.

"I'd better go," Trish says as she skips back into position, the ribbons in her high ponytail bouncing as she goes. "Enjoy the game!"

As Trish and the other cheerleaders assume their positions, Mindy and I find a spot next to Makkel and Cassidy, friends of mine from soccer who will be playing on the team this November, as well as Sabrina, a cellist in the orchestra with Mindy.

By the second quarter the Hawks are up fourteen to nothing. The energy on the field and in the stands is high, almost palpable.

I scan the crowd under a darkening desert sky, my pulse flickering off beat as I search for one person. I can't help it.

"Who are you looking for?" Mindy asks.

"No one," I lie, knowing very well who. I wonder if he's here, who he's hanging out with, who he's talking to. A girl?

My gaze springs over to Candace and then to the crowd of boys near the fence. I study the backs of each of their heads. Can't help it.

Cody couldn't have me over this afternoon for tutoring, or so he said. He told me he had a physical therapy appointment, a likely excuse. I wonder if he's trying to send me a subtle message.

Skateboards in my peripheral vision snag my attention. Lucas, Josh, and Dustin walk into the scene, each holding his own board and a QT drink.

Lucas finds me in the crowd before I'm prepared. I had no idea he'd be here. They've been so engrossed in putting their skateboarding stunts up on YouTube this week, I've hardly seen him. Besides, he hates football and pretty much all other sports.

Lucas kisses two fingers and lifts them up in a peace sign my way.

He smiles, and the three of them keep walking along the sidewalk past the student section.

"Hey, there's Lucas," Mindy says. "Where's he going?"

"I have no idea," I say, baffled.

Lucas glances back at me, his smile hiding something. I realize he's carrying something else, a big jumble of paper.

"Oh. My. Gosh," Cassidy says, coming to a halt after each word. "He is *so* hot."

Cassidy knows very well that Lucas is my boyfriend, so I whirl around toward her in surprise. The line of her gaze is nowhere near Lucas, however; her eyes are fastened on the sidewalk below, near the entrance.

"Mm-hm," Makkel agrees, her eyes focused in the same direction.

I follow their gaze, turning around to find a very tall, clean-shaven, and well-dressed Cody Rush. He pauses at the bottom of the bleachers and scans the crowd with a cocky tilt to his lips, his hands casually slung in his pockets like a male model who walked straight off the cover of *GQ* magazine.

He looks so different—looks like the Cody I remember from all those months ago who dove in out of nowhere and caught my tumbling bottle of caramel sauce. And something else is different. The boot is gone.

His searching eyes stop on me and the slight tilt of his lips spreads into a full grin with dimples.

My heart flip-flops inside my chest.

Instantly, he's greeted by a mob of guys from the basketball team and a couple of their girlfriends. He's back, both legs unobstructed and standing strong, nothing holding him back now.

Halftime starts, and Candace and her friends skip toward him from the other side of the fence. He walks straight past them, his eyes pinned on me.

I match his smile, every doubt evaporating as he draws near.

"Oh my gosh, Julianna," Mindy says, and I fear I've been caught. But Mindy isn't looking at Cody anymore, and neither are Cassidy, Makkel, or Sabrina. In fact, most people are turning around and looking up toward the top of the bleachers now, their attention far from the band that's marching onto the field for the halftime show.

I look up behind me, spotting Lucas and his friends holding a huge sign that reads JULIANNA, WILL YOU GO TO HOMECOMING WITH ME?

Shock numbs me from the inside out.

Mindy squeezes my hand and jumps up and down. "Oh my gosh, that is so cute."

She's right, it is cute. Lucas thought up a way to ask me that didn't involve a last-minute text.

Lucas points to me and waggles his eyebrows.

I smile, feeling the rush of heat to my cheeks under the stares of so many people.

Hands grab my arms, push my back, shoving me up toward Lucas. I ascend the bleachers and accept a kiss I didn't see coming. A few whistles and cheers ring out, increasing in volume when I say *yes*.

I laugh, bashfully looking down at our spectators—and Cody standing below.

He raises a grin when he sees me looking his way. Then he turns and disappears into the crowd of popular boys.

After a few pictures with Lucas near the banner, we start down the bleachers. I should be caught up in this moment, all eyes for Lucas. I glance down toward the group of guys along the fence, falling instead for a boy I can't have and shouldn't want.

Solitary confinement. When we arrive to visit Mama Saturday afternoon, that's where we learn she's been for the past forty-eight hours. A casserole sits on the table between us, one I spent the morning sweating over in anticipation of today's special visit when we can bring in goodies, something that's only allowed once a quarter.

Dad is speechless, his tall form hunched over the table across from Mama. My throat constricts at the thought of what she's been through.

"No way." Vic laughs. "You went to the hole?"

"Vic," Dad snaps.

Mama is near tears.

"Why?" I ask. "What happened?"

"It's a long story," Mama says and darts a cautious look from side to side, a habit I imagine she developed here. She leans closer. "A month or so ago, Dottie gave me a bottle of conditioner when I ran out."

"Dottie?" I ask.

"She's in my dormitory."

I lower my voice to a whisper. "The homicidal one?"

"Shh," Dad shushes. "Let her finish the story."

"No," Mama answers, "not that one. Dottie's one of the younger women in prison and one of the nicer ones, or so I thought. We sit by each other in the chow hall sometimes, and she's always offering me stuff. Like orange juice. She says she hates it, right, so I accept her offer from time to time. Then the other day I'm out of stamps, but luckily, Dottie shows up and lends me one, tells me she has plenty.

"Then on Wednesday Dottie approaches me for a favor. Right off, I knew it was trouble."

Mama closes her eyes and lets out a deep breath, lowering her voice even more. "She asked me to hide some stuff in my bunk for her."

Dad lowers his head into his hands and Vic nods with an almost amused little smile, like they both know the rest of the story.

"Drugs?" I ask, my voice pitched for her ears alone.

Mama nods. "I never should have accepted any of her help in the first place. Now she thinks I owe her. I should have known that no one in here is willing to do something for you out of the pure goodness of her heart. There's always a motive. I told Dottie no, of course. I couldn't risk getting caught with contraband and having my sentence lengthened. Dottie started the fight. I had to defend myself."

"Mama, throwing down in prison," Vic says like he's pinning a caption under the mental picture she just painted, and we're all supposed to laugh.

"Shut up," Dad says.

This is Vic's way of trying to lighten up the situation, to make us all crack a smile. Right now is not the time, though, and it's getting on all of our nerves.

"Don't end up in prison, Vic," Mama says, delivering perhaps the sternest lecture she's ever given.

Vic doesn't quite roll his eyes, but the expression on his face achieves that effect. He stands and starts toward the vending area. "I'm snagging a burrito."

"I'll go talk to him," Dad says and follows after Vic.

I look down at the casserole I made—roasted bell peppers, cheese, enchilada sauce, and corn tortillas. The guards dragged a knife through it several times before we were allowed to bring it in. Solitary confinement, contraband, inmates picking fights, and guards who treat you like scum; I hate that Mama is in this place, this hell.

Mama grips my hand across the table. "Don't worry about me."

"Kinda hard not to," I choke out over the lump in my throat.

"It's not all bad in here," she says, which can only be a lie. "I've learned some things."

My eyes snap up. "Huh?"

"It's true," Mama says with a surprisingly convincing nod. "I have."

"How so?"

"This place," she says, with a melancholy look around the ceiling and the walls, "as much as I hate it, it's taught me things."

I loathe every word she speaks. I don't like where this is going, not one bit. "Like what?" I ask with a cynical huff as tears blur my eyes.

"I spend a lot of time thinking," she says. "Sometimes I think regret is inevitable, like we're bound to regret any choice regardless. Every choice has good and bad associated with it. I convinced myself I was justified, you know, doing what I did. I still don't regret helping Vic and I never will. I just know now that there had to have been a better way."

Even though I can't stand the thought of Mama benefiting in any way from this, I realize I've learned things, too. I recall my initial reaction to Cody in Ms. Quinn's room, how I yelled and called him names and basically told him to piss off. I judged him far too harshly. Mama is too good, her heart so open and accepting, even to the harsh realities she's faced.

"I'm doing it," I say. "The pageant."

I summon a smile, opening my heart to change as well and determined not to back down.

"No," Mama says with a frown I wasn't expecting. "You were right. Wearing the crown was my dream, not yours. It was a foolish dream anyway, one I should have forgotten long ago. I guess some of us never grow out of wanting to be something we aren't."

It hurts, every word. I look around this prison, a place where Mama will never be anything but Sonia Flores Schultz—a convict— a mother who gave up everything to help her son.

I squeeze her hand from across the table. "Too many of your

dreams have been shattered already, Mama. I'm doing the pageant, no matter what you say. I'm doing it for you."

Her eyelids drop slowly, and when they open, twin tears slide down her cheeks. She hides her face in the crook of her arm, folding herself over the table as silent sobs shake her shoulders.

I dial Trish's number as soon as I get home. As luck would have it, Trish and Mindy are out shopping together, so I tell them both at the same time. "I'm doing the Miss City of Maricopa Pageant."

Shrieks and cheers overwhelm my ear. I pull my cell away. They're excited. I'm not sure what I expected, but this means a lot. I may not want a crowd at the pageant, but I definitely want my best friends there by my side. By the time we hang up, Mindy has offered her prom dress collection for me to choose an evening gown from and Trish has volunteered to help me with hair and makeup.

I put my phone down and smile. Listening to Mama talk about how prison has changed her has made me want to be better, too. I pull out the wad of cash Cody gave me. I haven't spent a dime yet, and that's good. At one point I would have been happy to accept payment from Cody and count it all as service, too. Now I realize it wouldn't be right. Time is running out and I need those service hours.

CHAPTER 27

Cody

The doorbell rings on Tuesday after school. Twice, with a long pause in between. I lean back from the desk in my room and call out for Lizzy before remembering she's at dance.

I alternate between walking and jogging down the stairs, loving this lightness of feet regardless of the stiffness. No boot—hallelujah. I run my hand over my short hair, liking the feel of that, too. I feel like my old self again. I've even started playing basketball again, a little here and there. Jordan, Zack, and Davy came down from Scottsdale for Labor Day yesterday, and we played some two on two. I've missed the feel of that leather against my palms.

I open the door, stepping back in surprise when I see Julianna. She didn't say a thing to me today, and she was nowhere in sight after school. I figured our tutoring sessions were over, and as far as I'm concerned, that's probably best. She has a boyfriend and she's claimed for homecoming.

"Oh, shoot," I say. "Did you walk? Sorry, I didn't see you after school."

"It's okay; I needed the walk," she says and bites on her lower lip, something I've decided she does when she's nervous. "I had a lot to think about."

The image of her in Lucas's arms up in those bleachers last Friday comes back. She's given me a lot to think about, too, and I haven't liked it. The first time I saw Lucas kiss her, over three weeks ago, when I wedged my crutch between them, I found the situation humorous. This time, not so much.

"Oh, well, I don't need any help today," I say, knowing I can't keep doing this, tempting myself with something I want but can't have. "Sorry."

"That's okay, I just—" She pauses, her eyes darting around like she's gearing up for something. "It's just that . . . I had to give this back to you."

She holds out the stack of twenties I paid her. "You've done so many nice things for me. I should never have taken it."

"It's your—"

"Don't try to convince me otherwise," she cuts me off. "I can't accept this."

I hold open the door and step aside. "Come in."

"Just take it, Cody."

"I'm not going to let you walk home, Jules. You might as well come in and grab something to drink before I drive you back."

She doesn't hesitate long. It's a good 105 degrees outside.

"Thanks," she says as I close the door behind her.

As we walk through the living room, I realize I never thought I'd see her here again. Sure, I suck at art, but I can get by. I don't need tutoring. And obviously she doesn't need the money as much as I thought.

I grab a water bottle from the fridge for her. "Why don't you want the money, Jules?"

"Don't get me wrong," she replies, "I appreciate it. I just can't accept it."

"Why?"

"Because . . . you've been so nice to me."

I take two steps closer, crushing the remaining space between us. She's here. Might as well enjoy watching her blush. "There's more to it."

Sure enough, her cheeks redden and she lets out a grunt of frustration. "You're impossible."

She slams the money down on the kitchen counter, and I clap my hand over hers.

"Fine," she says. "I need the service hours now, so I can't accept payment for the tutoring."

"Service hours?" I say, my curiosity rekindled over why she put up that tutoring ad in the first place. "What for?"

"For a pageant," she blurts out, her eyes widening with telltale embarrassment. Now her cheeks are chili-pepper red.

"Like, a beauty pageant?" I ask.

"I know. Hard to imagine."

"Not at all," I say with an appraising look sweeping from her beautiful face, down to her legs, and back up again. "You've got it made."

She definitely noticed me checking her out. Her gaze darts away from mine and she steps back, pulling her hand away. "So, I mean it. I can't accept the money."

She tosses the money on the counter.

"How many service hours do you need?"

"I don't know," she says. "Five to ten. Enough to show the judges that I have a solid start on my platform. Oh my gosh, I can't believe I told you about this."

"How many people know?"

"Not many," she replies. "And I'd like to keep it that way."

"That's a shame."

She shoots an incredulous look my way. "Why?"

"The bigger the crowd the louder the cheers. The louder the cheers the more a judge is swayed."

"That's not true," she says. "They judge on talent, on the contestant's answers to interview questions—that kind of stuff."

Even college scouts are influenced by spectator enthusiasm. "Say what you want, Jules. Everyone can be swayed."

She shakes her head and buries her face in her hands. "What a nightmare."

It's like she's putting herself through torture. "You seem *really* excited about this pageant."

"You're right, I'm not," she says.

"Why do it, then?"

"I'm doing it for my mom," she lets slip.

I nod, understanding well now and not about to press for more. "What's a platform?"

"A cause," she says and rolls her eyes. "Like cancer awareness or literacy."

"And what's yours? Torturing crippled guys?"

She looks back up at me with a playful grin. "Is that what I've done to you?"

I step closer and take hold of her wrist, slowly bringing her hand up in front of us. I pick up the money, place it in her open palm, and close her fingers around it. "I never complained," I say and hold her fist in my hands.

Her eyes meet mine before shifting away.

The garage door opens and Lizzy bounds in. Julianna pulls her hand from mine and steps back, bumping into a barstool. She quickly sits and starts drumming her fingers on the counter, like she's been sitting there the whole time.

"Hi, Julianna," Lizzy says and jumps onto the barstool next to her, still dressed in a leotard. She plops her backpack on the counter and unzips it. "I have something to show you."

"Oh, yeah?" Julianna says and slides the money across the counter toward me.

"Yeah." Lizzy pulls out a painting. "It's for my school's Evening of the Arts."

She sets the thick paper down in front of Julianna. It's a painting of a person; that's about all I can tell. For all I know, though, it could be an alien.

"Oh, my," Julianna says. "That is awesome."

She sure is a good liar when it counts.

"It's Mom," Lizzy says, clearly impressed with her work.

Mom walks in and sets down her purse with a smile. "Pretty good, huh?"

This is why I love Mom, and why I can never trust a compliment she pays me. I would have guessed Lizzy's painting was of a guy for sure. The person—Mom—holds her eyelids wide open in the painting, her jaw dropping open in shock like she just stepped in dog crap.

"That's great, Lizzy," I say and pat her shoulder, leaning my arm against the back of Julianna's barstool.

"I knew it," Lizzy says like she had in fact doubted the quality of her painting. "Bryson told me it looked like an alien."

Poor Lizzy inherited Dad's artistic gene, or lack thereof. I'm definitely going to Lizzy's Evening of the Arts. I don't care if the kid is ten, if Bryson makes another jab at Lizzy's painting, I'll make him regret it.

Lizzy pulls out her Evening of the Arts information sheet, slaps it down on the table, and then runs off, like she suddenly remembered her favorite TV show is on or something.

"This should be your platform," I tell Julianna, tapping Lizzy's Evening of the Arts brochure.

Julianna darts a nervous glance toward my mom, who is pulling a cookbook from her collection, as if she doesn't want my mom to hear.

"What?" she whispers.

"How else are you going to tie this tutoring into a platform?"

Julianna shifts uncomfortably. "I don't know, I figured I'd just title my platform something like *Education Is Good*."

"You're too talented for that," I say. "What about this . . . *Art*."

"*Art*?" she repeats, looking at me like I must be stupid. "Just *Art*?"

"It's a working title."

"Why art anyway?"

"Because you're good at it."

"I second that," Mom says as she turns and opens her cookbook. "Sorry; I didn't mean to eavesdrop, but I never got a chance to thank you for helping Cody with his art project."

"Julianna's competing in a beauty pageant," I say.

Mom closes her cookbook and flashes a smile. Julianna gives me the death look. If there's one person who can make you excited about something you're dreading, however, it's Mom.

"Oh, really?" Mom exclaims and walks over. "That's wonderful! My niece competed in one years ago. You know, sometimes pageants get a bad rap, but competing in one is actually hard work."

Flowers, dresses, weddings, big events . . . my mom eats this kind of stuff up. And besides, Mom is plain nice.

Mom's expression lights up like she just got an idea. "Do you already have an evening gown?"

"Uh, my friend said I could borrow one of her dresses."

Mom taps a fingernail against the granite. "Hold on," she says and heads for the stairs.

By the look on Julianna's face, I can tell she wants to be long gone, but now she feels obligated to stay.

"Advocating for the Arts," I say.

Now I have her full attention. She chuckles. "No, my dad is an artist. Trust me, Cody, the arts don't need advocating."

"*In Education,*" I say. "*Advocating for the Arts in Education.*"

"I thought you hated art," she says.

"I do."

She smiles. "Well, that's one thing we have in common."

"Really?" I ask. "That cupcake you made was definitely a work of art."

She looks at me appreciatively. "Fine, I dabble."

"I hear art classes are being cut next year," I say. "People are upset. Teachers don't want their classes cut. Students who love that kind of stuff are ticked. You'd have sympathy for sure and an instant following."

"That's exactly what I *don't* want," she says, visibly mortified at the idea of people knowing she's doing this pageant.

I figure it's like this: When you're taking a ball out of bounds and a spectator cheering for the other team yanks your shorts down from behind, revealing all—it happened, sophomore year—you might as well put on your best smile and own it.

"It's neat that you're doing this, Jules," I say. "For your mom."

She studies my face like she's afraid I'm teasing. "Really?"

"Yes," I say.

"Thanks," she says with a smile.

Mom returns to the kitchen with a stack of magazines and some plastic bags slung on her arm. She unloads everything on the counter, sliding the magazines toward Julianna with a measured look, like she's gauging Julianna's interest.

"Oh, wow," Julianna says and starts sifting through the magazines. Each one of the covers features bridesmaid dresses.

"You're welcome to take these home and look through them if you'd like. And I just had to show you this fabric," my mom says and opens one of the bags, "in case you're interested."

The first fabric is light blue. It shimmers, and Julianna gasps. Must be a girl thing. Mom's always been crazy for fabric. She used to sew a lot, back when Rachel and Lizzy were little.

Mom pulls out a red fabric and then a white, followed by an orange.

Julianna runs her fingers over each one. "Where did you get these?"

"New York," Mom replies. "The Garment District."

I remember now. A few years ago, on one of her trips to a bridal expo, Mom came back with a suitcase of this stuff to make prom dresses for Rachel. That was before Rachel started wearing all black and shutting herself in her room blaring rage music.

Rachel walks in, eyeing the bright and sparkly fabric like it might jump out and bite her. I introduce her to Julianna. Mom tries to pull Rachel into the pageant talk without much luck. In the end, however, Rachel does stick around, feigning interest. Or maybe she really is interested.

Rachel asks Julianna what her talent is. Julianna says singing.

Rachel leans up against the counter and twists a lock of blond and pink hair around her finger. "What song?"

"I don't know," Julianna says. "Any song will do."

"No," Rachel says with a firm shake of her head. As if her unsmiling face and thick black makeup around each eye isn't enough to demand that she be taken seriously.

I haven't seen Mom smiling this much at Rachel for months. Rachel was the musician in the family, advancing about as far as possible in piano lessons until one day she quit altogether.

"You don't want to sing just any song," Rachel says. "You want a song you can't help pouring your heart into, a song with lyrics that speak to your soul."

Rachel has always been a bit dramatic.

Julianna is nodding her head, though, like what Rachel is saying makes sense.

"You want a song that defines you and why you're doing this pageant," Rachel says, followed by a drawn-out silence. "So, why *are* you doing this pageant?"

Julianna laughs, and I realize for the first time how much she's relaxed into the barstool, talking with my mom and sister like they're friends. "To be honest," she says, "I don't want to do the pageant at all. It's for my mom."

Julianna doesn't mention prison or other specifics, but she does tell Rachel and Mom about how her mother used to have high hopes and big dreams but no luck.

"Life has never been easy for her," Julianna finishes, "but recently, life has really stunk. Now all of her hopes are smashed, and she definitely won't ever have her moment to shine."

Fabric, pageants, and shining—I am definitely out of my league here.

"Leave it to me," Rachel says. "I can find you some song ideas."

In light of Rachel's recent taste in music, I'm not sure this is a good idea. But Rachel knows a lot about classical and Broadway music, too, back from her days on the piano.

"Really?" Julianna says. "That would be great."

Mom offers to let Julianna borrow the magazines again, and Julianna accepts.

When Mom and Rachel leave, I pick up the money from the counter. "I imagine this kind of thing gets expensive."

"Pageants?" Julianna lets out a chuckle. "You have no idea."

I extend the money toward her. "Then you'll want this."

She eyes it warily. "I still have to pay the fifty-dollar entry fee and donate money to the Children's Miracle Network. Oh, and I need to find a local sponsor."

I pull out my wallet. "How much?"

"It needs to be a business, Cody."

"I know some people," I say. "My cousin manages the bowling alley in Gilbert."

"Thanks, but I think I can figure it out," she says and looks at the money in my hand again. "This still doesn't solve my problem, though. I can't take that. I need the service hours."

I hold up Lizzy's Evening of the Arts brochure. So much for distancing myself from what I want and can't have.

"Then we'll put on one of these," I say.

I should stay far away from Julianna Schultz, should never have gotten close in the first place. With her sitting in my kitchen right in front of me, I can't stop myself. I want to help her.

CHAPTER 28

Julianna

I can't believe he talked me into this. It's been ten days since Cody convinced me to switch my platform to *Advocating for the Arts in Education*, and practically the entire school is aware of it. All of the art teachers have been notified of my *Night with the Arts* event, thanks to Cody, and I've received overwhelming support from many.

Mrs. Legend even turned the event into a mandatory assignment, and most of the other teachers are offering extra credit. Any student is welcome to display an original piece of art, within reason of course. No obscene pictures or creations. Everything must be approved by a teacher in order to be displayed at the event, and that's a good thing. Someone already tried to approve a ceramics project made of nude-colored clay claiming to be Thor's Hammer from Bryce Canyon National Park. Yeah right.

My choir teacher arranged to have her choirs perform that night in the auditorium as well. The Art Club is helping pass out flyers. Highland's very first *Night with the Arts* is turning into an even bigger event than I could have imagined. And it's all going down on September 30, twelve days away.

I should be terrified. The entire school invited to an event with my name on it? The news of me competing in a pageant out there for anyone to hear? In truth I'm kind of excited; at least that's what I make of this bubbly feeling in my belly as I walk through school, spotting a flyer on a bench and another poking out from a locker. They're everywhere. Cody had them printed two days ago and started passing them out yesterday.

I spot Connor and Sam by the lounge between classes, each holding a stack of flyers. Thanks to Cody, even the popular kids are into it. Girls are twisting their locks of hair and popping their gum, asking each other if they're going. You'd think this was a bonfire or a party offering spiked punch and free beer.

My head is bowed as I make my way down the hall as inconspicuously as possible. I almost run into some girl, narrowly darting around her in time.

"Jules."

Her voice, not to mention the nickname, makes my head snap up.

"Rachel," I breathe out, relieved.

"I've got it," she exhales, the first brimming smile I've ever seen on Rachel Rush splitting her face. "The song," she says when I fail to catch on. "For your pageant. I've got it."

"You do?" I say, mortification creeping in. Me, onstage, singing. Alone. I haven't done that since my solo part in *Guys and Dolls* back in the eighth grade. Some people in the crowd snickered. Later, I found out it was Candace and her friends. Big surprise.

I haven't sung a solo since, even though I practice all the time in my room, while I'm cleaning, or any other spare moment alone I get.

"Yes," Rachel says. "I don't know why I didn't see it before. Such a common song—a classic—but it's perfect."

She whips out a folder and hands it over, along with a CD. "I found a shortened version. One minute and forty seconds. That's under the time limit, right?"

"Time limit?" I question.

"For talents in pageants," Rachel says. "I ran it by my cousin first; you know, the one who did a pageant a while ago?"

"Oh, yeah."

"Anyway," Rachel continues, "she said talents have to be under two minutes, so I found a shortened version." Rachel points to the folder in my hand that I'm guessing holds the sheet music. "I crossed out the measures and lyrics that are cut. I think this rendition still captures the essence of the story told, and it's beautiful."

The minute bell rings.

"Gotta go," Rachel says. "See ya, Jules."

I smile as she walks away, wondering if I have anything to do with her ease in opening up to me. I think about her family: Cody, charming little Lizzy, their flawless mom, and that awful special agent dad of theirs. All of them so perfect in their own way. It's got to be hard being surrounded by such perfection. Maybe having a feisty, nowhere-close-to-perfect girl like me around the house is a breath of fresh air.

Rachel made it easy for me to open up to her about the pageant. And she's right. I need a song that means something.

I'm standing at my open locker after fifth hour when a hand slams against the locker next to me. I look up, recognizing Lucas's leather bracelet. One of the green flyers is wedged between his hand and the locker.

"What's this?" he asks, sounding more confused than upset, like this is some joke.

I've been so busy this week, Lucas and I haven't seen each other outside of school.

"Rumor is you're doing a *pageant*?"

"Yes," I admit and turn to meet his eye. No use hiding it now. "Surprise."

He looks surprised all right, and not in a good way. "Jewel, a *pageant*?"

Said as though I'm about to play with Barbies or dress up and pretend to be someone I'm not, which isn't far from the truth.

"It's for my mom. She's always wanted me to do this."

"So?"

"So, I'm doing it."

"Just because your mom is stuck in fantasyland?"

Lucas is practical, not a supporter of anything girly. His ex left high school early to enroll in beauty school. That's when she became his ex. Still, he doesn't need to be rude about this.

"Someone told me Cody Rush is passing these out for you?" he challenges, like he's daring me to deny it.

"Yeah, he is. And I could use your help, too. I can use all the help I can get."

"What is it with you and Cody?"

"Nothing," I say, wondering if it's a lie. Lucas must have seen me with Cody more than I thought.

I've tutored Cody off and on since Lucas asked me to homecoming. Cody has kept his distance, holding his typical flirtations in check. So have I. It's for the best. Cody and I are friends, and he's a good friend. Supportive. Helpful. He always manages to make me laugh, and his strengths are rubbing off on me little by little. Making me think I can do things I never before dreamed possible.

Most of the time Cody and I end up talking about my platform and planning the *Night with the Arts*. He's brilliant. And confident and resourceful. And he can wield the kind of charm that gets him whatever he wants. He's everything I'm not, and although I find myself increasingly intrigued by him, he doesn't like me, not anymore. That much is obvious now.

"Why didn't you tell me about this . . . *pageant*?" Lucas asks, his nose wrinkling like he can't stand the smell of that word.

"Because I knew you'd react like this."

Clearly this was the wrong thing to say. Lucas digs his hands into his skinny sides. "Like what?"

"*This*," I say, gesturing to his rigid stance.

"Julianna," he says and pauses, his eyes widening like he clearly understands something I don't. "Pageants are . . . are—"

"Are *what*?"

"Stupid!"

That's it. "Maybe it's time you and I take a break."

The words slip out before I even realize that's what I want. It's the truth though, and it's only fair. I don't want to lead Lucas on when I don't feel the same way for him that I used to.

I begin to explain, even though I have no idea what to say. "It's just—"

"No, don't," Lucas cuts me off. "We both saw this coming."

We did?

He starts backing away like he's ready for that break now. "Let's just . . . talk about this later, okay?"

I don't get a chance to reply. I stand, watching Lucas disappear around a corner and wondering whether I did the right thing. Did I just break up with my boyfriend? And what about homecoming? Shock settles in as I walk to my next class.

It isn't until the end of the day that I remember Rachel's sheet music and CD. Distracted by Lucas, I shoved them in my locker and forgot. Making a quick stop by my locker, I pull out the folder and open it, my nerves bubbling up as my eyes devour the title and lyrics. Rachel was right. It's perfect. Too perfect, maybe. I can almost hear my mom speaking these words, her voice filling my head as the lyrics strike close to home.

A high-pitched squeal jerks my attention away. Holly is at her locker a few down from mine, her hand clamped over her mouth as rose petals tumble to her feet.

"Oh my gosh, oh my gosh!" she pants.

I make my way toward her, curious. Samantha Rusnak closes in from the other side. A bouquet—and not your typical bouquet—of flowers is situated in her locker. The flowers are fresh and exotic and arranged masterfully. Holly doesn't have a boyfriend that I know of.

"How did he get in my locker?" Holly asks before spinning toward Samantha. "*You* helped him, didn't you?"

Samantha smiles. "Of course! I knew you'd love it. Right?"

"Yes!" Holly says.

I spot a piece of paper in her hand. A homecoming invite. "Who asked you?"

Her face turns red at my question and she smiles. "Cody Rush!"

Samantha grabs Holly's hand and muffles a squeal of her own, sharing in her best friend's excitement. Their enthusiasm only underscores my shock and the fact that I've gone numb from head to toe. Speechless. I fish for something to say but nothing comes. The bouquet. Of course. Cody's mom made it. On the one hand, I'm glad it isn't Candace. Holly is nice.

"Congrats," I say, trying to infuse some artificial energy into my voice.

A text from Cody two minutes later as I walk down Hawk Hall pulls me from my trance. My pulse flickers back to life as I open the text.

GOT SOME B-BALL WITH THE GUYS AFTER SCHOOL. WON'T BE ABLE TO MAKE TUTORING. RAIN CHECK?

Basketball. Really, I'm happy he's back on his feet doing something he obviously loves. Still, my heart plummets, and I realize how hung up I am on Cody Rush, how everything he does affects me, no matter how much I want to deny it.

Sure. Have fun, I send back.

You need a ride home?

I study his words, sorely tempted. I'm clinging to something that isn't mine, though, and I have to stop. I type my response slowly, finally clicking send.

No thanks. I'm good.

Luckily, I spot Mindy when I reach the parking lot and she gives me a ride. I don't mention Lucas. I'm not ready to talk about it.

Mindy has been acting strange ever since English yesterday morning, and it's no mystery why. Trish was elated when she found out Cody was helping me with my platform, clapping and bouncing up and down in her seat while demanding details.

Enough was enough. Secrets can feel heavy with time, weighing you down. I told them all about Cody asking me to tutor him. In fact, I told them almost everything. All about how his dad was the fed who put Mama away and how Cody showed up at The Chocolate Shoppe. How he met Vic at a tournament. Got hit by a car. I kept my feelings for Cody locked away, hinting at nothing but my initial disdain.

"What's up?" I ask Mindy after a long stretch of road with no words between us.

"Nothing," she mutters, but I don't buy it. "I just can't believe you kept this all a secret."

"What?"

"You and Cody," she says with great effort, as though this has been on her mind all day.

Why did I keep it a secret? Truth is I liked him all along, even though I knew I shouldn't. A girl like me doesn't end up with a guy like Cody. Mindy has a crush on Cody, too. The way she's acting is proof.

"It was no big deal," I say. "And it was awkward, you know? His dad put my mom in prison. But Cody really is a nice guy and he needed help with art."

Mindy nods, hopefully satisfied, yet she doesn't say another word until "see you later" when she drops me off.

Tonight is the fifth pageant workshop and I plan to make the most of it. By the time I leave the house I'm a different woman, having spent way too much time with makeup and a flat iron in front of the mirror. I'm wearing the most fashionable outfit I own: a pair of white Capri pants that hug my butt, a lacy yet full-covering beige top, a red purse for a pop of color, and the highest pair of heels I own. Immersing myself in the trivialities of makeup and hair was a good distraction. From Lucas. From Cody.

I feel Dad's stare through the window as I walk toward Rusty. Thanks to Cody, I've discovered art is an interest I've denied myself for too long. I've been helping Dad with his projects. Fixing this and that. I'm good at it, too; Cody was right. I even caught an appraising look on Dad's face the other day when I finished my second coral reef.

I feel an odd sense of empowerment, a woman on a mission. I remind myself to wear heels more often. I need to make a quick stop by a copy center before the workshop. Big surprise: our printer/copier is broken.

I scan Rachel's sheet music in at a copy center, a pair of scissors in hand. Rachel is obviously a musician, the kind that can cross out measures, draw arrows all over, and still follow along without a hitch. My brain functions on a little more order, however. Copy, cut, paste. I'm compiling only the sections I'll be singing in the shortened rendition.

As I copy the second page, I get the prickly feeling that someone is staring at me. My eyes sweep the room while I copy the third page, catching a few eyes on me. I begin to wonder if I overdid it with the makeup before the sinking realization hits me: This is copyrighted music. Am I breaking some law? Suddenly I feel totally stupid, like I should already know.

For better or worse, I convince myself one copy is no big deal. Regardless, I pick up my pace. I sense the man at the copy machine next to mine looking at me and I dare a glance.

His gaze captures mine, and he doesn't pretend he wasn't looking. A mischievous smile plays on his lips as he stares unabashed.

"Hey," he says before I realize I was staring back.

I divert my gaze, but it's no use now. I paste on a grin. "Hi."

I'm not sure whether to ignore him or look back up. I choose the latter and notice the electrifying quality of his steely gaze. His eyes remind me of Cody's, which makes little sense. Cody's are green. This guy has the lightest blue eyes I've ever seen, almost translucent.

"Do you teach?" he asks.

"Teach?"

He drops a pointed look to the sheet music in my hands.

"Oh," I say. "No. I'm just copying and pasting the sections I need for a performance. I mean, it's my sheet music, of course," I rush in to justify myself, my excuse plunging out in a jumble. "A friend gave it to me. She bought it. At least I think she did. I mean, I'm pretty sure I'm not, like, breaking any laws here. . . ."

Thankfully, my tongue grinds to a halt before I do any more damage. Advice to self: leave now. I shove the last page facedown and press the copy button.

The guy saunters over and leans up against my machine. I raise my gaze to his, noting the muscles in his forearm, the tattoos on his biceps, and his generally impressive physique. His eyelid drops into a wink and he leans in to whisper, "Trust me, I'm the last guy who's going to turn you in."

A laugh bubbles up. I smile, realizing I'm blushing. Realizing the effect this attractive man has on me. And I think he's flirting with me.

This is all new to me. When I look into the mirror, I still see the shadow of the girl I was, the one with frizzy hair, glasses, and pimples. But I'm not that girl anymore. I'm wearing skinny pants and my hair is ironed to perfection. I look like a different girl, a much older girl. And that's the most awkward part about this. I'm pretty sure this guy is too old for me.

"Thanks," I say, trying to temper my grin and figure a smooth way to let him know that I'm still a minor. "I'd hate to go to juvie."

His eyelids close in a quick wince. *"Seventeen?"*

I chuckle. "Yep, and you?"

"Twenty-six," he replies.

Nine years. Barriers safely established, he extends a cordial hand toward me.

"I'm Damian Acklen."

I shake his hand. "I'm Julianna."

"I'll bet you already have a boyfriend anyway, am I right, Julianna?"

Cody flits to mind first and I kick myself for it. "Yes. I mean, no. Um, it's complicated."

Should I tell him the truth? *I broke up with my boyfriend today.*
"And his name is?" he asks.

This is more than irrelevant, but Damian is smooth and tall and dark and handsome, and I tell myself off for wanting to revert to my bashful ways. This is what people do. They talk. They flirt. This is a new me, a more confident me, and I'll be eighteen this January anyway.

"Cod—" I start to say before correcting myself. "I mean, Lucas. Sort of."

Damian's brow rises in question. "You sound sure about that."

I laugh.

Damian's smile broadens. "Now I know you're trying to get rid of me."

"No, it's not like that," I say, laughing and holding up the sheet music. "My *friend* Cody is helping me get ready for this pageant I'm competing in, so his name slipped out."

"A *pageant*?" he says. I've heard this question a million times in the past two days, spoken in various intonations. Some surprised, some upset, some appraising.

Damian's voice hints at nothing but approval, though, and I'm happy to be off the subject of Lucas, so I go on. "Yeah, the Miss City of Maricopa Pageant."

"Wow," Damian says. "Good thing Cody is helping you. That's a big endeavor to tackle."

Said as though he knows Cody, and we're all good friends. "Yeah, it is big," I babble on, checking my phone for the time. "Evening gowns, a platform with service hours, raising money. Oh, and I have to find a sponsor."

I point my index finger to my head and pull a fake trigger by lowering my thumb.

Damian smiles. And here's my chance to scram. I'm a busy girl with high heels and a tight schedule.

"Have you found one yet?" he asks. "A sponsor?"

"Uh, no, I haven't."

"Perfect. I'll sponsor you," he says, his assertive statement catching me by surprise.

I trip over my words. "It h-has to be a business."

He pulls a card from his pocket and extends it toward me. "I own a luxury sports car lot."

I read the business card: ACKLEN MOTOR GROUP.

I'm the least lucky girl in the world; I'm not even sure I know what luck feels like. Now, however, with Damian's business card in hand and my jaw hanging open, I'm pretty sure this is what it feels like.

"It's two hundred dollars," I say before I get too excited.

"Done," Damian says.

A sponsor. Just like that. I did it. No begging anyone for help. Not even Cody. I recall how I felt when I saw those flowers in Holly's locker, when I learned that Cody had asked her to homecoming. Then Cody canceled our afternoon tutoring, and I spent a good part of the day sulking about it.

I've fallen head over heels for Cody Rush. Today I fully realized that and it scared me. I can't keep holding on to something I can't have.

As I watch Damian drive away in his sporty black car, I think perhaps everything will come together. I'm not as hopeless as I thought after all. The tides have changed. My luck has made a turn for the better.

Everything goes along perfectly at the workshop. I've settled into the routine and so has everyone else. We're friends, really. Rebecca, Sophie, and Jenny. Even the overconfident Denica and I are becoming buds. Five girls competing against each other doesn't make for likely friends, but we are.

We quiet down. Lacy Baldwin starts us off. There are two more workshops to go before the dress rehearsal, and I'm determined to learn everything I can. Tonight we're learning how to walk in heels, followed by some onstage question coaching. When Lacy's attention is drawn to the back of the room, we shift around to see three girls walking in.

My stomach plummets.

"Hi," Lacy says, "welcome."

They say hi back, tell us they're new. I wait for one of them to glance my way, to acknowledge me, and yet I dread the moment they will. Anyone can join the pageant up until a week before the performance. Still, I'd gotten used to the idea of only five of us competing.

This is no coincidence. The *Night with the Arts*. The flyers Cody helped me make. Our whole school hearing about the fact that I'm doing this . . .

"Have a seat," Lacy says. "Introduce yourselves."

"I'm Aubrey," the first girl says as she sets her purse down and glances at her friends.

"I'm Laurel," the second puts in.

"Hi," the third girl says sweetly with a practiced smile. She flicks her hair over her shoulder. "I'm Candace."

CHAPTER 29

Cody

Being a good boy and keeping my distance from Julianna sucks. I've tried to lose myself in basketball. I won't lie; I've missed it and it's become more addicting than ever.

Luckily, my mom needs Julianna's measurements for some pageant dress mock-up she's making. And we have a crapload of stuff to do for the *Night with the Arts*. Lucas is going to have Julianna all to himself next Saturday at homecoming. But today she's mine.

Balloons, streamers, and music greet Julianna and me as we walk in. A sign reads: HAPPY BIRTHDAY LIZZY.

"Oh, no," Julianna says. "It's Lizzy's birthday? I should have gotten her something."

Inflatable water slides are set up in the backyard, surrounded by a mass of nine- and ten-year-old girls in swimsuits. Squeals ring out from the back door.

"Julianna!" my mom says as she rounds the corner. "Let me grab my measuring tape."

"If you're busy, seriously, no worries," Julianna says with a worried look around. "I can come back later. This is too nice of you anyway."

"Oh, it's no trouble," Mom says, waving off Julianna's concern.

"I'll just make a quick mock-up so you can see if it's something you'd like."

Mom takes a few measurements. Hips. Waist. Mom makes me turn around for the bust measurement, and Julianna blushes.

"Come on, we can work up in my room," I say when they're done, sick of that dang coffee table coming between us.

Stage crew, technical support, security: I run through a list of stuff we need to figure out for her event. Julianna's brows are raised as I go on about easels and tables, people needed for setup and cleanup. Her eyes shift around, glancing from me to the floor, from my John Wayne stand-up to my bed, which I'm leaning up against. Like this is all too overwhelming.

She's a doer, not a planner. Creative and willing to take initiative, but something gets lost in the planning phase. She freaks, gets all jumpy.

I take in Julianna's wide eyes and the way her knees are drawn up to her chest, her arms wrapped around them. She's tense. I want to run my fingers through her hair and ease her down on the carpet. Crush my lips to hers and blow her mind away with a kiss she'll never forget.

"Okay, let's make a list," she says and grabs a pad of paper. Her teeth bite down on her lower lip as she clicks her pen—another nervous habit. I know her better than any girl I've been interested in and haven't already made a move on. And there's good reason. She's different.

This whole situation between us is different.

My dad put her mom in prison. And I can't even remember the first time Julianna looked me in the eye, can't remember much of anything about that night. She thinks I'm conceited. I think she's stubborn. She thinks I'm a spoiled pretty boy, and I think she's pretty much the most amazing girl I've ever met.

That's why I want to help her: to show her I'm more than that. Because of her, the past six weeks at this new school haven't stunk as much as I thought they would. In fact, I doubt I'll ever forget them. She's given me hope. At first, nothing more than the hope of remembering what happened the night my leg was broken. Now it's more.

After a long summer of being babied, unable to do much for myself, let alone anyone else, it was nice to be on the giving end again, helping Julianna. She needed the money and I had the dough.

I reach out and grab her leg, digging my thumb into the muscle above her knee and receiving a squeal of laughter in return.

"Loosen up." I laugh as she bats my hand away. "You look like you're going to blow a gasket."

"I do not look that stressed," she claims, her smile still bordering on laughter.

I reach for her knee and dig higher this time. She bursts into a fit of laughter and squirms away. Now I know another thing about Julianna: her ticklish spot.

"Drop the pen and set the paper down, miss," I say as I get her other knee. She's laughing so hard, she fumbles the pen and paper, melting into the ground as she twists away from me.

A knock at the door startles us. The knob twists and my dad pokes his head in.

Julianna scrambles to sit up. She brushes her hair into place and scoots away from me, her eyes darting between my dad and the floor.

"Hey, Dad."

He levels a serious gaze at me. My dad doesn't have an abundance of pleasant expressions, and this certainly isn't one of them. "Don't forget. Shooting range this evening. Five o'clock."

"Yep," I say. "Got it."

He nods and shuts the door.

A long moment of silence. Then, "He scares me."

It was barely a whisper, and Julianna looks mortified that she let it slip out.

I laugh. "You're not the only one," I say, remembering friends and girlfriends in the past who had felt the same. "It makes him good at what he does."

Julianna stares at the ground. "It's his job to terrify," she says with a hint of irony, almost a mocking laugh.

"Just to get people to take him seriously," I correct her.

"I think most people already do," she says. "What if people simply make a mistake when they break the law?"

We've crossed into risky territory and I wish I could backtrack.

"Justice is his job," I say.

She looks me in the eye. "Well, justice is screwy. And it certainly isn't always fair."

"Maybe not, but someone has to draw the line between right and wrong."

"Is everything so black and white for you?" she counters.

I think about it and give my honest answer before thinking better of it. "Yes."

"What about mercy?"

This is starting to sound like church, which I don't care for. *Mercy?* Don't get me started. Where was mercy when Jimmy got sick? Mercy is a nice thought that pans out to be nothing more than an illusion.

No. All of life is chance. All we can do is work our hardest to defy the odds, to accomplish goals and get what we want. Telling Julianna I don't put any stock in mercy makes me sound like a heartless jerk, though. "I don't buy it." The admission tumbles out anyway, and I realize how fired up she's getting me.

"You don't buy it?" she asks, incredulous. "You don't believe in mercy?"

"Not really," I say, reminding myself that Julianna has no right to take her anger out on my dad. "Life is life, Jules. Rules are rules. Society dictates them and that's it; they are what they are."

She exhales a mocking gust of air. "Yeah, and the rules are *always* fair."

"I never said that."

"Then what *are* you saying?"

"That *life isn't fair.*"

"Well, it should be!"

"But it isn't!" I yell. "Where was mercy when Jimmy died, Jules?"

She's speechless.

"My point exactly," I say. If she wants to talk about fair, she chose the wrong one to argue with. "One day he was healthy, the next he was sick. Then he died."

Sympathetic curiosity shapes her expression. "Jimmy isn't gone, Cody."

"You can't tell me that."

"What, you think he's gone? Forever?"

"Yeah," I say, remembering his death and the eternal void he left behind.

"Gone for good, huh?" she says. "That makes death pretty scary."

"No, death isn't scary," I say, knowing something far worse: the pain of living with the consequences of hurting someone you love.

"What do you fear, then?" she asks, prying into depths never before explored, and for good reason.

"Failure!"

It came out as a roar. For once Julianna doesn't spit something back at me.

"I'm sorry about Jimmy," she says.

How did we even get on this subject?

"I'm sorry about your mom," I say in return.

"She felt she had to help Vic," Julianna explains. "He was on drugs. Needed rehab. That's why my mom did what she did. She got the extra money the only way she knew how. I'm not excusing what she did. Even she wishes she could take it back."

Silence crushes the air between us. Vic. Drugs. Like my dad told me in the hospital. We stare at anything but each other, and I try to think of the right words to tell her I'm sorry.

"Do you play?" she asks.

I follow the line of her gaze to the guitar in the corner. I recall that first time I saw her at Vic's house. I was playing a guitar in their living room. She didn't even notice me.

I shake my hand. "A little."

Okay, so I'm not completely challenged in the arts and music. After three years of me and Mom bickering over the piano lessons I hated, we settled on guitar lessons instead.

"Play me something," she says.

"Only if you sing," I challenge.

We level a gaze at each other. This is the way it is between us.

"Fine," she says.

I grab the guitar and sit on the ground in front of her, our knees almost touching. I play the first few chords.

"Know this song?" I ask and can tell I've got her thinking. I love how competitive she gets when she's mad. The soothing harmony slowly dissolves the contempt between us.

"Coldplay!" she calls out as I repeat the intro.

I nod. "Know the words?"

She looks hesitant, and I figure she'll chicken out.

But then, right on cue, she sings, hitting every note with perfection. Her voice fills my room, loaded with talent. Enters my ears, penetrates my chest. Reaches inside.

My fingers fumble on the strings, and I refocus on my guitar.

Verse transitions to chorus. Her soprano pulls me in. And somewhere along the way, I realize the lyrics of this song perfectly describe me and Julianna. Sitting face-to-face. So close. So far away. Loving someone you shouldn't want. Wanting something you'll never have. The song draws to a close, and when the last chords of the guitar blend together with her amazing voice, I've found yet another thing I love about Julianna.

"Wow," I say. "That was incredible."

The corners of her lips twitch. A fleeting, doubtful smile. There and then gone. "You're sweet."

She doesn't believe me.

"I mean it."

She gives me a look. "That's what you said about my cupcakes."

"I meant that, too. You're going to blow everyone away at that pageant."

This time she smiles for real, a subtle grin that makes the red in her cheeks deepen. "You're very sweet to me, Cody Rush."

Said as though she understands how crazy I am about her. How much I care. Mission accomplished. I want to set the guitar down and give in to her tempting lips once and for all, but I hold back. And it nearly kills me.

Plans for her *Night with the Arts* completed, I walk her outside to the Vette and open her door. She offers a smile in return and climbs in. One week from today she'll be like this with Lucas, all dressed up and off to homecoming. Laughing. Flirting.

Kissing.

Touching.

I don't let my mind go there.

As I drive Julianna home, I try to imagine Lucas opening her door for her. I try to imagine him making her laugh, making her lose herself in the moment. But I can't. My weak imagination is probably to blame. Either that or my pride. Still, I wish the challenge—the honor—of showing Julianna the time of her life at her senior homecoming was mine.

* * *

Dad grabs a few extra magazine clips from the showroom and slaps them on the counter.

"What are you rockin' today?" the guy at the register asks, wearing a God, Guns, and Guts T-shirt, along with a beard that's starting to look fuzzy.

"Glock," Dad says and finishes the transaction.

We situate our ear protection, blocking out all sound, and enter the range through a set of thick doors. The scent of gunpowder drifts in the air as we make our way to the third and fourth lanes. It's one of those smells I can't quite explain, can't describe why I love it, but I do.

We clip our paper targets to the string and punch a starting distance of fifty feet in, sending the targets flying down the tunnel of bullet-punctured walls. Dad lands almost all of his shots in the center ring. I hit most of mine on target, missing a few. We're the only ones in here, so we take off our ear protection to reload.

"Tell me about this girl you're spending so much time with," he says, lines of concentration etching his face as he studiously reloads.

"Julianna?"

"If that's her name . . ." Dad mumbles, always the chipper one.

"She's cool," I say.

"Good girl?"

"Yeah."

Nothing but the quiet click of bullets loading into our magazines breaks the silence. I get the feeling I'm about to go under some heavy fire myself in a figurative sense. I begin to feel sorry for our punctured targets.

"Rachel seems to like her," Dad says. Not what I expected.

Rachel has been better lately, taking a more active role in the family. Hanging around the table after dinner. Making eye contact. Taking her earbuds out. She even played the piano for Julianna the other day.

"Is she a good student?"

"Yes."

"Good family?"

Because I'm not sure how to answer I falter for a reply. I contemplate various ways of phrasing a positive response but realize they would all be a lie. Her brother has been on drugs, her dad doesn't exactly hold down a job, and her mom is incarcerated. Definitely wouldn't fly with my dad.

"She's helping me remember the accident," I say, effectively changing the subject.

This earns a strange expression from my dad, one I imagine mirrors my own. There must be a million better ways I could have redirected the conversation here.

"What?" he says, his brows pulling down over questioning eyes.

It's cold in here, a relief from the heat outside, and yet I feel a bead of sweat crawling on the back of my neck.

"Remember the photo-booth picture you found in my pocket the night of the accident?" I ask.

At first I don't think Dad remembers, but the confusion in his eyes dissipates. "That was her?"

"Mm-hm. And those pictures were taken that night."

"But she wasn't with you when you got hit?"

"No," I say.

"And you know, how?"

"She told me."

"And you trust her?"

This is my dad. Always an issue of trust. I can't blame him, though. Lies are the reason he has a job. Cheating, stealing, backstabbing . . . he sees it every day. Friends always ask if my dad's job is just like the movies and TV shows. They're typically surprised when I tell them it's worse.

"Yes, I trust her."

"I thought you were out with that friend of yours that night," Dad says. "Vic."

"Yeah, I was."

"Well, how did you end up in a mall photo booth?"

"I don't remember."

"Is that when you met Julianna, or had you met her before?"

"Uh . . . we had met before."

"How?" he fires back. "We'd only moved to Gilbert a week or so prior to that."

I get the feeling this is only a hint of what it's like to be interrogated by Special Agent Rush, and I suddenly feel sorry for the poor criminals out there. I take a deep breath, knowing my dad will wrench the truth from me one way or another.

"She's Vic's sister."

I am so dead.

"*Vic*? The son of that Schultz lady?"

"Julianna's different," I begin to say.

"No," Dad cuts in, his voice rising. "Absolutely not. What are you thinking? Their family is trouble. I put their mom in *prison*. I already told you to stay away from Vic. Same goes for his sister. Vic is not the kind of guy you want to hang out with. He was involved with drugs. "

Asphalt. A crisscross of metal—a shopping cart.

I pick up the joint, the distinct smell reaching my nose. Weed for sure.

"We're cool, man, we're cool," Vic says. "I'll get you the money."

I snap out of it, shocked at the flash of remembrance. Freaked out.

"Cody," Dad says, his voice cutting through the distant sounds of lost memories perched on the edge of my mind once again. "Do you understand me?"

Dad is more than upset and it's not hard to understand why. I'm not sure what to say, not sure what to think of that memory of Vic. The joint. Weed. *I picked it up*. Vic promising to deliver money?

A drug deal.

And I was involved?

"Yeah. Yeah, I understand," I say and step toward the exit. He's right.

I mumble an excuse, something about a headache, which isn't far from the truth. Dad ditches our session at the shooting range and walks out with me. We say little else, and I'm glad. I stare out the window as he drives us home, feeling his probing stare.

He's on full special agent alert mode, me being the subject of his scrutiny. And if I know my dad, it won't let up anytime soon.

CHAPTER 30

Julianna

"Good morning, Highland Hawks!"

Monday morning video announcements are underway during second period, but I'm too busy finishing my calculus homework to watch. That, and I'm preoccupied with thoughts of Cody and our argument on Saturday. He infuriates me sometimes, going off about justice and law. Self-righteous jerk. Then I realized we were talking about a lot more than right and wrong. Life is harsh; that much Cody is right about, and he would know. But how did talk of Jimmy and death turn into his admission of fearing failure?

This week's birthdays are announced, and several people in the class let out a whoop when Candace's name is mentioned. I look over at her in time to see Cody wishing her a happy birthday.

Candace beams, reveling in the spotlight. She can't stand *not* to be in the spotlight. I've always known this. Still, I didn't think she'd dash in and sign up for the Miss City of Maricopa Pageant the first second she caught wind of it.

I force myself to refocus on my math. I find less and less time for homework now. The *Night with the Arts* is a week and a half away and the pageant is two weeks after that.

When the homecoming dance is mentioned, my head snaps up to the TV and I forget all about calculus. Homecoming is this weekend. In the rush to get everything ready for my pageant platform, I almost forgot.

Homecoming royalty nominees have been selected via popular vote. Connor Dominguez, Chad Watkins, Pablo Lopez, and all the regulars are announced. The football stars, student council populars, and even a couple of beloved class clowns. Then—

"And Cody Rush," Nolan Sampson finishes and turns to Tracy Felberg, who will be announcing the female nominees.

I look over at Cody, who is hiding his embarrassment behind a grin. I'll bet no one else in this room can interpret his expressions like I can. Candace grabs his arm, practically bouncing in her chair as a few of the guys congratulate him with whoops of approval.

"Trish Perry." The first girl nominee is announced and I silently celebrate. *Go Trish*. I'm so glad she made it. The list goes on. "Jentrie Burk, Michelle Walker, Candace Landley, and Laurel Stevens."

Candace and Laurel feign humility as friends congratulate them. Then Candace turns to Cody and lets out a squeal. "This will be so much fun," she says and squeezes his arm. She's probably touched Cody's arm more than I have, which makes me sick. And jealous.

Lucas has avoided me lately, and I don't blame him.

HOMECOMING? I text him near my locker between classes. My teeth chew on my lip as I wait for his reply.

FRIENDS CAN STILL GO TO HOMECOMING. He finally texts back.

FRIENDS?

YEAH.

I'D LIKE THAT. I reply with a smile, feeling as though something unbearably heavy has been lifted off my shoulders.

The homecoming football game that Friday holds no appeal. In fact, I couldn't care less. Still, I go to support Trish.

It's a whiteout game. White shirts. White tutus. White cowboy hats. White, green, and black handprints slapped onto people's bare legs. Highland goes all out. We even have a T-shirt gun launching T-shirts and other sponsored items into the crowd. Highland is up by seven points at halftime. The crowd is going wild, and it won't be dying down anytime soon.

Side-by-side ATVS roll out as the homecoming nominees are announced. Butterflies gather in my stomach. I convince myself I'm nervous for Trish. I glance over to the open gate in anticipation, knowing very well who's really wreaking havoc on my nerves.

I've come to terms with the fact that Cody Rush will always do this to me. Some crushes you just never get over.

Justin Crowder and Sasha Baker stand in the back of the first ATV, dressed in formals and waving to the crowd as they are introduced. ATV follows ATV, a pair of nominees in each. The top three words each nominee would use to describe themselves are read off. Hardworking, egotistical, friendly, a beast, loveable, fun, chill, nice. People laugh and whistle.

Cody's ATV hasn't come out yet. I remember the way we sat in his room less than a week ago. Cody played that song on the guitar, challenged me to sing. I took his bait once more, something I'll probably always do. And I let my voice free, forgot my insecurities, and forgot the past. Music came alive in me that day, and I haven't been able to get enough since.

I've practiced my pageant vocal nonstop. To say that I've lacked confidence since my *Guys and Dolls* solo would be an understatement. My tough, spunky personality is more of a front, something I've wielded like a shield.

Cody fears failure like I fear success. Fear of reaching for my goals. Now I want to conquer that. I want this pageant. At least I want to sing. When I sing I feel like I can fly.

"Connor Dominguez and Trish Perry," the male announcer calls out. *Fun*, *happy*, and *crazy* are the words Trish chose. Connor's three are *athletic*, *immature*, and *party animal*. Both descriptions couldn't be more accurate.

"And our last male and female nominees are . . . Cody Rush and Candace Langley."

Pain sinks like a hunk of rusty metal into my belly and I look away. They're on an ATV together. I can't blame Cody. I have no hold on him, never gave him a reason to look at me as anything more than his tutor, the daughter in one of his dad's criminal cases, a poor girl in need of his pity.

Candace's three words are *sweet*, *cheerful*, and *flexible*. I'm not so sure about that.

"And Cody Rush held nothing back as he easily described himself with these three," the announcer begins. "*Beautiful, hot*, and *sexy*."

Cheers and whistles ring out, a little more from the girls than the guys. I roll my eyes, knowing Cody's lack of creativity is to thank for his word choice. Instead, he opted for a humorous reply like I should have known he would, one that was sure to get everyone's attention.

The announcer laughs. "Judging by the response from the females in the crowd, I'd say he nailed it."

I suddenly feel sick to my stomach. Can't stand to look at the bedazzled royalty nominees lining up on the football field. All thoughts of our guitar and vocal moment gone, I dash down the stairs, the sound of my feet hitting the metal bleachers barely audible over the cheers of the crowd.

"Julianna," Mindy calls out. "Where are you going?"

My heart hammers a path up my chest, swelling inside my throat. I pretend not to hear her.

Trish is announced as the runner-up, bringing my escape to a halt at the bottom of the bleachers. I cheer for Trish.

"Our Highland Hawk homecoming queen is . . ." the announcer draws out, "Candace Langley."

Candace's hands fly up to cover her open mouth. People cheer. Candace beams under the spotlight. Like she will when she takes the crown as Miss City of Maricopa in less than four weeks. I head for the exit.

"And this year's Highland Hawk homecoming king is . . ."

I don't need to hear it. Connor or Sam of course. The same two who have been at the top of everyone's list since freshman year.

"Cody Rush!"

The name booms out into the night air, echoes in my ears. Pulling me to a halt.

People stomp on the bleachers. Cheering. Screaming. The new guy—Cody—homecoming king? However amazing and well-liked Cody might be, I didn't expect this.

I stare.

I blink.

Cody walks forward at last, apparently just as shocked.

"Kiss, kiss, kiss," the crowd chants as he and Candace are crowned at the center of the football field.

I'm numb, my feet cemented on the ground as my eyes refuse to look away. A suspenseful moment passes, every eye on Cody and Candace as the crowd chants. Cody smiles bashfully—not like him—and I let out a breath I didn't realize I'd been holding. He's not going to do it.

But then Candace reaches up and pulls Cody's head down to her level, covering his lips with hers.

The crowd goes wild, mocking the hope within me. The kiss seems to last an eternity.

I turn and walk out for good this time, the stinging in my eyes making me realize how hard I've fallen. The major problem with falling is this: It's rarely a pain-free experience. But what did I expect? Life isn't fair. Especially when you want something you can't have.

The number that shows up on my cell at eleven o'clock on Saturday morning is one I don't recognize, and I'm about to ignore it.

"Hello," I say after caving to curiosity.

"Hi, Julianna?" a female voice greets me, and it sounds familiar. One of my friends? No. She sounds mature. Confident. Proper.

"Yeah, hi," I reply hesitantly, still unable to place the voice.

"This is Cody's mom. I hope you don't mind that I got your number from his cell phone."

I sit upright in my bed and toss the nail file I was using aside.

"N-no," I say, wondering what this is about. During a bout of insomnia at 2 a.m., I promised myself I'd scream expletives at the next person who mentioned Cody Rush to me. My dramatic determination to distance myself from Cody helped me sleep, if nothing else. Now, however, with Cody's mom on the phone, all curse words evade me.

"It's totally fine," I say. "How are you?"

"Oh, I'm great. Thank you for asking. I was calling to see if there's a time you could come by to try on this mock-up."

I also promised myself I'd stay away from Chadwick Estates, away from Cody's house.

"You bet," I reply. "When works best for you?"

"Well, I know you're probably busy today with homecoming."

Busy? I'm still in pajamas, I haven't touched makeup yet, and I have yet to pick out a dress at Mindy's house.

"No, today is fine," I find myself saying, already at my closet door and searching for something presentable to wear.

"Are you sure?"

"Yeah, absolutely."

How can I be anything but nice to Cody's mom when that's all she's been to me?

"Great," she says. "Cody is running some errands for me, so he won't be here."

Said as though this might be a problem. She has no idea how relieved I am. Hopefully she assigned him a lot of errands.

"I can be there in a half hour," I say.

Thirty-two minutes later I pull up in front of Cody's house. Rusty shudders, grinding to a halt before I kill the engine. I say a silent prayer that he'll hold out.

Cody's mom welcomes me in, and I follow her upstairs to her craft room. I gasp when I see three dresses hanging by her sewing machine and serger.

"It's the fabric," I say, my mouth still hanging open. "The fabric you showed me."

"Mm-hm," Cody's mom replies. "Your favorite three, if I'm not mistaken."

"Mrs. Rush," I gush.

"Please, call me Janice."

"Are they—" I'm too embarrassed to ask, too shocked.

"Well, they're made to fit you specifically, so I hope you want them."

I run my fingers over the fabric. "I do."

One dress is a rich blue, the sleeveless bodice tastefully decorated in sparkling jewels, the fabric fanning out at the waist into a full skirt. It shimmers in the light and has evening gown written all over it. The red dress is sleek and fitted with a slit. I picture myself onstage, singing as the spotlight catches the subtle diamond beadwork. The third dress is a beautiful coral. Knee length. A lighter fabric with intricate folds and twists around the waist.

"I meant to make a more professional dress out of this one," she explains. "Maybe top it with a white business jacket or something. You know, for your interview with the judges. But I guess I had evening gown on my mind." She laughs behind me. "You're welcome to wear it to prom tonight."

"Homecoming," Rachel's voice from behind us cuts in to correct her.

I think about Mama in prison, about how on my own I've been. A lump swells in my throat.

"I can't accept all this," I say, finally pulling myself together to face her. "This is way too nice of you, Janice."

Rachel is standing in the open doorway behind us, one eyebrow climbing into a high arc. "Believe me, you're doing *her* a favor."

Janice laughs. "It's true. And you might have convinced Rachel to let me make a dress or two for her."

Rachel grins. "Don't push your luck."

I try on the dresses. Janice steps out while I pull them on, but Rachel stays to help me zip them up. They fit like a glove. Rachel claps her hands together.

"You *have* to wear this to homecoming tonight," she says as we gape at the lightweight coral dress through the full-length mirror. "This dress with your dark hair—you'll definitely be the prettiest girl there."

Rachel is right about one thing: this dress is made to stand out. "I'm totally going to wear it," I say, my eyes refusing to let go of my reflection.

"He wanted to ask you, you know."

I easily tear my eyes away, my heart catapulting into a heady tempo as I search her face for an explanation.

"Cody," she confirms. "You're the one he really wanted to take tonight."

"H-how do you know?" I ask, equal parts shock, hope, and disbelief converging inside my stomach. "Did he tell you?"

"Not exactly, but I know him well."

It scares me how much I want to believe her.

"He's been a great brother." Rachel picks up a spool of thread and fiddles with the end. "After Jimmy died . . . I was in bad shape." She studies the spool, her finger twisting around the dangling thread as though the motion is therapeutic. "Even though we were really young, Jimmy and I butted heads. I still remember. We never got along. We were way too similar. I just wish we'd figured out a way for those similarities to bring us together instead of push us apart."

She sets the thread down. Flashes a tense smile. "Cody was there for me through the worst of it. He even bought me flowers last Valentine's Day, back when I was still in junior high. His buddy delivered them to my classroom."

Warmth pricks me, deep inside. Just when I think it's possible to thoroughly hate Cody Rush, he finds a way to weasel his way back into my heart.

"I wish he was taking you, too," Rachel says with a sneaky smile.

Here I am determined to keep my distance from Cody until we part ways at graduation, and yet his mom and sister are starting to feel like good friends.

I'm not sure how to reply, so I reach out and pull her into a hug.

Ten minutes later I make my way down the stairs with the coral dress folded over my arm. Janice wanted to finish a few things on the blue and red dresses.

"Thank you so much," I tell her. "These dresses are incredible."

"You're welcome," she says and smiles. "You'll have to let me know how everyone at Chadwick Manor treats you during the dance tonight, okay? The staff. The food."

I turn at the bottom of the stairs, curious as to why Janice Rush would care so much about the quality of our homecoming venue. Chadwick Manor is a colossal Tuscan estate that rests on six acres of lush landscaping here in eastern Gilbert. Not far from Cody's house, actually. Huge reception hall. Fountains. A waterfall. It's on the pricy end for a high school dance venue, so we've never had one there. I figured our senior class vice president—Candace—must have an in with whoever owns the place.

"Okay," I say.

"It was my mom's dream," Janice says, not making sense. "She loved the flowers and the gardens. The events. I took after her there. Owning a reception venue was her dream. She's gone, but it's been fun keeping that dream alive."

Chadwick Manor. Reception venue. Her mother's dream. I know the Chadwicks owned a good portion of Gilbert at one point.

"Wait," I say. "Chadwick is your maiden name?"

Janice's expression twists into something between a smile and a furrow of the brow. "Cody didn't tell you?"

Chadwick farms. *Chadwick Estates.*

Oh my gosh. I knew Cody was rich, but this is something else.

"Well, he—" My voice is defensive, followed by a delayed, "no."

Candace lives in Chadwick Estates as well. She's the senior class vice president and is in charge of homecoming. Now I know who her in with the venue was: Cody.

My gut coils as I remember the way she kissed him on the football field, practically stamping her claim on him for the whole school to see.

I climb into old Rusty and lay my new dress over the passenger seat. My goal of forgetting Cody tonight and immersing myself in homecoming with Lucas and our group—*at Chadwick Manor*—is as good as hopeless.

I recall what Rachel said about Cody wanting to take me to homecoming, and my foolish heart dares to hope she's right. I look at the dress resting on the passenger seat. Thanks to Janice, I'm going to look good tonight, that's for sure. I fire up Rusty, conflicted emotions clashing inside as I start down the road with Cody Rush on my mind.

CHAPTER 31

Cody

My head is a mess, everything knotted into jumbled chaos ever since that flashback I had at the shooting range. Dad asked if I trusted Julianna, trusted her family. How can I answer that? I can't even trust myself. I was part of a drug deal!

I dribble the ball. Bounce, touch. Between the legs. I toss it up and it falls right in the hoop. Uncanny. This afternoon has been like that, everything I toss up on our backyard court sinking into the net with a beautiful *swoosh*. Too bad I'm not in a game right now. Basketball is the only thing that successfully distracts me from the accident, from Julianna.

Mom calls from the patio, reminding me about homecoming tonight. And I'm full-on sweating.

I take a quick shower and throw on my tux. Put on some cologne. I grab the keys and head for the garage, almost forgetting the corsage Mom made. Luckily, she's on top of things.

A half hour and forty pictures taken by Holly's parents later, we meet up with the rest of our group for dinner. Then the dance. I never thought I'd go to a school dance at Grandma's reception center. Desert Mountain High was too far away. Yet here I am.

I walk up the stone path to the giant building, thinking of how I came here as a kid when it was being built. Everything has changed. My life went up in flames, it would seem, everything crashing down when we moved here and I got in that accident. All of my dreams, my goals—flattened. Or maybe these thoughts are a cop-out, an easy way to excuse yet another failure. Maybe basketball isn't a lost cause. Not yet.

The heavy bass shaking the dance floor pulls me from my thoughts. The ballroom is alive with music. Dancing. Swiveling spotlights. I lead Holly into the crowd where Connor, Sam, Pablo, and the rest of the guys from our group are dancing with their dates. Holly looks nervous, like this isn't her typical crowd.

The DJ is solid, though, spinning all the right tunes, the perfect mix of slow and fast songs. I crack a few jokes and Holly laughs. She loosens up after a few songs and eventually so do I.

Until I see her.

Everyone does. Her small waist is wrapped in tight folds of fabric, the length of her tan legs accented by a pair of heels that most girls would break a leg in. She's never looked more comfortable, though, or happier. She towers over Lucas by at least an inch, but she doesn't seem to mind. She stands tall. Confident. Tempting. My eyes drink her in, her hair hanging in loose curls down her back.

My dad's warning to stay away from her takes a leave of absence from my brain. The music, the lights, everyone around me, fade into nothing. For me, there's no one in the room but her.

Holly touches my arm, bringing the lights and music into focus again. Another slow song starts. Holly's friend Samantha has caught up to us. They say something about using the bathroom and I wonder if I should offer to escort them.

"We'll be right back," Holly says and walks off with Samantha before I get a chance, leaving only one person standing in my way.

Lucas.

He isn't seizing his opportunity to dance with Julianna, though, and that's his loss. His hands dig into his pockets as he talks to a friend. They flick a disgusted glance around the ballroom, like something about this place isn't to their liking.

"Do you mind?" I ask when I reach them, extending a hand toward Julianna and waiting for Lucas to look my way. He finally does, shock appearing on his face as he glances from me to Julianna.

Julianna turns as well, doing a double take as her jaw drops.

"Whatever, man," Lucas says, his upturned lip telling me to get lost.

"Thanks," I say, taking that as a yes.

I slip my hand in hers. I lead a speechless Julianna into the middle of the dance floor and slide a hand around her waist. "Dance with me?"

She casts a fleeting glance toward Lucas, like she's still in shock. "Do I have a choice now?"

"You could always slap me in the face. Leave me standing here alone."

She lifts a brow upward, a flirtatious expression crossing her face. "Tempting."

I wrap my other arm around her as well, crushing the distance between us. Slowly, I lean toward her ear, breathing her in. "Dance with me," I whisper, feeling her resistance ebb as she melts into me.

I close my eyes.

Her hands touch my shoulders, hesitant at first. Then she wraps her arms around my neck and I open my eyes, memorizing every detail about this moment. We turn in slow circles, her cheek on my chest, my nose in her dark curls.

"This is the song," she says, one of her hands gliding down to rest on my chest.

"Mm-hm," I reply, and slide my hands down as well, feeling the length of fabric along her back, a thin layer that rests between her skin and mine.

"You remember?"

"I couldn't forget," I say. This is the song we listened to in my car that day she broke down. I bought her a pair of sunglasses. She fell asleep in my living room. That was the first day I saw any chance of us getting together.

We dance like this, breathing in the same air. Problems fading into nothing. For a song that ends too soon.

I hold on to her long after the song ends and another starts. Her lips are so close to mine. A fast song shakes the ground beneath us and everyone is matching their movements to the beat.

Julianna begins to pull away, pausing when I don't let go.

At last I take a step back. "Thank you," I say, meaning it and regretting it at the same time—regretting the end of having her in my arms.

Her lips part, her eyes searching mine in a way that almost crumbles my weak resolve to be a good boy. Not to kiss someone else's date in the middle of the homecoming dance floor. I brush a strand of dark hair behind her ear, her blue eyes pulling me in regardless. Everything about her drawing me to her with a magnetic force I can't refuse.

Yet I somehow find the strength to walk away.

CHAPTER 32

Julianna

I grip the bathroom sink, needing something to hold me in place after dancing with Cody. We were so close—dangerously close—like two balloons covered in static, a charged force drawing us together. I recall his arms embracing me, his hands tracing the length of my back. His touch sending warmth over my skin. I check my reflection in the mirror. Blue eyes stare back at me, and my cheeks flush with color.

His lips were inching toward mine. I can't deny it: Cody Rush was about to kiss me.

And then he was gone. Disappeared, practically.

I stare at my reflection, trying to steady my uneven breathing.

Giving up, I dash from the bathroom. Decision made. I'm not turning back now.

I pass the drinking fountain, searching the hallways. I fling aside all thoughts of Cody's dad and my mom, all fears of Vic and my dad warning me against Cody. I turn down a maze of corridors, searching left and right. And then I see him. At the end of a darkened passage. Alone. Pacing.

"Cody," I say.

He turns at the sound of my voice but looks away again.

"Cody, look at me."

Nothing. He rests one hand on his hip, the other hand digging into his hair. Frustration oozes from his rigid stance.

I start toward him, not about to back down. "What's wrong?"

At last he turns. "*You*," he says, his voice reverberating through the empty hall, bringing me to a stop.

"You and me; this is all wrong. It always has been."

The words cut deep. Sting. "You don't mean that," I say, the hitch in my voice betraying me.

"You're right," he says. "What I'm trying to say is I love you."

His words hit me, melting every last barrier around my heart. He loves me. Three momentous words out in the open.

He runs his fingers through his hair again, messing it up. Suddenly, he looks more rugged than put together. Seductive. It reminds me of when he first came to school, a total mess sitting in that wheelchair. I loved that boy, too. As senseless as it is, I've always loved him.

"L-Lucas and I," I stammer, terrified of admitting my feelings for Cody in return. "It's over. We're just friends."

Cody shifts his weight from one leg to the other and gives me a look. "What do you want, Jules?"

Somehow I know this question is monumental, my answer pivotal.

I stare at him and falter. No one has asked me this in weeks, months. I think about all the things I've had my heart set on, worked to keep together, strived to accomplish. But looking at Cody now, it's hard to think of anything else.

What do I want? How do you place your heart out in the open like this? How do you tell someone they consume your thoughts, your dreams?

I want you.

The words tangle up, wedged like a knot in the back of my throat.

Cody brushes a curly lock of hair away from my face, his gaze following the motion. "'Cause all I want right now is to kiss you, and I'm sick of trying to think up more reasons why I shouldn't."

My breath catches in the back of my throat, my heart hammering with the need to reach out and give him what he wants—what *I* want.

Cody draws back, his hand falling to his side. Like he's about to walk away again.

"Then stop trying," I say.

His gaze collides with mine. My heart skitters in the heady silence. A muscle tightens in his jaw, like he's deciding the barrier between us was made to be broken. There it is; every carefully penned-up emotion breaking loose with an open invitation, leaving me exposed in front of the last boy I should have fallen for.

My pulse flickers as he moves toward me. He slides a hand around the back of my neck, his fingers gliding through my hair. His lips hover over mine, and a sigh unravels within me.

His lips brush mine, soft and slow, his eyes opening briefly—searching, asking. Giving me a chance to back out. I step into his embrace.

And then we mesh into one, all restraint gone—his lips moving over mine, his perfect mouth hungry for more, opening up something inside me I didn't know existed. Warmth spreads through me, setting my veins on fire. His chest rises and falls as he presses me against the wall, as though he, too, has taken leave of his senses. And I know in that instant that I've never been kissed like this before.

"Jewel." Vic's voice echoes down the hallway and I jerk away.

Cody steps back, his reaction delayed. Like he's just now realizing what we've done.

Homecoming. Holly. *Lucas.*

I cover my mouth with my hand.

"Jewel?" Vic calls again, followed by a squeal of giggles from Heidi as Vic says something to her with muffled laughter.

My heart swells as though it could burst and I ache to be alone with Cody, to explore his lips and this connection we've denied for too long. Yet somehow I manage to turn and leave.

CHAPTER 33

Cody

I return to the dance feeling like a classic jerk. I came to homecoming with one girl and kissed another in a darkened hallway during the dance. Still, I can't shake the memory of that kiss.

I search for Holly, finding her and Samantha with a group of friends near the refreshments. She sees me, too, and waves me over, looking anxious about something.

"I'm sorry," I say when I reach her, meaning every word more than she understands.

"For what? Never mind," she says and gestures to the stage. "They're about to crown the king and queen. I was worried you'd miss it."

King and queen—*homecoming king*. I forgot.

Holly shuffles me toward the stage, where Candace, wearing a dress that doesn't leave much to the imagination, is eagerly waiting with her date, Justin Crowder.

"Cody!" Candace says and pulls me forward.

"Hey," I say, my thoughts still caught up in that hallway with Julianna.

Our names are announced. Crowns are placed on our heads. Candace keeps her arm linked with mine. Then a slow song starts and

Candace is wrapping her arms around me. This has to be the worst part about being crowned a prom or homecoming king—the customary king and queen dance in front of the entire school, a spotlight bearing down on you.

"So, homecoming *king*," Candace says, her lips pulling into a pout as she fingers the lapel of my tux. "I'm glad we got to dance."

Which reminds me . . . I search for Holly, relieved when I see Justin asking her to dance. Good guy.

"Yeah," I say, a bit delayed.

"My feet are *killing* me," Candace complains as she steps in close, her leg brushing up against mine. "I've been practicing my dance number for the Miss City of Maricopa Pageant *nonstop*."

Now she's caught my attention.

"The pageant?" I ask, confused. "The same one Julianna's doing?"

"Oh, yeah," she says, her eyes rolling back. "She's doing it, too. Seriously, I don't think a kleptomaniac should be able to wear the crown, but that's just me."

My defensive side kicks in. "What do you mean?"

"Julianna," Candace starts, watching me closely, like she's gauging my reaction. She lowers her voice. "Did you know her mom is in prison for *stealing*?"

If only Candace knew. "Yeah," I reply, like it's no big deal. "I knew that."

"Well, Julianna is *no* better." Candace throws a careful glance around before looking back up at me. "We used to be close back in junior high, until she stole Pamela Redman's sweater. I saw Julianna take it, right there in the middle of drama class. Oh, and Pam's lip gloss, too." Candace looks off at nothing in particular. Thoughtful. Regretful. Even sad. Meanwhile, I try to decide if this story could hold any validity.

"As hard as it was," Candace says with a sigh, "I knew I had to distance myself from her after that. She hasn't changed either, so it's a good thing I did."

"That doesn't sound like the Julianna I know," I say.

Candace offers an apologetic grimace. "It's sad; a lot of people aren't what they seem."

If anyone should know that, it's me.

Dad has told me many stories. I've grown up listening to cautionary tales about people who hide their true tendencies with skill. They're all the same, happy to rat out someone else to save their own skin. Whether to ease their guilt or to put on a front, they start donating to charities and getting involved in the community. Oftentimes criminals are right there under your nose, the last person you'd suspect.

Julianna and her service hours flit to mind. I push these thoughts away. But then Dad's question at the shooting range last Saturday nags at me: *Do you trust her?*

I sure can't trust Vic. He lied to me about the night of the accident, said we were out getting something to eat. In reality we were involved in some kind of drug deal. Do I trust Julianna? The honest answer is, I'm not sure who to trust.

Candace changes the subject. Says something about decorations and refreshments. All about how wonderful my mom is for offering a discount on Chadwick Manor to the school. She goes on and on. I listen halfheartedly, unable to concentrate.

We've all done things we aren't proud of; no one's junior high years are free of shame. I remember what Julianna asked me the other day in my room, something like *what if people simply make a mistake?* She asked me what I thought about mercy. As hard as I try not to go there, I wonder if Julianna was talking about more than her mom.

The slow dance ends and I make my way back to Holly, unable to shake thoughts of Vic and lies. Thoughts of what Candace told me. Thoughts of everything my dad said at the shooting range, about how Julianna is off-limits. And for the first time I wonder: Should I have accepted that long ago?

CHAPTER 34

Julianna

Lucas wasn't searching for me, as Vic had suggested. Or at least it sure didn't look like it. I rushed back into the dance to find Lucas sitting on a bench with Tina East, both of them laughing. I caught him in a sideways glance, making eyes at Tina. I know that look. His eyes told all. Apparently I'm not the only one who has feelings for someone else. I felt oddly relieved.

Still, I feel the full weight of guilt as we stop for drinks at the QT after the dance. Lucas, Josh, and Dustin open the trunk and pull out skateboards. Josh and Dustin's dates talk and laugh as they watch the guys show off. Meanwhile, I can't seem to focus on the here and now.

I try not to think about Cody and Candace dancing together. I saw it. Everyone did. I recall the way Cody and I danced together. Most of all, that moment in the hallway when all restraint broke and he crushed my lips with his. My heart skitters at the memory.

Lucas leans toward me in the backseat. "Wanna watch a show at my house?" he asks, his eyes more interested in the neckline of my dress than anything.

I thought we'd decided to be friends. "I'd better get home," I say. "My dad wants me back by one."

"Your dad won't care," Lucas says, and he's right. It was a lie.

"*And* these shoes are killing me." I lift my foot, effectively inching away from Lucas as I show him the heels I bought with the money Cody gave me. "They're for the pageant."

Lucas gives me a look. *The pageant.* Obviously I picked the right change of topic to kill all thoughts of romance.

"Your house or Lucas's?" Josh asks me, meeting my gaze in the rearview mirror before his date tickles him in the armpit and he swerves, refocusing on the road.

"My house," I say over their laughter.

"I still can't believe you're doing this pageant," Lucas says. Not one ounce of respect in his tone, no hint of support. I don't need this now.

I force my gaze to the view out the window so I don't have to look at him. Or maybe so he has no chance to see the way his words hurt. I know Lucas hates anything girly, but I thought maybe for me he would make an exception. His friend. I thought he would care, if for no other reason than that I care about it.

I'm a mess of emotions at the thought of Cody—again—as Lucas walks me to my door.

"Thanks for tonight," I say. "We can still be friends, right?"

Lucas nods. "Friends."

He steps down from the porch, barely looking me in the eye. He pulls out his cell phone as he walks back to Josh's car, his thumb gliding back and forth across the screen. Texting Tina? I'm left on my doorstep, not sure what to make of the emotions coiling up inside. It's official: we're done. I don't know how I envisioned my first breakup going, but this wasn't it. Still, I know it's for the best.

Cody's empty seat in calculus Monday morning is like a crater on the side of the classroom, something I can't help staring at. He didn't text me—*all weekend.* Should I have texted him?

While Mortimer introduces the pop quiz, I replay every detail of our kiss, something I've only done a million times during the past thirty-two hours. Vic had called my name from down that hallway, startling me. And then *I* pulled away from Cody.

Maybe I should have texted him. Or called. The uncertainty nags at me all morning until I receive a text from Cody before lunch.

I fumble my phone as I scramble to open the text.

Coach set up a scrimmage after school. Won't make it to tutoring.

Not what I was hoping for. At all. I have no idea what to reply. I decide humor is my best option, anything to keep it light.

SLUFFING MATH TODAY? I text and send.

COACH CALLED ME IN. HAD TO TALK. EXCUSED TARDY.

So formal. My lip automatically pulls in between my teeth to give me something to chew. I reread his text. What to make of this I have no idea. I wish he'd loosen up, give me some clue as to what's going on between us.

K

It was about as basic a reply as any. It was also all I cared to give. Then he texts MISS YOU.

My defensive side is unwilling to believe my eyes. The longer I stare at his text, however, the more my insecurities fade. With those two words, Cody has kept me hanging on.

After weeks of one obstacle after another being thrown in my path, my recent turn in luck is invigorating. I'm off to meet my pageant sponsor now: Damian Acklen, owner of Acklen Motor Group. A *luxury* car lot. As I pull up to Acklen Motor Group, I realize just how luxurious it is. This is the first time I've been ashamed of old Rusty. I inch into a parking spot, terrified of scratching the cars on either side.

A gust of cool air envelops me as I open the swinging glass door and step inside. No one sits at the front desk. I stand on the polished tile, glancing around before spotting Damian through the open doorway of a nearby office. A lady wearing a tight skirt sits on the edge of his desk, her legs crossed. Black heels adorn her feet, a crisscross of straps wrapping up half the length of her toned and overly tanned calves.

Looking over her shoulder, she spots me and slides off.

"Hi," she says. She makes her way toward me, her obvious boob job bouncing with every step her heels make across the tile. Click, click, click.

This is more than awkward, asking for Damian. I hardly know him. Something about this whole place makes me uncomfortable. I tell myself to be a big girl and not let my self-consciousness get in the way.

"Julianna," Damian greets me, his hands slung in the pockets of his business slacks. A buttoned-up shirt hides the tattoos I know cover his arms, the light blue fabric accenting the blue of his eyes.

I exhale, relieved that he remembers me. He even remembers my name.

"Hi, D—er, Mr. Acklen," I say, opting for a formal title.

He chuckles. "Damian. Please."

I extend the paperwork for the sponsorship: instructions on getting his logo into the program for the night of the pageant and stuff.

"I'm sorry, it's kind of a lot," I say after explaining each paper.

"This is nothing," he says and tosses the stack onto the front desk where Boob Job is now sitting—his secretary, I gather. "Connie deals with this stuff all the time. She's the best," he says and glances back at her, eliciting a coy smile.

Damian gestures to the wall and I look, finding a collage of photos framed in polished, expensive-looking wood. Some of them were taken at the dealership, pictures featuring famous people who have bought cars here. Damian is in lots of them. I spot a picture of him standing near a wall of animal cages, holding up a giant check made out to the Arizona Humane Society. And it's a sizable sum.

"Wow," I say, "that's very generous of you."

Damian shrugs. "I like dogs and I like supporting a good cause. Connie handles our donations to the American Cancer Society, too. My dad passed away from leukemia years ago," he adds by way of explanation.

"I'm sorry," I say, thinking back on how tired and worn-out my dad looks. He and I have our differences, but really—what would I do if I lost him?

I feel better about the sponsorship money I'm asking of Damian. Two hundred dollars is nothing to him. Now it makes more sense why Damian so readily offered to sponsor me. He's obviously one of those rare guys who looks for opportunities to use his money for good.

"How is everything coming for your pageant?"

I return my attention to him. "Really good," I say, my exaggeration bordering on a lie. The *Night with the Arts* is two days away and I have a million things to wrap up. Mrs. Legend is e-mailing me nonstop, each successive message becoming more clipped and snippy.

"I'm putting on an event for my platform Wednesday night," I say, my thoughts tumbling into words as I remind myself to call the president of the art club to go over details.

"Platform?" he asks, looking genuinely intrigued. I remember how nice he was at the copy center when I first mentioned the pageant.

"*Advocating for the Arts in Education*," I explain. "The event is an art gallery and orchestra-slash-choir performance supporting arts in education. It's in the auditorium at my school . . . if you want to come. Seven o'clock. You're more than welcome."

"I'll be honest," he says, "the arts are not my strength."

I give a courtesy laugh. Generous *and* honest.

"The pageant is on the seventeenth of October?" he asks.

Good memory. Did he put it on his calendar? Was he planning on coming?

"Y-yes, and you're welcome to come to that, too," my big mouth blabbers out before I can stop. But Damian's been so nice. Inviting him is the least I can do, even though the idea of *anyone* coming to the pageant still unnerves me.

I remind myself of Mama every time I feel like bagging this insanity and taking the easy route. What's more, I want this for myself now, if for no other reason than to go for something with all I've got. To conquer my fears of singing onstage, of reaching for a goal only to be shot down by popular vote, like student council. Regardless of the outcome, finishing this pageant will feel like an accomplishment.

"Thanks," Damian says. "I'll see what I can do."

I'm finishing the last touches on my banner for the *Night with the Arts*, the giant spread of paper taking up the entire length of our kitchen floor. I sit up and blow a strand of hair out of my eyes, resting both of my chalk-covered hands on my knees as I admire my work.

Night with the Arts is written in bold, colorful letters across the banner, graffiti style.

With less than forty-eight hours until the event, I was beginning to doubt my decision to spend time on the banner. I had three new e-mails from Mrs. Legend when I got home, in addition to the two texts she'd sent that afternoon.

DON'T FORGET TO CONTACT THE HEAD JANITOR ABOUT OPENING THE JANITOR-IAL CLOSET, Mrs. Legend wrote in one message, and ONE OF MY STUDENTS IN ADVANCED PLACEMENT STUDIO ART SAID SHE HASN'T RECEIVED AN E-MAIL RE-MINDER. DID YOU NOT SEND IT OUT YET? she asked in another.

I added it all to my ever-growing to-do list and put it aside for an hour while I unwound, losing myself in orange and purple chalk. Now, staring at the finished banner, I'm glad I took the time to put my own personal touch on the night, my artistic contribution.

Dad walks by and eyes the banner curiously. I snag my camera from the counter and hand it to him.

"Take a picture of me, will you?" I ask, remembering the take-pictures-of-platform-planning-for-portfolio item on my to-do.

Dad is still staring at the banner.

"It's graffiti," I explain, admiring it with him as I straighten my aching back.

"I caught onto that with the *N* and the *A*," Dad says, making a funny expression as he examines my work. "But the rest of the letters look kind of . . . cute."

"*Cute?*"

"Yeah. Crafty."

I study my banner again, seeing what he means. I take in the criticism. No time to redo it now. And besides, I haven't been an angel to him lately either.

I regret it, this falling out we've had. No specific fight or anything, just little moments during the past several months that brought us to where we are now. Snide remarks I'm not proud of. In frustration over our financial situation, I've dismissed his creativity, angry at his chosen trade. I sure haven't built him up for his artistic flare.

"My *Night with the Arts* event is Wednesday night," I say, taking a minor step in the direction of making amends. "I'd love to have you come. You're so artistic. It would be great to have you there."

Dad's lips twitch, barely a grin. He's always aloof, so hard to read. "I'll try."

"Thanks." I smile. "And my pageant is on the seventeenth of October."

"Oh, yeah," he mumbles and fidgets with the camera. "About that. I may have a snag in my schedule."

Schedule? Since when has Dad had a schedule? The only calendar we have is two years old and we use it as a fly swatter.

"The Tempe art gala is that day," he explains. "It's a festival held each fall at Tempe Town Lake—"

"I know what it is," I say. "I've been there with you."

"I thought I'd enter Hephaestus," Dad says and gestures to the

254 • *Laura Johnston*

scrap metal project that still inhabits our entire kitchen table. I wasn't aware the pile of metal had a name. Clearly Dad sees something in it that I still fail to understand.

"It ends at six thirty," he says, "so I might be able to stop by for the end of your pageant."

An empty promise. Not even a promise. And I know better. All of the artists and vendors stay after to clean up. He'll miss the whole pageant.

I heave a deep breath. "It's fine," I lie. Mom specifically asked him to help me with this pageant, and he agreed. To this day, he's done nothing. And here I thought he'd be proud of me advocating for the arts.

I pull out my ponytail and fluff my hair, checking my reflection in the blackened sliding glass door. "Can you take the picture now?"

"You should leave your hair up," he says. "Makes you look more like an artist."

"Just take the picture!" I yell.

He snaps one picture, not even waiting for me to smile. Then he sets the camera down and heads for the garage.

The front door slams shut and Vic shuffles in. A wadded-up ball of clothes flies in my direction, landing on my banner: a litter of gym socks and a shirt that looks like a mechanic took it off after a long day at the shop.

"Wash those, 'kay?" he says on his way to the stairs. "I'm out of socks."

My phone buzzes with another text. I sit speechless as Vic dashes up the stairs. If this is another text from Mrs. Legend telling me what to do, so help me... Not that I can complain. I need her help.

I rub at my tired eyes, sick of everyone telling me what to do. Telling me my best isn't good enough.

I check the message, relieved to see it's from Trish.

OH, HONEY. FAMILY DISNEYLAND VACAY OVER THE WEEKEND OF YOUR PAGEANT. MOM JUST PLANNED. HAS TICKETS AND EVERYTHING. I WANTED TO B THERE FOR YOU! SO SO SORRY.

I push away thoughts of Trish *and* my dad missing my pageant as another text buzzes in. Mindy.

WHEN YOU COMING OVER TO TRY ON THESE DRESSES?

I completely forgot. Mindy told me I could borrow her prom dresses for the pageant. That was before Cody's mom made me those incredible evening gowns.

A third text. Stress mounts. This one is from Stasha, the vice president of the art club.

ANY WORD ON THOSE BACKDROPS? DID MISS HARDING GIVE US THE GO-AHEAD?

The backdrops. I almost forgot I was supposed to check with the drama teacher about borrowing a set of lampposts for the stage. Actually, I did e-mail her; I remember now. At least I'm almost sure. My in-box is so full, though, anxiety kicks in at the mere thought of searching through it for her response.

I am so behind.

Yep, go ahead, I text, reminding myself to stop by the drama room tomorrow to double-check.

Everything will be okay; it will. Still ... One text lingers on my mind: Trish's. Until now I didn't realize how much I was counting on my best friend being there to support me. Not to mention my own dad.

CHAPTER 35

Cody

Coach called me in to talk about basketball—a *tournament*, no less. The Arizona Preps Fall Showcase. Everyone who knows anything about high-school basketball here has heard of it. The event is attended by some of the top national and regional scouting services in the country. It's an opportunity any aspiring college player would jump all over.

Coach Layton thinks I'm ready. Wants to work with me. Physical therapy has helped a lot; that and the weight training I've done in class. I've built up strength I didn't realize I had and yet still somehow maintain a light touch on the ball. If I believed in miracles, this would be my only explanation after everything I've been through.

I want this tournament, want this scholarship. Even more now, after I was so convinced my chance was gone for good. Getting a scholarship—even making the team—would be a feat after the summer I had, a triumph over the break in my leg. And it could all be mine at this tournament on the night of October 17.

One problem: that's the same night as Julianna's pageant.

The *Night with the Arts* turns out to be a madhouse, and that's good. I guess. I'm swamped with tech crew and helping out backstage with the orchestra and choir. I hardly see Julianna. Just snippets of her running to and fro, answering questions and posing for pictures. What possessed me to suggest Julianna do this, I'm not sure.

One kid forgets to spit out his gum before performing and gets it wedged in his French horn. Some of the lights aren't working right for the tech guys. Then one of the backdrops tips over—some lamppost—and breaks. Stasha, the vice president of the art club, frets over the broken glass. I'm cleaning it up when some lady I recognize as a teacher marches toward us.

"Who gave you permission to use these lampposts?" she snaps, anger practically steaming out of her.

"Julianna," Stasha says.

"Who?"

Crap, Stasha's about to cry. "Julianna Schultz," Stasha says again. "She's the one in charge. Miss Harding, we're so sorry."

"Well, she's going to have to pay for this," Miss Harding says. "She's in enough trouble for taking it in the first place without permission. Not only have you stolen backdrops from my storage, you've broken them, too!"

Said as though we broke each pane of glass in all five lampposts intentionally; shot them out with a BB gun or something. I roll my eyes.

"I'll pay for it."

Miss Harding shoots an indecipherable look my way. "Well, you'll have to go through the proper channels."

Proper channels? Come on. Miss Harding explains school financial protocol, most of which I'm too tired to take in. I apologize on Julianna's behalf and assure Miss Harding I'll take care of it.

The foyer where the gallery was is almost cleaned before I really see Julianna. Trish is giving her a hug, saying something. I pick up on the words *I'm sorry.*

"Really, Julianna," Trish says, her voice audible as I draw closer. "I wanted to come to your pageant so bad, I swear. Mom won't let me get out of this trip."

"It's okay," Julianna says. "And it's *Disneyland.* You love Disneyland."

Trish squeezes her hand before turning to leave.

Julianna smiles when her gaze meets mine, her tense posture deflating as she takes the remaining few steps toward me. "We did it."

"Congratulations, Jules."

She straightens the collar on my polo shirt, her nearness unwinding any residual tension I feel from the evening. "Thanks for all of your help," she says, her full lips drawing into a grin as she looks up at me. "Good to see you, by the way. It's been a while."

I remember the last time we were together: that kiss at homecoming I couldn't get off my mind. Until Coach Layton brought up the tournament Monday morning. Between the tournament and Candace's story about Julianna stealing stuff in junior high, I've been preoccupied. My parents love the Langleys, Candace's parents. They trust them.

"I know; sorry," I say. "I've had a lot on my mind."

"Oh, yeah?"

"Yeah," I say with a tired smile and slide both arms around her, joining my hands at the small of her waist. She doesn't relax in my arms.

"What did your coach want to talk to you about?" she asks.

"A tournament he thinks I'm ready for. The Arizona Preps Fall Showcase," I reply, unable to stop the smile I feel coming on every time I think about it.

She looks up at me, her eyes studying mine. No shock over my big news; no excitement whatsoever. I figured she'd be surprised, at least, happy for me even.

"Is Vic competing in the tournament?" I ask.

"I don't know," Julianna says, reminding me of what a dysfunctional family she has. "I've heard him mention that tournament before, though. When is it?"

"October seventeenth."

Her expression registers a state of deep thought.

"Same night as the pageant," I confirm.

Tension weaves its way through the silence between us.

"Congrats!" she says, a little forced. "I mean, is your leg going to be okay?"

I don't need the reminder. Recruiters know what happened to me over the summer, know what kind of injury I'm trying to come back from. They'll be watching for any signs of my leg affecting my game.

"Yeah," I say. "It's good."

"So you're doing it," she says, part question, part statement.

My first thought is, how can I not? Then I remember what I overheard Trish saying, her apology over not being there for Julianna's pageant. Julianna's mom won't be there either.

"No, it's the night of your pageant." The answer stumbles out. Didn't think it through. Hadn't decided for sure. I guess I just did. "I mean, I want to be there for you."

She exhales, long and deep, her eyes closing slowly as a smile spreads over her lips. "Thank you."

The gratitude laced through her voice makes me think I made the right choice, and yet I'm still conflicted. I'll have plenty of time this winter season to impress recruiters. Even as I tell myself this, however, I wonder if it's true.

Every option here sucks. I doubt Julianna has ever had the kind of support from her parents that I've had from mine. My parents wouldn't miss a game for anything. Julianna needs someone.

She glances down the foyer and straightens with a start, as though she just remembered something. My arms drop as she scoots away and gestures to two guys walking toward us.

"Cody, I want you to meet my sponsor," she says. "Damian Acklen."

His name and face register with a flash of remembrance.

ACKLEN MOTOR GROUP.

It's him: the owner of that luxury car lot. Something about his presence here feels wrong.

Damian directs a finger at me with a slick smile. "I remember you. Cody, right? Still got a thing for those Jags?"

Good memory. Too good.

"Oh, you know," I say. "Once you have Jags on the mind, they're hard to forget."

His lips pull into a grin as I recite what he said to me that day I stopped by the lot.

"Wait, you know each other?" Julianna asks, her eyebrows pulling together.

Damian gestures to the guy beside him. "This is my brother, Fin," he introduces, as though he didn't hear Julianna's question.

The tattoo sleeve covering Fin's arm is the first thing I notice, followed by his jacked biceps and overall thick build. He's not much shorter than me; not much older either.

And Julianna knows them?

Fin says something to Julianna. I glance from her to Damian and his brother, dressed like a punk in a black tank top that shows off every one of his tats. I do a double take, realizing his tank is red. Yet I swear, a second ago, it was black.

The passenger door opens and a man steps out. Black tank and jeans, flat-billed hat, a tattoo sleeve covering his entire arm. Caucasian. Strong. He actually doesn't look much older than us.

Us.

I blink hard. *Us.* Me and Vic.

I pin a sharp look on Fin—Damian's brother. The guy in the black tank and jeans? My heart delivers a series of fast punches against my chest. Was there even a guy in a black tank and jeans? The recollection is poised on the edge of my memory, fuzzy at best. I look at the tattoo sleeve covering Fin's arm and he notices.

"One of the lampposts broke onstage," I say and take Julianna's hand. "I need to show you."

"What?" Julianna exclaims, giving me her full attention, as I hoped.

"Follow me."

She turns to Damian as I lead her away. "I'll be right back."

CHAPTER 36

Julianna

Cody leads me into the auditorium. I can't believe it. *One of the lampposts broke.*

We only make it halfway down the aisle before Cody turns around, bringing both of us to an abrupt stop. "Jules, you have to stay away from them."

"Who?" I say, confused, my mind still focused on the broken lamppost.

Cody darts a cautious glance left and right. A few members of the art club are cleaning onstage. Other than that, we're alone. "Damian and his brother," he whispers.

"What? *Why?*"

"Because they're trouble."

"Trouble?" I ask. "What are you talking about? How do you even know them?"

"I think they were involved in the accident."

I was confused enough before. Now I'm baffled. "When your leg broke?"

"Yeah," Cody replies and shoves his fingers through his hair, messing it all up.

This is a huge accusation. I look up at Cody, at his disheveled hair

262 • *Laura Johnston*

and wild eyes. His eyes make another furtive sweep over the empty auditorium.

"Cody," I say, treading carefully, "I thought you got a concussion that night. When the car hit you."

"Yeah, I did."

"And you forgot everything."

"Bits and pieces have been coming back," he claims.

Cody has told me this before. "Like what?" I ask.

Uncertainty flickers in his eyes. He heaves a deep breath, his gaze pleading with me to hear him out. "There was a drug deal. I think. And I remember running into that mall scared. Something went wrong."

I feel like I'm listening to a four-year-old with an overactive imagination spinning a story about dragons in his closet.

"*You* were involved in a drug deal?"

"No," he says, his voice defensive, followed by a delayed, "Yes. I mean . . . I don't know."

"Cody—"

"Vic was involved, Jules. He had to be."

Now he's got my attention. Vic and drugs. Very possible. Still, I don't want to believe it. Not after everything Mama sacrificed for him.

"I think I should go talk to the detective about my case," Cody says. "Tell him what I remember."

"And Vic?"

"That too."

"Cody," I start, more than nervous on Vic's behalf. My family has fallen apart enough already. "You say you *think* you remember a drug deal. You're not sure?"

Again he hesitates. "Not exactly."

"Cody," I exhale.

"You've just got to stay away from Damian, Jules."

To be honest, the only thing I feel like doing is shutting out all the voices telling me what to do: my dad nitpicking everything I create, Vic ordering me to wash his clothes, Mrs. Legend and her meticulous checklist. And now Cody is telling me to stay away from Damian.

It's been nice being on the receiving end of Cody's help. I couldn't have done any of this without him. Still . . . for once, I set my sights high and accomplished something. I got the owner of a luxury sports car lot to sponsor me.

"I'm pretty sure Damian is a good guy," I say. "He donates to the Arizona Humane Society. And some cancer charity, too, ever since his dad died of leukemia."

"All the more reason for me not to trust him," Cody replies, completely shocking me. "What's he trying to cover up?"

"What's your deal, Cody?" I ask. Seriously, is he listening to himself? "Why don't you trust anyone?"

The dagger-sharp look he shoots me would kill anyone with less of a backbone. "Why don't *you* trust *me*?"

"Because you sound *crazy*," I exclaim. "You got hit by a car! Of course everything you remember about that night feels scary. You say you ran into the mall scared. What if your brain is making it all up?"

A muscle in his jaw flinches. "I think the problem is I've been *too* trusting."

What he's getting at I have no idea. I let out a deep breath, energy spent.

"Can I trust you?" he asks. "Because I sure can't trust Vic."

This slam on a member of my family, however true, is not what I need right now. "*You* don't trust *me*." I state the obvious. "Why?"

"I never said that."

"Why?" I repeat.

"Candace told me about some sweater and makeup in junior high," he says at last, the mention of Candace making my gut twist.

Sweater. Makeup. Pamela Redman's lip gloss and sweater. I can't believe Candace told him. What's more, I can't believe Cody listened. No doubt Candace skipped over the part about her claiming that Pamela stole the sweater and lip gloss from *her* and that I'd be doing Candace a favor by getting them back.

"She told me you stole them," Cody says. "Is it true?"

If I wasn't about to cry, I'd shove him in the chest and say something—anything—to defend myself. Nerves frazzled from stress and too little sleep, I take it all in, willing the tears to stay where they belong.

"Never mind, Jules. It doesn't matter, and I'm not trying to upset you," he claims. "I realize we all make mistakes."

Yeah right. He said so himself: He doesn't believe in mercy. Right and wrong. Hardcore justice. You cross the line, you're out. Remembering the wallet that was turned in to reception a few weeks ago doesn't help. Tears threaten to spill over as I recall being tempted to take money from it. *But I didn't.*

"But the lampposts,.too," he says. "That teacher was ticked, said you guys took them without even asking."

A mistake. A huge, huge mistake. I completely forgot to stop by Miss Harding's room yesterday to ask.

Cody lets out a deep breath. "I'm just getting tired of trying to figure all this out, Jules. You, your family."

"Then stop trying to figure it out," I say, letting my defensive side kick in. "You don't trust me? *Fine.* Trust Candace."

This conversation is about a whole lot more than Damian or Candace or lampposts and lip gloss. Staring at Cody's perfect face now, I realize this really never was meant to be. Me. Him. It was always going to end like this.

Tears wet my lashes. *The end.* I'm reluctant to believe it. My heart aches as I think about the end of this beautiful, screwed-up connection Cody and I have. I blink the tears back, brushing past him and starting up the aisle before he can see. "I'll pay for the broken lamp."

"Jules," he calls after me.

"Don't, Cody." *Please don't follow me.*

He does anyway. "Jules, come back. I already told the teacher I'd pay for it."

"No," I say, spinning around. "I don't need your help. I'm sick of feeling like your charity, sick of you telling me what to do."

He throws his hands out, his expression incredulous. *"Telling you what to do?"*

It was unfair; I know that. But I can't articulate anything through this mess of emotions. "Just go to your tournament, Cody. I don't need you at the pageant."

"Jules . . ."

My heart feels like it's splitting in two, yet I say it anyway. "We both know that tournament is where you belong."

He gives me a long hard look, his jaw set, his face unreadable. "You know," he says, "I think you're right."

Then he turns and leaves, the sound of the auditorium door banging shut behind him bringing everything to a close with a sharp pang.

"Sorry," I say when I return to the foyer where Damian and Fin are glancing at the last few art pieces left behind. I wiped any sign of tears away and came right back, relieved to find Damian still here. I wonder if this was how Mama felt: so many responsibilities, so much to hold together. So often she looked frazzled, as if she was always one step behind. I took for granted everything she did for us.

Damian smiles, an almost sly grin that reaches his eyes. It's a characteristic expression of his, I decide, a smile that could hint at a secret.

He extends a manila envelope. "Everything you need for the sponsorship."

I accept it. "Thank you. I should have offered to pick this up from your office. I didn't even think about it."

"No big deal."

Fin alternates glances between his phone and the blackened glass doorway, like he's watching for someone. Kind of tense. I see the resemblance between them, something in the shape of their faces and their body build, even though Damian's eyes are blue and Fin's are brown.

Shane from the art club brings a ladder into the foyer for me. "Thanks, Shane," I say and position the ladder beneath my banner overhead.

"Here, let me," Damian says. I politely refuse, but he insists.

"Thank you."

Damian scales the ladder. He's too nice. "No problem," he says. "That your boyfriend?"

"Who, Shane?"

"No, Cody."

"Oh," I say, infuriated all over again as I recall Cody's accusation that I stole Pamela's sweater and lip gloss. "No, he is *not* my boyfriend."

Everything Cody said comes back, all about how he thinks Damian and Fin were involved in the accident. "Wait, how do you know Cody?"

"He stopped by Acklen Motors a few weeks ago," Damian calls down from the top. "Seems to have a thing for Jaguars. Have you two been together long?"

Fin holds the bottom of the ladder with one hand, his other still holding his cell. He glances up at me and gives a quick grin before looking back at his cell. I'm having a hard time seeing how they could be trouble.

"No. And he's just a friend," I reiterate and then add, "The most unlikely of friends."

"Oh? How so?"

"His dad's an FBI agent." It slips out, the most straightforward answer to sum it all up.

Fin's head snaps up.

I let out a laugh, aware that the stress from tonight is letting thoughts spill out unchecked.

Fin and Damian exchange a look. This information seems to have caught their interest. I guess it is pretty cool to know an FBI agent.

Holding one detached end of the banner, Damian shifts to glance down at me. "FBI?"

Not that I'm about to tell Damian my mom is a convict. "Yeah. And, I mean, my dad is an *artist*. Basically, Cody and I—and our families—are about as different as they come."

Damian takes in a slow breath before stepping down the ladder. Fin no longer seems interested in his phone.

"How'd you two meet?" Fin asks.

Superodd question, but whatever. Fin's brother is giving me two hundred dollars in sponsorship money and they both showed up to my event tonight. After weeks of wanting to tell someone about me and Cody and not having anyone to share it with, I let the story spill out, all about how Cody showed up randomly at The Chocolate Shoppe one night at the beginning of the summer and bought a bunch of chocolates for me.

"He was smitten," Damian says as he positions the ladder beneath the other end of the banner. "No surprise there."

I chuckle. This is almost more fun than talking to Trish. Disparaging thoughts flitter in as I recall wondering all summer whether Cody would ever stop by again. "Not exactly. I didn't see him again until school started. We're just friends."

Friends who kissed four days ago like nothing could ever tear us apart.

"I heard he got pretty banged up in an accident over the summer," Damian says. "Leg injury, concussion—"

I look up, regarding him through narrowed eyes despite every effort not to. "How did you know about the accident?"

"It made the local news," Damian explains, like this should be common knowledge.

"It did?"

"Yeah." Damian hooks a thumb down in his brother's direction. "Fin's into basketball. Follows all the high-school sports."

Men and their sports. Makes sense. I never read about sports.

"Yeah," I say, relinquishing some of my anger toward Cody. "He has had it rough. I mean, the accident happened that same night he gave me the chocolates. He doesn't even remember meeting me."

Damian looks down, his eyes flashing with interest. It really is a bizarre story. Sad but crazy. One of those stories you can only laugh about later because what else are you going to do?

Damian steps down and hands the banner to me. "So, he doesn't remember giving you the chocolates?"

I wad the banner up and shove it under my arm. "Nope."

"Did he give you anything else?"

Fin is all eyes, waiting for my reply. I think about the photo-booth pictures, about the past several weeks of pageant preparation and how far I've come. I certainly wouldn't be here if it weren't for Cody, for his encouragement. Cody has given me a lot. This thought adds to the regret swelling within me. Cody and I—whatever we had—are no more.

"No," I say. The banner is down now and everyone is ready to head home. Besides, I've blabbered enough about my screwed-up love life.

"Thank you for the sponsorship," I say, realizing this might be the last time I see Damian.

"You bet," he says and draws out his wallet. "In fact, you're going to need more than that to get ready."

Cash is drawn out. Fifties. *Hundreds.* I stare at the stack of money, my eyelids refusing to blink.

"Here's three hundred—make that four hundred—for whatever you need to buy. Shoes, clothes . . . not enough?"

I blink. Damian's eyes are searching mine.

"Five hundred, then?" he asks.

I've never seen so much cash in my life. "N-no. I mean, *yes*, but . . . you don't have to."

He puts the money in my hand. "And here's an extra hundred for two reserved seats the night of the performance. Fin and I want front row. Can you do that?"

"Uh—y-yeah. Absolutely."

"Great," he says, his voice filled with the kind of confidence that only a man who isn't used to being told *no* can have. "We'll see you then. October seventeenth."

"Right," I say, my tongue feeling awkward as the right words evade me. They turn and leave. "Thank you!" I call out.

I watch Damian and his brother walk toward their black sports car, still shocked by the strange feeling of so much money in my hand.

Really, Damian has been nothing but kind.

CHAPTER 37

Julianna

Unanticipated excitement bubbles up when I open my eyes and realize what today is—October 17. The pageant. Never in a million years did I think I'd look forward to it. But I do. Until I swallow.

My throat pinches with pain.

My throat. My *voice.*

I sit up, denial rushing in. My talent depends on this. *I need my voice.*

Sunlight streams through my window, forming wavy lines of light on my bed thanks to my warped blinds. I brave another swallow, dread slicing through as my throat throbs in response.

I drink lots of water. I avoid talking—anything to preserve my voice. My interview with the judges is at 11:00 a.m., so I'll have no choice but to use my voice then.

My skin is clear, my eyes bright. I think of the positives as I dress in my interview outfit, a lightweight neutral dress with a white blazer on top. Now, looking in the mirror, I wish I'd spent more money on this outfit, the first one the judges will see me in. It's amazing what you can buy with four hundred dollars. It's also incredible how fast you can run out. Clothes, shoes, and coordinating jewelry for multiple outfits.

Dad is already at the Tempe art gala when I leave. He took Rusty, leaving me and Vic with the used Buick he bought a week ago. Vic is still sleeping, so I have the Buick all to myself. Only me and an unfamiliar car and a million nerves. Walking into the interview room with six judges watching my every step is unnerving for sure, but as I move to my spot in front of them, I tell myself that at least there's no audience for this.

They start by asking me about my platform, *Advocating for the Arts in Education*, and I tell them all about my *Night with the Arts* event, directing them to my platform portfolio for reference. The judges nod in approval. I can tell they're impressed.

Then they delve into current events, posing questions ranging from violence in other countries to bullying online. Separation of church and state, stem cell research, specific controversial court cases, the environment, you name it.

I do my best, feeling pretty good about both my responses and my presentation. Then it's on to the wrap-up miscellaneous questions.

Wrap-up—*almost done.*

"Would you like to be famous?" one judge asks. "If so, in what way?"

A trick question for sure. After hesitating for a beat, I opt for a comical tone, like I imagine Cody would. "Absolutely," I say with a smile that hints at a wink. "I'm going for Miss America, right?"

Six smiles. One lady is beaming at me, a delegate from the Miss Arizona organization named LeAnn. I think I've at least won her over.

"What's a down day for you?" LeAnn asks.

Again I stick with humor. "Waking up to a broken air-conditioning system in the middle of August and stepping on a scorpion on the way to the bathroom."

LeAnn bursts into laughter and a couple of others laugh along. Another delegate from the Miss Arizona organization touches a hand to her chest, like the mere thought of such a day is horrific. Try living it.

"How do you set goals for yourself?" a judge named Jerry asks me, a stern guy who hardly cracked a smile at my previous answer.

These questions are harder than I imagined. "I'm learning that the best goals aim to make me a better person, to help me conquer a fear or stretch me in some positive way."

I'm not sure where that answer came from, but I'm glad. It's the truth, something it took being asked for me to realize.

One final question. And I need to nail it. I've done well so far. I think. This interview is worth 25 percent of the competition score. Now, standing here as one of eight contestants, I wonder what it would be like to win a thousand dollars in scholarship money and wear the crown. A *thousand* dollars. I keep my shoulders squared, my feet sturdy.

"When has your life most dramatically changed as the result of a random external event? How did it affect your life?"

I swallow hard once. Twice. One event jumps to mind, but I won't go there. Not Mama. Not now. Last question. I part my lips to blurt out some vague response, anything that will suffice so I can get out of here, but I know they'd prefer something specific.

"At the beginning of this year my mom was indicted for mortgage fraud."

I instantly have the keen attention of every judge. In this case I'm not sure it's a good thing.

"My brother had a drug problem and we couldn't afford rehab on top of the other financial demands of life."

Drug problem. Couldn't afford rehab. My heart thuds against my rib cage like it's telling me off for being such a ditz. I've already committed, however, so I can't stop now.

"She felt she had to help him, so she took matters into her own hands. It took me a long time to accept the fact that she was wrong, and I'm still adjusting to life at home without her."

This statement is something of an epiphany, and it reminds me of the second part of the question. *How did it affect my life?*

"I used to be angry about my mom's imprisonment. But really, anger does no good. I've learned that. Above all, I've learned that regardless of the bad luck or obstacles thrown our way, each of us is in control of the course of our lives."

I smile and offer each judge a handshake in parting, knowing I'm screwed. I'm still beating myself up over my last response as I pack for the pageant that afternoon.

Information packet: check. Backup CD with the accompaniment for my song: check. I run through each of my outfits: the cowgirl hat, boots, and skirt for the opening number, my evening gown, my talent gown, my swimsuit, and my interview suit for the onstage question— heaven help me—each outfit bagged with coordinating jewelry, hair accessories, and shoes. Curling irons, lotions, and all the best in hair products and makeup—thanks to Cody and Damian's money.

I drink a ton of water, feeling the effects of so much talking on my sore vocal chords. Then I pack everything in the Buick and run inside for my purse and keys.

"I need the car," Vic says the moment the keys jingle in my hand.

He's watching TV, flipping channels from one sport to the next.

I take in a deep breath, not about to waste words fighting. "What for?"

"Got a date," he says. "Me and Heidi. It's been a year. We're celebrating."

Moments like this remind me what a softy Vic can be. He remembers the anniversary of their first date and he's taking her out.

"That's why Dad left the new car. Said Rusty's been acting up."

"But my pageant is tonight."

"I'll take you," he offers, surprising me.

Easy enough. Dad said he'd try to make it to the end of my pageant, so I'll catch a ride back with him. Vic turns off the TV, and together we head for the car.

It's been a long time since Vic and I have been alone, no Heidi in the front seat. We talk about his date tonight. He's taking Heidi to RigaTony's, her favorite restaurant in southern Tempe, not too far from the pageant.

As we make the forty-minute drive to the Performing Arts Center at Maricopa High School, I'm reluctant to admit I've missed Vic, the Vic who used to spend time with me. Believe it or not, I even miss the Vic who teased me incessantly. The Vic who gave me no personal space, flicked my ponytail into my face, and stole bites of food off my plate. Even his locker pranks have stopped.

"Thanks, Vic," I say as he hangs my outfits on a hook outside the dressing room.

He nods and turns to leave, looking uncomfortable so close to the girls' dressing room and yet obviously appreciating the view as Denica struts out in a short robe, offering him a smile and a little wave on her way.

"Hey, Jewel," Vic says as I open the door to the dressing room.

I turn back, praying Vic refrains from whatever derogatory statement he's about to make. Vic is about as different from the other members of our family as could be. Where our mom is musical and a dreamer, Vic is anything but. Where our dad is artistic, Vic couldn't care less. His life has evolved around playing basketball on city courts and getting into trouble on the side. And here I stand in front of him with an evening gown draped over one arm and two pairs of heels in my other hand, about to compete in a beauty pageant.

"Good luck."

He's already walking away before I can process what he said and the sincerity with which he said it.

"Thank you," I say, but my throat is so clogged with emotion, it's hardly loud enough for him to hear.

Nerves escalate as seven o'clock draws near. For *all* of us. Jenny fidgets her legs incessantly; Sophie's fingers are bound to have joint damage after all of the rubbing and knuckle cracking; Candace, Laurel, and Aubrey are on their fourth layer of lipstick, I've chewed off all of mine, and Rebecca looks like she could be sick. Only Denica seems cool and confident. Genuinely keyed up. Then again, she did this last year.

Candace ignores me and I'm glad. I still can't believe she lied to Cody about the sweater and lip gloss, stretching the truth to make me sound like a thief instead of the naïve girl I was. Let Cody think what he will. I push resentment away, won't let it get to me. Not now. Not tonight.

The photographer and videographer set up their gear. The tech crew gets ready. I double-check with the ticket booth at the front door, making sure Damian's two tickets and reserved seats are ready for will call.

With Trish in Disneyland, my dad at the Tempe art gala, Mama in prison, and Vic off with Heidi, Damian and his brother might be my only supporters in the crowd tonight. I doubt even Mindy will be here. She's been evasive ever since I told her I wouldn't need to borrow her dresses tonight.

I don't let myself think about Cody as I get my cowgirl outfit on with the rest of the girls in the dressing room. I've avoided all contact with him during the past two and a half weeks. When I saw him heading off to the school gymnasium yesterday with Connor and a couple of the guys, a basketball slung under his arm, I seized the opportunity to dash over to his house to pick up the two pageant dresses.

Rachel told me she and her mom would be at the pageant if not for Lizzy's dance recital. It made me happy for Lizzy; such a cute girl with so much potential and her whole family supporting her. And yet I've wondered how Cody's family is planning to split this night between Lizzy's recital and his tournament.

I try not to think of Mama either. If only Trish were here. She would have been my personal cheerleader tonight, probably would have recruited a crowd. Now, as I stand in position behind the closed curtain, I decide a crowd of supporters wouldn't have been such a bad thing. Better than no one here cheering my name.

As the curtain parts, I remind myself why I'm doing this. Mama. All for her. To see her smile when I tell her about this night. I work up a smile, regardless of how alone I am in this or how badly I messed up the interview.

The western song blares from the speakers and an overwhelming crowd begins to cheer. I stare out at the audience in shock. Nearly every seat is filled. I pull my thoughts together in time to plaster a smile back on my face and start in on our choreographed dance.

Candace is rocking it next to me, shaking her hips and tossing her hair around like a true dancer. I step in beat with the music, but I feel stiff and inept. I curse my mother all over again for getting me involved in this.

Damian and Fin catch my eye. Front row, right behind the judges. Damian winks at me, and my smile involuntarily broadens. The judges wear various expressions, most smiling. LeAnn leans forward in her chair with a permagrin while Jerry looks like he's staring at the stock exchange.

The entire pageant feels like a throwback to simpler times. Before long I've relaxed more than I thought possible. Not even the swimsuit portion is as awful as I anticipated.

Unfortunately, my nerves return in full force before the talent portion. I take in a few deep, controlled breaths and hum through some drills in the dressing room, extending my range with each drill. My voice has loosened up as the day progressed—thank heavens.

Rebecca's Irish dance is impressive. Laurel proves herself an accomplished violinist. Aubrey does her cheerleading routine. Jenny's ventriloquism act is cooler than I expected and Sophie's pre-performance finger warming pays off during her incredible Rachmaninoff piece on the piano.

Candace and I are the last performers. As I watch her unbelievable modern dance performance, I pray for my voice to hold together. Candace's dance is impossible to beat. The round of applause she receives at the end sends panic through me. *I'm next.*

"Good job," I whisper and offer a smile. She walks off stage, all smiles as she marches past me.

The talent portion is worth 35 percent of my overall score. *Thirty-five.* This is big.

I'm tempted to back out until a random thought slips in: it could be worse. A lot worse. I could be stuck in a cell, months and even years of life—real life in all its everyday monotony and beauty—taken away from me. Truly alone.

And yet here I am, dressed in the kind of dazzling red gown and heels I never dreamed of wearing. I might be alone, but that might not be such a bad thing. Standing here backstage, I decide perhaps it's in the silent, solitary moments that we dig deep for strength. Reach for our goals.

I pull my shoulders back and hold my head high, drawing on the presentation skills we practiced in workshop. I walk into the spotlight.

My piano accompaniment begins to play, and I begin the mental countdown until I join in. I take a deep breath and close my eyes, imagining an auditorium of empty chairs, only me and the microphone and the song Rachel picked out.

I sing the lament of the anguished Fantine from *Les Misérables.* "I Dreamed a Dream."

I read the abridged version of the book for English my junior year, but I never thought of the universality of emotions, the vast reach of its message. My voice carries over the microphone—clear, resonant, emotive—lending my confidence a set of wings as I continue.

I think about Mama. I think about her hopes and dreams, just like Fantine. I imagine her darkened prison dormitory at night. Mama's dream was different from the hell she now lives, too.

I finish the last verse, deep emotion poured into every line. That's it, three short verses, my eyes closing as the words sink in deep. One minute and forty seconds of music lingering in my ears and sweeping me away.

The crowd erupts into applause. My eyelids flash open and I take in the sight. People cheer, people whistle, people *stand.* All around, one by one, until a good portion of the crowd is on their feet in the kind of ovation that can only be brought on by music that reaches inside the soul and draws something out.

My chest swells. I stand frozen, just a girl under the spotlight who was never meant to shine.

I did it.

No, I didn't do it. Not alone, at least. In fact, I wasn't alone in this at all.

As I step away from the mic and bow like I've practiced, I recognize how much help I've had along the way. From the art club to Mrs. Legend, Barbara and Donna, Cody's mom, Vic dropping me off tonight, even my dad's criticism. Perspective shifts as gratitude rushes in. One person, above all, I have to thank.

As the applause dies down, as the spotlight fades and all that's left are lingering feelings soaring at an all-time high, I understand. This is what can happen when a boy like Cody Rush believes in a girl like me.

CHAPTER 38

Cody

Dribble, dribble, hold. Dribble, dribble, hold. Foul shot. Focus. The basket is all mine. I fix my eyes on the rim and block out all sounds of spectators in the bleachers, the ball perched in my hands. Can't let the pressure get to me. I've practiced this shot a thousand times. Thirty seconds and the game is over. This could be the winning shot. I've got this.

The ball flies in a high arc and sails right through the net. The crowd cheers.

The opposing team makes a mad dash for the other end of the court. We're all over them on defense. Sweating. Energy high. Determined.

They pass. Dribble. They try to get a shot, but we don't let them.

Taylor Payton from Mountain View goes for the big three, the buzzer ringing as his ball soars toward the basket. Nick Frederickson from our team jumps in vain to block. We all hold our breath. The ball hits the rim and rolls away from the net.

73 to 72—we win.

Jumping. Celebrating. Butt slaps all around.

Parents cheer from the bleachers. I find my dad in the crowd. His smile is a mile wide.

This is big for a lot of us, winning at a tournament like this. Getting the blocks. Shooting a high field goal percentage. Top national and regional basketball scouting services from all over the country are here. Scouts are looking for athleticism, performance, body size, skill, and more. And they aren't about to recruit a player who'll be nursing an injury.

I'm here. After the accident this summer, I didn't think this would be possible.

Cody Rush develops into serious prospect once again after recovering from leg injury sustained early this summer. That's what the Arizona Preps Web site said in a post last week. I followed my instincts, like Jimmy used to say. When I was twelve, I ditched baseball and all the associated raw memories of the sport my little brother loved. And I dedicated myself to the sport *I* love. College ball—it's so close.

One more game to go.

"I'm proud of you," Dad says and claps his hand on my shoulder between games. It means a lot. More than he knows.

Lizzy has a dance recital tonight. It's been on the calendar for months now, and Lizzy is performing some solo thing. Last dance of the recital. It's a big deal, the kind of opportunity not many girls at her dance studio get, I guess.

Mom was torn. Wanted to be at both. Dad gladly opted to come support me. Lizzy wanted him to see her solo, however, so he promised to leave early to catch the end of the recital. He's got maybe another twenty minutes here.

"I can't wait to see what your senior-year basketball season holds in store," Dad says. I can tell he wants to stay. "Make sure to get me the schedule of your games as soon as it's out and we can put them down on my calendar."

Said like I'm already on the team. Tryouts aren't for another couple of weeks. He's right, though. I've got as good a shot as ever at making the Highland team, maybe even scoring a scholarship. Hopefully tonight.

Music blares. Guys are warming up for the next game.

I'd better get over there. "Thanks, Dad."

Dad turns back toward the bleachers but stops. Turns back. "Oh, and Cody, good luck with your last game," he says with a clever smile. "Trust your instincts."

I've heard Dad say that a million times—his phrase. But after so many flashbacks about Jimmy lately, I realize that expression was more Jimmy's than his. And I can't help but think of Jimmy.

The next game is intense. Solid players on both teams. We're neck and neck through the first three quarters. I'm so focused on the game that I fail to see when my dad leaves. I glance up at the stands during a time-out. Gone.

A scout from ASU is here. They've been following me since my sophomore year, and I would kill to play for them.

My injury will be a factor. They've been watching for any signs of my leg affecting my game. I know it. I grin as the buzzer wails and play resumes, knowing I haven't given them a reason to doubt my recovery.

Christian Garcia from Corona del Sol makes a steal for the other team. He dribbles it down the court and passes it off to Garret Wilding for a smooth layup.

"Come on," I say to my guys around me, trying to keep our spirits high. Momentum going. "We've got this. We've got this."

But then Andrew Cook misses a shot for our team and the opposing team gains possession before we can recover. We're falling apart on defense. Garcia makes a three-pointer.

65 to 71. They're pulling ahead and there's only eight minutes left.

We rally. Get the momentum going again. Or maybe it's in my head, because another guy on my team misses a layup and we fail to recover. Then I miss a block.

I glance at the stands inadvertently in time to see the ASU scout shift his gaze from the court to his notepad. He jots something down and it messes with my head.

I force my attention back to the game. Can't lose focus now.

Offense. We've got this. Adam delivers a nice pass to me and I take the shot. A spasm of pain pulls every muscle in my leg tight. The ball sinks through the net, hopefully deflecting any attention from the fact that I'm favoring my leg now.

68 to 71. We're closing the gap. But I'm no longer focused on the game.

My leg.

I run through the pain, keeping my steps even. Not about to let any hint of injury show. Five more minutes. I have to hold out. If I can at least get ASU's interest now, they'll pay more attention to me this season.

I do my best, but I can tell I'm no longer on top of my game. The ache in my leg escalates as I take the ball downcourt. I pass it off the first chance I get and check the clock, my heart beating against my chest from more than exertion.

Hammering. Pounding.

Not here, not now. Not during this game. I push memories of the accident away. It's the last thing I want to think about. Yet my efforts do little good.

A rush of blood through my ears harmonizes with a deep rumble approaching from behind. A familiar sound. A rich, chilling purr.

The Jaguar.

I whirl around, barely see it coming.

I'm standing at the three-point line. Can't move. It *was* a Jaguar. I remember now. And I *had* seen it before. I was watching it, already suspicious for some reason. Was it following me? And then I saw something else, the dark sky ahead.

I freeze, my heart lurching at the sight. I recall the weather alert on my phone that almost got me caught. Dust storm.

It billows inch by inch. Swallowing the city whole. Thick. Fast. A coughing fit erupts. Darkness closes in.

I barely catch a pass. Didn't see it coming. I don't have a clear shot from here, or maybe I do. I'm too distracted to know for sure. I pass it off to Adam. My phone. I remember my phone. Or at least a weather alert on my phone.

I whip out my iPhone. My thumb hovers over it, hesitating. My dad, police, my dad, police: the options ricochet in my mind before I go for something else entirely, the choice my brother Jimmy probably would have rooted for.

I press record.

"So when do I meet Ian?" Vic asks the drug dealers.

"You don't," the guy in black says.

Fragmented memories fly back, jumbling together. But the details, however out of order, are clearer now than ever.

The meaty guy in black seizes a fistful of Vic's shirt—Fin.

Fin. I know it was him. Fin, Damian's brother. The tattoo sleeve. The tank top. One of the drug dealers was Damian's brother. Was Damian the other dealer?

Apprehension claws to the surface as I think about Julianna.

I got the entire drug deal on camera.

"Get the money, Vic," Fin says, his lips curving into a twisted grin. "That sister of yours, the one with the tight little body? I wouldn't mind getting my hands on that."

The buzzer rings. We lose 69 to 74, but I don't care. All I can think about is Julianna. She thinks I'm crazy, though. Doesn't believe me. I regret the fight we had in the auditorium, regret bringing up Candace's accusation. So much pressure had been building that I snapped. I got the drug deal on camera, though. There's hope. But where did my phone go?

There was a gun, I remember. I panicked. But Vic got out of there. I threw a rock to distract the dealers. Vic claimed they were alone. Fin and the other dealer were about to get in their car to leave, and then . . .

My phone makes a deafening beep, a discordant echo that shakes every cell in my body and puts my pulse on hold. I muffle the sound too late. I glance down.

EMERGENCY ALERT: Dust Storm Warning in this area till 11:00 P.M.

And then I was running. Fin saw me, chased me. Which means he must have recognized me the other night at Julianna's event.

I dart into the road, headlights blinding me as an SUV screeches to a halt. My arm flies out, muscles clenching with fear.

My phone was knocked out of my hand. It hit the pavement. Skidded. I scooped it up and sprinted through the parking lot.

I bring my phone up to eye level as I dash around a row of cars. A crack slices through the screen. I curse.

I dare a glance behind me as I approach the mall entrance, relieved. I've lost my tail. I hope. He's nowhere in sight. For now.

I whack my phone against my other hand. Nothing.

I vaguely remember the Buckle. My phone was dead. I snagged a new shirt and hat and paid for them.

I toss my old shirt and shattered phone into a nearby can.

A trash can. My phone, the recording—they're gone.

People are patting my back, applauding me on a game well played. I'm having a hard time staying in the present. We lost the game. I fell apart during the last five minutes, doing my team no good. I shift into autopilot as we exchange high fives. I gather my things. My leg is stiff now, reminding me of the long summer I spent recovering from that night.

Headlights blind me in the instant before the bumper rams into me—my leg.

Muscles, a bone.

A shattering pain.

I hit the hood, my shoulder ramming the windshield before the car brakes and sends me flying in the other direction. Thrown several feet ahead until I slam into the ground, the asphalt scraping off the side of my face before my skull meets something hard and unforgiving.

And everything goes black.

"Is he dead?" a bottomless voice asks.

It wasn't a hit-and-run, not exactly. They got out of the car: two of them. The same two drug dealers? One of them was searching under my arms, searching my pockets one by one. Which means they must have seen the photo-booth pictures. They knew I was with Julianna. They wanted the phone, but it was gone. In the trash. The video destroyed.

A muffled cry of pain. An Arizona license plate.

I willed the numbers into memory: 1039.

I recall the numbers that have been perched on the verge of my memory for weeks. 621039. I was remembering the car that hit me.

Tinted windows, shiny hubs, six spokes.

Six.

F-Type, two doors.

Two.

621039

And then the frame around the license plate springs back: *ACKLEN MOTOR GROUP.*

Julianna consumes my mind. She's at the pageant now. Her sponsor might be, too. Damian, the owner of Acklen Motor Group. Fin's brother. I know I'm not crazy. Julianna is in danger.

"That was one well-played game, Cody," a man says. I look up to find the head recruiter from ASU standing before me. And he's not the only one. A recruiter from OSU and another from USC stand nearby. Deep in memory, I'd made my way to the foyer without realizing it.

This is really happening. Recruiters. *ASU.*

"Thank you," I say and shake his hand. My moment. My lucky break. I did it. A triumph over this leg, this injury, *that night*. And yet I can't fully live it. Can't shake the feeling that I should be somewhere else.

Trust your instincts.

"We'd love to have you come on over for a campus visit," the scout says, but I can't concentrate. Did he really say what I think he just said?

All I can focus on are those three words ringing in my ears—trust your instincts—three words from a voice I haven't heard in a long time: Jimmy's. His voice is audible—in my ear—as though this were another flashback. I look around, an irrational fragment of my mind expecting to see little Jimmy standing behind me. But this is no flashback, and Jimmy isn't here.

Trust your instincts.

The memory of Jimmy's voice so clear in my mind does something to me I can't describe, makes my throat tighten up. It doesn't make sense and yet it does. Every time I've remembered pieces of the accident, memories of Jimmy inevitably followed, as if someone or something was trying to tell me something.

"I'd love that," I say and hurry for the door before I can talk myself out of it, no doubt leaving the scout more than confused at my abrupt departure. And possibly even screwing over my chance at a scholarship. But my eyes have been opened, and I finally see everything.

Ian is short for Damian.

Adrenaline pulses through my ears as I dash across the parking lot toward my car, my feet barely touching the ground. 8:55 p.m. I might be too late. It's an hour's drive from here to Maricopa High School, where Julianna's pageant is. Forty-five minutes if I push it.

CHAPTER 39

Julianna

We stand onstage, eight contestants in evening gowns and heels as we wait to hear the judges' verdict. The competition was stiffer than I imagined, each girl putting on an impressive show of talent, fitness, poise, and intelligence. Well, almost everyone got the intelligence part across.

Candace's answer to the on-stage questions left a bit to be desired. When asked why she would like to become the next Miss City of Maricopa, she hardly took a breath before rushing in with, "So that I can stand as an example of the type of girl who should wear the crown."

Not bad, I guess. But the next question was how she thought the United States should aid refugees of war in other countries. This time she took a number of hesitant breaths before answering, "I think . . . they should be freed. Yes, they should definitely be freed. And given food."

Sophie and I exchanged questioning looks backstage. Did Candace think they were asking about *prisoners* of war?

As I stand beside the seven other contestants, I run through the scoring breakdown, knowing Candace's blunder won't matter. The on-stage question is worth only 5 percent of the overall score, while the talent is worth 35, evening wear 20, swimsuit 15, and private interview 25.

Candace's dance can't be beat. She nailed the most important two minutes of the entire competition. Her evening gown was unlike any other, too, a white, tastefully beaded, off-the-shoulder dress that accented her fake tan, bleached teeth, and perfectly set updo. That, and she outdid us all in the swimsuit portion with her ruffled bikini.

Homecoming queen, Miss City of Maricopa . . . however cocky Candace's first on-stage question was, she was right. Candace Langley is crown-bearing material.

Sophie and Denica, in my opinion, are the only ones who stand a chance against Candace. Sophie's Rachmaninoff piece blew us all away. Her smile is contagious, her yellow evening gown matching her personality. And she answered her on-stage question like a champ. Then there's Denica, who's a repeat contestant, one of the attendants to last year's Miss City of Maricopa, Lacy Baldwin.

"Thank you all for coming out tonight to support our amazing contestants," Donna says into the microphone, addressing the darkened crowd beyond the stage. "We nearly doubled our ticket sales this year and we are so thrilled to have you all here to share in this moment when the new Miss City of Maricopa will be crowned."

A prickly feeling begins in my toes and radiates upward. This is it. Now that I think about it, the winner could be any one of these girls standing beside me.

Denica had every right to be excited about the swimsuit portion. She certainly gave Candace a run for her money. Rebecca is kind, and she's a talented Irish dancer. She would make a great Miss City of Maricopa. Laurel and Aubrey are beautiful and talented. Then again, maybe the judges were in the mood for a less conventional talent and were impressed with Jenny. Her ventriloquism act was definitely original.

The reigning Miss City of Maricopa, Lacy Baldwin, joins Donna onstage, wearing an evening gown, sash, and crown. Really, every girl standing at my side deserves a crown.

Donna asks the band for a drumroll. "Our second runner-up, and winner of a two-hundred-fifty-dollar scholarship, is . . . Sophie Spinetti!"

People clap and cheer as Sophie steps forward to accept a bouquet and a sash from Lacy.

"Our first runner-up, and winner of a five-hundred-dollar schol-arship, is . . ."

Denica, I think. No, Laurel. Then again, I really like Rebecca and would love for her to win first runner-up to Candace.

"Candace Langley," Donna announces.

I hesitate before clapping, surprised. Denica beat Candace? Or was it Laurel?

Candace walks toward Lacy Baldwin, hiding her disappointment as she takes her bouquet and sash.

"Now, one of these final six ladies will be our new Miss City of Maricopa," Donna says. "She will not only win the title, she will also win a thousand dollars in scholarship money, as well as serve as a role model to others in her community. Our new Miss City of Mari-copa is . . . Julianna Schultz."

I clap twice before the name registers. My mind must be playing tricks on me, a conclusion quickly shot down by the fact that every-one is staring at me. Including a smiling Donna and an eager Lacy Baldwin, who holds a second crown in her hands. *My* crown?

Me?

Cameras flash. The cheering is overwhelming. I step forward, see-ing the faces in the audience better now. Stasha, Sean, and other members of the art club are here. Even Mrs. Legend sits a few rows back with her husband. And Mindy . . . she came. Other people from school are here, too, whether for Laurel or Aubrey or Candace or me, I'm not sure. And Damian. He puts two fingers between his lips and whistles.

My cheeks burn in an obvious blush and I smile.

A crown is placed on my head. My brain staggers to catch up. Lacy situates the Miss City of Maricopa sash on my shoulder. I ac-cept the huge bouquet she hands me—nothing quite as amazing as the ones I've seen Cody's mom put together but beautiful.

Cody's mom.

Cody.

Rachel. Mrs. Legend. The art club.

Equal parts gratitude and guilt wash in. Gratitude to these people, for this moment. Guilt as I think of how undeserving I am. Desire and ambition follow as I resolve to prove myself, to do my best, to be everything this position calls for. And then it settles in: I am Miss City of Maricopa.

I interviewed, performed onstage—actually went for something. And *succeeded*. And I won a *thousand dollars* in scholarship money. College. This taste of success is overwhelming.

And then I remember Mama.

She's going to flip with excitement. Moisture gathers in my eyes as I imagine telling her. I have her to thank for this.

Donna thanks everyone for coming. Then news reporters are onstage, asking me questions. The night hurtles past in a haze of smiling faces, flashing cameras, hugs, and glitter.

Mindy comes up onstage and gives me a big hug. "You looked beautiful, Julianna. And you won!"

We share a girly moment complete with giggles that could certainly be classified as *giddy*, one of my least favorite words. Right now I don't care.

When I'm finally packing up my things, I realize how late it is. And that I don't have a ride home. Dad never came.

I check my cell phone, finding three calls from him. And one from *Cody*. No voice mail.

I check my text messages, finding one from Dad.

RUSTY BROKE DOWN ON THE WAY TO YOUR PAGEANT. COULD BE THE TRANSMISSION. WILL HAVE TO GET IT TOWED. CALL ME.

I try to call, but it goes straight to his voice mail. Great.

I look around the empty dressing room, just me and pieces of sequins on the floor. Some residual makeup on the counter. Even Mindy is long gone by now. I call Vic, hoping he's still at RigaTony's with Heidi, less than a half hour away.

"Hello?"

"Vic," I say, relieved. "Hey, listen, I know you're—"

"Hello?"

"Vic? Can't you hear me?"

"You didn't honestly fall for that, did you?" *Beep.*

I let out a grunt of frustration, forgetting how obnoxious Vic can be, even in his voice- mail greetings. "Vic, Rusty broke down. Dad couldn't pick me up from the pageant tonight, so I'm stuck. I know you're out with Heidi, but can you come get me?"

I gather my things as best I can and head out. Some guy from the tech crew congratulates me as we pass in the hallway. I thank him, wondering how I'm going to get home. I'm sure Donna is still

288 • Laura Johnston

around, but how embarrassing is that? Her new Miss City of Maricopa doesn't even have a ride home from the pageant.

I reach a fork in the darkening hallway, feeling like a total loser as I accept the fact that I'm stranded.

"Incredible performance."

I turn toward the voice, finding Damian and Fin.

"Thank you," I say, equal parts relieved and surprised to see them still here.

Damian leans up against the wall beside me, his close presence over my shoulder reminding me of that day in the copy center when I first met him. We exchange small talk about the pageant and then they offer to walk me out to my car.

"Actually"—this is rich—"I don't have a car. Or a ride home."

"No problem," Damian says. "We'll give you a ride."

"Yeah?" Such a relief.

They offer to help carry my stuff out. I gladly hand over my dress bags, the act of separating my things making me realize I forgot something.

"My pageant heels," I say. "Hang on. Sorry. I think I left them in the dressing room."

"We'll buy you a new pair," Damian says, which makes me laugh. Still, I note the impatient edge to his voice. He's ready to get out of here. This night—this entire pageant—wouldn't have turned out the way it did without Damian Acklen.

"Just a sec," I say and open the door of the dressing room.

I call Vic one more time, not about to fall for his stupid voice-mail greeting this time. "Vic," I say after the beep, bending down to look for my shoes under the counter. "Never mind. My sponsor, Damian Acklen, and his brother Fin are giving me a ride home. Thanks."

Sparkly heels catch my eye. I snag them from beneath the counter.

"Julianna!" Donna catches me outside the dressing room, looking dead on her feet after such a long night and yet still keyed up from all the excitement.

Crew members are packing up props and cleaning. I glance over my shoulder toward Damian and Fin and try to break away, but Donna fires up talk about upcoming events. A fund-raiser next week for the Children's Miracle Network, speaking at a school flag-raising ceremony, possibly even having me sing the National Anthem at sporting events. The list goes on, reminding me of how very real this is. So much responsibility and yet so much potential. I'm grateful. It's like a whole world of possibility has been opened to me.

"Sorry it's such a long drive," I say to Damian and Fin as we finally make our way into the parking lot.

"Nah," he says over his shoulder. "It'll give us time to talk."

About what, I'm not sure. It dawns on me how very little I know about Damian and his brother. Two strangers, really. And they're giving me a ride home.

When I spot Damian's black sports car—a *Jaguar*—I recall what he said about Cody going to Acklen Motors. Why? Damian told me Cody has a thing for Jaguars. And yet Cody didn't want me anywhere near these two. So why would he go to Damian's luxury car lot? Because he loves Jaguars or because he was suspicious? Just how much of his dad does he have in him?

"Something wrong?"

I look up, realizing I've stopped walking. I force a smile.

They're trouble, Cody told me. He thinks they were involved in the accident.

"No," I say. "I'm fine." But it's a lie. Suspicion creeps in, constricting my throat.

Cody said he remembers a drug deal—with Vic—and he remembers running into that mall scared. I discounted it, told him he was foolish. Yet now I recall the way he was at the mall that night, his eyes darting around, his forehead perspiring. He wasn't the cool, confident Cody I've come to know since.

Is it possible that Damian and Fin know Vic?

I didn't trust Cody, just as he didn't trust me. He believed Candace's story.

Thoughts ricochet in my mind, driving me crazy. Fin asked me how Cody and I met. Did he already know? I shake the ludicrous thought away, but more thoughts flit to the surface in its place.

Damian had heard all about Cody's injury—from a news article, he said. It made sense then, but now I can't shake this unnerving feeling that something doesn't add up. And it makes me wonder: Why exactly is Damian Acklen here?

I pin my gaze on him as he opens his trunk. To support me, yes, but why? Out of the goodness of his heart? To be a good sponsor, adding another charity to his list? Or does he like me?

This possibility is so farfetched it nearly makes me laugh. Rich,

290 • *Laura Johnston*

attractive, successful Damian Acklen certainly has a dozen beautiful women after him. What is his motive?

Denica's warning shuffles back to memory, all about the worst part of winning being the creeps that follow you around afterward. But Damian is no creep. He's the wealthy businessman, the owner of a luxury sports car lot who donates to animal and cancer charities.

All the more reason for me not to trust him, Cody had said when I told him that very thing. *What's he trying to cover up?*

And here I am, *about to get in Damian's car*. I tell myself off for being so distrustful. I'm beginning to remind myself of Cody.

"I'm going to call my brother real quick to make sure he isn't on his way," I say anyway.

"No need," Fin says, extending a hand to take my things from me.

Suddenly, something about this situation has me wanting to back away. Find another ride home. Run.

Tires squeal. A flash of headlights blind me as a car whirls into the parking lot. A Corvette.

Cody.

His Vette screeches to a stop and he jumps out, his jaw tight, his eyes narrowed in on Damian. The sight of him makes my heart stagger, skipping a beat in its already erratic tempo. He's here. The relief pouring in makes me realize how nervous I am.

Damian and Fin have turned their attention, too. Cody takes three measured strides to Damian before punching him in the face.

I scream as fists start flying, and my heart catapults into my throat. Fin dashes around the car to get in on it. No words, just fists.

Someone is on the ground now. Cody? I've dropped all my things. Call the police? Yes. I scramble for my cell phone before someone behind me yells. A woman. Donna.

She and members of the tech crew are across the parking lot. Fin pauses. Now I see blood on his fist, and I realize it must be Cody's.

My gut sinks.

And yet Fin's face doesn't look so good either. Damian turns his attention to Donna as well. Blood gathers on his lower lip.

Fin backs away, making his way to the passenger door of the Jaguar in a flash. Then another car zips into the parking lot. The Buick. Vic pops open the door, but Heidi stays inside.

"Fin," Vic calls out, the name putting my pulse on hold. They *do* know each other. Which means Cody was telling the truth. He *does* remember. A drug deal gone bad. Vic got Cody into this whole mess.

"It's gone." Cody's voice.

I bite down on my lip as I round the Jaguar to see him on the ground. Blood drips from his nose, weaving a red trail over his lips and down his chin. I gasp and cover my mouth.

"The recording," Cody says. "The phone. It's gone. I threw it away. Now leave her alone."

Damian looks satisfied with this as he gets to his feet and steps back to his car. A smile slithers over his lips.

The *recording*? The *phone*?

The Jaguar pulls out of the parking lot before Donna even reaches us, its deep rumble fading into the distance along with its taillights. Cody gets to his feet.

"What happened?" Donna is at my side now. "Are you okay? Oh my—"

Color drains from her face as she takes in the sight of Cody's bloody nose. "I'm calling the police."

Her phone is already drawn out.

Cody wipes the blood away with the back of his hand. "It was just a misunderstanding."

"You need medical attention," Donna counters.

"We'll get him to a hospital." Vic. He's at Cody's side now, his hand clasping Cody's shoulder like a best friend as he urges him back to his car.

Cody shrugs him off. "We wouldn't have been in this mess if it weren't for you."

"Cool off," Vic says, keeping his voice low.

"Did you know?" Cody asks. "About the recording? That's why you've kept your distance ever since the accident, huh? You claimed you didn't know me and you were glad I'd lost my memory."

Vic glances our way and so does Cody. Vic steps toward his car, facing away. Heidi stands outside the open passenger door.

"His dad is FBI," I say to Donna, as though a link to the FBI lends some credibility to Cody, the one who started the fight. The thought of having police show up has my nerves on edge. I want to leave, to pretend none of this happened. At least give my mind some time to assimilate the events of the night.

Now that Vic and Cody are done, Donna won't stop talking, and yet I struggle to process a single word she says. Something about being a witness if we need one, and will I be all right?

"Yes, yes, I'm fine," I say as Donna helps me pluck my dress bags from the ground. Cody is here, too, bending down to help. Donna flinches at the sight of him.

"I've got this," he says and gathers up everything, easily carrying three dress bags, two pairs of heels, and my makeup tote in one arm. My bouquet in the other.

"Jewel, get in," Vic says, gesturing to our car.

But Cody is already putting my things into the back of his.

"I'll take her home," Cody says.

I dither back and forth between the two cars before hopping into Cody's. The familiar leather seat and close confines of his car calm me, the purr of the engine comforts me. Once we're in fifth gear on the freeway, Cody takes my hand in his, and it feels good. Safe. Before long, however, the silence between us that was once relaxing becomes uncomfortable.

"I'm sorry," I say, still baffled at the confirmation that Vic knows Damian and Fin. Vic must have come as soon as he heard my last message, the one when I told him I was getting a ride home with Damian Acklen and his brother Fin. "I didn't believe you—your story—and I should have."

Cody glances down at our clasped hands with a hint of a smile before returning his gaze to the road. "It's okay."

I wish he'd say more. Damian and Fin are drug dealers, rich drug dealers. And Vic knows them. This reality spins around in my head, part of my mind refusing to accept it.

"Are we—" I pause—"in danger? Me, you, Vic . . ."

"No."

Said with such assuredness.

"Without the recording, I'm no real threat to them," he says.

"What recording?"

"Of the drug deal," he explains. "That night, with Vic. I told Vic I didn't want any part of it, but I didn't get away in time. They showed up; Fin and some other guy. I recorded it all."

"And Damian?" I ask.

"He showed up later that night during the dust storm. He hit me with his car—that Jaguar. I recognized his license plate when I drove up just now. He searched my pockets for my phone, but it was already gone."

"So you remember?" I say. "The accident . . . the mall?"

He shakes his head, the muscle beneath the five o'clock shadow on his jaw clenching in frustration. "I don't remember much between throwing my phone away in the mall and getting hit by his car."

"You *threw it away*?"

"It was damaged," he explains. "Totally shattered."

"Oh," I say, but so much of this still doesn't make sense. "But I don't understand why Damian would come back around. Wouldn't he want to stay away from you? Wouldn't he worry about jarring your memory?"

"Thing is," he says, "I gave him a reason to worry that my memory was already coming back. I stopped by his car lot. The Acklen Motor logo caught my eye, and it looked familiar."

"And he recognized you."

Cody nods.

Did he give you anything else? I recall what Damian asked me at the *Night with the Arts*, and my shoulders deflate. It seemed like an odd question then. Yet I realize now what was behind it. What was behind everything he did.

"Damian thought you might have given your phone to me," I say. "At the mall."

Cody nods again, and it all clicks. Here I thought I did some amazing thing by landing a wealthy sponsor on my own.

"Damian was getting close to me to get information, to tie up loose ends," I say, receiving another silent nod from Cody.

"He's one of the smart ones," Cody says. "The smart drug dealers. Their distributors don't even know who they are. I'm pretty sure Vic didn't know Damian, not before tonight at least. During the drug deal he asked Fin when he'd get to meet 'Ian,' meaning Damian, and Fin said he wouldn't.

"If one of the lower drug dealers gets caught, they'll almost always rat out the higher-ups to get time off their sentences. The smart dealers insulate themselves. Having a perfect cover-up business to account for mounting income is a smart move, too. An owner of a luxury car lot like Damian would have an easy time spending lots of dough without getting flagged by the government.

"But he was also stupid because Fin is his brother, and I got him on camera. A recording like that is perfect evidence. Irrefutable. If I somehow still had the recording, or access to it from you, Damian would have every reason to be worried."

"But you don't," I say, obviously bringing his enthusiasm down a notch.

His deep exhalation is almost a grunt. "No."

"But you remember, Cody," I say. "You remember the accident. Can't you tell the police?"

"Yeah, I can. But the accident was more than four months ago, and I did get a serious concussion. Memory loss. My memories are worth nothing, especially in court. Can you picture me taking the stand, a kid who's had *amnesia*, testifying against guys like Damian and Fin without any solid evidence? Defense attorneys would have a royal laugh at my expense, and they'd have every right to."

"What about Vic?" I ask. "Couldn't he testify?"

"Yeah, but would he?"

"Good point."

It's only eleven o'clock when we pull up to my house but it feels so much later.

"Congratulations, by the way," Cody says with a smile, his eyes dropping to the boxed crown in my hands. "I knew you'd win."

I certainly didn't. I didn't see any of this coming. The interview, the pageant, the fight between Damian and Cody—it's hard to believe so much happened in one day.

"I'm sorry, too," he says, the porch light from my house illuminating his green eyes in the darkness. "I trust you. That whole thing with Candace and the sweater story—I shouldn't have brought it up."

"It's okay," I say.

He lifts my hand and presses his lips to my knuckles, holding my gaze as he repeats, "I'm sorry."

In light of everything that's happened, Candace's twisted story and the fact that Cody might have believed her shouldn't matter, but his apology means the world nonetheless.

Did he give you anything else?

The lingering excitement of the night refuses to leave me alone long enough for me to fall asleep. Damian's question won't leave me alone either.

The glittering crown rests on my dresser in the darkness. I stare at it, thinking back to that visit with Mama at the beginning of the summer when all of this started. I recall the sweltering Arizona heat as we left the prison, the brown landscape dotted by cactus reminding me of how trapped I felt. I see this place differently now, see myself differently.

Did he give you anything else?

The question repeats in my mind as I toss around in bed.

I'm not sure which Dad was more surprised to see earlier tonight when I returned home: the crown in my hands or Cody Rush helping me bring my things in, his nose still carrying a trace of blood.

"You won," Dad pointed out once Cody left.

I nodded. "And Hephaestus?" I asked hopefully.

Dad shook his head. I can't say I was surprised the hunk of scrap metal didn't win an award at the gala, but I felt bad for my dad anyway. "Next year," I assured him and headed for bed.

Vic comes home late. I hear him crash in his room at 1:47 a.m. Part of me wants to barge through his door and demand the full story, while the other part of me aches to remain in denial. He was dealing drugs after Mama went to prison, which means her sacrifice for him was for nothing. He hasn't changed at all.

Despite my restlessness I fall asleep, but the craziness of the night maintains a tight clasp on my subconscious. I'm at The Chocolate Shoppe. My apron is a mess. It's been a long day and I'm about to close. But then I fumble a bottle of caramel and hold my breath as it dives off the counter, plummeting toward the ground before someone sweeps in and catches it.

I look up to find two very green eyes staring into mine.

"Got it," he says, one side of his smile tilting upward into a crooked grin with killer dimples.

Cody.

It's a dream, a very pleasant dream as I relive that night in broken fragments, everything from him ordering chocolates to the photobooth pictures to parting ways in the mall parking lot.

"Hey," I call after him as he walks away. He turns, still walking as I hold up his chocolates and stuffed dog. "You almost forgot."

He shakes his head, walking backward with a wide smile. "They're for you," he calls out.

I look at the bag of chocolates in my hand—all of *my* favorite chocolates—and the dog, stunned.

The dog.

I spring out of bed, feeling light-headed and confused. *The dog.* Cody did give me something else that night.

The glow of early dawn slithers in through the broken slats of my blinds, illuminating my closet door with a hazy blue light. I throw open the closet and search through my things on hands and knees, remembering how I threw the stuffed animal in here in a senseless rage after seeing Cody at school that first day. And then I forgot all about it.

My hand brushes past something soft and fluffy and I drag it out. The dog.

I stare at the cute white dog, wondering what on earth would possess Cody to take the time to buy a stuffed animal at the mall when he knew he was in danger.

What if Cody's memory failed him yet again? Is it possible he didn't throw his phone away after all?

I squeeze the dog, shifting the stuffing aside as I feel around. Nothing. No phone.

I let out a resigned breath of air. It was worth a try. Some of the stuffing has fallen out, littering the carpet at my knees. Curious, I pull the dog up to eye level, finding an opening in the seam—almost like someone tore it open.

I shove my finger inside and feel around, wondering if I'm crazy. Or could it be? A tiny piece of something hard touches my finger and I pinch, drawing it out to reveal a flat little square. A SIM card. For an iPhone.

I sit on my bed and stare at it. The clock on my wall ticks with the passing of time. My initial feelings of triumph ebb as I consider what this could mean—for Vic. Fin and Damian aren't the only ones this recording will bring down. Am I actually considering this? Handing over incriminating evidence on another member of my family to Special Agent Rush?

Minute after minute passes until two hours have gone by.

I find myself at Vic's bedroom door a moment later, slowly pushing it open to reveal a still-sleeping Vic, his sheets a tangled mess around him. The earthy, stale scent that is so my brother reaches my senses. It's foul and yet, at this moment, oddly endearing. My throat tightens. Vic is a mess and is most likely involved with drugs again. When will it end?

He stirs in his bed. I should dart down the hallway, close the door, or at least flinch at the thought of Vic finding me in his room uninvited, but I stand my ground.

His brow twists in confusion when he sees me.

I hold up the SIM card, feeling the sting of tears in my eyes and wondering if I should have gone behind his back after all. But he's my brother. The only sibling I have.

"This is it, Vic," I say. "Cody's recording of the drug deal. It wasn't thrown away after all."

Vic sits up, his feet touching the floor as he buries his head in his hands and exhales.

I brace myself for his tirade. "Cody doesn't know I have it."

Vic stands. I swallow hard, reminding myself to be strong. He walks toward me, navigating through the piles of laundry and trash on his floor.

He plucks the SIM card from my fingers, towering over me.

"It will catch up to you someday, Vic," I say past the lump in my throat. "One day, sooner or later."

Cody's argument about right and wrong comes to mind, and I agonize over whether I'm doing the right thing. I close my eyes as though I can block out reality. Here I am handing this valuable piece of evidence over to the person it incriminates. How can I go on being Cody's friend keeping this piece of the puzzle from him? He was the victim that night. The truth is the least he deserves.

Vic's fingers touch mine, and I open my eyes. He places the SIM card in my palm and closes my fingers around it.

He nods once. Twice. "I know," he says. "And this belongs to Cody."

Brushing past me toward the bathroom, Vic leaves me in his open doorway without another word.

CHAPTER 40

Cody

I stare at the box in my closet. *Cody's Room: Jimmy's things.* I slide the lid open with ease this time, knowing Jimmy would have wanted this. Forgetting, I've learned, is rarely the solution. He would have wanted me to remember all the times we shared, from the very best to the bitter end.

The deck of old-fashioned baseball cards rests on the top. I smile. I shift through the Ninja Turtles, spotting a few other action figures I hadn't noticed before. And then the time machine. My smile broadens.

"It's a time machine," Jimmy had answered my questioning stare when I found him hunched over the LEGO creation.

"You traveling ahead in time, Jimmy?" I'd teased him.

"No, I'm coming back in time someday."

"What for?"

"In case I grow up someday and lose my imagination, like all the adults say you do. This way I can come back and remember all these genius ideas I've got."

Jimmy was a lot of things. Humble wasn't one of them.

The sketchbook is the hardest part. My hand brushes over the thick cover, wiping away some dust. I open it at last, finding one of Jimmy's earliest sketches of our family. The second is a sketch of him as a kid dressed in full Luke Skywalker attire with Yoda on his back. Another of himself with a bat raised over his shoulder on home base. The picture of the Scottsdale Stadium catches my eye, the one I watched Jimmy draw on his eighth birthday.

Time Machine Figure 1: NBA Star Cody Rush

I smile at the caption above the next drawing. The sketch is of me as an adult wearing a red Chicago Bulls jersey. It's a pretty good depiction of me, actually, the older me Jimmy never saw. I turn the page to find another time machine picture. This one is of me behind the wheels of a nice sports car. So far, I'm loving the future Jimmy drew for me.

Page after page, picture after picture of the future as Jimmy saw it. I've never seen these until now.

Time Machine Figure 7: Special Agent Cody Rush

There I stand with my gun drawn, an oversized badge at my hip. But where is Jimmy? I turn the page, finding it blank. This was it; the last picture Jimmy drew. I flip back and stare at Special Agent Cody Rush again. It's only me, no Special Agent Jimmy Rush at my side. In fact, every time machine picture has only one person in it: me.

A few other odds and ends are scattered along the bottom of the box: a Buzz Lightyear and some plastic binoculars I remember getting in a kid's meal. I place everything except the sketchbook back inside. Time machine. Ninja Turtles. Baseball cards last of all. I situate the lid on top and put it back in my closet. Things Jimmy would have wanted me to keep.

I take the sketchbook to my desk and place it where I can see it. Today. Tomorrow. Maybe I'll leave it there forever. Special Agent Cody Rush stares back at me from the page.

He should go inside. I recall the thought I had that day when Jimmy and I were pelting lizards with our airsoft gun in the backyard, the day he got sick. I ignored that instinct and it's haunted me for years.

I grab my wallet and keys, glancing back at my room as I shut the door. There will always be too much quiet, a voice that's missing, empty spaces where Jimmy's things would have been. But maybe, as his time machine pictures suggest, Jimmy was okay with that.

I brush my teeth before heading out for the night. Hot date. Nine o'clock. I spit and rinse, placing my toothbrush back on the second shelf from the bottom as always. A new brush rests on the shelf below mine. Unwrapped but unused. Like it has for the past eight years. I take in a deep breath and let it go—everything. And I put the toothbrush in the trash.

"Have you been in here before?" the dark-haired, blue-eyed beauty asks me from across the counter.

I lean up against the display of chocolates and work up a mischievous grin. "Unfortunately, I don't remember."

It's true; I still don't recall coming into The Chocolate Shoppe that night or taking the photo-booth pictures.

Julianna places her palms on the counter and leans forward, a flirtatious smile playing at her lips as she inches toward me. "Hmm, well, you're missing out."

"Am I?"

She nods, her bottom lip drawn between her teeth in the enticing way that makes me want to pull her right up over the counter and kiss her breathless.

"So, what can I get for you?" she asks as she puts on a new set of gloves. "Are you buying for yourself or someone else?"

"Someone else."

"Someone special?"

I nod, crossing my arms and leaning on the counter to bridge the distance that's been between us for far too long. "She has no idea."

Julianna smiles, the corners of her lips curving into her everreddening cheeks. "Well," she says and stands tall again, digging her hand into her hip. There's that attitude I love. "Then you'd better buy her some chocolates to let her know."

"Think that'll do the trick?"

"Mm-hm."

"We're on then," I say. "Get me a box of nothing but the best."

Julianna points out her favorite chocolates, boxing each one. Plenty of milk buttercream and lots of Rocky Road.

"Throw in a few of those almond buds, too," I say.

She lifts a skeptical brow. "You sure this girl of yours likes nuts?"

"Those are for me."

She laughs. We both tease and laugh as we close down the shop for the night and head out. We eat chocolates and take photo-booth pictures, recreating our first unofficial date. I plan on never forgetting this one.

Picture number one: chocolates in our mouth.

Picture number two: chocolate-covered smiles.

Picture number three: a chocolate-tasting kiss. I could get used to these.

I interlock my fingers with hers, drawing her hand up between us like that day in my backyard when we were covered in mud. Julianna looks into my eyes and whispers, "I love you, too."

The machine flashes. Picture number four down.

"I should have told you that night at homecoming," she says.

I look at our hands, enjoying the feel of her fingers in mine.

"And I wanted to tell you thank you," she continues. "For the other night at the pageant. For coming. Thank you for everything."

"I only wish I could have been there to hear you sing again," I say, recalling the day she sang while I played the guitar.

"How about a personal performance sometime?"

I smile. "We're on."

Julianna's expression turns solemn. She lets her hand drop. "I have something for you. Vic and I have something for you."

"Vic?"

She nods. Takes a deep breath. She reaches into her purse and draws something out.

"What is it?" I say, unable to see what's between her fingers in this dark photo booth.

She grips whatever it is in her fist before turning it over to me. "It's yours, Cody. You didn't lose it. Turn it in to the police; give it to your dad—whatever you need to do. Vic knows, and he's ready to face the consequences."

I stare at the tiny SIM card in her palm. A SIM card. For an iPhone.

I look up in disbelief. "Is this . . ."

She nods.

"How?"

"You gave it to me that night, only I didn't know. You hid it in the stuffed dog."

"What stuffed dog?"

She pulls the curtain aside and points to the stand of stuffed animals down the hallway. "You can buy me another one if you really want to re-create that night," she says, one corner of her lips curling up playfully.

"The recording," I say as I take the SIM card. Here it is. Solid evidence that will answer so many questions about that night. I look back at her, carefully reading her expression. Turning this in can only mean more heartache for her family. "Are you sure?"

She nods.

"Is Vic sure?"

Again she nods.

Dad will be happy, satisfied even. Julianna's turning this in will sway his opinion of her for sure. Mom, Lizzy, and Rachel all love her. He's bound to come around after this.

"Come on," Julianna says, pulling back the curtain and climbing out.

I follow her, stepping on some type of card on my way. Trash, probably. A punch card for the carousel or a food court restaurant. But as I step away, the card catches my eye and I can't look away.

"Come on," Julianna calls out, already ahead of me. But I can't stop staring at it. What are the chances?

"What is it?" Julianna asks, back at my side. She bends down, picks it up, and flips it back and forth like a piece of junk she's considering tossing. "Hm, a baseball card."

She tucks it into the front pocket of my shirt and gives my chest a pat.

I look down at the pocket, frozen. Deep in thought.

Our discussion of right and wrong, mercy and justice weighs on my mind. Julianna was right. Life isn't fair. I've known that ever since Jimmy died. But I've learned a few things since that first night here in the mall, things I don't fully comprehend and may never really understand. That maybe life isn't all chance. Maybe some things happen for a reason. Maybe, even, Julianna and I were brought together that night by a force beyond our control.

"You were right, you know," I say.

"Right about what?" Julianna asks. "That you're a pretty boy?" She snags the photo-booth pictures from my hand and throws me a wink. "Don't let it go to your head."

She grabs my hand with a flirtatious smile and leads me to the exit.

"So, what now?" I ask. "My part of the date is over. The second half was yours to plan."

She holds up a plastic bag. "Two cupcakes, specially made. Then basketball at a park. I wore my tennis shoes."

I throw her a curious glance as I open the mall door for her.

"Don't judge," she says and steps out. "After spending everything on that pageant, I'm tight on funds again. Had to get creative."

"Basketball, though?" I ask. "Are you sure?"

She pinches the rim of my hat and tugs it down. "The sport might be growing on me."

Cupcakes and basketball? My luck keeps getting better.

"You know, I can take you to a show or something if you'd rather—"

"Uh-uh." She cuts me off. "I expect you to bring your best game. I've never seen you play and I'm curious to find out if you're as good a ball player as you are a kisser."

"So this is *that* type of competition?" I ask, receiving a playful nod from her in return as we walk to my car. Her bottom lip is pulled between smiling teeth.

Game on.

Read on for an excerpt from Laura Johnston's evocative young adult novel *Rewind to You*, available now in ebook or print on demand.

WISH YOU WERE HERE

One last summer before college on beautiful Tybee Island is supposed to help Sienna forget. But how can she? This is where her family spent every summer before everything changed, before the world as she knew it was ripped away.

But the past isn't easily left behind. Especially when Sienna keeps having episodes that take her back to the night she wants to forget. Even when she meets the mysterious Austin Dobbs, the guy with the intense blue eyes, athlete's body, and weakness for pralines who scooped her out of trouble when she blacked out on River Street.

When she's with Austin, Sienna feels a whole new world opening up to her. Austin has secrets, and she has history. But caught between the past and the future, Sienna can still choose what happens now . . .

"A fabulous, fresh new voice in YA."
—Kay Lynn Mangum, author of *The Secret Journal of Brett Colton*

"Laura Johnston scores a touchdown with this coming-of-age love story."
—Kelly Nelson, author of *The Keeper's Saga*

"This poignant, sweet romance gripped my heart from beginning to end."
—Jennette Green, author of *The Commander's Desire*

I toss my cell in my purse and take a deep breath, inhaling the sugary scent of vanilla and pecans. It's the smell of River Street.

Let's make a pact.

The words I heard my dad speak when I passed out drift back to my mind. But what was our pact? A crippling ache seeps into my heart as a thought settles in: *I'm already starting to forget him.*

I walk back toward my car, brushing these thoughts aside as I try to enjoy the simple things: birds chirping, an artist painting the Savannah River, a pair of shoes I'm tempted to buy. But I step in a wad of fresh gum and a bird craps in my hair like I was target practice, and I quickly admit this trip to River Street was a total waste. Darkness closes in, and streetlamps cast shadows around me as I walk back through the park, one heel sticking to the pavement with every step.

I distract myself with my phone in time to see a text from my mom.

CAN U PICK UP SOME LUCKY CHARMS ON YOUR WAY HOME? I FORGOT. GET A BUNCH.

Oh, man. The Legos thrown across our living room will be nothing compared to what will happen in the morning if we don't have Lucky Charms. Not that I blame Spencer. If he didn't put his foot down every once in a while, Mom would have both of us eating a bowl of hot wheat cereal and a green (aka grass) smoothie at every breakfast.

Knots unwind in my stomach when I spot the stone staircase that leads to my car. Ha! *Mom had no need to worry,* I think, pleased with myself.

The catcall whistling from the shadows doesn't register until they step under the dim streetlamp, two of them. Despite myself, I gasp.

"Hello, sweetheart," one of them drawls with a wink. "Wanna take a walk?"

Oh please. One whiff and I can smell alcohol on his breath.

I step back, surprising myself by how quickly I form a profile. Five feet ten inches, maybe. Baggy shirt and way too much cologne. The other guy is easily in his thirties as well, yet his spotty mustache makes him look fourteen.

"Excuse me," I say, and move to get around them, but they shift to block my way.

Cologne jabs Mustache in the arm playfully. "Hey, the lady doesn't want to be bothered."

I welcome the slightest bit of reassurance. *There still are gentlemen in this world,* I tell myself just before they burst into laughter. I march a path around them.

"Aww, come on, baby. We're just playing. You want to have some fun tonight?"

I step over a puddle of mud. "Absolutely not."

By the time I look back up, they've materialized in front of me, blocking my way again. I glance around, searching for backup. Anyone. Like a slingshot snapping against my chest, anxiety seizes my nerves.

I clutch my phone, prepared to break into a run and dial for help if I have to. But who would I call? Mom? No way. Brian would rush to my aid, but he'd have a royal laugh after I so confidently assured him I'd be fine. And Kyle is three states away. 911 is always an option but a bit of a dramatic one at this point.

A group of people walk through the park within earshot. But they are laughing hysterically (probably every bit as drunk as these two), oblivious to the ridiculous fix I'm in, and besides, really, I can handle this. I hoist my purse strap on my shoulder and dig one hand into my hip, gathering gumption.

"Listen," I say, hoping I don't look as flustered as I feel. But Mustache drapes his arm over my shoulders, and a chill quivers up the back of my neck.

I slap his arm away. "Back off, Mustache." The nickname slips off my tongue.

He gives an amused laugh. "Ooh, she's a feisty one."

Rock 'em sock 'em? That's a joke. I clench one fist, wondering how much damage I could do. I tighten my grasp on my purse, wishing I had some pepper spray or an umbrella or even a high heel I could wield as a weapon. Still, one scream and someone will surely hear.

"C'mon, sweetheart. We're just having some fun," Cologne slurs.

"And I don't want any part of it, so get out of my way."

Mustache sighs. "Aww, you're going to miss the fireworks."

Fireworks. My eyes lock on the space behind them, caught in an abrupt trance. I'm speechless. Immobilized. Oddly numb to everything going on around me as the suppressed memory of fireworks crashes back to the forefront of my mind.

Please, no. Not fireworks. Despite the muggy air, goose bumps ripple up my arms as the chilling memory creeps to the surface. I jolt as a sharp crack rattles my ears. A burst of light illuminates everything, casting a red glow on the faces of the two men. I shudder, daring a glance at the falling specks of fire.

Today is June fifth, a Friday. I forgot. The first Friday of every month, fireworks shower the sky over River Street. Fireworks rupture above me, an explosion of colors. Thundering. Crackling. Fizzling. Just like they did *that night.*

My heart slams against my chest. Suddenly I feel as though I'm sinking in water with no way of swimming out, fighting to breathe. Another explosion splits the dark sky, and like a cannon, sends a crack pulsating through the air.

It happened almost one year ago on the Fourth of July. We should have been here in Georgia, but we weren't. Because of me.

I picture my dad and me in the Jeep that night, the smiles on our faces. Images flash through my mind, dulling my vision. The fireworks were so intense I could almost feel them vibrating my Jeep as my dad and I zipped over the bridge. Fireworks so stunning, I didn't see the motorcycle veer into our lane.

I jerked the steering wheel instinctively. I overcorrected, glimps-

ing the two motorcyclists the second before our Jeep tipped, rolled, hit the barricade, and then—

They say we hit the barricade mid-roll and flipped right over it, vanishing from the sight of any witness on the highway. As for myself, I can't remember anything between that and the moment I woke up with water spilling into my mouth, as the river swallowed our Jeep. The windshield caved in, and water flooded in so fast I never got that last breath.

The tart smell of fireworks saturates the muggy Savannah air, so thick I can almost taste it. Cold sweat creeps to the surface of my skin, like it did earlier tonight when I looked at the picture of my dad and me. Right before I fainted.

Spots begin swimming across my field of vision. Numbing tingles course up and down my arms.

Not again.

This silly trip to River Street isn't only a waste, it's a disaster. I feel a hand wrap around my arm, but their words and laughter are as muddled as my vision. They pull me along. I draw in a shaky breath. "Leave me alone!"

I fight against them, but the blood rushes out of my head, my arms, my legs, leaving every muscle useless. I'm like some stupid damsel who can't do a thing to save herself.

"Let go!" I hear the shrill pitch of my voice and realize just how terrified I am. But the seconds stretch on, and I know I'm alone.

In the corner of my blurry field of vision, I glimpse another figure advancing, someone who must have heard me yell. Mustache backs off after my scream, but this timely hero yanks him away regardless and shoves him to the ground.

"Hey!" Mustache yells, climbing to his feet. Cologne comes to the aid of his pal, seizing a fistful of this guy's shirt and yelling something up into his face. Mustache and Cologne look like dwarfs compared to this guy. I try to steady myself so I can get a look at this saint of a man who is helping me, but all I can make out from his blurred silhouette is that he's tall and seriously built and he wears a baseball cap.

I grab my head and try to pull myself together, my lungs short of breath. I'm angry at how weak I feel, how useless. Voices argue, short and to the point. The last thing I see before my legs melt into numbness is how fast Mustache hits the pavement after my baseball cap hero punches him.

My dad. Although reason fights against it, it has to be him. This feeling of calm. Safety. His arms barely catch me before I hit the ground. He leans over me, cradling me in his arms.

"Are you okay?" His voice comes as an echo, something barely there and fading quickly.

Then a bright light replaces everything.

"Are you okay?"

My heart squeezes at his voice, and my head jerks up. The blinding light surrenders to the scene before me and I see him clearly.

My dad.

The sight of his deep, caring eyes renders me speechless.

Dad gestures to my leg. "Are you okay?"

I glance down, feeling the pain at last. Fresh blood seeps from a cut on my shin.

"Oh, yeah—" My voice breaks. I clear my throat, and as I do, the weightlessness of the moment sucks all the pain of the past year away.

He's here.

This may only be a dream, but he's here. My dad is behind our home in Richmond with a shovel in one hand and a glass of apple juice in the other. And then the recollection strikes.

I saw him like this earlier this evening, after I fainted in the beach house. A hint of apple juice reaches my nose, the perfect blend of sweet and sour, and it all comes back. He was holding the juice when I fainted the first time, too. Juice squeezed from apples off our trees. Nothing could be more vivid than that scent. But what are the chances of having the exact same dream twice in one day?

He takes a sip, lets out a sigh of satisfaction, and offers the tall glass to me. I glance around at the garden we stand in. Our garden, the place where I used to sneak my dolls out for a tea party. This was a place I could get muddy and my mom couldn't protest. Our property was always immaculate, fruitful. I never understood how Dad did it. Life and happiness flourished around him, something I miss.

I look down at my muddy shovel, suddenly remembering that time I whacked myself in the shin with my own shovel. Memories flutter in, scattered pieces filing back into place. This incident in the garden occurred hours before the accident. How could I have forgotten?

I smile. "If we don't suffer a little, we won't remember it, right?"

Dad smiles and extends the juice again.

Cold liquid trickles down my throat as I drink, as refreshing as the memories it evokes. I'm at a loss for words, shocked at what's happening. So I lean back against the picket fence and decide to simply relish this miracle.

Dad shifts his gaze to the sunset just visible above the thick trees. "You know, Sienna, there aren't too many moments quite like this."

I nod, because whatever is happening right now is definitely not normal. It feels so real. I wish it would last forever.

"Let's make a pact," he says, and I feel seven again, making a promise with a best friend. "Let's remember it, okay? This moment."

Ah, *the pact*. I look around, the beauty of this place sinking into memory with ease: our tiered fountain, the apple trees, the vines around each post of our gazebo. Finally, I nod.

"And when times get rough," he says, "we can rewind to this moment and remember the taste of a job well done. We can remember how great this day was."

A lump swells in my throat as I recall who was behind the wheel that night: *me*. "Okay, it's a pact."

I'm so focused on my dad that I don't notice the white speck flittering across my vision, then two and three specks. My dad becomes a blur, and a wave of nausea hits my stomach as I'm jerked away from him, swept away from the garden altogether.

"Can you hear me?" someone asks. I feel a hand on my shoulder and another one cradling my head. I open my eyes, totally confused as the blurry outline of a figure bent over me comes into view. And the baseball cap.

"Hey, there you are," whoever is holding me says, his voice lowering into a tone of relief. With a twinge in my heart, I realize it isn't my dad. My balance stabilizes, my body grounded again in reality. Besides a pounding headache, I'm pain-free. My shin is fine.

"Ugh." An ugly-sounding something stumbles from my lips as the nausea dissipates. I blink, remembering that I need to get home. I try to push myself into a sitting position, but before I can, he scoops me off the ground. Startled, I reach for his shoulders for balance. And *oh my*. Something about the muscles beneath my fingertips makes me draw back and then wish I hadn't.

I open my mouth to assure him I can walk, but I glimpse his sharp jaw and strong chin, and the connection between my mind and my mouth floats away. My eyes travel over his lips and then to his eyes, and my heart freaks out. Skips a beat. The most impossibly blue eyes I've ever seen stare back into mine, and I lose not only my train of thought but all control of my gaping eyes as well.

One side of his mouth pulls into something of a grin, his face inches from mine. His eyes trace the outline of my forehead down to my chin and linger on my lips. Then his gaze meets mine again. He raises a brow. "Are you all right?"

"Y-y-yes." My voice comes out like a frog's croak. "Fine. Thanks."

"You sure?"

"Mm-hm." Another attempt to steady my voice. I try to get my flirt on, flashing a smile as I assure him, "The ground can walk just fine."

That puts a smile on his face.

"I mean, *I* can walk just fine. On the ground. You can set me down." I bite my tongue before I do more damage.

"Right," he says doubtfully. Something in the way he holds me, the brazen expression on his face as he looks into my eyes, tells me I should be careful.

"I'm good. I promise."

He sets me down at last. Now that I'm out of his arms and can think straight, I finally get a rational look at him. Dark hair, only visible around the edge of his baseball cap. Thick hair. Total girl magnet. He's at least six inches taller than my five foot seven. All right, even out of his arms, my heart rattles around so fast I fear another blackout, or whatever just happened.

He watches me as I wobble. "You gonna be okay?"

I nod even though I feel like a ballerina who rolled off a stage. "Where did those, um, those—"

"Those losers?" he asks.

I nod.

He smiles. "They bailed."

No wonder. Another glance at his—ahem—*intimidating* physique, and I decide I don't blame them. He's hot, okay, hotter than any guy has a right to be. And unfortunately, it's impossible for him not to know that. He's one of *those kind*. He even looks amused, as though he's reading my fascination from my face. Meanwhile, I can't do anything but stare into his blue eyes, feeling like a dental patient after a heavy dose of laughing gas.

I run a hand through my hair, suddenly reminded of the bird poop in there. And the gum on my shoe. This keeps getting better.

Then I flinch when I spot a swarm of gnats by my head, and one flies into my eye.

"What the—" I mutter.

"You okay?" he asks. Again.

"Yeah," I lie, bending over and blinking. And stepping right into the puddle of mud behind me. Sound advice to myself: *Leave now!*

Reminding myself I have a plan—buy Lucky Charms and head home—I let my one bug-free eye jump between this cute guy and the display of fireworks behind me, gearing up to leave. I always have a plan, my life a programmed route from A to B. It's safe, predictable. Maybe that's why I haven't budged.

"Thanks," I say, and turn to leave for real this time, but not without sneaking one last glance at his gorgeous face. My stomach somersaults when I catch his eyes on me. Fixed on me. And not in a *you-are-a-ditzy-klutz-who-won't-make-it-off-of-River-Street-alive* kind of way. Like, in a good way. His stare glues my feet to the ground, holding me near. Blood rushes to my cheeks and I smile, despite myself.

He extends a hand with an unbearably charming smile, probably practiced. "I'm Austin."

Laura Johnston lives in Utah with her husband and two children. Growing up with five siblings, a few horses, peach trees, beehives, and gardens, she developed an active imagination and always loved a good story. She fell in love with the young adult genre through her experience in high school as well as her job later as a high school teacher. Laura enjoys running, playing tennis, sewing, traveling, writing, writing, and more writing, and above all, spending time with her husband and kids. REWIND TO YOU was her debut novel. You can visit her at laurajohnstonauthor.com.

LAURA JOHNSTON

"A rapturous, beautiful debut with a romance
that seeps into you like a sizzling Georgia summer."
—Amber Hart, author of *Before You*

REWIND
TO YOU

www.ingramcontent.com/pod-product-compliance
Lightning Source LLC
Chambersburg PA
CBHW021308250626
47155CB00002B/431